ONE THOUSAND AND A NIGHT

AS TOLD BY LARISSA, UKRAINIAN CONSTRUCTION SHOCK WORKER

ESSENTIAL PROSE SERIES 229

ONE THOUSAND AND A NIGHT

AS TOLD BY LARISSA, UKRAINIAN CONSTRUCTION SHOCK WORKER

MARINA SONKINA

With the assistance of Alexandra Berlin

GUERNICA EDITIONS

TORONTO—CHICAGO—BUFFALO—LANCASTER (U.K.)

2025

Guernica Founder: Antonio D'Alfonso

Michael Mirolla, general editor
Paul Carlucci, editor
Interior and cover design: Errol F. Richardson
Cover Art Work: Wlodzimierz Milewski

Guernica Editions Inc.
1241 Marble Rock Rd., Gananoque, ON K7G 2V4
2250 Military Road, Tonawanda, N.Y. 14150-6000 U.S.A.
www.guernicaeditions.com

Distributors:
Independent Publishers Group (IPG)
600 North Pulaski Road, Chicago IL 60624
University of Toronto Press Distribution (UTP)
5201 Dufferin Street, Toronto (ON), Canada M3H 5T8

First edition.
Printed in Canada.

Legal Deposit—Third Quarter
Library of Congress Catalog Card Number: 2024949910
Library and Archives Canada Cataloguing in Publication
Title: One thousand and a night as told by Larissa, construction shock worker / Marina Sonkina.
Names: Sonkina, Marina, 1952- author
Series: Essential prose series ; 229.
Description: Series statement: Essential prose series ; 229
Identifiers: Canadiana (print) 20240515811 | Canadiana (ebook) 20240516001 | ISBN 9781771839662 (softcover) | ISBN 9781771839679 (EPUB)
Subjects: LCGFT: Novels.
Classification: LCC PS8637.O537 O54 2025 | DDC C813/.6—dc23

Contents

PART I

PART II

Author's Note

The events described in this novel take place before Russia's full-scale invasion of Ukraine in February 2022.

Main Characters

Larissa (Lyalya): a foreman living in Ukraine
Nikita: her son living in Ukraine
Adelle: Larissa's mother
Lyuba: her daughter living in Germany
Danya: a little boy adopted by Larissa
Irakli: Lyuba's lover, a physicist and an amateur artist
Victor Erofeevich: a decorated colonel, in love with Larissa
Samsonov: Larissa's first husband
Timofey (Timmy, Tim) Doroshenko: Larissa's second husband
Natasha: Tim's first wife
Kasyan: Timofey's father
Valia: Kasyan's wife
Olesya Smeluk: Kasyan's lover
Clavdia Smeluk: Olesya's sister
Seraphima: Larissa's friend
Vanessa: Larissa's friend, head of a pharmacy
Edic Portugalsky: an impresario with a part-time job in the KGB

PART I

Chapter 1: Commander-in-Chief

"Am I scared to live alone in my dotage? Is this what you want to know? Scared I'll take a nosedive when no one's around? Well, what can I tell you? Sometimes, at night, these thoughts do come: What if I croak? How long will my body lie there stinking until the door is broken open? But it won't be me anymore, so why bother? You know, people get used to everything, even the thought of dying. As Tolstoy said ... how does it go? Wait a minute, I'll tell you: 'There is nothing terrible in the world. There is no situation in which one would be completely happy and free. And no situation in which one would be completely unhappy and unfree, either.' See?"

"You know this stuff by heart?"

"Oh yes, my memory isn't quite gone." Lyalya shot me a glance and reached for the pack of cigarettes from the balcony table of the Bogdanovich Apartments, one of the many pensions dotting the sea boulevard along Kotor Bay, where I rented a place for a reunion with my aunt.

Her tenacious memory contained a motley mosaic of quotations with which she loved to pepper the conversation, as often as not out of place. She'd shower us, her Moscow relatives, with her favourites; back then, we used to laugh about this to ourselves.

"It's so beautiful here!" A cigarette between her fingers, with their swollen joints, Lyalya filled her chest with air in small greedy gulps. "The sea, my God! I've never seen such blue before. And the mountains! See the buoys on the water? If one sways, all the rest give a shudder. That's how it was for me and my friends. If one was in trouble, everyone would respond ... But that's changed. Everybody's in it for themselves these days. When death is close, I'm suddenly alone in the whole world ... That's the rub."

"Move in with me," I said, half-jokingly.

Aunt looked at me closely. "Last time, they denied me the visa. Do you think Canada will have pity on me now that I'm on my way out?"

She made herself more comfortable in her balcony chair, stretching out her girlishly smooth legs. Gazing at the low mountains across the bay from the balcony, she lit her first cigarette of the day and went on to polish off a bowl of strawberries between puffs.

"Did I tell you? I still volunteer about thirty hours a week, handing out medication to seniors. Mind you, they're all younger than me, but half of them can barely walk. Me? I walk from house to house, no buses for me, thank you very much. What do I have my legs for, right?"

At eighty, took part in amateur swimming competitions against forty-year-olds, and, well, earned some medals, she informed me bashfully.

"The air of Adriatic! Divine nectar! Gods on Parnassus don't have it this good! Look, I brought you something."

Lyalya effortlessly got out of her chair without any support from her hands and returned a minute later carrying a tiny plastic bag.

"These belonged to your great-grandmother Rachel. I kept them all my life, but now they're yours. Why don't you try them on?"

The earrings were unassuming: flat gold crescent moons, mass stamping. A provincial saleswoman or a kolkhoz worker might have worn them. An unusually rich kolkhoz worker, that is. The golden hook was too thick for the hole in my earlobe. I felt my face pucker with pain but went on to squeeze the earrings into my lobes to please Aunt.

I was born ten years after Rachel was executed by the SS in Ukraine—in the city of Dnieper, called Dnepropetrovsk then. These two crescents were the only material proof of her existence. It was strange to gain this sudden access to her bodily life through this useless bit of trivia: the holes in her ears were wider than mine.

***

"Do you like Yevtushenko's poems?" Aunt was asking me as we were preparing for bed, our first night in this "paradise on Earth," as she referred to Montenegro.

Two beds, one wide and the other much narrower, were positioned side by side in a large bedroom. A couple of nondescript paintings glanced at us indifferently from the wall; a false-leather, diarrhea-yellow armchair stood near the larger bed, and next to the smaller one, there was a simple plastic chair. The only things that lifted the bedroom out of its bleak boredom were bedspreads. I thought the two quilts, patterned with bright hexagons housing red poppies and roses, had a touch of Mediterranean flavour, perhaps Greek, but Phoebe, one of two designers in the quilt studio I owned, could've easily done something like that.

"So you don't like Yevtushenko? Well, I do. The trouble is, my eyes are getting worse. I can't read much, not even with glasses."

"Let Nikita buy you an e-book. You can always increase the font."

"No I won't!" she replied. "I want to read *my* books. From my *own* bookcase! I got this whole collection! Anyway, don't you like any poetry at all? What about Voznesensky? 'Our neighbour, good old Buggybitchin, wears pinkish long johns in the kitchen. He's getting balder, getting fatter ... But he can juggle antimatter!' Great, huh?"

My arrival had apparently brought Lyalya's youth to her mind and—tangentially—the poets of the sixties, the idols of the young to a degree reserved for rock musicians in the West. Their glory was long over, but once, during the Thaw, they drew full stadiums of enthusiastic admirers. Why did she suddenly remember that?

I looked at her callused, arthritic hands, then at her face, which seemed much younger than her hands. And I felt sorry for her: All her youth, she'd been drawn to a different life, to a different world than the one fate had palmed off to her. Her affectations notwithstanding, this desire was sincere. The Books (a word Lyalya always pronounced with a capital letter), the classics from Shakespeare to Mandelstam—a literary world vastly different from her harsh profession—accompanied her through life like a picture of a fiancé who keeps postponing the wedding.

"Try me! I can recite Yevtushenko by heart for, hmm, at least half an hour."

"Maybe later, Lyalechka, okay?" I let the southern sun warm my face, and an irresistible desire for idleness, for total immobility, filled my body. "You've always been great at remembering things, that's for sure."

"Yeah, and you know why? I build my mental muscles, like I build the physical ones by swimming."

Between the puffs, she put four strawberries into her mouth, one by one, and rolled her eyes as if she had just hitched an express train to paradise.

"Do you remember how you used to smear your face with strawberries?" I asked. "Back then, you wouldn't waste them by eating."

"Oh, yes, I did! A long time ago that was." She chuckled. "When I still had a face, not this pickled apple. Sour cream is even better, though your skin stinks after."

When I was a child, Auntie would repeatedly terrify me by nonchalantly strolling about the house in her underwear, her face covered with blood-like splotches, her copious hair tied up in a turban after a good soak in egg yolk followed by a nettle water rinse.

On occasion, the strawberry mess was replaced by gobs of cottage cheese, smears of sour cream, or cucumber juice with honey.

"And do you remember," I said, "how, when I wanted to get rid of my freckles, you suggested I bury my face in an anthill, and I believed you and tried it? Do you remember that?"

"Oh … well." Lyalya chuckled again. "I guess I might've played a little joke on you. I had to babysit you in summer, and I wanted to go out with boys."

Chapter 2: The Reunion in Montenegro

I CAME TO MEET Aunt in Montenegro, one of the few countries she could travel to without a visa as a Russian citizen living in Ukraine. A few years before, I'd invited her to visit me in Canada, but the Canadian embassy in Moscow refused her the entrance visa on the pretext she might not want to return to Ukraine. And now that Russia was waging an undeclared war in Ukraine, having taken Crimea, there seemed to be even less hope that we'd ever be able to meet in Canada.

When I saw her slender, girlish figure in a sports jacket at the Tivat airport, it struck me how little her body had changed in the twenty years since we'd last met: the same light steps and straight back of a ballerina, though to my knowledge, she'd never danced in her life. Only when I approached did I see the changes. Her hair—once an unruly, wiry, chestnut-brown mass—was all grey, collected in a copious knot and tied up with a cheap pink elastic atop her head. Her face had withered, the puffiness under her eyes spreading down her cheeks, giving her features a babyish look. Her once milky skin now had age spots, and her large eyes, which I remembered changing colour from aquamarine to cornflower blue depending on the light and her mood, had lost their lustre, enmeshed in wrinkles.

She looked at me intently, then quickly averted her gaze, as if we both agreed to conceal our mutual shock at time, this surreptitious and relentless sculptor that had betrayed us both, adding a wrinkle to her forehead, a furrow to mine, muting the lustre of her aquamarine eyes and my brown ones, discolouring our lips and cheeks, and pulling the edges of our mouths down to the default expression of perpetual melancholy, which neither of us, at this moment, actually felt. My aunt was always of a more elegant, compact build, living mainly on veggies, salads, and cigarettes, while I'd gobble up bread and sweets as I pleased. As a teenager, I envied her and once was able to pack myself into a clingy little dress of hers, and even take a couple of steps—but without breathing. Now, I instinctively tucked in my protruding belly, hoping to look slimmer in her eyes.

In the taxi taking us from the airport to Kotor, Lyalya had snuggled up to me, tightly holding my arm with both hands, as if I could fall out of the car or change my mind about this long-awaited get-together.

I was a little scared of the week ahead: seven days and nights together. But I'd prepared a list, places of interest: medieval fortress cities, chapels and monasteries hiding in coves, boat rides along the bay …

The taxi driver—dark-skinned, bearded, handsome—spoke no English, and I tried to catch his reflection in the mirror, from which two pictures were dangling on a cord: one of Putin, the other of a saint, apparently a local Montenegrin one, complete with a halo but looking like a jack from a game of cards. With every jolt of the car, Putin swooped down on the saint, then retreated.

***

The blue bay framed by the greenish mountains and the languor smeared throughout the Mediterranean air had a calming effect on Aunt. She spent the first day sitting motionlessly on the balcony, gazing—regretfully, it seemed—at the mountains, at the trees under the balcony, and at the small boats bobbing on the waves, almost at our feet.

It was strange to see Aunt so still; I couldn't remember her sitting. She was always either doing things or telling others how to do them. Micromanaging her family seemed justified: Who could rival Lyalya's accomplishments on the battlefields of life? Who was more deft, more savvy in practical matters? Neither her first deceased husband nor the second one; nor her son Nikita, his cancer in remission; nor her numerous friends or former bosses. Only the blunt and stubborn wilfulness of her daughter, Lyuba, could challenge her own.

But Lyuba had moved to Germany, where she learned the language from scratch, became a successful neurosurgeon, and now presided over the lives of her own family: two daughters and a lethargic husband, a chemical engineering student in Ukraine, now a garbage collector in Germany, whose job was a constant nagging shame to Lyuba, the only stumbling block that she was powerless to overturn to fully consummate her success story.

Indeed, Lyalya had an uncanny ability to "obtain" what was "unobtainable" in Soviet times, when the planned economy produced an abundance of rockets, bombs, and spaceships but very little of the strategically irrelevant stuff required merely to keep the body and soul together. Transformed from consumer goods into mystical objects of desire, canned meat, buckwheat, salami, medication, clothing, shoes, bedsheets, needles, kitchen utensils, and toilet paper were acquired through ruses, stratagems, schemes, or charm, depending on the circumstances. On a few memorable occasions, she even got hold of oranges.

Then there was the matter of shelter. My aunt's complicated plots could stretch a tiny apartment like pantyhose, enlarging the living space through a sequence of exchanges till her family achieved relative comfort, with children finally sleeping separately from their parents and grandparents.

Yes, Aunt was good at bending life, at squeezing drops of comfort from dicey and often hostile circumstances. A hustler and fusser by nature, necessity, and vocation, she used her prodigious energy to cultivate loyal friendships and useful connections, to receive and return favours, and to seduce enemies into friendship or at least into temporary alliances; she bribed when needed, and perhaps took bribes. She was a commander-in-chief who made sure her family and friends stayed afloat in the precarious world into which fate had thrust her shortly after the declaration of World War II, in spite of her mother's desperate attempts to get rid of the accidental pregnancy by means of five hundred rope skips and a clandestine—her husband was at work—jump with a parachute.

Chapter 3: The Departed

"THERE'S NOBODY LEFT NOW," Lyalya said, counting down on her left hand. First her mother, immobilized for the last six years of her life, followed by her mother's two lapdogs, which went on a hunger strike after the death of their mistress. Most recently, Tanya, her daughter-in-law (not that there had been much love between them). Before that, Timofey, her second husband. Her three closest friends—Seraphima, Vanessa, and Lisa—were also gone. In her city, cancer was quick to take people to a better world, "for which you can only hope after a good look at this one," Aunt said. The death of Samsonov, her first husband, she preferred not to talk about: "Shameful life, shameful death."

We were silent for a moment. The summer days were long, and from the balcony, we could see the sun slowly rolling over the ridge of the high bluff across the bay. What I really wanted to ask her about was Danya's passing. But somehow I didn't dare.

"How is Nikita, by the way?" I asked instead.

Her son (and my cousin), Nikita, was the only relative left in Ukraine.

"The latest X-ray was all right, thank God. I cook a week's worth of food for him every Sunday; borscht, veal paddies; twenty, thirty at a time."

"Thirty? That's a lot of paddies!"

"Lasts him a week. He comes on Sunday to pick up his food; we have tea and a little chat."

Before leaving for Montenegro, I got a phone call from my cousin Lyuba, Nikita's sister. Germany, Canada, Ukraine, Israel—our family sprawled all over the globe.

"Why does Nikita go to see Mom and not the other way around?" Lyuba asked.

The last time we talked had been fifteen years before.

"Would it be such a big deal for Mom to come and do his laundry, clean up a bit? The poor lamb is all lost since his wife's death. I'd never neglect a son of mine like that!" Lyuba said (the number of her sons being zero).

"Is that what my daughter says? That I'm neglecting her brother?!" Lyalya's eyes narrowed with anger. "Is it she who cooks for him? She who schleps groceries all the way from the market?"

Why on Earth had I mentioned that phone call, I thought, listening to the gentle prattle of the Adriatic. But it was too late.

"Me going to that pigsty? What for? To lose my sleep next night?" Lyalya forcefully extinguished yet another cigarette, then flopped back into the armchair, her arms crossed over her chest. "Has Lyuba ever seen her brother's apartment? Wallpaper hanging off the walls in streaks, half of the door hinges gone, piles of dirty laundry and dishes everywhere. It wasn't much better when his wife was alive, mind you … I'd given them two thousand rubles for renovations … Could have thrown it right into the rubbish bin instead! And my daughter wants me to go there and clean up?"

I tried to soothe her.

"If anything, your son should be helping you," I said.

But that failed to appease. "I don't need help, thank you very much!" She brusquely leaned toward me. "I'll never forget! July or August it was. Anyhow, hot like hell! I went to his place. He was standing in front of me, barefoot. And I saw his toenails—claws, I tell you, good enough to climb a tree! Am I supposed to cut them for him or what? Don't get me wrong," she said, calming down by and by, "Nikita and I are on excellent terms, and I don't mind the cooking. Look, he's living with a single lung; he's an invalid. Can't walk a few stairs without huffing and puffing. Every time he's due for an x-ray, my heart leaps out of my body …"

"What does he do with his time?" I asked after a pause.

Lyalya sighed. "Chasing goblins with his pillowcase, as they say. The huge cat he has, called Rokha, twenty kilograms or something. They spend their days playing hide and seek."

"I thought he still worked. He's now what? Fifty-five?"

"Fifty-seven. Well, they stopped paying his salary a year ago. The factory went bankrupt. So I told him to quit. I said, 'I don't see them coughing up any dough for you ever, son; they are taking you for a ride. Enough is enough!' At least he has his disability payments."

"Can he live on that?"

"Nobody can live on Ukrainian handouts! I help him out, of course. If it weren't for my Russian pension, I don't know how we'd pull it off."

As a Russian citizen living in Ukraine, Lyalya had to travel to Russia for her pension: no transactions were possible between the two countries even before Russia had started the war in Donbas in 2014, much less now, in 2019.

Several times a year, she'd take two trains to a weirdly named town—Crystal Goose—and bring back cash in a pocket sown into her bra, keeping vigilant against robbers all night.

"But don't you need the money yourself?" I asked cautiously, thinking of all the years she'd been supporting her son and his family.

"What for? All I need is … well, for him not to die before me, I guess."

Chapter 4: Nikita's Trophy

"When they found out about Nikita's cancer," Lyalya said, "I was on my way to Moscow to get my pension. So there I am, unpacking my suitcase, when Tanya calls me: 'Nikita has a lung sarcoma. Come at once; we don't know what to do without you!' My mind went blank at first. I had just arrived, hadn't got my pension—how could I help without money? But soon enough, I got my ass in gear, got hold of my pension in a wink, returned to Ukraine, and then straight from the train station to the chief surgeon, Ukropov, my suitcases in tow. I know everyone there. Remember I'd worked there during the hospital's construction? So I say, 'Cancer? Sergey Sergeyevich! How can it be? This is my only son!' And he—such a round little man, nothing to see above his desk but a head in horn-rimmed glasses—won't look me in the eye. Says they must operate urgently. And I say, 'What if you don't?' He says, 'Then Nikita's heart won't stand the pressure for long.' Not much to ponder there, right?

"So I race over to them, to my kids, straight from the hospital, still with my suitcases: 'That's that,' I say. 'They need to operate urgently.' Nikita was never the brightest, you know, so he says, 'I seem to breathe easier today. It's getting better all by itself!' And Tanya, well, brains and good looks just won't go together sometimes. 'Yes, don't you worry. He'll breathe it away!' Breathe it away? Well, I couldn't beat about the bush after that. 'Another week, and it will be too late,' I say. 'Ukropov himself told me.' So I kicked Nikita into surgery, spent all the time in the hospital, day and night, Tanya sitting at home all the while, the hospital 'affecting her nerves,' if you please. After the operation, I gave Ukropov two hundred dollars in cash, and he didn't bat an eye, though in Ukraine, medicine is officially free of charge. 'Sergei Sergeyevich, what's the prognosis?' I asked. 'What should we expect from fate and God?'

"To this, Ukropov said nothing, only shrugged his scrawny shoulders, playing with a pencil and looking at me as if he was seeing me for the first time. Well, I realize that he needs some more grease. Fifty dollars more, and he puts the pencil away. 'Your son will live. The prognosis is good. He'll be under observation.'"

Lyalya sighed again. "Was it Montaigne who said that life was fragile? So many in Zaporizhzhia die because of the smelters. But my son, he got his cancer from asbestos, way back when he was a ship electrician. Insulation for boilers, pipes—they all used asbestos. Nobody gave a damn!"

Nikita had been an adventurous boy who decided to flee the drabness of dusty industrial Zaporizhzhia and embrace the freedom of the high seas. A ship mechanic, fixing piping, pumps, and boilers, Nikita sited every port of the world from Singapore to Vancouver to Sidney to Marseilles. He showered his mother with nylon blouses and stockings, cheap leather jackets, umbrellas magically closing and opening at the push of a button, Italian scarves printed with anchors and chains, cigarette lighters—the cheap merchandise from back-alley stalls that sailors buy for their kin.

For ten years, his mother felt like a queen; her bargaining and bribing power increased multifold. "He was a good boy, would always bring me piles of stuff," Aunt said dreamily. "We didn't quarrel back then. I mean, he wasn't around much, but I could assert my authority; in those days, he still listened. And so strong! What's left of him now? A husk! But then … I have a bit of a temper, you know. Once we had a huge argument about something or other, and I ended up slapping him in the face."

"Your grown-up son?"

"Sure thing! If he refuses to listen to his mama …"

"He didn't fight back, did he?"

"God forbid, no! Well … he just grabbed me silently, like that, lifted me off the ground and put me on top of the fridge. Then slammed the kitchen door behind him. Remember the fridges we had back then? The tall ones, with rounded edges? There I was, screaming at the top of my voice: 'Take me down, for God's sake!' But he was gone. Well, I scrambled down somehow."

Lyalya laughed heartily, throwing her head back in abandon. I wondered what pleased her so: The prowess and strength her son used to have? His audacity? Or the memory of physical contact, odd as it was, the contact she was missing now?

***

After a decade at sea, Nikita moored in Zaporizhzhia and married a girl whose languid indifference to life was matched only by her extraordinary beauty: the doe-eyed, dark-haired, porcelain-cheeked Tanya seemed to have stepped out of the pages of an ancient Persian manuscript.

Her beauty was the product of a chance encounter between an Iranian cabinet maker and a straitlaced girl from a small provincial town in the Moscow region. Tanya was conceived on a stack of roughly planed boards in an unlit corner of the lumber factory to which her mother had been sent as a technician in the heyday of Soviet-Iran friendship, when Russians built dams, factories, plants, and power stations for their southern neighbour. Needless to say, Tanya would never see her father. An exotic flower among the nettles of Middle Russia, the girl grew up indulged by her mother and hissed at by her neighbours.

Nikita spotted Tanya on a beach in Odessa during a two-day leave from his cargo ship *The Communist Cause*. Abandoning *The Communist Cause*, he took his trophy to the registration office.

After the anemic life of a tender lily, Tanya succumbed to bone cancer at the age of fifty. "She kept asking me for wood shavings," Lyalya told me. "Kept them under her pillow and smelled them all the time. The only thing that gave her comfort in the weeks before her death."

***

A melancholic chime sailed over the waters, the bells unseen. The chapels nestling in the steep slopes seemed to be growing from the stone like limbs from a tree; as daylight faded, they turned from light tan to dark brown, blending with the face of the mountain. The fading light illuminated clouds and their rosy underbellies were reflected on the water.

"You know what my trouble is?" Aunt said. "That I have nobody left to talk to."

"But look, I'm here! We've got a whole week together. We'll talk and see things. There are some great churches here."

Lyalya frowned. “I didn’t come here for sightseeing, you know. I came to talk to you.”

And so we talked. For seven days and nights, we talked. At bedtime, exhausted by her commanding energy, I would crawl into my cot across from her queen-size bed, the likes of which she had never seen before, and pull the blanket over my head as the cadence of her low, chesty voice washed over me, wave after wave.

Chapter 5: Senga Sengana

"We'll walk together," Lyalya informed me on our first morning while rubbing some facial cream into her cheeks. "Eight kilometres a day, at least. Four to Kotor and four back. A doctor friend of mine said that each time your foot hits the ground, it pumps blood to your heart."

For the next seven days, we were pumping blood to our hearts walking along the quay to Kotor and back. Shorter than me, my Aunt moved forward in determined strides, her back ramrod straight. I, trying to conceal my shortness of breath, was catching up to her with my short, fretful steps. We never tried a different destination, strawberries at the Kotor market turning out to be the greatest attraction for my Aunt.

Approaching the stalls with a sour expression on her face, Aunt increased her pace and skeptically survey the heaps of food: herbs, mushrooms, nuts, cucumbers, Turkish sweets, fish, and all kinds of sea delights. The sellers stood motionlessly at their trays, hands crossed on thick bellies under spotless white aprons. Nobody shouted, drummed up customers, or praised their goods. Something clearly rankled Aunt. Was it the cleanliness and order, the silence, the abundance of merchandise on display she could not afford to buy? The pursed lips on her stiffened face seemed to say: "I know you're all here to hoodwink me! Good luck, folks!"

She kept strutting forward, looking neither at me nor the sellers, as if their quiet manner was a personal insult. If I lost sight of her straight back, I knew where to find her: at the strawberry stalls. There, she'd be immediately transformed, dashing from one tray to the next, picking, choosing, tasting, and leaving without saying thank you. I had no way of knowing what guided her choice; all this bright, red freshness looking equally enticing to me.

Managing to save fifty cents, Lyalya would finally dive out loaded with kilograms of sweet-smelling berries.

"You sure you need so many?" I asked the first time.

"Come on! It's Senga Sengana! The best strawberries ever, worth killing for! Don't you smell it? You need to smell it!"

"We could buy more tomorrow …"

"Tomorrow, my bum! A kilo of strawberries a day keeps the doctors away, and tomorrow never knows! As Churchill put it." She grandly waved away my confusion. "Well, Churchill, or Chaplin, what do I care, both start with *ch*. Maybe the market will close tomorrow. Then what?"

Loaded with shopping bags full of strawberries, we'd return along the quay toward the Bogdanovich Apartments, sitting down on a bench to rest on the way.

"Here! Eat! You won't find anything better than Senga Sengana!" She smoked her cigarette, gobbled up a few handfuls of strawberries, and finally relaxed, as if an important duty had been fulfilled. "Look! Will you look at the clouds? This one is sitting right on top of the mountain! This fatty! Dangling his fat legs, see? I haven't seen the mountains in forty years. The last time I did was in Norilsk."

As if encountering the world for the first time, she took delight in its details and overall design. She marvelled at the deep fiords, which let enormous ships moor right at the ancient walls of Kotor; at the concave, dazzlingly white bow of a fifteen-storey cruise liner that served as a background for a picture I took of her; at the motley horde of tourists the liner would disgorge each morning. Out of curiosity, she followed the tourists into the ancient town, where they were gradually sucked in by cozy restaurants in narrow back alleys and boutiques full of trinkets. She tried to guess the tourists' nationality by their clothing, but her interest in people and souvenirs was fleeting. What really drew her were buildings and the azure of the Adriatic.

While she inhaled the tangy smell of the sea, she quickly figured out why frayed pieces of rope and strips of plastic mesh were attached to long lines bobbing over the surface of water: mussel farming. The regularity and straightness of these lines delighted her.

But sometimes, her face would darken with resentment, and I wondered what nagged her in this peaceful, cozy place, with cream-yellow houses climbing the mountain like sheep.

"What a life! Why can't we live like that? What kind of life did we have, generation after generation? You tell me!"

She looked mistrustfully at the people sipping their beer at the docks, reading newspapers, staring at the motionless waters. Lyalya's lips pursed as she both admired and resented the lazy peacefulness of the world around her. What seemed to me a modest, low-key place, a wannabe-upscale resort on the Adriatic, was all glitter and luxury to her.

Chapter 6: Cossacks Writing a Letter to the Turkish Sultan

As soon as we returned from our morning stroll, Aunt would take her clothes off and strut around the flat in her underwear, a habit she'd acquired in her youth, when there were no air conditioners to mitigate the sweltering heat of Ukrainian summers. All her numerous female relatives, none of whom were alive anymore, had done the same. I avoided looking at what her smart clothing had been concealing a moment ago: the hanging skin of her underarms, her scrawny straight hips, her now flat buttocks.

I remembered, as a child, my grandmother and her sisters puttering around their hot, airless apartments in underwear, their copious flesh bulging out of their patched black drawers and their oversized bras, homemade from linen, as they fussed over a large steaming copper bowl of rose petal jam. Ever since, whenever I detect the faintest fragrance of dog roses, the images of half-naked, plump, middle-aged women surface in my mind, a circle in a steamy kitchen, fresh bunches of roses on the floor next to each. They wipe drops of sweat off their foreheads, remove rose petals from the prickly stems, and drop them into the basin as casually as if they were potato peels.

Too precious to be consumed by adults, rose petal jam was a treat for well-behaved children on very special occasions. It was in a different league from cherry or apricot jams, cooked every year on a near-industrial scale and poured into tall jars covered with pieces of paper encircled by brown string. Cherry and apricot—those rows of plebeians—slept in the massive ornate cupboard, waiting to be dispatched by train with relatives returning to Moscow and Leningrad to weather their severe winters devoid of fruits and vitamins.

***

To pick dog roses, my grandmother and aunt, then in her twenties, would embark on an exhausting, sun-drenched journey to the island of Khortytsia, crossing on foot the giant Dnieper dam, Stalin's legendary project of the thirties designed by Americans, the fact forbidden to ever be mentioned. Trailing behind, I'd make faces, sticking out my tongue at the relentless sun and the lifeless sky, this motionless world of heat.

I remember my grandmother would stop, gently taking my hand. "Hang on, darling, just a little bit longer. Look over there! See Khortytsia? Once, the famous Zaporizhian Sech was there."

Opening my eyes with effort, I'd fearfully look down at the powerful silver-lilac glean of the river, with a large island on its back. I'd see my grandmother and her sisters making buckets of sauerkraut, cutting through the tight heads of cabbage with short knives they called *sechki*. My sleepy imagination would turn the Zaporizhian Sech into fields of cabbage with female figures in white shawls inclined over the vegetable beds with sparkling *sechki* in their hands. The sun hit the steel blades, and they scattered into dazzling fragments with a slight glass chime. I'd peel my sandals' soles off the heat-softened bitumen and take another step.

It took a few years until the innocent cabbage field of my imagination was replaced by the military camp of the drunk Cossack outlaws that settled on Khortytsia in the sixteenth century. We learned about it in school, in grade six or so. For two hundred years, a successful Cossack brotherhood from Khortytsia made raids on everyone who wasn't an Orthodox Christian believer and on foreigners in general: Poles, Tatars, Turks, Jews. The Cossacks burned, plundered, skinned the prisoners' feet before releasing them, and they cut the babies out of the bellies of pregnant Jewish victims.

A few years later still, when a teacher pointed at Repin's painting *Cossacks Writing a Letter to the Turkish Sultan* at the Tretyakov Gallery in Moscow, I saw the heroes of the "national liberation movement" up close: their half-naked sweaty bodies, their broad red trousers girdled with bright sashes, their round heads, shaved but for a single forelock, their moustaches so long that they would stick their ends behind their ears.

The Cossacks are writing a letter to the Turkish sultan refusing to obey his authority. Repin painted a vivid picture of their sneering faces. "Twenty kinds of laughter! Every Cossack in the painting laughs in his own way!" The teacher raised her voice, feeling personal pride either in Repin or the mirthful, murderous letter writers.

The image of Cossacks went on to haunt me through my school years. The initial shock of disgust caused by the painting was intensified by Gogol's brilliant story *Taras Bulba*. In the exam paper in ninth grade, I wrote that I saw nothing heroic in these thugs whose lives were all about bathing in blood and drinking themselves stupid.

Gogol's genius would not let him distort life, I assumed, which is why he released monsters in the bright light of truth onto his pages. He did not hesitate to describe how the Cossacks punished each other for crimes against the brotherhood, burying people alive in a grave and putting the coffin with their victim on their chest. But still, Gogol sung these marauders as national heroes. Why? How to explain the romantic passion for fighting, violence, and murder in a painfully timid writer who was happiest at his mother's side?

I still don't know why I wasn't kicked out of school for this essay. It did play its role a year later, though, when the school authorities decided to use it to expel me from the Komsomol for a worldview incompatible with a young Communist's duties.

I had my share of shame at the whipping post of Komsomol meetings and was already beginning to repent when suddenly the campaign stopped. Either my tormentors moved on to larger prey or were too lazy to complete what they'd begun (rarely enough, such things did happen). Anyway, suddenly my troubles died down, like witchcraft in Gogol's phantasmagorias.

But if the main purpose of my persecutors was to intimidate me, in that they fully succeeded.

Chapter 7: Angelic Seraphima

I KNEW MY AUNT would want to swim in the sea, no matter the temperature. There were a couple of beaches along the embankment leading to Kotor, but it was still early May, and hardly anyone was in the water. Though we didn't do much but walk and talk, Lyalya always seemed to be moving: cooking for the two of us, doing the dishes or cleaning the apartment, arranging my things, her own somehow always in order. To me, her very name intimated a giggle and a carefree movement. "Lyalya" had been my aunt's childhood name, her toy name, tiny bells jingling, as I never thought of it as a name for serious, glum adults. Later, she changed it to an official-sounding "Larissa," a name I could never bring myself to call her by. When and how did she become Larissa Semyonovna Samsonova instead of Lyalya Solomonovna Sternberg? She shed her Jewish maiden name by marrying Samsonov—that much I knew. But the patronymic? Her father's name was Solomon, not Semyon. How do you un-father your own father?

"To Russians, Samson and Hercules are Russian. They believe that Christ was Russian, born in the village of Ostapovo!" My aunt laughed. "But imagine, just imagine, the production meetings at my work! Lyalya Solomonovna Sternberg! Come to the podium! Every head turning: 'Who the hell is that? Jewish? How did she get here?' Weirder than Kafka, that would be!"

"Was Samsonov by any chance related to the ill-fated general Samsonov of World War I?" I asked. That commander of the Second Army who lost one hundred and forty thousand Russian soldiers to German encirclement in East Prussia? Who couldn't face reporting the disaster to Nicholas the Second and committed suicide—a relation?

"What? My alcoholic Samsonov related to a Tsar's general? Ha! Your Highness, General Samsonov! Now, that sounds grand! So I've been calling him all wrong all the time: pantless boozer, I said, fershnickered putz! Turns out I should have been calling him 'Your Highness!'" And Aunt dissolved in laughter, her head thrown back.

From her mirth, I got the impression that she'd never heard of General Samsonov of World War I. Which was not surprising. Having orchestrated the revolution in Russia, Lenin was sponsored by the Germans on the promise—which he kept—that he'd pull Russia out of the war. Then 1917, the year of the revolution, became a watershed, a demarcation line: all preceding events, including World War I—The Imperialist War—were declared non-existent or unimportant. With history being constantly rewritten, the *Homo sovieticus* knew or cared little about that old war, soon enough superseded by World War II—The Great Patriotic War—with its colossal loss of thirty million lives.

After the divorce, Lyalya kept Samsonov's last name.

"For my sister, your mother, changing her name was easy because she was older," Lyalya said, folding my scattered clothing into an orderly pile. "All it took for our father was to 'lose' her birth certificate during the war. He couldn't pull the same trick for me though. But I wasn't really giving it much thought till one day I got a phone call from the archive department of the city hall, which I had built about ten years before."

An architect by training, with a second degree in civil engineering, Lyalya ended up working as a contractor for major civil projects, supervising engineers, designers, and construction workers. An unusual job for a woman. Especially a woman with a Jewish name, a dancing gait, eyes of pure aquamarine, and a copious braid reaching her waistline.

"There's some serious problem with the sewage, they tell me. People refuse to show up at the city hall for work, the stench is so bad. No certificates have been issued in the halls of bureaucratic power for at least two weeks. The result? The whole city is inundated with unregistered newborns and the recently deceased. No plumber in the city can fix the problem! Whom are they calling? Me! And I go, 'Am I a plumber or what? I finished building my city hall ten years ago; my liability lasts for three; what do you expect me to do now?' So I hang up."

Aunt always referred to the construction projects she worked on as her very own. It was always "my hospital," "my school," "my registrar office," "my city hall" …

"Three days go by. Another call: 'Larissa Solomonovna, it's an emergency. Other than you, who can help us?' Fools are never sown—

they grow on their own! Can't they repair a damned bit of a canalization? So I took pity on them. I had a handsome guy on my team, Gold Hand Gosha, we used to call him. Good at breaking women's hearts; four rivals for his favours had submitted to the Party bureau a letter of complaint—you know how people would come to the Party with their personal problems back then? Like, your husband is cheating on you—go discuss it at a meeting! Anyway, you know what Gosha said? 'All I fix are pipes, not hearts. I'm the best pipe fixer in town, and you go to hell.' So they did. They left him alone. And his harem? You can't cut Gosha Gold Hand in four, so women had to make peace with each other.

"I promised city hall to send them Gosha in return for one small favour. I needed to have my name changed, I said. 'Name change? No problem! Just drop by!' So I arrive, and what do I see? The place is deserted, every office vacant. But in one drab room, with brown paper peeling off the wall, a girl is typing away with her right hand, pressing a hanky to her nose with the left, and there's an albino mouse at her feet, gnarling savagely at an orange peel. It looked at me, then at the portraits of the furry-browed Brezhnev, wiped its pink muzzle with its paw, and scampered away through a hole in the wall.

"'That's surreal!' I say to the girl at the typewriter. Her name, as it turned out, was Seraphima. I mean, an albino mouse in a city hall! Eating orange peels, of all things!

"'I guess it hates the stink, so it took to orange peels,' says the girl. She keeps banging at the typewriter with such speed as if she needed to catch the next plane to Paris. 'What's the rush?' I go. 'Who's gonna give you a bonus for your "five-year-plan-in-four-weeks" work? The mouse or what?' And she kvetches: 'If Vezuvy comes and the report is not finished, he'll cut me to pieces!' And I ask, 'Who the hell is this Vezuvy?'"

Chapter 8: Honey Shores, Milky Rivers!

TURNED OUT THAT VEZUVY, who was the director of the archives, kept stalking Seraphima through the bleak labyrinth of the city hall. Each time she tried to vanish around the corner, he threatened to fire her.

"Forget Vezuvy," Lyalya said to Seraphima. "You owe him nothing. You can bang on the typewriter at my department instead."

And with these words, she pulled the sheet out of Seraphima's typewriter and tore it up.

"So Seraphima gets all fluttery and indecisive, but a fancy took me to save that girl from that stinky place. 'Look,' I said, 'right from the start, you'll be getting the same salary as here, plus peace of mind. If that's not a nice bonus, tell me what is.' The poor thing rushed to hug me, and later we became the best of friends; no water would pour us apart."

Aunt got animated, her face lit up, and I recognized the young woman of bygone days.

"Shall we go for a walk now?" Lyalya winked at me. "A brusque one, eh?"

"But I want to hear the story."

"I can walk and talk you know!"

"I'm still fighting my jetlag, and you said your back is hurting a bit. Are you sure you want to walk?"

"Mens sana … Forgot my Latin. How does it go? In healthy body, healthy mind, right? Who said that? Seneca or Caesar? Hold on: who wrote *Twelve Caesars?* Suetonius? That must be him, then. *My back won't give any slack! Give me a ride in Cadillac!* I'll have my cigarette, you'll rest, and then we'll go."

We took our positions on the balcony. When I sank into the chair, it squeaked mournfully, but my aunt's didn't make a beep.

"What was I saying? Oh, yes, Seraphima! When I first saw her, I thought, my God, if there are angels in heaven, they must look like her. Did her parents know how she'd turn out and that's why they gave her such a name? Only her hair was jet black, and angels are supposed to be blond, no? But then, she was a Bosha."

"A what?"

"An Armenian gypsy. They look like Armenians—lived among them for centuries—speak a different language, though, and the way they live ... their men never work, Seraphima told me, only women do. Once a woman gets married, she starts her day job: going from door to door begging for the essentials. She'll knock at your door and coax you into giving her what her family needs to survive. If you refuse, she'll tell you stories—they're known to be good storytellers—and keep coaxing you, cajoling, pressing. People don't hate the Bosha because they never steal. The whole art, Seraphima told me, was to talk you into giving things away voluntarily."

"How did she end up in Ukraine?"

"Lost her parents in the Nagorno-Karabakh War, at the end of the eighties, remember? The Azeri killed them. Seraphima somehow made it to Zaporizhzhia, alone. She spoke very little Russian then. Anyhow, I gave her a job, took her under my wing, but not for long, as it turned out.

"Men parted with their marbles over Seraphima's beauty, and before long, she got into trouble again! Our boss, Nikanor Timofeevich, nicknamed The Tractor because the floor trembled under him. Like a rusted piece of agricultural machinery, he was. A big fish at my construction bureau, and the only boss over me. So where do you find The Tractor after work? Rubbing his paunch against a billiards table, playing against his secretary-cum-lover. Now The Tractor dumps that secretary and invites Seraphima to the billiards table. Seraphima had never held a cue. But as the saying goes, when I say jump, you say, 'How high?' I don't know what she saw in this fat cad, a miser and an ass licker to boot. Ahh ... the soul of another is a dark chamber." Aunt sighed, shaking her head in disbelief. "Maybe Seraphima just got lonely? In a strange country among strange people? Anyhow, to make a long and sad story short, she fell head over heels in love with The Tractor. I tried to warn her, but, you know, try changing lenses in somebody else's pink glasses! I watched her slipping down the slope, women wagging their tongues behind her back: Look at her new stilettos! A month's salary worth! And her Red Moscow perfume! She must have had office couch duty again!

"It was the winter of the following year was, I think, when The Tractor took Seraphima to Sochi on vacation. Charging the trip to our agency, of course. And whom does he order to organize it? His jilted secretary! So what does the secretary do? She calls The Tractor's wife and spills the beans. The wife hops on a train and goes straight to the hotel in Sochi that the ditched secretary had organized for the lovey-dovey! Up she walks to the reception and right away demands the keys to their room."

"They'd give her the keys?"

"Sure! She's the wife, after all. In the meantime, the lovers are taking a promenade along the beach. You know how it is in the south: Honey shores, milky rivers! Lemons and oranges on the trees! Palm leaves whispering love sonnets in their ears! Infatuation always makes people foolish, don't you think? The two return to their room laughing, hugging, and kissing. While the wife is watching … guess from where?"

"You said they gave her the key …"

"From a crack in the wardrobe! That's where she hid!"

"Like in a joke? In vaudevilles, it's the lover who's supposed to be hiding in the wardrobe."

"Well, this time it was the wife. When she saw they weren't in the room, she hid in the wardrobe. You know those heavy dark armoires."

"Wait a minute, who would ever do such a thing in real life?"

"You think I'm making it up? Seraphima herself told me!"

"And you believed her? Didn't you tell me that gypsies, the Boshas, earned a living by making up stories?"

Lyalya pursed her lips. Be these wonderful fabulations Seraphima's or her own, to buy into them meant to turn a grey deep-frozen filet of the quotidian into a living sparkling fish.

"Let me finish," Lyalya said solemnly. "Wait till you get to the nub of it! Before hiding, the wife noticed Seraphima's purse on the chair. She quickly goes through it, grabs her passport, and then crouches in the wardrobe to wait. You think it's hard to watch your husband making love to another woman? I wouldn't dispute that! But then she finds out that the shit is deeper than she thought: Her very own husband ups and asks Seraphima to marry him. Who'd keep quite after that?!

"So the wife jumps out of the wardrobe, waving the passport in front of the naked Seraphima. 'You, slut! Like hell you're going to get married to my idiot! I'm not giving you this thing back. Not till you pay me three hundred rubles! Go dance now!' Men are cowards, you know. Don't be a dickhead, come up with something, right? But The Tractor—well, he pissed his pants with fear! Or he would've if he was wearing any. So he says to Seraphima: 'Oh dear, the wheels have fallen off! Shit has truly hit the fan! We still have a week of vacation left, and my wife's health can use the sea and sunshine. So you know what, Seraphima, go back to work, why don't you?' And he coaxes the wife out of the wardrobe and makes up with her in front of Seraphima, but the wife refuses to return the passport. Without it, where can Seraphima go? As the saying goes: without a piece of paper, you're just a bug, with a paper, a human being. The wife dug in her heels: three hundred rubles, and no haggling! That was about three months' salary at the time. Where would Seraphima get such a fortune?

"I don't remember now how she managed to return. Maybe she took a bus. All I know is when Seraphima told me that story, I summoned my gals and said: 'Look, we need to brainstorm. Rain or shine, but we have to get Seraphima's passport back.' So we put our heads together, and here's what we end up with: We're going to have a little chat with The Tractor's wife and straighten her out. And when she gets her thinking straight, she'll be begging Seraphima to take her passport back and pay some on top."

"But how would that work?" By now, I was intrigued.

"Ah, it wasn't rocket science, let me tell you! Manya, my subordinate, was in charge of all the construction materials, Anna was in charge of the personnel, and Sonya of finance. If The Tractor doesn't get construction materials on time, is he going to build a hospital out of thin air? If there are no workers, who'll do the job? And if there's no financing, his five-year plan is shot! That means he'd be fired, and before his wife can count to ten, her hubby would be dead horse meat. You see my point? She did too. All her life, she'd been pampered, rolling like cheese in butter. Mink coats, dinner parties, silver plates, the whole shebang! If her hubby lost his job, the party would be over. That's how we got Seraphima her passport back."

Chapter 9: The Admiral

I VAGUELY KNEW THE story of Aunt's first marriage to an abusive alcoholic, the marriage that took her from her Ukrainian home to the Siberian wilderness. But why did she marry Samsonov? With her pragmatism, I couldn't imagine love playing a large role.

"Have you ever been in love, for real?" I asked one evening, as we were readying for bed.

Aunt raised her right eyebrow. Her fingers, cleverly twisting her bangs onto the rollers, froze for a moment.

"As Ivan Turgenev said: 'The mysteries of life are great, and love is the greatest.' Do you agree? I couldn't have put it better. By the way, do you remember Victor?"

I didn't, not immediately. But then—the vague memories of my childhood summers in Ukraine came into focus. Just like the blinding glare of Dnieper would crystallize into separate flashes once I put glasses back on my myopic eyes.

I first combed through the coterie surrounding Lyalya since her girlhood, but he wasn't part of it. I remembered the faces of adolescent boys and grown men, all turned to her, as she, with a shrug of her shoulders, concealing her thirst for attention, showcased her cartwheels, backflips, and splits in the courtyard near a table where the old men from the adjacent apartment buildings got together to play dominoes in the hot, sticky summer evenings. Obliged to babysit me but unwilling to miss her fun, Lyalya would often drag me into the raucous company of her admirers (I don't remember a single girl there, except herself and me) telling them I was her daughter—me about five, her sixteen.

And then I did remember Victor. The first time I saw him was not in Zaporizhzhia but in Leningrad (we must have been visiting our cousins), in the Summer Garden, sitting next to Lyalya, who was posed demurely on a bench. Serious, dark-clad ramblers, mostly middle-aged women, were strolling arm-in-arm past the statues of Greek goddesses and gods. Lyalya, by then eighteen, in a slinky polka-dot-blue dress with a white turndown collar, her thick braid reaching her slim waist, her enormous aquamarine eyes gazing wistfully into the distance, alert as a troubled bird. Unusually quiet, she was sitting, ramrod straight, on the edge of the bench, next to a man in a military uniform, whom I took for an admiral on account of his dark blue jacket and the golden stars on his epaulettes. (He proved to be a retired colonel, but the fancier "Admiral" stuck to him in my mind, and this is what Lyalya and I used to call him between ourselves.) He was very old, the Admiral, over thirty. With his trimmed moustache and carefully parted greyish hair, he looked like a foreigner from postwar trophy films. I could barely recognize Lyalya's demeanour, her lips gingerly touching the tip of the ice cream that the Admiral had treated us to. Her quick glance stopped the dangling of my feet, and I stiffened in vexed uneasiness.

I was convinced then that the invisible but powerful force coercing Lyalya to freeze next to this taciturn old man was a mysterious self-punishment, that she was bored to death. Only years later did I finally understand the sorrowful drama playing out between the two: the Admiral's fear of scaring away this precocious flower, the mask of restraint he put on to camouflage his ardour, Lyalya's alert uneasiness and awkwardness in response to the old-fashioned courtship of a much older man, a decorated war hero and a friend of her father's. Her shyness, which I had taken for boredom, would later be replaced by an exalted if tormented attachment to this man.

It was my grandfather, Lyalya's father, who put an end to the romance.

I asked her about it the next day when, after a long walk, we found a restaurant on a deck looking out onto the water.

"After all these years, I really can't blame my father," she said, looking at the menu. "I guess I'd have done the same if it was my daughter."

The only customers at that early evening hour, we were facing the Adriatic. On the opposite side of a narrow bay, on the mountain slope, there was a semi-destroyed fortress of grey stone. A narrow path descended from it, disappearing in the dark greenery, then surfacing again. From afar, the forest looked like tightly curled moss.

"Looks like an expensive place." Aunt touched the cutlery on the starched tablecloth. "Why not eat at home? I could make some fish soup."

"Listen, we see each other every twenty years! Do me a favour, don't even look at the right side of the menu. Just order what you like. Do you like octopus? Fresh from the Adriatic?"

"Octopus?! How about some normal fish?"

I read the English version of the menu, translating "salmon," "trout," and "mullet" into Russian.

Aunt picked the latter and leaned over the table, a conspiratorial expression on her face: "I wonder what kind of fish you eat in Canada?"

"Different kinds, I guess. I like salmon."

"Oh yes, salmon's fine! Say, do you remember how we had to eat whale meat all the time? Nothing else in the shops! I was working in the Far East back then. Whale hunting was a free for all there, so some local bigwig came up with the brilliant idea of showering the shops with frozen whale instead of fish. First in the Far East, and then all over the country. Why the hell not!"

"I wonder where all the fish went. I mean, with the size of the USSR, and all those rivers and lakes …"

"Yeah, right. Remember the song?" She began to sing under her breath. Fortunately, the restaurant was still empty.

Fields and rivers of my Soviet homeland
always fill me with the deepest feeling,
In the world, there is no other country
where you breathe so happily and freely.

She saw my expression, stopped, and mused: "Then again, you know what Turgenev also said? 'If it depended on our superiors, we would all be eating with our feet!' Exactly so: we eat with our feet, we turn back rivers. Were you old enough to remember? How they decided to change the direction of the Irtysh, the Ob, the Yenisei! Only the Perestroika made them come to their senses. And the dams, goddamn dams blocking the rivers!"

***

I remembered a snowy, windy February, myself in felt boots, hopping from foot to foot in a queue at the fish shop. The crowd behind me kept pushing, until my mother and I were finally pressed into an open door, and there, in the gap between the many shoulders (always black or dark brown or grey; the country of my childhood knew no other colours for clothing), I noticed an aquarium with live carps, eyes like magnifying glasses. After a long time waiting in the cloudy breath of the freezing crowd, we reached the counter. A sullen-faced woman in black sleeves and a dirty apron carelessly wrapped the living, tail-swinging carp in a newspaper without giving us a glance. Nobody looked at anyone. We carried this living swaddled thing home. While my mother was taking off her coat, I rushed into the bathroom, turned on the faucet, and let the carp splash into the water. I remember my fascination when I saw the fish mouth with its reddish lining greedily swallowing the breadcrumbs that I hurled into the bathtub! And I remembered my despair when, the next morning, I found my new pet floating among the slime of scattered bread, tummy up.

I was about ten when the snakes of queues disappeared from the city because there was nothing to be bought. Only algae waving sadly in the aquariums. Later still, the water was poured out, the algae thrown away, and the glass parallelepipeds remained empty, dimly reflecting the light of the shop lamps.

"You want to drink something?" I asked. "Tea, coffee? They've got freshly squeezed juice too."

After we were done eating, we ordered two juices, and while Aunt fitted the drinking straw to her lips, I looked behind her. A girl in a bright yellow swimsuit was coming down the stairs of the embankment. She reached a small patch of sand and tried the water with her toes. In May, it must have been freezing, but she gingerly walked in and swam off with quiet, easy strokes.

Looking at this girl, I thought of Lyalya's early love again. "I'm still wondering: What made you part with the Admiral? If he was the man you loved, I mean?"

"But I already told you. My father put an end to it."

"Wasn't he a war buddy of the Admiral?"

"Sure he was. Four years at the front line together. I nearly drove a wedge between them. They had a man-to-man talk. I was listening at the door. My father was talking rather grandiloquently; you know how he was sometimes." Lyalya tried on a deeper voice: "'Victor, do not obscure the sun on the bright sky of my daughter's future! I never had a son, only two daughters. Now tell me, do you think it's fair to deprive me of a hope for a grandson who might become a famous scientist, or a Polar explorer, for all I know?'" Aunt spread her arms and shook her head, just like my grandfather, her father, used to do.

"He said that?"

"Yes, he did."

Her gaze followed the girl in the yellow swimsuit, who was now coming ashore.

"It's all water under the bridge now, but for many years, I couldn't accept it," Aunt said, collecting the plates on the table. She never let the waiters do their job.

***

As a child, I wanted to rectify the injustice done to the Admiral, who had suddenly disappeared, his name becoming taboo in our family. I wanted him back, if only for the sake of his splendid uniform. It was much later, as an adult, that I learned the real reason for his expulsion from our family: on the very last day of the war, a mine had exploded a metre away from him, ripping his stomach open, and blowing off his manhood.

For years to come, Lyalya kept pining for the stars of his epaulettes and the clean smell of his eau-de-cologne, till a young man by the name of Samsonov pressed her against the cement fence behind the Institute of Architecture and Design as she was returning home with a diploma in her hand. "You will be mine," Samsonov said, "and you better believe it."

"Let go, you brute!" Lyalya said, fighting him away with the roses she received for her graduation.

Chapter 10: Does the West Need Ukraine?

"The only good thing about Samsonov was that he could tell jokes with a poker face," Aunt said the next morning as we embarked on our daily walk toward Kotor, a medieval walled town with ancient fortification sitting in the loop of Kotor Bay. The promenade skirting the shore was almost deserted.

"You remember Samsonov, don't you? Some husband that was. A scumbag!" I didn't expect her to be quite so harsh. But on she went: "He'd wrap my braid around his fist—like that—and slam my head against the wall. No wonder Nikita tried to run away from home. But why are we talking about Samsonov here, amid the palm trees?" She frowned.

"Let's not," I quickly said. For a while, we walked in silence. Lyalya stopped to watch a man with a fishing rod in his hand and suddenly broke into laughter. I looked around wondering what had caused it.

"Ah, it's nothing. Remembered a joke Samsonov used to tell me. So a woman calls up a friend and says, 'My old man went fishing and hasn't come home yet. I've been waiting and waiting. At 5 p.m., he didn't show up. At 7, he didn't show up. At 10, he still hadn't come home. I'm sure my dickhead is spending the night with some whore again!'

"'Don't be silly!' her friend says. 'You know, there can be a perfectly harmless reason. Maybe he drowned!' That's exactly how I came to feel about Samsonov. I often wished he'd drop dead!" my aunt said, forgetting it was her idea not to talk about her ex. "After the divorce, though, he went all the way down. Got to the point when he wanted a bribe from his own daughter for that letter!"

"What letter?"

"The letter of permission, don't you know? We've really been out of touch, let me tell you! Well now, when Lyuba decided to emigrate to Germany, the state demanded she get permission from her father. An adult married woman, can you believe it! So Samsonov ups and says, 'Pay me, and you'll get your permission.' It wasn't peanuts he was asking for either. He hadn't seen his daughter since the age of five, had nothing to do with her after I divorced him and left Siberia—and here he goes, demanding baksheesh! Of course, Lyuba doesn't have that kind of money. So he says, 'Your mom's pockets are deep. Dive right in!' Well, we got the money together somehow. But he didn't get to use it. Gave up his ghost in an alley; the money was gone, of course. They say he had a hard time making ends meet at the end of his life, knocking on doors, fixing old irons, almost begging. So when he got his bribe, he drank himself stupid and froze to death. He had been a really good electrician, mind you!" Aunt took a breath. "Anyway, enough of that. Let's go watch the ships!"

As we were approaching the tall ramparts encircling Kotor, a cruise ship slowly moved out of the harbour. The sight was majestic, but it didn't make much of an impression on my aunt.

"All these tourists. What do they get to see? Hop on, hop off, is that the phrase? Nah, I wouldn't want to spend my holidays like that! What we're doing is best." She sighed and looked at me sharply. "Tell me, it must be lonely living abroad, eh? Do you have close friends? Anybody to talk to heart to heart, like you and I do?"

Is she asking about my life, or the life of her daughter in Germany, I wondered.

"Oh, things are different in the West," I said. "Sure, I have friends. But people don't carry their souls on their sleeves. They prefer … How shall I put it? Not to burden others with their problems. Nobody wants to appear weak or needy. Poor, distressed. No grand emotional outpours."

Lyalya squinted. "What do you mean?"

"Things seem to be more controlled, more regimented: work, sex, friendship; each in its own slot."

"Cold fish, in other words, your Canadians, eh?"

"More restrained than Russians, that's for sure. But people are busy, you see. I'm busy too. Everybody's on a tight schedule."

"Same at home these days. Especially for the young. Busy making money. In the old days, you know, you'd just drop by, sit in the kitchen, talk past midnight. A good talk is such a relief … Not anymore. So your Canadians, what, they never visit each other?"

"Of course they do! But people don't just knock at your door. When you invite guests, you give them a couple weeks' notice. When they say goodbye, you don't cajole them into staying for hours; you don't force more food or drink on them."

Lyalya looked at me with sorrowful eyes: "And what if you need help?"

"Oh, they'll help. I mean, people help if you ask. I had a lover once, and when I lost my job, he asked if I wanted him to help me look for a new one."

"A piece of work, your lover! I would have scratched his eyes right out for that!"

"But why?"

"You act, you don't ask!"

"He was quite a decent man, by the way … an architect, like you. But he didn't want to presume—who knows, maybe I didn't want his help, or had some other plans. So he had to ask first."

"What do you mean, 'other plans'? No job means no bread on the table! He simply doesn't know what it's like to starve!"

"You're so strict, Auntie!"

"Ain't I right, though?"

"It's just that you can't assume you know another person's needs. You can't interfere without asking."

"And you like it?"

"You learn to accept it. Distance is not such a bad thing. It gives you space, a kind of freedom."

Lyalya scrutinized me with suspicion. "And you don't feel lonely?"

"Well, you get used to that too."

"Poor girl! I'd have hanged myself! Me, I'd have never adjusted to that life! Never! And who knows? Maybe it's good that Lyuba changed her mind."

Lyalya looked at me like she was expecting an answer, something that would finally relieve her of the pain.

I noticed how pale and haggard her face suddenly became. Had she managed to build a protective cocoon around what happened almost ten years before between her and her daughter? Did she now believe what she was saying?

"German is a hard language to learn," I said.

"German was not the point. You know me: if need be, I would have learned it."

After having lived in Germany for about three years, Lyuba had invited her mother to move to the country. Her zeal in manoeuvring through the labyrinths of bureaucracy was unparalleled. After much effort, she achieved her goal: the permission was granted, paper work done. Wasting no time, Lyalya packed up, said farewell to Ukraine, and moved to Germany. She stayed with her daughter's family for a month—by the end of which she realized that her daughter's welcome had worn thin. No explanation was ever provided. No questions asked. Lyalya simply packed up and returned to Ukraine. For years afterward, she wouldn't mention her daughter's name.

I quickly navigated away from the painful subject.

"You asked me about Canada," I said. "You see, in Canada, one out of four or maybe five is an immigrant. People came from all over the world. How could you know your neighbour, especially in a big city? There's no shared past, no shared experience. What do I know about the childhood of the Chinese girl whose family lives two floors below me? Or the Hindu boy from Rajasthan who is now my doctor? Or, say, the South African from my Italian book club? Nothing! But what matters to me is this: As a nation, Canadians are tolerant. They respect law, common civility; that's the thing! We don't have racial conflicts like Americans do. Between Blacks, Whites, Latinos."

"Hmm, what don't you say … In Ukraine, gypsies are hated. People from Uzbekistan, Tajikistan, all these *Gastarbeiter* are despised. The Ukrainians are goddamn nationalists! And always have been. They just don't like others, especially Russians."

"Hardly a surprise."

"You think? There are no Russian programs left on TV. And the new law on language? Russian children cannot learn their mother tongue! How is that? With eighteen million Russian-speaking people, huh? And the economy? Ten million are working their asses off in the West! Changing the diapers for babies and old people in Poland, in Portugal, in Spain … What is Ukraine hoping for? That the West will accept them into the European Union? Trade with them? Buy their inferior steel? Ha! Like last year's snow, the West needs Ukraine! The West doesn't care! When soldiers were recruited to fight in Donbas, mothers had to knit socks and sow underwear for them because the government couldn't dress their soldiers! Corruption from top to bottom! I can only hope that Eastern Ukraine will finally separate and join Russia."

"You got a new president now. Maybe things will get better."

That got Aunt huffing and puffing: "What can he do, this comedian? How can this nice Jewish boy rule a country like that? His oligarchs will eat him up without a hiccup while he's boning up on Ukrainian grammar."

"Why would he?"

"He barely speaks Ukrainian! He had to hire teachers before the elections. Ah, you can't imagine what Ukraine has come to. Remember, you and I couldn't talk on the phone for most of the last year! Half of the city didn't have a connection. Why? Cause people steal the cables—there's copper inside; it's worth quite something. As soon as there's a new cable, people dig it up again. It's worse than in America!"

"Do you think Americans dig up telephone cables?"

"Well, don't they? I watched a program about American swindler schemes on Russian TV. The Mormons, in Otah or Atah or something, those polygamists! They marry young girls, herd them into a house, and each wife with a child collects money from the government like a single mother."

"'Welfare,' it's called."

"Whatever it's called, is that true?"

"There might well be a few cases."

"Or another one they show on Russian TV, pretending they didn't finish building their house! I like that one! If two planks of the roof are missing, the house isn't finished. Then they don't have to pay taxes. Clever bastards, right?"

***

When we returned to our flat, Lyalya, as usual, settled on the balcony with a bowl of strawberries in her lap and a pack of cigarettes in front of her.

May days are long. The peaks of the mountains opposite were still illuminated by the setting sun, but dense purple shadows were already wrapping their feet. In the dusk, the air was thinning; it seemed fragile and palpable, as if you could touch your finger to it and make it ring like crystal.

"I don't like the twilight," Aunt said, lighting another cigarette. "It feels as if the day was dying in your arms … And always that thought: How can I account for another day that passed? How can I defend the way I spent it?"

"To whom?"

"Yeah, well, to no one, I guess. God is high up, and the Tsar is far away, as they say. And there's hardly anyone left for me here on Earth either to give account to. You know what's important? That there's somebody there who remembers you as a child. When such a person dies, a piece of you, the most important piece, as I realize now, dies with them."

A discorporate honk of a steamship began wandering through the gorges. Be it this lonely mooing or Lyalya's word, that made me, too, feel sad.

"It's the age," I said. "We're getting old."

"No, it's not that!" Aunt exclaimed, turning her whole body to me. "It all depends on how your life went, how the cards lay down. If you can travel anywhere in the world, meet interesting people, have all these new experiences, if you can just off and fly to the Bahamas whenever you please, you won't go digging in the past!"

I looked at my Aunt in surprise: Did she really think the Bahamas made such a difference? Like everywhere else, people in the West might have problems, get sick, even die—but apparently the old Soviet myth about the eternal feast of life beyond the border is indestructible.

"When you go to the Bahamas, you bring yourself along," I said. "I know how you feel. I, too, used to believe things were better elsewhere. But what if it's best to stay where you were born?"

"You regret having left?" Aunt asked.

I shook my head.

"Honestly?"

I hesitated for a moment with the answer.

"Well, I don't. I mean, rarely. I think if you continue living where you were born, your past is somehow redeemable: you remain connected to it by myriads of invisible threads of which you may not even be aware. Sure, nothing stays the same back home, the names of the streets, even cities change. But the land itself, its smell, the landscapes, the faces, the language, yes, the language! The way people talk and laugh, the way they mimic—everything signals to you: As long as we're here, your past self hasn't perished. You're whole. But once you leave your country, you … how shall I put it? A part of you dies, just as you yourself has said. No place—no matter how comfortable—will become as dear to you as the shabbiest hut of your childhood. You simply can't call any place home again, that's what I mean. Some places are more comfortable than others, and that's about it."

"Perhaps it's a good thing you didn't go to Germany, after all," I said. "Emigration is hard, especially at the start and surprisingly, at the end of the journey."

"How do you mean, at the end?"

"Well, when you're already settled, and have more or less earned your place under your new sun, and put all the efforts and fuss behind you, instead of looking forward as before, you look backward, and then you begin discerning the call that you had no time to hear before."

"A call?"

"Yes. Call signs from a distant shore. Many simply choose to return. But at the beginning, it's again different. The newcomers get tired, not just physically but emotionally tired … tired of constant silent struggles. Dried up, hardened. They yearn for the warmth of the familiar, for a cozy place to rest. If there is no such thing, they invent one. The home country begins to seem rosy."

Lyalya breathed a sigh. "Lyuba never talked to me about any of that. She's a well-respected surgeon with a good salary; they send me pictures of their nice house; she calls me from time to time, sends me parcels."

"See, she does think of you."

"Oh, please! I know my daughter: Guilt, that's what it is. But what happened to her heart, tell me! She was so close to me, so caring. And now—stone hard, she is. All cold and polished. Maybe immigration has done to her exactly what you're describing: killed her heart!" She paused.

"Kids! Why do we want to have them, you tell me! What for? In the end, what do we get for all these years of hard work? Loneliness?"

"You're not serious, are you? I always thought having children was the most wonderful thing in life!"

"If you believed that, and that's what you wanted, why did you decide not to have them?"

"Wasn't much of a decision, really. Just circumstances. You'd have to have somebody you'd want to have them with, right? Somebody suitable. Somebody you can trust and relate to. I'm not saying a soulmate, a perfect match—that's a tall order—but at least a kindred spirit."

"A perfect match! A kindred spirit! Ha! As the saying goes: *Love me the way I am! A good one, anybody can love!* Men … there's always something wrong with them, or haven't you noticed? If it's not this, it's that. That's the law of nature. Newton's second law!" Lyalya gave a deep sigh, as if she felt a personal responsibility for men's warped design. "As Gogol said, if I could glue the lips of Nikanor Ivanovich to the nose of Feodor Petrovich, etc., etc., etc.! But can we do that? No! Well, then, we have to tolerate them, to compromise. You've been living alone all your life, never married. I don't know how you do it. Of course now, I'm alone too, but when I was younger, I absolutely had to have a man! A husband!"

"Even though you're so … so capable, so self-sufficient!? I can't drive a nail into the wall, but you?!"

"For a nail, you call a handyman. That's not what I need a man for. Sure, I can do this and that and hundreds of other things. But at the end of the day, you ask yourself: Whom are you doing it for, Lyalya, eh? Just for yourself? That's ridiculous! Thank God, I've never had an empty home. Men cling to me like leeches."

Feeling the coolness of fresh sheets and adjusting my body to an unfamiliar bed with a mattress that felt too firm, I thought that as much as I would've liked to have children, the fear of letting a man into my life was always a more powerful force. In my youth, I didn't lack admirers, but with the passage of time, I grew to love the gentleness of my peaceful, uneventful life. I suspected that my aunt was not adverse to drama; I, on the other hand, abhorred it. The turmoil and the uncertainty that come with relationships—I could never handle it. I do not consider myself an artist. To stitch together pieces of fabric for a quilt is an intimate affair between me and a needle, but as soon as I start to draw out my design or put together the template, the anticipation of extraordinary worlds that I am about to bring to life fills me with joy! If fancy takes me, I can create shimmering diamonds to trick the eye of a spectator into all kinds of optical illusions. The bygone world of English gardens, with roses climbing to the thatched roofs and coming to life under my hand will satisfy the nostalgia of both young girls and middle-aged women. Exotic plants, intertwining their lithe bodies, will dazzle a perspective buyer with a more vivid imagination, thanks to their burning magenta, dashing emeralds, and mysterious chartreuse.

I feel perfectly happy in these contained worlds of my own creation. Yet, I'm not some kind of a withered spinster seeing nothing beyond my sowing machine! My horizons are wide open! When my business grew, and we were selling quilts internationally (long before the Internet), I had a chance to travel to the most remote parts of the world. Hunting for new patterns, for new ideas, became a passion of mine. I'd sit with old grandmas in remote Kenyan villages and learn from them. I travelled as far as Central Australia to see the aboriginal fabrics of the Aranda people, known for their whimsical patterns. True, the pleasures of domesticity have eluded me, nor have I known great love or great passion in my life, but I learned to find contentment in the way my life have unfolded.

"Are you asleep already?" My aunt's chesty voice wedged into my musings. "Speaking of life without men, it's like cooking borscht with no salt, no pepper, no tomatoes, just beets and potatoes. Blah! You can still eat it, but it'll get stuck in your throat. I've always liked strong-willed, powerful men with, you know, determination in their eyes. He decides something, and he does it! He doesn't sit on the fence, dangling his legs in fear: 'Should I jump, or should I sit here till cows go back home.' But whom did I end up with instead? Pushovers, weaklings!"

"But, Lyalya … how shall I put it nicely?"

"Go ahead, just say it."

"You are a powerhouse, a locomotive going full speed. If they get in your way, they get smashed. Otherwise, there'd be a constant power struggle."

"I know. I've figured that out myself a long time ago. In the past I thought, 'God almighty! Why do I have to make do with these wet blankets all the time, these fence sitters? But I wisened up. Now I've got the answer! They need my help, that's why. They need me to keep them from falling. I've always had to keep my arms open to give them a soft landing. And me, what would I do with a man who needs nothing? We'd be like two celestial bodies passing each other in the empty universe. No interaction. I'll tell you something that I never told anybody … Are you awake?"

"Yes. All ears."

"Here's the truth: I'm tired. Tired of being me. Tired of holding my arms stretched out. You know what I wanted all my life? How I imagined my man? My real soulmate? First of all, I imagined his bosom. That's the most important part for me! Stop laughing. Not in that sense, silly! Ever since I was a very young girl, I thought if I had a man, all I wanted was to bury my head in his chest. So he protected me from the world, you see. And I'll have nothing to be afraid of. I even had this fantasy of being a tiny creature."

"Like a fairy?"

"No, a real human being, but tiny enough that he can carry me in his pocket so I'm always protected. That's where I live: in his pocket."

"And you don't see the light of the day?"

"Why? He'd take me out. I'd sit in his palm, and we'd chat. But as soon as there's some danger, I'd duck back and be safe again, see? Wherever he goes, I go too, in his pocket. So if he, for example, talks to somebody, I can hear everything, but I don't need to participate cause he'll do all the talking for me. And I can just rest or fall asleep if I wish."

"And what does he feed you? Nectar?"

"Must be nectar, I guess."

Chapter 11: Off to Norilsk

When I opened my eyes the next morning, the first things I saw were my aunt's legs stretching over her head on the floor, her toes almost touching the ground. She uncoiled, then bent forward, reaching her toes, uncoiled again, and moved into a back bend. I suspected that without an audience, her morning routine would've been slacker. Was she trying to impress me?

"It's chillier today," I said, reluctantly getting out of bed.

Lyalya got up and went to the kitchen to start making breakfast. Helping her was forbidden from day one. "At home, you can work to your heart's content!" was all she said. Subsisting on coffee and cigarettes, she kept a watchful eye on me, making sure I consumed fried eggs, porridge, and yogurt every morning. But no bread. "Your nectar is ready!" she'd announce, and we'd sit down at a tiny kitchen table for a meal.

"How old were you when you moved to Siberia?" I asked. "I hardly know anything about your life there."

"Siberia? I was twenty-two, I guess. Just graduated from the architecture university."

"Did you really have to follow Samsonov there when you married him? Couldn't you two have stayed in Ukraine? It's quite a bit warmer."

"Sure, I could've. In fact, he'd have preferred to stay in Zaporizhzhia. After all, he was born in Ukraine. No, the folly was all my own. Independence! Freedom from my family! The romance of it! How did the song go those days? 'We'll melt the permafrost and make a garden blossom!' Besides, I wanted to put some distance between me and Victor."

The Admiral happened to be living in Zaporizhzhia.

"So off we go to Norilsk! The further the better! Beyond the Arctic Circle! The most northern city and the coldest city in the country! Big bonuses for 'severe climate conditions!' And the most polluted too. I thought Zaporizhzhia was dirty. Little did I know! They'd found the largest deposit of nickel in the world there, or so they said. Chimneys belching out sulfur dioxide day and night … Your spit would be black on the white snow. They called their river Norilka 'the blood river,' because of all the red goo in it. And one other thing. Nobody was talking about it at the time, and we, young enthusiasts, had no clue, but people there knew who had built the city: the *zeks*. Slave labour. One of the largest camps was close by; ten thousand dead? Two hundred and fifty thousand? Nobody knows. Each house in Norilsk stands on a pile hammered into permafrost, about ten metres deep. We had a neighbour, an old woman. She was once digging her potato patch in summer, and human bones came to the surface. That happened every spring; she was quite used to it.

"We figured Samsonov could get a job as an electrical engineer at the Norilsk nickel smelter. And he did, except he started drinking right away. I remember our first winter: total darkness, temperatures of minus fifty Celsius, snowstorms, blizzards … It hurts to breathe. Every gulp of air burns your lungs, and if you happen to be on the road in a blizzard, in five minutes the truck will be buried in snow. So you wait till a tractor pulls you out. That is, if your lights are still working. If not, they'd find your corpse the next day.

"And the summers. The summers are another story! They come suddenly, without any warning: You leave your house in boots and your warmest jacket, and suddenly it's plus thirty-five Celsius! In the tundra, mosquitoes and flies will eat you alive. But there's beauty too. I remember I picked a small flower in the tundra, a little lilac star, and as I held it in my palm, the petals began opening from its warmth. In those short summer days, as far as your eye can see, you walk on a carpet of flowers: reds, burgundies, purples, blues, yellows … They say the desert is like that too, breaking into spectacular bloom for a short while. In summer, the ice on the lakes thaws for a little while. I got to swim then, and I'd swim far out … But one thing you don't want to do is touch the bottom. It's permafrost. And the mountains are bright red, or pink! Even these ones here are not as beautiful. So yes, there were things to love there. And we weren't afraid of hard work, or the frost, or the mosquitoes. We were young, you see, that's the thing!"

Waving the rings of smoke away from me, Lyalya kept dragging on her cigarette. "When we arrived in Norilsk, I had hoped I'd be able to work as an architect. An architect! In Norilsk! Fat chance. I think I never told you what I ended up doing. And you'd never guess. Imagine, I became a model! They needed somebody to show dresses on TV. They took my measurements: Twice the wrists had to equal the neck, twice the neck had to equal the waistline. I fit the mould."

Chapter 12: Life in Siberia

"THAT WAS THE FIRST and last time Samsonov had forced his will over me," my aunt said finishing her coffee, and hardly touching anything else. While I was picking at my plate, Lyalya washed her cup, cleaned up the counter, swept the floor, all the while filling me on the details of her life in Siberia.

Her husband's jealousy forced her to quit the modelling job three months after she started.

But she wasn't one to be broken.

Smiling, charming the taciturn northerners into chatting, Lyalya ultimately managed to get as close as she could to her profession. She supervised the construction of hospitals, schools, and housing projects, travelling all over Siberia, as far as Vladivostok.

An actress at heart, she unconsciously mimicked the way people talked and dressed. But what thawed up even the most mistrustful hearts was her vivacious cordiality, her laughter, and her sincere desire to help. The world, in constant need of assistance, could certainly rely on her. And people responded in kind. The wives of workers brought her warm clothing knitted in the long winter months, veggies grown in their hothouses, and berries gathered in the tundra during the short summer weeks: foxberries, cloudberries ...

"Then, on New Year's Eve, we'd have a proper feast for my whole team. With *kholodets*, my crown dish: You boil pigs' feet and cows' knees for four hours. Cut some fresh garlic into soup bowls, lay pieces of boiled meat on top, and then pour the broth over it all. Then you leave the bowls outside in the cold to thicken. So each guest gets a personal perfect bowl of meat jelly. Dumplings, I did them with three sorts of meat. Once, I made five hundred pieces! Well, me and Zina, my neighbour."

I finally finished my breakfast. While Lyalya was washing dishes, my eyes were drawn yet again to her enlarged, knobby, reddish joints that didn't seem to belong to her body.

"Arthritis?"

"Oh sure, all this washing in cold water in Siberia."

"No hot water?"

"In Norilsk?"

I blushed under her gaze. "Tell me, were you ever afraid?"

"Afraid? All the time! I fear lots of things; white mice, for instance."

"No, seriously. Being a boss over tough men in Siberia, former prisoners, some of them—and you the only woman?"

"Can't complain, really. I never felt any hostility. The men always respected me. Besides, I wasn't the only woman. The only female architect and a construction supervisor, yes, but there were women labourers, plasterers, and painters. It was physically hard, my job, that's true enough. Say I'm building a high-rise: the elevators aren't running yet, there's no heating. You have to climb all the way up to the twentieth floor to inspect the building, and it's minus forty outside. But I never had any problems with my workers. They were good to me. Respectful. The bosses, the bureaucrats, that's another story … But afraid? No."

Lyalya was putting the dishes in the cupboard, and for a moment, while her hands were shuttling back and forth, she stopped, and her gaze softened, fixed at one point.

"Well, I'll tell you. A long time ago … in the late sixties, I think it was … Lyuba was three or four then. They found new oil deposits in the taiga, about five hundred kilometres from Tomsk. They herded the former *zeks* to start exploitation. They had to remain in Siberia under police surveillance. Some were criminals, some political prisoners, all kinds. And they had to live somewhere. I was sent to build cottages for them, to figure out where to build, to measure the terrain, to calculate the construction materials needed, the usual. No roads or anything. I arrived by helicopter. Me and Vitaly, my pilot. Have you ever ridden a helicopter in a strong wind? I was puking all the way up there. Finally, we land on a small clearing in the taiga. I must've been looking like death from that ride. The men encircle me. My pilot, Vitaly, they push him to the side. Men looking me up and down, like they'd never seen a woman before, and maybe they hadn't in God knows how many years. And there was silence. I don't know how long it lasted—three minutes, maybe? But I'll never forget that silence. That's when I got scared. Then one of them told me to drop my pistol. But I knew better than travelling without a pistol through Siberia. So I go: 'Dropping this? You don't want to be responsible for me becoming a tiger's dinner, do you?' There are some chuckles, but then another guy says: 'How much for your ass?' I go, 'Not for sale. And if it was, in all your life, you wouldn't earn enough dough for even my pinky. So calm down, buddy!'

"Again, some laughter from the crowd, but the guy who told me to drop my pistol shouts: 'Cut it out, you suckers!' Then he steps out of the circle and comes right up to me. 'Our new boss, are you? Take my free advice: Bug off to where you came from. We're free folks, we need no minders, least of all one in a skirt.'

"Well, that was plain unfair, and I said so: 'Do I look fit to boss anyone around? Look at me! Ask my pilot: I messed up the whole goddam helicopter puking. The reason I'm here is to take care that your noses and other important body parts don't get frostbitten! You're used to sleeping in barracks, aren't you? I'm going to build you cottages like you're at a Black Sea resort!'

"And once I say that, I hear a little chuckle, then another, and another, like a ripple washing over the crowd, and suddenly they are all roaring with laughter: 'She's going to build Winter Palace for us, this cunt!' And after that, everything went smoothly."

We were silent for a while.

"No," Aunt said, "I wasn't afraid of the people. What the state did to people, that was scary. In the cities, we didn't know, or we pretended not to know, but in Siberia, you couldn't hide it. Okay, let's get ready, or we'll miss out on the morning, and the strawberries will be gone. We can chat on the way."

She took off her apron, and we went to Kotor for strawberries.

Chapter 13: The Murder

"You asleep?" Lyalya asked, braiding her still pretty thick and long hair before bed and deftly winding her bangs onto curlers. "Are you asleep?"

"No, not yet," I said, drifting away.

"I should let you sleep, I talk too much."

A moment later, her voice broke the silence again.

"You asleep? I shouldn't bother you. I often have insomnia, do you? You know what I do when that happens? I try to remember every capital of every country in the world, especially the African countries; they're the toughest ones."

"Why bother?" I said in a foggy, sleepy half-voice.

"What do you mean, why bother? You need to exercise your memory muscles. You don't want Africa, you can think of Einstein's equation instead. What do you mean you never knew it? It's simple. $E = mc^2$. I can explain. Really not that hard."

"Lyalechka, my darling, can we postpone till tomorrow? Why don't we try and get some sleep now."

"Ah, I must tire you out." She sighed. "Sleep, baby, sleep." She fell silent for a moment, but then I heard her breathy, muted voice again. "All this talk about my life with Samsonov … it drives my sleep away. Racks my soul. You know, I should be really hating him for what he has done to me and my kids, and yet, I feel sorry for him. Especially when night falls, I feel, how to put it … strangled by pity … the kind of life he had. He keeps holding on to me, holding on."

Her voice was trailing off in the absence of an answer, but I didn't want to disturb the cozy cocoon of sleepiness by talking.

"His mother was murdered right in front of him. Then the orphanage, the wandering all over Russia. Is it his fault he turned out the way he did?"

I bolted up in bed, all sleepiness evaporated.

"What do you mean, murdered?"

"Exactly that. Murdered, by her lover."

***

My childhood memories of Samsonov never associated him with violence, but then I rarely saw him. He sometimes needed to come to Moscow for some reason or other. Our one-room apartment served as a transit point for numerous relatives who visited the capital on business or for fun and culture "to have a sniff of civilization." My mother would always let him stay with us. What did they have in common? What could they talk about? Nothing, it seemed, but there they were, drinking tea in the kitchen, even joking. I remember Samsonov's stubbly hair, the shiny stones on his cufflinks, the perfect trouser fold, the starchy cuffs, and the stench of cheap cologne.

Something gloomy and dangerous seemed to emanate from his heavy, puffy face, his smallpox spots, his buffalo-strong back stretching to the limit his well-ironed jacket. It was impossible to imagine him as a child.

By and by, I learned the story from Aunt. In the thirties, the state had unleashed an expropriation campaign, forcing Ukrainian peasants to hand in everything they owned. This led to massive hunger and the death of about ten million people. Samsonov's father, a peasant from a small village in Ukraine, was one of the victims. He had hidden a bag of grain in a dugout at the cemetery, was arrested and sent to Siberia. His wife fled the next day with her two small children.

Up to the seventies, the Soviet peasant's life was not unlike that of serfs under the Tsar. Forbidden to have identification papers, they were now owned by the State represented by collective farms and were not allowed to relocate or look for a job elsewhere.

For almost a year, the fugitives were on the run, hiding in cargo and cattle trains that rattled them across the vast expense of the country farther and farther away from devastated Ukraine, to the East, beyond the Ural Mountains. The destination Samsonov's mother was hoping to reach was the city of Tumen, where her brother Petr lived, her only surviving relative.

I was listening to Lyalya's muted voice in the quiet of the night. I'd heard similar stories before, different variations on the same theme: men, women, and children hunted down by their own country, the country they were taught to love since early childhood, and did love and rhapsodized in exalted songs accompanied by thunderous military orchestras.

That a wife of an "enemy of the people" managed to escape arrest, to flee with small children, to survive, was a miracle.

"What was the name of that woman, your ex mother-in-law?" I asked.

"Samsonov has never mentioned it. I found out accidentally, from neighbours in Zaporozhje."

****

Luck smiled at them in Lipetsk, a city only four hundred kilometres away from Moscow and far away from the Urals. That day, the mother said she'd go looking for some food, and the children waited for her in the factory boiler house, where some kind soul let them warm themselves. An hour later, the mother returned and let herself fall on the boxes without taking off her padded jacket or her felt boots. The children feared she'd lain down to die. But then she sat up, took off her wool headscarf, and began weeping, choking with relief: "Here we are, children, I've got a job, they let us, let us be ..."

The children were looking at her, perplexed. The word "hired" meant nothing to them. They were hungry. And she didn't bring any food.

For the mother, the exultation lay not so much in the pay, which was meagre, as in the illusion of permanence. The fugitives would now have a roof over their head: a room in a dormitory and access to food. The mother would do enough tasting while cooking to go without meals; for her children, she'd regularly manage to filch something from the factory kitchen, usually a pair of meat rissoles wrapped in bits of newspaper and hidden in the legs of her rubber boots.

Fate had brought them luck, or so they thought, by an unexpected means—at the personnel department of the plant, the mother chanced to meet the chief of the local police, Koburov, an older heavyset guy with the crooked legs of a cavalryman. Noticing a young woman in a worn-out jacket, her delicate face thin with worry, Koburov ran his tongue along the gums with a gold front tooth, as he usually did when he saw a good-looking lass.

"What are you doing here, Swan Princess? You're not local, are you?"

"We're from Ukraine."

"Got that far, eh? Have a hubby?"

The woman lowered her eyes.

"Any place to stay?"

Again, she didn't answer.

Koburov moved closer to her. "A bird of passage. No nest, no home? You know I have to arrest you as an itinerant?"

For the first time, her wide-open doleful eyes looked directly into his with dark intensity.

"'Black eyes, burning eyes … how much you scare me,'" the policeman crooned. "Cossack blood, ah? Hot stuff." Koburov came closer. Her old blouse let him glimpse the contours of her breasts. She smelled vodka on his breath.

"Can you cook? For eighty people or so?"

She nodded.

"Lyda," Koburov shouted across the room to the girl in the human resources window. "Zhizhin told me you were looking for a cook. Here's one for you. Register her for three months to replace Chubrikova for starters."

The girl in the window raised her brows. "Ivan Alexeevich, Chubrikova is coming back from maternity leave in two months."

"Then register her for two. What are you staring at me for? I'll talk to Zhizhin myself, I'm telling you."

Ivan Zhizhin was the secretary of the plant's party committee. Nobody could be hired without his permission, but that would be no problem; they were buddies and drank and bathed at Koburin's banya.

"Give her a cot at the dorm," the policeman added casually, his sharp, estimating glance taking in the whole of the young woman's body.

She said very quietly, with her lips alone: "I'm not alone. I have children: a boy of seven and a girl of five."

"Kids? Why didn't you say at once?" He frowned, hesitating for a moment. But didn't backtrack. "Well, the Soviet power takes care of mothers raising the future generation of Communists, right? If that's the case, let's find you a separate room in the dorm. For now. Put the children to bed in the evening and wait for your guest. We have to drink to your new job, don't we?"

Since that day, Koburov would come to the factory dorm every second evening, bringing a bottle of vodka, which he quickly emptied. After dinner, when the children fell asleep, he'd maneuver their mother toward the bed separated from the corner where they slept by a calico rag hanging from the ceiling.

Every night, the children would be awoken by wild growls of the stranger. The girl whimpered with fear, and her brother became convinced that what the policeman was trying to do at night was to kill his mother.

"Why does your breath stink?" the boy once heard. "I told you not to eat garlic, didn't I!"

"I had a toothache, that's why," Mother whispered fearfully.

"You stupid village bitch! Next time, go see a doctor instead. Never mind, come here, just shut your mouth." The policeman must have done something terrible to Mother, her son thought, as she groaned with pain and then broke into sobbing. An hour later, the policeman would be gone. Mother said he had wife and kids at home.

At other times, when night fell and the sounds of tired, dishevelled life of a dorm finally died away, little Samsonov heard the policeman complain: "Stop lying there like a chump! Are you a woman or what?"

"Shh, you'll wake up the children."

"Fuck them! You've got a real man in your bed, you should appreciate it. Now stop crying, will you! Are you ill or what? Always sobbing … Come here, I'll heal you the only way that works!"

Now Mother was stealing an extra rissole for Koburov, three all in all. They had dinner together, as a family, and the policeman would quickly consume his. Then anger would rise in him to a boiling point. "Who are you stealing food from, you kulak spawn? The Party and the people! If you bring another one, I'll lock you up, you'll see!"

One day, he broke the rissole in half, stuck one half into his mouth and threw the other in Mother's face. The boy jumped up, and his little fists rained upon the offender. The bullet intended for the child hit the leg of a chair. The second bullet killed the mother.

***

The two orphans reached Tumen a month and a half later. The elder sister could barely make out their Uncle Peter's address in their mother's scrawl on a crumpled piece of paper. They had hoped Uncle Peter would take them in. But shortly before their arrival, he had moved in with his mistress, as it turned out. When they knocked at the door, his recently abandoned wife half-opened it. "You can stay overnight, here on the floor," she said, reluctantly letting them in. "I don't have enough for my own children, much less for relatives of his. Why doesn't his bitch adopt you?" she said under her breath. But the children heard her.

Nevertheless, on the day of their arrival, she took potatoes from her children's plates, halved them, and silently gave the halves to the orphans. Her own children eyed orphaned cousins with scorn. After dinner, they pushed the intruders into a dark storeroom.

"Take care you don't kill them dead!" their mother shouted.

Next day, Samsonov and his sister did what they were used to doing when their mother was alive: they took to the road again.

They were apprehended fast asleep on a dirty train station floor strewn with cracked sunflower seeds. The siblings spent the rest of their childhood on the metal bunk beds of various orphanages.

In spite of his share of petty thefts, Samsonov managed to avoid the colony for young delinquents and even enrol at an institute. He turned out handsome and tall, with the body of an athlete. Natural smarts got him a degree in electrical engineering.

As an adult, he never reconnected with his sister.

***

I looked at the clock. It was after three in the morning. No chance of falling asleep at that hour anyway. Huddling up in the cold room with a blanket on my shoulders, I sat up in bed.

The moonlight coming through the window softened the features of Lyalya's face, making her look younger. The metal curlers on her forehead sparkled in the pale light, looking totally out of place.

"I don't know why, but the longer I live, the sorrier I feel for my ex." She sighed in the dark. "I used to think: no matter how bad your childhood was, it's no excuse for being an asshole! After all, you have your whole life to cure the ills of the past, to build up your life brick by brick, right? As Chekhov put it, 'All your life, you have to squeeze the slave out of yourself drop by drop.' But Samsonov, he remained a slave. And I should have helped him, but didn't."

"Oh, come on, now. Why would you blame yourself for his life? He was a grown man! Didn't you just say that everybody is responsible for their own life?" I was irritated from the lack of sleep.

Aunt yawned deeply. "Oh, I don't know ... maybe ... night thoughts are night birds: they peck your brain out if you're not careful. Let's go to sleep, pumpkin. It's almost dawn."

She rustled, making herself comfortable, and soon I heard her laboured breathing.

Chapter 14: The Golden Horde

"Do you want to know why in Russia, not to mention Ukraine, people will never live well?" Lyalya asked the next day while eating strawberries on our way home from Kotor market.

"Why?"

"Because we're too chicken to repent! Without repentance, nothing can change. We'll be running on the spot. You know, Lyuba told me things about Germany: every pupil knows about the Holocaust. Germany took responsibility for the war. They've probably had it up to here, the Germans, but still every pupil is forced to learn this story! The way you stick a pup's nose into its own shit so it learns not to shit in the house ever again, pardon the expression. And look: The Germans restored their place among the nations. They should be respected for this. And we Russians? We destroyed who knows how many—forty, sixty million?—of our own people! And who gives a damn? The Russian troika is rushing along, as Gogol said. All nations are giving way to Russia. Like hell they do. Nobody needs Russia, people either fear or disdain it. Nothing will happen in Russia without repentance!"

That word again! It didn't sound at all like Aunt.

"Repentance? But how will you separate the victims from the executioners? Everybody was involved. You know yourself: Those who tortured and shot others in the twenties would become victims of terror in the thirties. Then they suffered the same fate, wave by wave … unravelling an anaconda feeding on itself."

"I agree!" Lyalya said. "And let me tell you: while Putin is in power, there can be no repentance. He'd be happy to return the Soviet power if he could. He admires Stalin, I'm sure!"

"Of course he does! He's a KGB man, after all."

I felt relief. At least Aunt wasn't a supporter of Putin. I suspected that her anti-Ukrainian sentiments would naturally push her toward Russia. But I'd been too fast with my conclusions.

"Still," she said, looking at the mountains as if inviting them to witness her words, "I might not like him personally, but I think Putin is good for Russia. Russia needs a strong hand. He won back the Crimea, and I hope he'll win back Eastern Ukraine too!"

"Are you serious?" I asked. "Under international law, Crimea belongs to Ukraine."

"What law is that? It's all a mess made by Khrushchev! He just wanted to give a little present to his Ukrainian compatriots—drunk, he probably was, or hungover. In fact, the Crimea has always been a part of Russia!"

"Not always. Only since Catherine the Great."

"That's not enough for you? Have you been in the Crimea lately? Well, I have, and let me tell you: The Ukrainians have turned it into a hole, into a cloaca! Putin will rebuild it. Putin will save Russia. He leads with a strong hand. He has stopped the Wild East of the nineties. You don't know how bad it was! Russia needs a dictator."

"How can you hate your own people so much?"

"Whom? Russians or Ukrainians? I don't hate either. I was born here, in Ukraine. I built hospitals, schools, houses all over Ukraine and Russia, including Siberia. I love Russia. But I know Russia too well. That's why I'm telling you: democracy in Russia will never happen."

"But it's possible in the West! Russia is part of Europe. I'm not saying that democracy has no shortcomings—"

"Shortcomings my bum! Impossible is what it is—in Russia, I mean."

"But why?"

"The people. No respect for the law. And everybody's stealing."

"When Russians move to the West though, they work well and respect the laws."

"Yes, other people's laws, they can respect, but not their own. At home, they can only steal. They can't help it. The Russians are a fine people. But spoiled by the Golden Horde."

"What?!"

"The Golden Horde. The Tatar Yoke. Read history! Nothing has changed since its rule seven hundred years ago. The principle is the same. There is the khan, and the khan has absolute power, be his name Stalin or Putin. Nature abhors a vacuum, as Seneca said."

"How can you compare? These are completely different societies—the Middle Ages, the Tsarist Empire, the 'dictatorship of the proletariat,' and what's going on now, after the Perestroika, whatever you want to call it."

"They only seem different. Timofey and I have often argued about it. I was outraged at first too, but now I see he was right. Kings, communists, reformers—it's all still the Golden Horde. Seven hundred years ago, Russian princes would amuse the khan and his bootlickers by crawling toward him on all fours and then backing off on all fours because you can't show your ass to the ruler. That's just what everybody does today. Back then, the princes were after letters of privileges, they'd tear each other to pieces for them. And what did these letters say? 'Don't burn my hut, burn my neighbour's hut instead; ease up on the taxes, and I'll be licking your Tatar ass and crawling on all fours my whole life.' So what has changed? Tell me! Nothing! A friend from Siberia sent me a letter recently. They had a flood or something, and one villager complained directly to Putin. He invites her to the Kremlin, just like Stalin did in the past, with the milkmaids breaking the milking record. Promises her some help and shakes her hand. She returns to her village, and you know what? She doesn't wash that hand for one week—another week. And the villagers, they line up to touch that hand. Eh? What would you say to that? Timofey was a good judge of history, he put things clearly. Putin understands what his people need and slings it in their muzzles! Here, guzzle it up! After him, another will come, and it'll be the same. The Golden Horde, as I told you."

I didn't know what to say. Hard to argue against such a radical indictment!

Despite my silence, Lyalya wouldn't calm down. "All my life, I've been fighting the bureaucracy of the Golden Horde! Lenin had no inkling what they'd make of the idea of Communism! How did the Devil put it in *The Master and Margarita*? 'How come, no matter what one asks for, you don't have it?' Bricks, they didn't have. Concrete, they couldn't make because they had neither gravel nor sand. Aluminum was in short supply. Cement, I couldn't find with a candle in a daylight. Nails, you had to order from Belorussia in exchange for ten kilograms of oranges, and where the hell could I get oranges?

"A good thing my Georgian friend Zurab was the director of a collective farm. He'd send me oranges from Tbilisi to Russia, and I'd move them on to Belorussia! Or let's say I needed some bulldozers. The administration has one bulldozer per hundred thousand square kilometres of taiga! I say, no bulldozers? Fine, send me some shovels instead. We're going to dig the foundation ditch for an industrial plant with shovels. They took it seriously, poor buggers. So I got one hundred shovels, all dull—they had nothing to sharpen them with! I sent them back by the next train.

"That was our life! Begging, crawling, licking boots, bribing. That's what gave people in my position heart attacks. And the deadlines. Fulfilling the plans, monthly, quarterly, yearly. You have to hand in a hospital on time, but you don't have enough construction materials. So what do you do? You cut corners, do a slack job. You know that's not the way to build—in a year, max, you'll need serious repairs. But you've got hundreds of people on your payroll. If the building isn't handed in on time, none of them gets paid. So there you are, lying awake at night calculating how long the building will stand before the walls start sagging and praying to God that, in the operation theatre, the ceiling won't collapse on the heads of the surgeons."

"It wasn't the 1930s or the 1940s," I said. "They wouldn't have put you in jail, so how about quitting?"

"And how about feeding your family? I'm not complaining, mind you. I loved my job. I'll be gone, but my hospitals, my kindergartens, my schools will be standing. In Siberia, in Ukraine, in Russia. And that's something. Don't you think?"

Engrossed in conversation, we missed the right turn and were wandering around, lost. The two-storey houses lined up along the embankment all looked alike: yellow or white plaster, geranium pots on narrow balconies and large "to rent" signboards.

"See how these are built?" Aunt asked. "Firmly, with love, with a sense of ownership. A pity I didn't buy some land here awhile back; they say it went for peanuts. I could design and build a house myself.. But it's too late now."

"True enough. If Montenegro joins the European Union, everything will become more expensive."

"The EU? Who's gonna let them in?"

"It's a matter of time. They've been admitted to NATO, after all."

"Why do they need NATO for? Who's threatening them?"

"Your dear Putin, for example."

"Oh, stop already with Putin! You use him like a bugaboo. Do you think Russia cares about tiny Montenegro?"

"Doesn't it? Who almost arranged a putsch here a few years ago? Who was going to disperse the local parliament and kill the prime minister? Who? And then to put a puppet government in place—just so they don't ever think again about joining NATO? Have you heard about it?"

"And you believe this?"

"Here, twenty people involved in the conspiracy were arrested."

"See how propaganda works in the West, just as well as in Russia! But sweetheart, why on Earth are we talking about politics? All those politicians, damn them all to hell!"

Chapter 15: The Ghost Town of Perast

The next day, as usual, we got our three kilos of strawberries in Kotor (I couldn't persuade Aunt to buy any less) and sat down on the bench at the fortress wall.

"Let's have a little day trip!" I said, looking at a grandiose white ship majestically moving into the harbour. "We haven't seen anything yet."

Lyalya gave a crooked grin. "Tell me honestly, are you bored with your aunt? Are you? It's so lovely here, with the gulls screaming. When I was young, I loved going to the Dnieper to watch the seagulls. They all seem gone now. You know"—she sighed—"I was as antsy as you are back in my day, always dying to go somewhere: new places, new people, and now, I'm done with landscapes. All I need is a chance to talk to someone close once in a while. I still can hardly believe we really managed to meet!" Lyalya snuggled up to me and hugged me. "Eat some strawberries, my little girl!"

"I will," I said, unscrewing the green stem from a sweet ripe berry. "By the way, I booked a tour for us. Not a long one, just half a day."

Aunt took her hand off my shoulder, and her face closed down immediately. "When did you manage to do that?"

"Back in Canada. Tomorrow at nine, they'll be coming to pick us up."

"Back in Canada? Ah, we'll have to go, I guess."

She sighed.

***

In her black baseball cap and yellow rubber coat, the guide looked like an exotic bird. The bird's name was Natasha. She pushed herself out of her Soviet-made car with a jerk, the tails of the yellow coat flying, the elastic miniskirt gathering under her belly like an accordion. She twisted her head back and forth, again, just like a bird, and her jet-black hair, pushed through the back band of her cap, sliced the air like a whip. Natasha looked to be about twenty. As for the young guy at the wheel, he didn't introduce himself, nor did he turn his head in our direction.

"Off to Perast now, and then we'll hop over to the island, and then they'll have a snack," Natasha said to the driver as she let herself fall into the front seat at his side. "Nineteen baroque palaces, fifteen Catholic churches, and all that jazz." She looked over her shoulder at us. "Can you walk?"

"Do you see a wheelchair anywhere?" Aunt said.

Natasha seemed somewhat embarrassed. "No need to take it the wrong way. It's just, well, one client, an older woman, climbed up to the chapel all right, but then she couldn't make her way down. We had to drag and carry her."

"Never mind, let's go!" Aunt said. Physical infirmities were not exactly her favourite subjects.

The car began climbing the steep serpentine path around Kotor Bay. Below, the bowl of the sea was shining, bright and round. Little houses with red-tile roofs and white, plastered sides were snuggling up to the shore and the mountain.

"You live here? When did you come over from Russia?" Aunt obviously wanted to soften the effect of her wheelchair comment.

"I'm not actually from Russia. I'm from Kharkiv."

"Ah, a fellow countrywoman! I'm from Zaporizhzhia," Lyalya said. "So do you like it here?"

"You bet!"

"And the language?"

"No problem! It's similar to Russian somehow. Three months, and Bob's your uncle! I came here for two weeks, to visit my boyfriend. That was four years ago."

"Yes, these things happen," I said.

"Actually, I wasn't going to stay, especially since I broke up with that guy. So I was wondering what to do with my life. Walking along the beach, repeating to myself non-stop: 'Go back or not, go back or not?' Suddenly I see an adder stone under my feet." Chattering away, Natasha, was clearly addressing Aunt, her fellow countrywoman.

"A what?" I said.

"A pebble with a hole in it. You can wear it around your neck. Here it is!" Natasha turned her head to us and pulled at a black ribbon around her neck, granting us a look at an unremarkable grey stone. "Adder stones are lucky. But you have to stay where you got one. Otherwise, it won't work. This stone came to me, you know, or else it called me. Well, anyway, I came back from the beach as happy as a lark! I felt so light, like a feather! The mountains all around me, the fjords, the beauty of it! By the way, we're driving along a fjord now too. Like in Norway. You ever been to Norway? Me neither. I'm going next year. So anyway, the adder stone decided my fate!" She turned to the driver. "Stop right here."

The Volvo came to a halt at a wooden pier.

On a piece of land that separated the Bay of Kotor from the mountains, the town of Perast sparkled with white-stone palaces.

"Built by Venetians. Everything here is just like in Venice."

Natasha made a wide gesture with her hand and head, which sent her ponytail flying. "Have you ever been to Venice?" she asked me, apparently concluding I was the only one of her two elderly clients who could have possibly had the experience. I kept silent. The new, renovated houses with white-stone façades were nothing like the dark palaces of Venice, blackened by time and water.

"Well now. At the time, the trade was in full swing, but then the Ottoman Turks attacked Perast, and it all went downhill. But the people in Perast defended themselves bravely."

"Strange. The place seems to be so open, no fortifications. But maybe they"— Aunt was talking, but the rooster cry of Natasha's cell phone interrupted her.

"Hello!" Natasha shouted. "Can't talk, I've got people here!"

But before she could hide her cell phone in the yellow folds of her coat, it screamed another *cock-a-doodle-doo*!

"What the hell," Natasha mumbled and hissed into the phone: "Are you deaf or something? I just told you: I can't! Or rather: I don't wanna! What is it that you don't understand? I'll make it clear enough in the evening!" And back to us she turned. "Anyway, what had we been talking about? That I mentioned, that other thing too. Oh yes! Did I say that Perast is almost empty of people?"

"How's that?" Aunt was surprised.

"Well, about four hundred people live here in summer, but in winter, there's simply nothing to do."

"What a strange town."

"Oh, that's not the strangest thing yet! Look over there, across the bay." Natasha waved toward the mountains. It seemed that someone had shaved off a patch of dark green hair from the slope opposite the bay. The bald patch was filled with villas, complete with columns and porticoes. But something was wrong with this silent gathering of ghostly palaces. The windows were black pits, as if after a fire.

"The most luxurious hotel complex on the Adriatic! Only without window glasses or doors. A Russian billionaire started building it but never finished. It seems he's been caught red handed. Now they're looking for a new sponsor. There are a lot of rich Russians here. They bought up all the houses in Montenegro. Their new dachas, that's what they are." Natasha snorted and shook her head.

"If they don't find the money quickly," Aunt said, "everything will turn to dust. Houses can't live without people."

"Now that's funny." The driver entered the conversation, smiling at Aunt. "I thought it was people who couldn't live without houses. Ha!"

"Sure! If the temperature inside is the same as outside, the house collapses." Aunt dived happily into her professional field, giving the driver a radiant smile. Her blue eyes were glittering.

Natasha frowned. "Okay, Igor, you go take a walk for a while, have a coffee or something, and we'll go to the island."

In the middle of the bay, two tiny islands stood out against the bright blue. The left one was empty, except for a gloomy crowd of pyramidal cypresses. The island on the right was just as big as the church upon it, which seemed to rise right out of the water. The milky azure of the dome resembled a baby bib and looked artificial against the deep blue sea and sky. A four-tier bell tower was moulded to the side of the church.

Aunt turned to Natasha. "So what is so special about the island?"

"There's a cool legend about it, I'll tell you in a sec. And anyway, if you are in Perast, you just have to go to the island!"

"Which one?" Lyalya asked, making no secret of her displeasure. "The left or the right one?"

"The one with the cypresses," Natasha said. "That's a cemetery, the island of the dead. We want the one with the church."

I looked closer: indeed, the island with the dark cypresses looked like the San Michele Cemetery, the one on an island not far from Venice.

"You get your tickets in that booth over there," Natasha said, stepping aside and pulling out her cellphone.

"Don't," Aunt whispered into my ear, slightly nudging me in the ribs with her elbow. "You paid her for the tour, didn't you? Let her buy the tickets!"

"She won't," I whispered back. "Besides, they are just a euro fifty. Let me pay."

She shook her head. "What does she want there? I have had my share of islands, you know."

We stepped into a shaky boat. A guy in jeans, a tee-shirt, and black boots, who'd been lying across the seat, woke up and reached for the motor.

"So the tour," Natasha said when we moored. "We're on an artificial island. Some say it's a legend; some say it's a true story. Anyhow, in ancient times, a sailor ended up on a cliff here after a shipwreck. There he was, dying. And then the Virgin Mary appeared to him. And guess what happens next? That's right, she saves him, of course, and he promises to build her a church for it. But how? There's nothing but a rock here, after all! And the water's deep, you know, cause it's a fjord, right? So the sailor says to his friends from Perast: 'Let's build an island!' Well, they tried to weasel out of it, but in the end, they started bringing rocks here in their boats and taught their children to do likewise. A year passed, two years, a hundred, two hundred, them schlepping and dropping all the while. By the way, there's still a holiday tradition to bring stones here on a boat. So by and by, there appeared an island. They built a church in honour of the Virgin Mary, and the sailors still give presents to her. Before a long journey, they go to this church and leave something. Right, here we are. Let's go down the stairs carefully, and on to the museum."

The museum was nothing but a stone cellar stuffed with all sorts of rubbish on rough wooden shelves: sloppily made porcelain plates, square irons, old bedwarmers, copper ladles, rusty padlocks. An old gramophone was cozying up to a soda siphon and an oil lamp.

"How did this thing get here?" Lyalya asked, surprised.

"What? The kerosene lamp?"

"No, there, on the lamp." She nodded toward an oval silver church amulet with an image of the Virgin Mary, the baby in her arms.

Natasha's ponytail swung up, drew an arch in the air, and rushed up the stairs. We followed it.

The picture gallery on the second floor smelled of dust and mice. Two paintings were hanging on the wall, a bit crookedly. One sported a smug, red-haired gentleman in a black shirt with a white front, painted by the clumsy brush of a provincial artist. In his right hand, he was holding a banknote, the left was leaning on a painted trunk, and in the middle, there was another one—yes, indeed, he had three hands!

"It's called *The Bribe Taker*," Natasha said.

The second piece turned out to be not a painting at all but a skilled embroidery. In the centre, the Virgin Mary was raising her hands toward the sky, angels fluttering around her.

"Have a closer look. Don't you notice something?" Natasha asked. "There, you see, the angel on top has golden hair. And this one, below, has white. Can you guess why? The embroiderer used her own hair! Her fiancé put out to sea. She went grey waiting for him."

***

We returned to the apartment at dusk. Lyalya was unlike herself: gloomy, taciturn.

"Tired, huh?" I tried to melt the ice.

"I'm fine." She frowned even harder.

"Okay, no more trips. Promise!" I said. "We're going to spend the rest of the time walking up and down the shore. Tell me, though, do you think the bride is a legend, or is she real? Embroidering with her own hair, waiting her whole life, and all that."

"That she waited, I can believe, but the hair—I doubt it. I might also be waiting for someone, but do you see me embroidering with my hair?"

"You're thinking of Lyuba again, right?"

"Not consciously, but she comes to mind, yes." Then Lyalya suddenly grabbed her head. "I'm such an old fool! I left the creams in my suitcase! They should be in the fridge, all but the German one. The German one, in its package, it won't spoil. It's from her."

"Why are you giving it to me, then?"

"She'll send some more."

"See, your daughter loves you! She sends you presents."

"Trying to atone for her guilt, that's all!"

"Well, why don't you … finally forgive her?"

"You know what Montaigne said?"

"Who?"

"You read Montaigne? He said, 'Bad advice does most harm to the adviser.'"

"Fine," I said, touching Lyalya's shoulder. "But please don't be angry with me, at least. I thought you'd enjoy the trip."

She turned her face to me. "Me, angry? Why on Earth would I be! Don't I see you're doing it all for me, darling!" Easily moving from irritation to exalted tenderness, she hugged me tightly. "Forgive an old fool! Sometimes I have these moods, I don't know … It's not about Lyuba either. Something got to me on that island, you know? Maybe it was that amulet."

"What amulet?"

"Come, you saw it too! On a kerosene lamp. As soon as I saw it, the whole tour was wasted." She scowled. "Never mind. Are you hungry?"

I nodded, went to the kitchen, and opened the fridge. Lyalya gently moved me away from the fridge, directing me to sit down while she took a command post at the stove.

At dinner, carefully picking out fish bones, I said, "This guide, I dunno. She seemed quick as a bird but, at the same time, lazy as a lemur."

"Have you ever seen a lemur?"

"Let's go to Madagascar and see one sometime!"

"Right after dinner." Lyalya grinned.

I looked at her. "Lyalya, do tell me: What happened to you after we went to this island? Your mood seemed to have changed."

"Curiosity killed the cat! You won't let it alone, will you? All right. I'll tell you."

Chapter 16: The Island of the Dead

THE SKY IN THE window of our small kitchen turned a deep, dark blue. The lamp under its simple, fringed shade was cozy, homelike. The melancholic slow sound of church bells filled the air, gliding to us from a chapel far away in the mountains. Lyalya closed the checkered curtains, leaving the night behind the window, excluding it from our conversation.

"I must have told you," Lyalya said, moving a platter with salad toward me, "how I spent a few weeks building shelters for former convicts in the Tomsk region, in the taiga, right? That year, I was given an Orthodox amulet, just like the one we saw today, hanging on that lamp. But I didn't take it. I was afraid to, for a reason. Enough with the bread, have some more salad! And chew more slowly, will you?"

I nodded. Yes, of course I would. I'd chew salad, crunch carrots, give up bread. I'd do anything to find out about my aunt's history. My history. My country's history.

"I was sent for three weeks to an oil refinery back then," Lyalya said. "I had to draw up all the documentation, put the entire project together. Architect, builder, chief engineer, and contractor, all in one. They gave me accommodation in the village of Nazino, on the bank of the Ob. Nothing but swamps and taiga all around. In winter, minus fifty degrees Celsius; in summer, mosquitoes, flies, and heat. I had the pleasure of the latter season. The nature there is hard on people, but beautiful too! At night, it was as light as day. Every evening after work, the pilot Vitaly would fly me to Nazino in his helicopter, and in the morning, we'd fly back to the taiga. The village was tiny, a dozen huts at most. The people there are Khanty, a small Indigenous nation with its own language and customs. They believe in spirits, have shamans, and all that—but they are good, kind people. Well now. I lived in a house with a woman, her three small daughters, and her old mother. Three generations, all female, living together—quite peacefully, mind you! The only trouble was the air was heavy in that house, it always stank of fish … I was lucky it was summer! In the warm months, Khanty wash at least sometimes, though very rarely, despite the river right in front of them. In winter, they don't wash at all! The woman often went to the Ob to fish with a net. They ate the fish raw, except for the pluck—that, they fried in fish oil. Most of the time, they lived like Paleolithic gatherers or something; forest berries, mushrooms. On weekends, I went mushroom picking with Banat, the woman with whom I lived. Do you know Siberian mushrooms? Squirrel's bread, they're called? You pick one from the moss: it's strong, on a thick little stipe, sweaty with dew, quite a picture! Nowhere else have I seen such mushrooms. So anyway, we were living together quite cozily. Only I was missing my children something terrible. Especially Lyuba; she was so small back then!"

"Did you leave Lyuba with Samsonov?"

"Oh, come on! Of course not. I sent the children to my mother in Zaporizhzhia in the Ukraine. At night, I couldn't sleep, kept imagining her little hands, kissing each fingernail in my mind, kissing her head, remembering the way her hair smells, such soft golden hair, not at all like the wires on my head. The more time I spent with Banat's daughters, the more did I miss my Lyuba."

"How long did you live with the Khanty, you said?"

"About a month."

"And then?"

"And then, all hell broke loose!" Staring in front of her, Lyalya exhaled with effort and shook her head. "Well, okay. The project was over, thank God, I was about to go home, but then the old grandmother fell ill. At first, nobody noticed: she hardly ever walked anyway, used to lie in the corner on a rag all day. But then we saw she had a fever. Right after her, Banat got it too. Same thing, a fever, shaking all over, and then I saw it. A carbuncle on her arm! I had some experience in Siberia, I knew what it was: anthrax. Contagious as anything. And sure enough, the next day, the youngest girl had a carbuncle on her little hand. There was no hospital, of course, no doctor.

"So what to do? Vitaly happened to have a capsule of erythromycin in his helicopter, but only one. Who should get it? I give it to the youngest girl, all the while thinking to myself, 'We'll all get infected now, and it will all be over.' So I try to persuade Vitaly to evacuate them to Tomsk by helicopter, but he refused because the helicopter could only carry one passenger. I say, 'Take at least the youngest girl!' 'Nope,' he says. He doesn't want to take responsibility for the child. And I see he's afraid to catch it. 'Then take Banat,' I say. 'She's an adult.' I don't even mention the old woman; what chance would she have? And just as I seemed to have finally persuaded Vitaly, Banat grew stubborn. Leave the children alone with their dying grandmother? No way!

"Then I see her and her mother whispering about something, arguing, it seemed. Then Banat starts to cook a potion. She drinks some, gives some to the old woman, and then she dresses her up: the weirdest rags, a chain of shells and deer vertebrae. She sits her mother down by the wall, propped up by logs on both sides, gives her tambourines. And now the old woman hits a tambourine, and Banat begins to spin, faster and faster, as if in a trance. Her braids fly in circles, the tambourine rattles on, driving the souls of the dead away from the hut. Shamans believe that the dead send diseases to the living. At the end, both mother and daughter fell on the floor and stayed there until morning, exhausted.

"The night passes, though I don't sleep a wink. The next morning, Gulsara, the oldest girl, eight years old, has scabs all over her skin. Well, I think, we're all dead if I don't act right now! I say to Banat: 'You want to die—it's your business! But what right do you have to orphan your children? Do you know what will happen to them? Do you know what an orphanage is like?! I'm the boss here. I order you, right now, you get into the helicopter and go to the hospital! And you bring over a doctor. Explain the situation, you're the mother, but don't return, stay in the hospital till you're cured. Understand?' I promised her I'd look after the children. What did it? My bossy tone or the fear of the orphanage? I don't know, but off she went.

"So I'm left in the hut with old Kaima and the children, everyone ill. I'm trying not to panic, but I know what the taiga is like and how cut off we are. Tomsk is more than five hundred kilometres away. A week will pass until you get to someone. In the evening, the old Kaima motions me over and says, 'I'm dying. I have nothing else to give you in thanks, but take this doll, it will protect you.' And she takes an amulet with Virgin Mary off her neck ..."

Lyalya got up to pour me some tea. She took a pull of her cigarette, sat down, and continued, waving the smoke away from me.

"Well, the old woman takes off this amulet on a dirty string—and I'm afraid to take it, of course, horrified of the infection. Kaima sees it and says, 'Don't be afraid. This doll will save you from death. It doesn't let me go, it keeps me here, but it's time for me to start the long journey. Take it, free me!'

"'Where did you get this amulet, Kaima?' I ask 'Did some Russians give it to you?'

"'A woman left it as a keepsake. She lived with us before the war.'

"And she told me that story. There was an island in the middle of the Ob, not far from Nazino. The villagers called it the Death Island. That Russian woman had escaped from it; came out of the taiga at dusk. She could hardly move and did not speak. And kept pointing at the rags wrapped around her calves.

"It turned out that in 1933, six thousand 'special settlers' had been brought to the island, mostly from Moscow and Leningrad. Stalin had ordered two million 'undesirables' to be deported to Siberia. People were grabbed in the street and thrown into a car. On the way (first by train, then by barge), they were hardly ever fed. The survivors were unloaded on the island without food, clothes, or tools. The guards shot those who tried to escape."

Lyalya fell silent. We avoided each other's eyes. After a pause, she resumed her story.

"There was a terrible famine on the island. In the first two weeks, about three thousand people died. Some of the deported had been real criminals, murderers. They formed gangs, and bloody chaos began. When the guards buried the corpses, they saw that jaws had been broken to get at golden teeth."

"What use was gold on the island?" I asked, putting aside my cup of tea.

"The guards took it in exchange for tobacco. When the guards left, the criminals started hunting people. They … I can't even say it … They killed and ate people, fried their hearts and livers in campfires.

"So this one woman by some miracle managed to escape and hide with Kaima. She had no ankles. They had tied her to a tree and eaten them off. According to Kaima, the woman looked about sixty, and she was not even thirty. She lived with the Khanty until the war. Before she left, she gave Kaima the amulet, which she thought had saved her from death. I was squeamish to take it from Kaima then. But I did. Who knows? Maybe it saved me from anthrax."

"What happened to that family?" I asked, a lump in my throat.

"Banat survived. The children didn't. Kaima and the middle girl, Zayna, died in my arms."

"Have you seen that island?"

"Yes. There are no traces of horrors left. Only the grass grows lusher than anywhere else."

"Did you ever tell anyone about it?"

Lyalya shook her head. "Who cares about our past? You know, when the USSR collapsed, when people learned the whole truth, at first, they were glued to their TVs. Morning papers were sold out before you made it to a newsstand. But the interest quickly waned. The new generation rushed to make money, to build capitalism. Who's got time for the past?"

We fell silent again. An inner anxiety, a dull dissatisfaction stirred in me. Millions of innocents tortured, turned into ashes—and nobody cares? I thought of Perast, of another island created in memory of saving one single soul. Centuries of work. Stone to stone. To collect evidence, pebble by pebble, that was what we needed.

"Once the witnesses are gone," I said, "nobody will be able to tell the story."

"But that's not the point! There are documents, thousands of pieces of evidence. But people now pretend nothing has ever happened. The victims are dust; their executioners live in comfort on fat pensions. Seventy percent of the population believes that Stalin was great. That he won the war for us!"

"A Stockholm syndrome?"

"What's that?"

"When victims get to love their kidnappers, get attached to them."

"Oh, who has come up with such nonsense!? They don't know what they are talking about!" She fell silent, then continued. "Stockholm syndrome! In Russia, those who went through this hell were not allowed to talk about it. Your grandfather, for instance. He was a war correspondent during the war. He liberated Ravensbrück, a women's concentration camp. Did you know that? That's the thing. My father never said a word about what he had seen there. Neither to his daughters nor to his wife. I only found out later, from Victor. After the war, a whole generation was silent. Did you, did people your age, hear anything about the Holocaust? It was all concealed.

"Propaganda was cunning. It worked with half-truths. The shootings were reported, after all: 'So many civilians died here.' Only that these civilians were shot because they were Jews. Not a squeak about that!"

I said, "'Jew' was unspeakable, remember? Like a four-letter word. How did they put it instead? 'A citizen of Jewish nationality.'"

Lyalya got up from the table, joined her hands above her head, leaned in one direction, then in the other, as if movements could shake off the gravity of our conversation. She lit another cigarette, but this didn't calm her down.

"You say we kept quiet!" she said vehemently. "Yes we did. How else could we survive? We kept quiet so as not to go to jail, not to ruin the lives of our children. But also … how can I say it? You see, to explain gas chambers, you have to put them into the context of familiar human experience, and how would you do that? You can say 'gas chamber' or 'Death Island,' or 'they ate human flesh.' But what do these words mean if the mind refuses to understand them? How can you grow back into normal life with such knowledge? It's—it seems like blasphemy to worry about puny everyday things after that! Look around you: What do people care about? What to buy, what to eat. And there is a good reason for that. Otherwise, you can just go and hang yourself. Anyway, your tea has gone cold."

"Maybe it takes time," I said after a pause, "a distance of time. I've heard a story about a woman in Israel. She lost all her children in the Holocaust. Ten all in all. After the liberation, she swore she wouldn't die until she gave birth to another ten. A new soul for each of the dead ones. This wasn't easy, especially as she was over thirty."

"And?"

"And she did. Gave them birth and brought them up."

"Well, I don't know. I can't judge or anything"—and a shiver went over her, as if she were freezing—"but how can another soul replace the deceased?"

“It seems to have worked for her, if she gave herself this mission. But tell me, did Haim also keep quiet?”

“Oh, Haim. Haim was special. You could say he saved me then, after the taiga.”

Chapter 17: Happiness

THE NEXT MORNING, I found a children's colouring book in the hallway, forgotten or abandoned by the previous guests. On the cover, two crimson horses were chewing blue grass under yellow clouds. The wind in the picture was apparently blowing in two directions at once, making one horsetail flutter to the right, the other to the left.

I remembered how, more than half a century ago, one of the times when Lyalya came to Moscow, she had a sudden itch to ride a horse. I begged her to take me along. At the equestrian center I was offered a piebald pony. All I dared was to stroke the thick silky bangs that covered its eyes. I did not even try to mount it.

Lyalya got a red mare, so old that it seemed indifferent to the world around her. There she stood, her head bowed, sometimes shivering all over, sometimes reaching for a bunch of dandelions nestled in a crevice of the asphalt. Lyalya pulled on the reins, stood up in the stirrups, but nothing helped: the old dame wouldn't budge. But then, all at once, she struck the ground with a hoof, neighed—and bolted! There was a glimpse of Lyalya's hair, a glimpse of the mare's tail, and I saw a maddened centaur racing furiously in a circle. I was about eight years old, and I bawled with horror.

How could Aunt, who had never ridden before, rein in the obstinate beast? I remember how she leaped lightly from the mare, struck her on the rump with her fist in punishment, and then rushed to me. "Well now, what are you crying for, silly! Nothing can happen to me, you know? Nothing, ever!"

That evening, in the presence of my parents, Lyalya chattered and roared with laughter without the slightest reason, and I laughed with her, following the silent but stern command of her eyes. After that incident, rumours of trouble reached Moscow and Leningrad. Lyalya became so addicted to horses, relatives shook their heads in disbelief, that she almost gave up architecture. It was a close call, though ultimately she did not end up as a stable hand or jockey.

Now, looking at the crimson horses grazing in the children's colouring book, I remembered that old story and felt an almost painful urge to return, be it for a minute, into our carefree youth, when Lyalya was full of unbridled, dangerous joy, agility, strength, and sly artistry; when there were no deaths of loved ones, no fear for the life of her son, no thoughts of her own loneliness in old age, so carefully concealed from me.

Outside the window, a cloudless Mediterranean sky was gaining in benevolent blueness, and I felt like shouting to the invisible power pulling the strings of our destinies. "Hey, there! We survived! No matter how the beast bucked and kicked under us, we somehow managed to stay in the saddle! We're still here, not shackled, not enslaved! Our causeless laughter is the laughter of victory over fear and slavery!"

Aunt walked out of the bathroom, her hand pressed against the small of her back. She was obviously experiencing some pain but would refuse to discuss it.

Ignoring the pain, she swept the floor, put away the broom, and took a medicine bottle from a drawer.

"Here, have some after breakfast."

"What is it?"

"Fish oil."

A sickening smell hit my nose, a smell I've hated since childhood. Once upon a time, in a very different life, in a Soviet kindergarten, it was forcibly poured down my throat. ("You won't leave the table until you drink up—come on, open your mouth!" "You can't go to the bathroom until you drink up—and be quick about it!" "You won't ..." And so on).

I had no means of staging an uprising at the age of six, in the Soviet kindergarten, but I certainly could on vacation in Montenegro with my eighty-year-old aunt.

"Lyalya, dear, do you remember how old I am?" I gave her an expectant look.

"You can be a hundred for all I care! For me, you're still a little girl. Drink up, and I'll tell you about Haimele."

I couldn't help but laugh. Aunt had not changed.

***

"Anyway, Haim—we called him Haimele—once came to visit us in Norilsk," Aunt was telling me as we were strolling along the embankment, pumping blood to our hearts as usual.

"So I fly from Nazino through Tomsk to Ukraine, get the kids, and return with them to Norilsk. Sure thing, nothing good awaited me at home. Samsonov was like a mad dog on the loose after all the time alone. But I kept thinking of Nazino, imagining Grandmother Kaima and the girls. I had promised to save them, and I didn't. They were dead.

"And then suddenly Haimele comes to visit! He and Aina were living in Siberia, too, back then. Haim was great fun, and the kids were all over him, especially Lyuba. And Samsonov, he was a lamb when Haim was around; he even did the dishes. Haimele would take off my apron from me and drag me out to go skiing, never mind the temperature outside. He bathed in winter too, kept climbing into ice holes almost until his death. A crowd, all swaddled up warm, would come stare at an eighty-year-old swimming in a frozen lake. Minus thirty degrees, the water like a burn, it evaporated at once, no towel needed.

"In the evening, after dinner, Haimele would entertain the kids. Once, he placed a grain of wheat on the table, passed his hands over it, said some mumbo-jumbo. Then handed Lyuba a blunt penknife and told her to split the grain in half. It had world happiness inside, he said. If she only managed to let it out, all wars would stop, and people would become forever happy.

"So imagine the scene: Lyuba keeps trying, but the knife slips off. And Lyuba never had much patience. So she flings away the knife and turns on her loudest wail, the main weapon in the fight against adults.

"And Haimele, you know what he does? 'Let's compete who's loudest,' he says! So they're both screaming as all get out. But who could out-scream Lyuba? Haim pretends he has given up, falls to the floor like a boy, kicking his legs in the air and laughing. 'Lyuba, help! Ah, the giggly monsters will tickle me to death! Oh, save me, catch that little speckled one under my arm!'

"Lyuba turns off her siren and starts to crawl over Haim, looking for the giggly monsters. And he keeps going, 'Here, you see, the one in striped pyjamas, with a tail! It's stuck in my beard!'

"He jumps to his feet and pretends to be shaking off the monsters. 'Here's one in my pocket! And this one's crawling right into my ear!' Lyuba's doing her best to help. 'Well,' says Haimele, 'now that we're rid of the giggly monsters, let's get back to that grain! Let's cut it open, let world happiness out, and make everybody happy!'

"But Lyuba suddenly goes for broke. 'I don't want to make everyone happy!' she says. 'I just want to make myself happy.' And Haimele says, 'But see, once you make everybody happy, you'll be happy too!' Well, you can't fool my daughter like that. She just ups and swallows the grain. 'Nope! The grain will grow inside me and make me happy first!'

"That's what your cousin has always been like, ever since she was knee high."

Chapter 18: Haimele the Magician

I MUST'VE BEEN ABOUT five when I saw Uncle Haim for the first time, and he soon became my favourite among all relatives. He'd sometimes stop in our small Moscow apartment on the way from Siberia. What would bring him to Moscow? Either it was never mentioned, or memory fails me.

According to the family lore, Haim was the spitting image of Tsar Nicolas the Second. I could only confirm this much later, after the collapse of the Soviet Union, when pictures of the ill-fated monarch materialized on mugs, tee-shirts, and cheap icons in church kiosks. Yes, the resemblance was uncanny—that is, if you could forgo the difference in expressions: the bland solemnity on the Tsar's face and the nonchalant grin on Uncle Haimele's. Tall, slim, moving with elegant ease, Haim often displayed a most unusual behaviour for people of his generation; he smiled.

Something else, too, was unusual about him. In the grey dowdy Soviet world of the fifties, where was he getting his bright ties with asymmetrical patterns, his checkered jackets, and his leather shoes with thick soles?

Winking at me, as if I were his co-conspirator, Haimele would reach into his jacket and produce a guinea pig. The pet would run up to his breast pocket and ferret around, throwing onto the floor an artificial rose, a handkerchief, a ribbon, before re-emerging with a carrot in its paws, which looked just like a baby's hands. Petting the guinea pig with his index finger, shaking his head from side to side in disbelief, Uncle Haimele pretended to be moved to tears at the sight of the toy-like furry cutie that had mysteriously turned up on his outstretched palm munching a carrot. And while his head was shaking, his feet were tapping faster and faster, as if his head had no control over them. The outstretched arm with the guinea pig would also get a life of its own, and a bewildered Haimele would start spinning, chasing his own arm till it appeared from behind his back with a dove—or rather, a garden variety grey pigeon. The sudden transformation was as bewildering to me as it seemed to Uncle Haimele. His eyes rolled, and his brows went up while the tips of his lips kept drooping down till his face froze into a mask of total incomprehension. Clearly, it wasn't his fault that miracles kept happening to him. He just couldn't help it.

I was convinced that Haimele was a magician.

When I became a teenager, the pigeon and the guinea pig stopped materializing. Instead Uncle Haim would show up on a porch with a bouquet of fresh lilacs and tulips, hugging my mother and laughing: "Julia, darling! The mountains I had to climb! The waterfalls I had to swim across to finally see you!"

I noticed traces of moisture on my mother's cheeks and nose as she sniffed the fresh flowers, her eyes closed. She blushed and laughed and became younger in front of my eyes, as if the flowers were imparting to her their delightful essence. I felt the nagging of jealousy. Neither I nor anything in our grim life could make her as happy as Uncle Haimele's visits.

Our tiny apartment consisted of two rooms separated by a two-metre corridor. My paternal grandparents occupied the larger room, vacant of almost all human belongings except for a piano, which only my mother and I could play—and secretly at that, when the grandparents weren't home. For as long as I can remember, they weren't on speaking terms with my mother, and therefore, entering their room was forbidden to us.

"You know where the key for the door is, honey-bunny? Go get it!" Haim prodded my mother.

"What if they come?"

"Nah, the stinkers will rot at their jobs at least till nine!" Uncle Haimele never called my grandparents by their real names. Instead, he invoked their exceptional ability to "pollute the vistas of human life," especially the life of his niece—that is, my mother. He was right in his assessment: my paternal grandmother, a diminutive, tight-lipped woman and an important party bureaucrat, lived for her work, considering lipstick, high heels, laughter, and any unplanned joy malicious growths on the sombre body of Communism.

Her husband, Joseph, my grandfather—a taciturn, stern, and handsome philanderer—rarely showed up at home before midnight, sometimes skipping sterile domestic nights altogether. He loved beautiful women and took close notice of his son's young wife. "You shouldn't lift such heavy things," he'd say in his wife's absence, taking bags of groceries from the hands of his daughter-in-law. "Let me help you."

But as soon as grandmother came home from work, the door of their room slammed shut, and all life sank into the slime of heavy, wary silence.

Grandfather hardly spoke to me, and it remains a mystery what kind of man he was. In the family archive, there was a note signed by Lavrenty Beria himself, the most influential of Stalin's secret police chiefs, threatening grandfather with execution in case of failure to perform a military task. The Moscow railway plant, which my grandfather had been managing during the war, was evacuated to Kazakhstan and ordered to urgently switch to the production of missiles. There were no trees in the Kazakh desert and thus no material for containers in which to send weapons to the front. But grandfather, apparently, had found a way. After all, he hadn't been executed.

My grandmother's hatred of my mother was visceral and unbending, propped by an impenetrable wall of silence endured for over twenty years.

There's nobody left to ask, and I can only guess what had fuelled and sustained this hostility over such a long time. Perhaps the fact that my grandparents had to share the apartment with a newcomer from another city? I doubt it could've been the main reason, for in those days the cohabitation of several generations—often in the same room—was assumed.

I suspect that in this "classless" society, the hatred was a matter of class more than anything. My mother was the daughter of a well-known writer and journalist; she herself had graduated from the prestigious philological department of Leningrad University, had listened to lectures by luminaries like Eikhenbaum and Propp—all of which was totally alien to the party bureaucrats that were her in-laws. Or perhaps what really rankled them was my mother's independent nature, her acerbic intelligence and cutting wit? Was it too much of a contrast to their son, a good-natured, placid drifter of no special talents or vocation?

I remember the phrase with which Grandfather Joseph greeted my grandmother every evening upon arrival: "Anna! My slippers!" Dismissive of his wife as he was, why did he uphold so hypocritically her boycott of my mother, whom he secretly admired? Perhaps he didn't want to rock the boat, or didn't care enough to interfere.

Only once in his life did Grandfather Joseph remove his mask and openly acknowledge his admiration for his daughter-in-law. It came about a few hours before his death.

He was fifty-nine when he was struck with throat cancer. Of all his relatives, he preferred his daughter-in-law to visit him in a hospital as he became sicker and more helpless. A year before his death, he lost his voice and could only breathe through a tube in his throat. The hideous bubbling sounds that came out of this aperture scared me. My mother, not shying away from the heavy smell coming out of the tube, sat at his bedside for hours, stroking the emaciated yellow hand lifelessly lying in hers.

A mystical event that no doctor could explain happened the night before his death: not being able to speak for almost a year, my grandfather suddenly found a clear voice and dictated to a ward neighbour a farewell letter for his family. He thanked his wife for their long life together and asked her to forgive him. Addressing his son, he praised his son's wife, Julia, and said that if something were to happen to him, she alone would save him.

Many years later, the grandfather's words turned out to be prophetic. It was Julia who had nursed her husband, my father, back to life after his almost fatal stroke. It was she who continued to look after her invalid husband for the next thirty years until his death.

Joseph's son has never handed over to his mother her husband's farewell letter: the idea of shattering the fortress of enmity, erected so scrupulously for so many years by his mother, scared him. The old woman passed away without ever learning that her husband had asked her for forgiveness and thanked her for their long life together on his deathbed.

When I listened to Haim's bel canto, his *bravo, bravissimo, pronto, prontissimo*, I became convinced that he wasn't a circus magician after all but a leading baritone at the Bolshoi theatre. As the flourish of his last notes died, my mother closed the lid of the piano, locked the room, and restored the key to its place in a drawer. Her uncle would move to the kitchen to another stage of a performance: cooking. God only knows where Haim would get salami and nuts and canned fruit and even fresh tomatoes in the middle of winter. He took pride in usurping the kitchen, rolling his sleeves up, being in charge of a feast. Watching him fuss around the kitchen, I would reinvent him again: this time, he'd be the chef at *Prague*, an exclusive restaurant in Moscow.

I was so disappointed when I learned—much later in life—that Haimele turned out to be neither a magician nor a Bolshoi theatre baritone nor a chef in the most fashionable restaurant in town, but somebody totally mundane: a doctor responsible for the sanitation of Dnepropetrovsk in Ukraine. Had I known how deadly that profession was at the time, would I have respected him more? A medical man, and a Jewish one at that, he was bound to become a victim of the campaign known as "the doctor's plot." Accused by Stalin's henchmen of poisoning the drinking water in the city, he was sentenced to "ten years without the right of correspondence," a euphemism meaning execution. By some miracle, though, the sentence was replaced by twenty years in labour camps.

Chapter 19: Haimele's Real Story

A MAGICIAN, AN OPERA connoisseur! A doctor! And even that was not all.

Before becoming a doctor, Haimele Sternbloom had commanded a Red army battalion, participating in the bloody defence of Tsaritsyn, later famous for a battle of World War II (renamed Stalingrad after that battle, and after Stalin's death, renamed again, to Volgograd.) When Haimele got arrested in the thirties, his parents believed that the Party would soon acknowledge its error: a decorated Red Army veteran could not have been a traitor, a saboteur, an "enemy of the people."

When in 1941, Germany invaded the Soviet Union, Haimele's parents again succumbed to a widely spread belief that all the prisoners would be released from the camps. What gave them such hopes? Were these rumours intentionally spread by the NKVD, as KGB called itself in those days? Later still, the Sternblooms bought into the idea that the Germans, a civilized nation, wouldn't harm Jews who played Bach in their homes and had Goethe on their bookshelves.

In 1941-42, the retreating Soviet troops carried out mass shootings of Russians who'd been imprisoned before the war. They were shot without trial, the bodies buried in unmarked graves. But by the end of 1942, huge losses at the front forced Stalin to change tactics. By his order, convicts from Siberian camps were sent to the front and enrolled in "suicide battalions." Many were ready to buy freedom at the cost of their lives. However, this decree did not concern the "enemies of the people," the victims of the totalitarian regime accused of such crimes as Haim was. They were released only after Stalin's death.

The scarier and madder the world became, the stronger was the flame of hope in people's hearts.

The city was being bombed, the Germans had reached its outskirts, the inhabitants of Dnepropetrovsk were evacuated, but Haim's parents, Moses and Rachel, stayed put. When their son is released from the camp, he shouldn't find the nest empty!

Countless human grains of sand disappeared without traces in the bloody mess of history. Only occasionally, according to an unpredictable whim of fate, a grain of sand might be blown far away from its Golgotha and fly on.

Shortly after the end of World War II, there was a reshuffling of bosses at Haimele's Magadan labour camp. A new director recognized the emaciated, scab-covered goner: he'd been the man under whose command the director had been slashing enemy heads at Tsaritsyn. Haimele was released two years before his term, in the winter of 1944.

Crossing the vast desolate land, now from East to West, from Magadan to Ukraine, Haimele finally reached Dnepropetrovsk, his hometown, recently freed from the Germans. A pile of rubble covered with snow sat on the corner of the familiar street where his parents' house used to stand.

The details of what had happened to his parents, he would only find much later, when the family received a letter from Sternblooms' neighbours, witnesses of their roundup.

***

The Germans had entered the city of Dnepropetrovsk on August 25, 1941. About a month later, thirty thousand Jews were murdered.

The execution of the Sternblooms followed the usual SS scenario: the door was knocked in with rifle butts when the Sternblooms failed to open; the old man and woman were beaten; their table silver and Rachel's rings were taken away; and then Haim's parents, together with hundreds of other Jews, were marched along the Karl Marx Avenue toward the Polytechnic Institute. For fun, SS members made the arrivals crawl in front of them in the dust on all fours. Those who could not crawl quickly enough were whipped. Those who tried to get off their knees were shot.

The Sternblooms were sixty years old.

"The Ukrainian neighbours who later sent us this letter," Aunt said, "they were the ones who directed Germans to my grandparents' house."

"What makes you think that?"

"How else could the SS have found out who was Jewish and who wasn't? Without the help of neighbours and the local police, making the lists of future victims would have been impossible. The woman who had sent us that letter after the war. I remember her and her husband—Kravchenko, their name was. I used to play with their daughter. My grandfather had delivered her."

***

In those now unimaginable times, before the Sternblooms were killed with thirty of their relatives, what had their lives been like?

My maternal great-grandfather, Doctor Moses Sternbloom, was an unusual man for his time and place. A doctor and a pious Jew, a fine connoisseur of German literature and philosophy who read medical literature in German and French and translated Heine as well as Hebrew Talmudists into Yiddish.

When I came to Canada, I was able to smuggle from the USSR only one family album with old photographs that miraculously survived. On one, a light-haired man with a thin face and a neat beard. The perceptive glance of his bright eyes reveals a calm sense of self-esteem. Next to the photograph, Rachel (his wife, and also his cousin, as was often the case in the diaspora): a generously ample body; a full, round face in a halo of curly grey hair, like a cap over her head, a double chin cozily resting on a lace collar. Her face seems indeterminate, hardly expressive of anything but an absent-minded good nature. Looking at this portrait, you can hardly imagine that before the revolution, Rachel, the mother of a large brood and a dedicated housewife, had learned Italian with passion, had even gone to Italy to take singing lessons. Was it from his mother that Haim inherited his love of the opera and absolute musical hearing? The two earrings and this picture, that's all I have from Rachel.

After the revolution, most of the three-storey house that doctor Moses had built for his family was expropriated. The Sternblooms and their six children were crammed into two rooms in the attic, while Russian and Ukrainian factory workers occupied the rest of their house.

Gradually, over the years, the working class intruders became part of the family. Dr. Sternbloom used to treat them and deliver their babies. When the Nazis came, they did what many Ukrainians had done: reported them to the police.

The fate of the Sternblooms' two sons, also doctors, were tragic reflections in a diabolical mirror. Both ended up in labour camps, Haimele as an inmate, and his brother, Abraham, as a doctor for prisoners. Haimele survived; his brother was murdered during a prison riot. The circumstances of his death were never disclosed to his family.

By the time the war broke out, the Sternblooms already had grandchildren; all three generations were living under the same roof. Rachel, the matriarch, resisted favouring one child or grandchild over the others. Was it her heart or her sense of duty that made an exception for Leah, the daughter of her imprisoned Haimele?

Little Leah was growing up without a father; Ruth's daughter-in-law had to live through the war without a husband; and the grandfather and grandmother felt a guilt as unwarranted as eternal before both, and thus coddled and indulged them more than the other children and grandchildren.

At night, the cannonades would not stop as the Germans were rapidly approaching Dnepropetrovsk. Among the deadening explosions, the insomniac Dr. Sternbloom somehow discerned a quiet but persistent knock on the door. Barefoot, so as not to wake his wife, the doctor walked to the door and looked through the peephole. And then his knees gave out and his heart skipped a beat: he recognized his youngest son, Benjamin.

Benjamin had gone to the front with the first draft, becoming a radio operator somewhere near Dnepropetrovsk. Along with others, his unit was retreating to the east under the unstoppable onslaught of the German offensive. He had spent half the night sneaking back to his parents to tell them what was being kept out of the government reports. Dnepropetrovsk was about to be surrendered; out of the three bridges connecting the city to the unoccupied left bank, two had already been blown up; the third was expected to collapse any moment under heavy German bombardment.

The old man was standing there in his underwear, facing his son, blinking with inflamed lids from lack of sleep.. "Benny, my son ... alive ..."

"Are you all right, Dad? I'm fine, fine. Listen! I don't have much time. I came to pack you and Mom. You must flee! A little longer, and it'll be too late."

The old man touched his son's cheek as if to make sure he wasn't a dream. "What are you saying, Benny?"

"I'm saying, you have to flee. the Germans are on the outskirts. The last echelons have already been evacuated. You have to get out of the city on your own, no other choice. But I'll help you. Let's get going. I have an hour. If I don't get back to my unit by dawn, I'll be shot as a deserter."

"But this is … wait, you must be hungry! We've got … we've got some potatoes here. We're old people, your mother and me. How could we flee, Benny? Where? And the library? And the Torah! You remember, don't you? It used to belong to your great-grandfather. It will fall to bits if we try to carry it."

The son stared at his father. "The Torah, Dad!? You take warm clothing and blankets, that's all you need!"

"But it's summer now. By autumn, we … we surely will be back? The Torah won't survive all the pere … pere … peregrinations."

Dr. Sternbloom couldn't move, his body suddenly going limp. His son held him and hugged him, pressing the old man's wrinkled face to his chest for a minute. He felt his father trembling. "You wake up Mom. I'll take care of the rest."

"If you say we need to hurry, then, well, we need to tell Ruth to wake up Leah, poor little one," the old man muttered, but he made no move, still utterly bewildered.

In the morning, the Sternblooms and Ruth started out across the long bridge by foot, their belongings and little Leah in a pull cart. The bombardment continued. Time and again they had to stop for Leah: frightened, she needed to pee every few minutes. They had only walked half of the bridge when the old people were overcome with fatigue. Her feet bloated, Rachel had a hard time walking. Ruth hesitated, considered getting rid of all their stuff and letting her-in-laws sit in the pull cart. But how would she and her daughter survive the evacuation without warm clothing?

There was no time to think. She quickly made her choice.

As the grandparents turned around and started walking back along the bridge, little Leah had no chance to say goodbye. She had finally fallen asleep among the bags. Not even the exploding missiles could wake her up.

Chapter 20: Moses' and Rachel's Children

It seems utterly surprising now that nobody in the family ever rebuked Ruth for her role in the death of her in-laws. Had Moses and Rachel's children truly forgiven her and kept no grudge in the years to come?

It was my grandmother Adelle who took it on herself to help Ruth and her daughter after the war. Her devotion to them bordered on servitude. I could never understand why she had to wash Ruth's and Leah's clothing, scrub their floors, shop and cook for them.

Clearly, my grandmother blamed nobody but herself for the death of her parents. She was the daughter; Ruth, the daughter-in-law; and she, the daughter, had failed to persuade her parents to leave the city while it was still possible.

Religious holidays were forbidden in the Soviet Union. Adelle didn't go to a synagogue (if there were any left after the war), and I don't think she was religious. But every year on Yom Kippur, the day of Atonement and Repentance, she fasted and drew into herself, perhaps silently asking the elusive God to forgive her sins, and atone for the death of her parents.

***

When, in 1955, Haimele was finally released from the camp, he briefly came to visit his daughter and wife in rebuilt Dnepropetrovsk. Former prisoners were not allowed to live in the major cities. But Haimele didn't intend to stay with his old family. By that time, he had a new one. His common-law wife and a baby girl were waiting for him in the village of Kostino, not far away from Norilsk.

"What was his second wife like?" I asked. I came up to the open window and looked at the sky, where a few stars glimmered in the twilight.

"Kristine? Oh, she was very plain compared to Ruth. Ruth was a real beauty. A mane of black hair, an ivory complexion, and those soulful eyes. She turned heads, Ruth did. I'm surprised she never remarried. Then again, how many men were left after the war?"

"Kristine was Latvian, right?"

"Yes, a wisp of a girl, blond, thin, as flat as a board front and back. Never talked much. But she was half Haimele's age, mind you, and my uncle loved young women. The older he got, the younger his lovers became. It was Kristine who nursed him back to life after the camp."

"Was he in such a bad shape?"

"Physically, certainly. The beatings had half-destroyed his kidneys, and he had an open ulcer and broken ribs."

Kristine had shared the destiny of many in her small country. When in 1940 Soviet troops invaded Latvia, her husband fled, leaving his young wife and their baby to their own devices. Kristine survived the journey to Siberia in a cattle car; her baby boy died on the way. She survived the camp too, but she returned toothless. A wardress had tried to beat her into cohabitation. Haimele became her idol, her love, the fundament on which to rebuild her shattered life. But it proved too shaky. In spite of the three children they came to have together, Kristine couldn't marry Haimele. Ruth was refusing to grant her husband a divorce till her very death. Secretly, Kristine began to drink. By the seventies, she had turned into an alcoholic. Her end was tragic, as far as I knew.

"Did she really commit suicide?"

"She did. A terrible death, it was. Haim was over seventy when he eloped with some thirty-year-old to a resort in the Crimea; that was the last straw for Kristine. When she found out, she took poison."

PART II

Chapter 21: Timmy, a Harmless Man

Aunt's second marriage, to Timofey (whom she called Timid Timmy when she was in the mood to taunt him), proved more lasting, but it was also "lacking in vigour—you know, what a healthy, active woman needs," as she put it.

"He was harmless, and kind in his own way," she said. "Pampered my children, especially Lyuba. Her own father, Samsonov, didn't love her half as much as Timid Timmy. And she, too, adored him!"

"Not a small thing."

"Am I saying it is? But you see ... There was no fire in the man, no playfulness! Too boring, especially at night, if you know what I mean. What can I say? Timmy loved the quiet life, all he wanted was not to be bothered. Playing solitaire with my mother. Imagine! Breeding goldfish. He'd stand in front of the aquarium for hours. 'Now stop admiring the stupid fish!' I'd say, 'Look at what's going on around you!' And he'd be all: 'What do you want me to do, Captain? I can't change the world, can I?'

"Now toponymy. God help us! What kind of a hobby is that? What are all these obscure geographical names to you personally, I say. To me? To your step-children? Those old maps he hunted for, stinky old books that crumble in your hands. Mr. Know It All would spent evenings in some archives. Why? To escape me, that's why."

"A rather innocent hobby, by the sounds of it."

"Innocent? Yeees ... But you have to decide which world do you live in? This very real one or the weird world of your fantasies? All my life I was pulling him back to here and now, with my both hands I was pulling, and all my life he was slipping away. The discoveries I made when I started sorting his papers after his death. You wouldn't believe it."

"For example?" I asked, raising an eyebrow.

"The letters were the worst, I guess. He had written to Amerigo Vespucci, to Copernicus, to Chekhov. Is it madness or what?"

I looked at Lyalya in bewilderment, unsure if I should believe her.

"Don't get me wrong. He was a decent man. If I had asked him for the moon, he'd get it. Talented too. Could fix things great, or make something from scraps. He had the most clever pair of hands, but he wasted all his energy on nonsense. Spent six months working on a copy of a sixteenth century miniature sundial. Six months, do you hear! You could fold it up and carry it in your pocket; the arrow was tiny, and all of it was engraved with all kinds of things, pictures of wind creatures, their cheeks inflated. Nord, Levant, and all that jazz. And they would even show the time at night, by moonlight, with a mere five-minute error. Wonderful! But who the hell needs such a thing? Don't we have wrist watches? He behaved weirdly too. All dumb and numb, somehow, as if he'd been hit with a sack of flour over his head. And you know what I couldn't stand? His voice. He didn't talk, he whispered. What was he whispering for? Who was he afraid of?"

"How did you meet him?"

Lyalya took a breath, lit a cigarette. "At work. Timmy was a construction engineer assigned to my project. I always earned more money than him, by far, but that never bothered me." The way she said it, I had no doubt it bothered her all along. "What annoyed me is that he would hatch the most phantasmagorical plans! Just like *Oblomov*, remember the novel? 'I'll build a bridge, on that bridge I'll put stalls, and in the stalls, I'll put rich merchants.' That sort of thing. I mean, anybody can dream up fancy pictures at a drawing board. You get no dough for that! You need to make the project real, to push it through all the bureaucracy—and that he could never do. That was my job. I'd come home after work and get busy, one hand cooking, another cleaning, a third one rubbing my mother's back. Then there was the kids' homework to be checked too, and him? He'd shut himself up in the bathroom and read. Kept saying nonsense, like 'You just wait till we get rich, Larissa dear. I'll make a million, and you'll quit your job.' That had been his mad idea all the time. When we met, he was as poor as a church mouse, with one pair of torn socks and no roof over his head. I can darn socks, no problem. But get a place to live? That's another kettle of fish altogether."

"You mean he was homeless?"

"He was sharing a room in a factory dorm with six other guys. One room, seven men, four cots. They took turns, slept on the floor half of the time."

"But why? Didn't he have a Zaporizhzhia residence permit?"

"Yes, he did. But he was divorced. Had left everything to his wife and daughter. In our city, all men were either divorced or married, not a single single—which is why I had to take him in the first place."

"More proof of his kindness!"

"Sometimes kindness is hard to tell from stupidity. His wife was openly cheating on him, and he just shooed it all off, no hard feelings!" Lyalya sighed and shook her head as if a bumblebee were stuck in her hair. "You want to know how it happened? Timmy comes home from work early, in the middle of the day, and discovers his wife in bed with—guess who?—his best friend."

"What else is new?"

"Well, Timmy wasn't a cynic like you! Didn't gossip with the babushkas in the courtyard either. They could have enlightened him all right. Anyhow, he threw into his duffer bag a pair of shirts and a change of underwear, picked up a jar with his goldfish and was gone."

Not such a bad ending to the wife-and-best-friend anecdote, then. Everybody survived, except possibly the fish.

***

When Timmy and Lyalya got together, the question of a living space became urgent. Lyalya's apartment had two rooms, one tinier than the other. The smallest, she shared with her mother. The slightly larger served as a living room, and also as a bedroom for both her children, with a closet-like corner partitioned off for the boy. Lyuba, then six, suggested her "new Daddy" sleep on a cot in the living room, next to the ancient cupboard with about a hundred jars of jam. Lyalya wasn't too delighted with the idea.

Living space had to be fashioned out of thin air, and Lyalya turned for help to Patermufti Obkomchik, the mayor of the city, who happened to be her lover. "I've got news for you, Patty, which I'm sure you've already heard. I'm getting serious with Timofey Doroshenko, a guy from my office. You know my situation at home. Packed like sardines, we are. I need an apartment. Has to be in his name, though, as I'm already registered at my mother's, and I don't want to lose that one."

"When do you need it?"

"At your earliest convenience."

"Hmm ... I've already promised one to my wife's nephew," said Obkomchik and began rubbing his nose vehemently, which usually didn't bode well. Lyalya gave him such a look that he quickly left his nose alone, visibly shrinking in size.

"Timmy and I," she said, lowering her voice for added effect, almost spelling it out, "can't wait for long, you see. Your nephew is hardly such an urgent case!"

My aunt laughed. "Tongues were wagging, of course. Gossip spread like fire. And I don't blame them! In their place, I would've been furious too. There were so many single women at the office, with no husbands, children, lovers—nada! And here I am, parachuted onto their heads from Siberia: a braid up to my hips, eyes like that! (Lyalya joined the thumb and index finger on each hand, put the improvised binoculars to her eyes.) And here is Doroshenko, a handsome divorced man with manners, his hair still intact, and whom does he court? Me, a woman with two children, and Obkomchik's mistress to boot! Women were buzzing in Timmy's ear like mosquitoes: Don't you see the black Volga at the curb? Obkomchik picks her up every day after work! Even Obkomchik's wife must have gotten wind of it by now! But Tim paid no heed to any of that. 'Whoever was collecting pollen from this flower before me,' he said, 'is not my concern. If you want to catch the future in your net, first let the past go.' He could get suddenly poetic like this."

Chapter 22: The Great Pyramid of Giza Drops

Tim never found out who his true benefactor was. Till his last day, he believed that a two-bedroom apartment in a new brick building—with no cockroaches, in the most prestigious street of Zaporizhzhia—was his reward from the Party for his exemplary work. Needless to say, the furnishing of the flat was left to Lyalya.

Her lifelong friend Tamara, director of a furniture factory, had only to place one call to organize the home delivery of a white Finnish bedroom set and two sofas, also white, things the likes of which ordinary mortals could only glimpse in rare foreign movies or in their dreams on a lucky night.

Carpets were delivered right from a carpet factory in Kazakhstan. Its director happened to be renovating his country house bathroom, and Lyalya promised to send him tiles in return. Appliances didn't come with an apartment, nor could they be found in retail. A Zil, a clumsy roundish fridge suffering from hiccups at night, was a dream. Who would've guessed one could be obtained in exchange for a puny bottle of drops, all of whose weight was in its name: The Great Pyramid of Giza?

In spite of his diminutive stature, the chief engineer of the kitchen appliances plant, Zinovy Kroshkin, had a god-like status with the inhabitants of Zaporizhzhia.

His prestige and power were directly proportional to the residents' need for refrigerators, stoves, and washing machines, all of which were produced at his plant. For a while, nobody knew that, every night, Kroshkin turned into a frightened, stammering ghost. The reason was his wife. Exactly at midnight, she would start screaming four-letter words, spouting and gushing them till about 3 a.m., leaving her husband in a cold sweat, his extremities trembling uncontrollably.

The origin of this strange illness was unclear, the consequences unpredictable. The curses clearly addressed Zinovy, and he wouldn't have minded this that much, but the poor man seemed to hear the names of Soviet leaders, both alive and dead, in the stream of dirt.

And loud enough for the neighbours to hear too! He was beside himself with fear, losing weight and, it seemed, even height, tiny as he was to begin with.

Having spewed out the most terrible obscenities, his wife would pass out. Zinovy would struggle to fall asleep, counting sheep until morning, listening melancholically to the tide of his wife's snore. In the morning, his head would split with pain and premonitions.

Over the years, all possible remedies were tried, yet nothing could hold back the hurricane of curses.

And then Zinovy began to make a will. It was at this activity that Lyalya caught him when she entered his spacious office on the second floor of the Electric Motor Progress factory. She hadn't knocked, and he was so immersed that she got a glimpse of his writing before he noticed her. The sight of the powerful bureaucrat writing, with a shaking hand, "After my death …" first confused her, but not for long.

"What are you up to? Stop the nonsense!" she demanded and produced from her handbag a tiny bottle with the inscription *The Pyramid of Giza.*

"What is this?" Zinovy asked, barely moving his pale lips.

"A gift from Vanessa, the pharmacist. When your little darling begins to swear again, you grab her by the tongue and try to get, well, at least ten drops down her throat. It's a mighty remedy! Should take hold in a week or so."

The prophecy came true. The Pyramid of Giza was a wonder drug. At night, Mrs. Kroshkina began to coo like a loving dove and snuggle up to her husband like a kitten. In the morning, she'd bring him a steaming coffee in bed on a tray painted with African giraffes.

Tearful with gratitude, Zinovy Kroshkin made Lyalya and Vanessa gifts of three refrigerators, three stoves, and three washing machines.

"Why so many?" Lyalya asked.

"They break down, don't they? You'll need some back up."

***

I'd been listening to the story with growing bewilderment.

"So you really think some magic drops could heal such a weird disorder?" I asked.

Lyalya grinned. "Are you kidding? It was just a soothing tincture, some motherwort essence, and alcohol. But, as Seneca said, 'The truth and the lie look alike; in their posture, their manner, and their taste.' Since then, by the way, everyone went plain mad for that tincture! After all, that woman wasn't the only one swearing at night. The whole city was full of rage, especially when the wind was blowing from the west."

"And this Vanessa—who's she?"

"A friend of mine, God rest her soul. Three years ago, she left this world. She was the only one who knew the secret of the Great Pyramid of Giza, or so people believed. She herself said, 'Get off your asses, comrades! We've got that wonderful steppe right here. Go gather some motherwort, steep it in alcohol for a few months, strain it, and the tincture's ready!' But no. People believed that it would only help if she made it. Superstition, yes, but then again, understandable. That place wasn't good for living. People were suffering. So many diseases, heart attacks, strokes. People dying from their worries. I guess the nightly hysterics of that woman were like a safety valve of sorts."

"And why was the tincture called that?"

"Someone joked that these drops are harder to get than climbing the Great Pyramid of Giza; that got it started."

That's when I heard, for the first time, what role Aunt had played in the life of that motherwort gatherer, Vanessa.

Chapter 23: Napoleon's Carriage

Vanessa Khrabrova, head of the central pharmacy in Zaporizhzhia, was one of the few people in the city with whom Lyalya couldn't establish any kind of friendly relation for quite a while. Vanessa was certainly useful, as she could get any medicine, but as much as Lyalya tried, the woman did not respond to her noisy chumminess. Silently, without raising her head, she packed up the powders and pills in her gloomy pharmacy with a stucco ceiling and walls lined with dark oak. Silently, without a smile, she handed them to customers.

Things changed after a fire in the pharmacy. It took almost an hour until the fire brigade arrived. And although during this hour Vanessa had managed to put out the flames herself, dragging buckets of water from the bathroom by the dozen, there was still a lawsuit against her.

She was partly to blame, to be sure.

Why did she have to go tell the police that the fire was the fault of some woman who'd had a smoke in the pharmacy's restroom? Now, Vanessa was facing several criminal cases at once. First, criminal negligence: no strangers were allowed to enter that restroom. Second, the squandering of Soviet property: the drugs destroyed in the fire had belonged to the state. And third—and this was the main thing—the destruction of a unique exhibit, an ancient carriage that had stood in the back of the pharmacy, in an aisle between two cabinets, as long as anybody living could remember.

"A carriage? In a pharmacy?"

"Why not? Do you know a place where an ancient carriage would be of any more use? There was nothing special about it either, except for two naked mermaids, their tails entwined on the doors. Where this carriage came from, no one really knew, but the local KGB started a rumour that it once belonged to Napoleon himself. Like, he was scramming from Russia in it, leaving his army to die in the snow."

"But it was a fake, to be sure?"

"No, it was real enough. I mean, I don't know about Napoleon, but the guys from the Kremlin Armory Chamber came to inspect it and confirmed it was French work, early nineteenth century. Then they demanded the city hand it in to the Armoury Chamber; they have quite a carriage collection there. But our city officials suddenly got all plucky! My Patty—remember Patermufti Obkomchik?—had just become mayor, so he up and says: 'We cannot give this away: this is our main visual aid in the patriotic education of young people!'"

"Wait … the carriage is French, isn't it? How does patriotic education come in?"

"Oh child, you have no idea how things were done in Soviet times, have you? We had delegations from capitalist countries in Zaporizhzhia, experience exchange and all that. French, British visitors. Communists, to be sure, but still, who knows what they might be up to, our KGB thought. So you take a Frenchman to the pharmacy, put him in that carriage, and tell him the anecdote about Napoleon, how he was scramming from Russia in this very carriage and in deepest shame. The Frenchman (or a German or Englishman, for that matter) will get the hint. And after this ideological processing, he'll be fit to see the blast furnaces, the productive power of the Soviet country.

"Of course, some asked silly questions: 'Why do you keep a carriage in a pharmacy?' But there was a reply at the ready: 'A pharmacy? No such thing, comrades! In our country, all diseases have long been eradicated! This is a special veterinary laboratory for the treatment of elephants.' Because, you know, as mammoths come from Russia, why not elephants?" My aunt slapped her knees, bursting with laughter, but then sighed. "When the carriage burned down, Vanessa was dragged to court. They threatened her with prison even though she herself got burnt." That's when Lyalya came to her rescue.

"Tell me honestly: did you do it for the business connection? To get access to medicines? You weren't exactly friends."

Aunt's eyes sparkled at me, steely with anger. "Connection my bum! Should there be justice in the world or not? They were ready to crush her. For what kind of a crime? Besides, it was really Timmy who helped her, not me. Tim was living in that dorm back then, but every evening, he stayed at my place till late. It was quite cozy, the children and my mother fast asleep, me in the kitchen, making lunch for the next day, and Timmy next to me with his maps. A cold rainy autumn. I hear something quietly scratching at the window. A branch, I think first; we lived on the first floor. But then I see her: the head of our central pharmacy. I could hardly recognize her, a kerchief around her head, her hands in bandages. I let her in, pour her some tea, ask what's wrong. She doesn't even try the tea but asks straightaway: 'May I ask your husband for help?' Tim wasn't even my husband then. But never mind.

"So Vanessa gets out a worn piece of paper. 'This is the testament of Prince Khrabrov, former owner of the manor in which the pharmacy is located. The mansion, with all its contents, belongs to his descendants,' it says. 'Can this fact be confirmed by data from the city archive?' Vanessa asks, anxiously.

"Timmy produces a magnifying glass, takes a closer look. 'Yes,' he says, 'the history of that house is known. This is indeed the former mansion of Prince Khrabrov. There are papers in the archive confirming it; I've seen them.' And then he looks questioningly at Vanessa. She doesn't falter, Vanessa, but says straightaway: 'I am the heiress of Prince Khrabrov.'

"She was the great-granddaughter of the last owner, it turned out. She hid it all her life, and that was perhaps part of the reason for her aloofness. But at this point, she decided that it could hardly get any worse. So she came up with the idea to prove that, since the mansion belonged to her ancestors, the carriage and the rest were rightfully hers and she thus hadn't squandered any state property.

"At least she wasn't naive enough to think she'd get her mansion back. Still, mentioning her noble roots might have just as well done her more harm than good—but she ended up lucky. By some strange whim of fortune, the argument pleased the judge. Perhaps it was the idea of a princess working as a humble apothecary in a house that once had belonged to her family. Vanessa went free. And by and by, we became friends."

Chapter 24: The Moors' Castle

I REMEMBERED HOW, as a child, during my summer visits to Zaporizhzhia, my grandmother Adele took me to look at an elaborate mansion, a magic castle, I thought. The powerful stone walls were adorned with patterned brickwork and turrets. The façade featured openwork balconies with spiral half-columns, and the entrance was decorated with porticoes and intricate mosaics. In short, there was nothing like this luxury building in the city or, indeed, anywhere near it. Vanessa's pharmacy occupied the first floor; the upper floors were nailed shut.

The mansion showed Prince Khrabrov's peculiar taste, acquired on a visit to Istanbul in 1879. Awestruck by the celestial beauty of the Süleymaniye Mosque, the prince secretly converted to Islam. Upon returning home, he switched his coat for a khalat robe and would not leave the house without a turban. But that didn't seem enough. On a plot between kitchen gardens and cattle sheds, he built a miniature replica of the mosque. His luxurious residence adjacent to it was ever since then called the Moors' Castle.

The archives contained a paper listing the treasures of the eclectic assemblage acquired during the prince's travels to the East and West: weapons and hunting horns studded with gems; carpets; oriental furniture of the finest craftsmanship; paintings, sculptures; and, yes, a golden carriage by a French master. The richest man in Ukraine, the prince counted many important people among his friends, including the Patriarch of Russia. One day, the patriarch happened to be visiting Zaporizhzhia on his way from Crimea to Kiev. He glanced at the mosque, at the Moors' Castle, and could not stop a fit of coughing: "Kh-h-h … didn't we defeat the Turks at Pleven?!? Kh-h-h! Did one of them dare erect this blasphemous temple in the heart of Russia, not far from the sacred city of Kiev?" The patriarch turned his back to the Moors' Castle and crossed himself several times.

But it was explained to him that there were no Turks in Zaporizhzhia and that the mosque belonged to his friend, Prince Khrabrov, who'd abandoned his native Orthodox faith and converted to Mohammedanism on a whim. The patriarch spit on the ground, made the sign of the cross in four directions, and, exclaiming "begone, fiend!," excommunicated Khrabrov.

After learning about this, they say, the prince only grinned into his curled moustache, and instead of presenting the patriarch on his eightieth birthday with an antique signet ring, as he had intended to, he gave it away to the sixteen-year-old Daria, his servant and mistress.

Which of the Gods decreed that the most fortunate suffer the same afflictions as the poor?

Blindness struck the prince soon after the excommunication, and no doctor was able to return to his eyes the celestial glitter of the mosque or the proud beauty of the Moors' Castle with all the treasures he'd amassed. In despair, the prince let a healer come all the way from Egypt, the land of sorcerers, hoping he'd return him his eyesight.

"Allah Akbar!" the Egyptian said, prostrating himself in front of the prince. "God will cure the faithful. By his will I shall help you." Then he scrambled back to his feet, reached for an embroidered sack on his belt, and applied to the prince's eyes a red powder extracted, he said, from a ray of sunshine at summer solstice. And, the story goes, the prince could see!

Bedazzled, he covered his eyes. The glory of the world seemed too much for him to bear. "Do you have more of this potion, just in case?" he whispered, fearful that the miracle would suddenly stop.

"Master, I've used up all I had. Allow me to return to the land of my ancestors!"

"If all you need are the rays of the sun," the prince said, "then esteemed doctor, our summers can be as hot as in Egypt. If you stay here, at my estate, I'll fulfill any wish your heart desires!"

"My only wish is to be at your service," the cunning sorcerer said. "The secret of the concoction is not to be disclosed to anybody, but if you grant me a lab and a pharmacy, Allah willing, I'll be able to squeeze the potion out of our Ukrainian sun."

"The whole wing of my modest abode is yours," the hopeful prince exclaimed. "Allah be thanked!"

The sorcerer got off his knees and, pressing both his hands to his heart, walked out crabwise.

A week later, after the sorcerer moved into the mansion, Khrabrov took to bed with a mysterious ailment. Three days later, he peacefully went to meet his maker.

Shortly before his death, the prince acknowledged the two sons he had with Daria as his rightful heirs. The children were still young when the Egyptian took over the whole mansion, adding their mother, Daria, to his booty.

Records are silent on how long the Egyptian luxuriated in the Moors' Castle. Neither is it known how the sons got rid of him when they got older. It's even possible that he died a natural death.

Like their father, the brothers were passionate treasure hunters, and they kept enriching the collection after their father's death. Unwilling to sell the mansion, they continued to live there with their wives and children until the revolution. After the October coup d'état, however, their paths diverged. The older brother, Vasily, left Russia on the last steamer from Crimea to Constantinople. He failed to persuade the younger one to flee abroad with him.

Hoping to preserve his father's collection and to protect it from the Bolsheviks, the younger brother, Innokenty, stayed. He was lucky: the mansion was neither burned down nor wrecked. More than that, Innokenty was even allowed to live in the cellar of his own mansion as the boilerman, and even to give guided tours. Innokenty did not have much time to appreciate the grace of the new rulers; soon, he died of grief.

After Innokenty's death, the precious art collection was plundered, the porticoes and the pediment disassembled into bricks, and all kinds of junk was stored on the upper floor. But in 1930, a pharmacy opened on the lower floor of the desolate mansion.

***

Once the elder brother, Vasily, arrived in France, he turned into Basil Bravo—but the new name did not save him from extreme poverty. At one time, he, like many Russian noblemen, worked as a taxi driver, then got a job as a simple factory hand at Renault. His grandsons, however, made their way in the world, becoming lawyers and doctors. His grandniece, the lycée teacher Ivette Bravo, started a secret correspondence with Vanessa Khrabrova. Rare as the letters were, Vanessa learned that she was the great-granddaughter of Prince Khrabrov and that the Moors' Castle where she was running a pharmacy had belonged to her ancestor.

"I can try to get you a copy of the document from the archive," Timmy said. "But what use will it be? Nobody will return you the mansion."

"That's understood!" Vanessa said. "I'm ready to pay the penalty for the destroyed medicines. But I'm not ready for the clink!" She winced and began to loosen the bandage on her arm, which was apparently causing her pain.

Tim looked around fearfully. "Okay, okay, I get it but …"

"Look," Vanessa said. "I have nothing to be afraid of. I wasn't the one who set the pharmacy on fire. I'm going to write to Etienne Bravo! They won't conflict with the French police, right?"

"Now that made my skin crawl!" Lyalya exclaimed. "Well, me thinks Vanessa has gone totally bonkers! To mention the French police to the Soviets?! So I tell her the naked truth: 'The only way out of this mess is for you to confess and repent. Confess and repent, Vanessa! Tell them you let that woman use the toilet; say she had a child, and the child badly needed to pee. Tell them anything you want, but leave the French police out of it! With luck you'll get away with a reprimand.' But Vanessa won't listen. 'Etienne Bravo is my nephew. You don't think they know about my foreign connections, anyway? Don't they read my letters? And I won't lie about the woman either! I let her go to the toilet alone, she had no child!' All mighty and righteous, like. Well, she had a point there.

"'Sure they do,' I say. 'They open letters from abroad, but why get all cocky about it?'

"Vanessa falls silent, and I keep thinking: *zharit' pchelku—malo tolku*! To fry a bee will bring you no meat! Some parts are missing from this puzzle. And right I was!

"Turns out that a month before the fire, the first secretary of the regional committee came to her pharmacy in person for an aspirin. And she—did she fall from Mars or what?—charges him the price of the medication. Having to pay? Him? The first secretary? I bet he almost had a heart attack on the spot. People like him don't forget such humiliations. Vanessa suspected that he was later ordered to set fire to the pharmacy. After all, why did the firefighters take an hour to come?

"'If that's the story,' I say to Vanessa, 'you'll need to grease the wheels.' Vanessa doesn't even get me. 'What do you mean? Grease the wheels how?' she says, and I say, 'The question is not how, but how much!' But Vanessa gets on her high horse again, talking about her reputation and whatnot.

"'Well,' I say, 'you want to go to jail, this is your right in our country. But did you consider your fellow citizens? How will they manage without the Great Pyramid of Giza and other crucial medicines? Why don't you stay here overnight and sleep on it?'

"Vanessa must have realized that she was getting into dangerous waters, and she stayed.

"In the morning, I ran to Patermufti's office, and not a word to Timmy. I told the mayor the whole story and asked how much grease Vanessa needed to give to the first secretary so that he leaves her alone. Patermufti, he was a wise old bird. 'Two thousand at least,' he says, 'after all, she hurt his ego.'

"But where could we get that kind of cash? Well, I started collecting money in the city. In secret from Vanessa. And people were happy to pitch in! She had helped so many, she was well liked, despite her reserved character."

Lyalya sighed.

"That was a narrow escape, but it all went well. The losses were written off, the pharmacy was restored, and the carriage was replaced by a model of the cruiser Aurora, you know, the one that gave the signal to storm the Winter palace."

We fell silent. Lyalya lighted another cigarette.

"Did Vanessa know who had saved her from jail?" I asked.

"She thought it was Timmy and me. But it was the whole city, really. Let's get some wine in Kotor tomorrow! We should drink to the rest of Vanessa's beautiful soul."

Chapter 25: A Housewarming Party

LARISSA'S LIFE NEVER GAVE her a chance to put to use the acting talent that she undoubtedly possessed. But the artistry in her nature broke out in storytelling. The images drawn by her stormy imagination often seemed fantastic to me. But, to paraphrase Tolstoy (as Aunt often did), in literature, you're free to stray from the truth in any way, except regarding the protagonists' psychology. And indeed, she did not invent her protagonists but masterfully illuminated them with an unusual light, embellishing them with baroque moulding: her motto was not to be a bore, else, as she put it, "flies will start to fall from the ceiling, dead with ennui."

Were her stories about Soviet life true or fictions that she herself believed? Did it matter? What was true was that the toad eyes of phantasmagoria protruded from the mysterious mud of Soviet everyday life like a periscope. What scenes one could observe, what landscapes! "The laws of physics don't apply to us! A country of total suuuur!" Lyalya said, abbreviating the word "surrealism" to a bird's whistle.

In her youth, Aunt had been known for her hospitality, abundantly enjoyed by her many friends, neighbours, and colleagues. Lyalya would always remember the long feasts with tenderness. Her tenacious memory treasured even the smallest coins of the past, its fleeting words and situations: she remembered what people had been wearing, what jokes and toasts had been made ...

As soon as she settled down in the new apartment, Larissa invited guests to a housewarming party. She despised hierarchies, so the humble plumber Gosha might be enthroned, say, at the right hand of the furniture factory director Tamara Scooperdyaeva, who liked to say that a woman in possession of good Finnish furniture had no use for a man. The electrician Vardan would find himself next to the brooding apothecary Vanessa; the romantic Seraphima, eternally thirsting for lofty love, would sit next to the hero of socialist labour Spiridon Pushistikov.

What made the angelic beauty Seraphima connect her life (albeit extramaritally) with the bald, fat, used-up Spiridon? Some, moved by envy, answered this with a sideways glance at the Hero of Labour order modestly sparkling on the lapel of Spiridon's baggy jacket. Cynics grinned and hinted at the obscenity of the profession that had brought Spiridon not only the order but also to a place in the Supreme Soviet. Jokes were made about the syringe, which Pushistikov allegedly kept close even at night, putting it under his pillow. After all, an inseminator without his syringe is like a soldier without his gun! That was the logic ascribed to Pushistikov. This profession—despised by the envious—had brought our hero the honours and comfort, which, or so some believed, the orphaned Seraphima couldn't resist.

The reader may be wondering how the insemination of cattle could lead Pushistikov to the juiciest Soviet pastures, complete with a state dacha, a non-communal apartment, and a chauffeured car?

Well, now, let's leave the hospitable dinner table at Lenin Avenue for a while and make our way to a village, to the collective farm field. Far away, on the dusty ground, there is a group of people, tieless but in carefully buttoned white shirts under black jackets, despite the heat.

A fat figure stands out between them: a Hero of the Soviet Union, a threefold Hero of Socialist Labour, the Chairman of the Council of Ministers of the USSR—Nikita Khrushchev. Look at the sun-pierced crimson ears carelessly glued to his watermelon head! Aren't they exactly like Pushistikov's ears? And when the chairman gets angry, his lips curve in smear precisely the same way as Pushistikov's. (Does this random similarity perchance explain the dizzying success of our inseminator?)

Khrushchev was shaking a cob of corn at the noses of his silent retinue, as if driving nails into the incorporeal blueness above him. "So America thinks it's the dog's bollocks! But we're nothing to be sneezed at either, right? We'll outrun you and overrun you, American imperialists! Death to greedy capitalist sharks!"

At the word "death," a lark fluttered up from the ground and soared into the sky. There, in the azure height, the chairman's curses became a barely discernible chime, but the people below understood the meaning of each word.

"And what are we going to beat the American sharks with? With this very cob! With sweetcorn, our *kukuruza*, our field queen!"

He brandished the cob in his fist as if it was a club; the retinue applauded. "Where does the power of the American proletariat come from? That's right, corn! Aren't we every bit as good as them? Why should we eat bread and potatoes like in the olden days, blast it? Don't you want your children and grandchildren to eat meat? Down with the hay, then, and give us corn straw instead! With corn, we'll have five times more cattle! What did Lenin say? Communism is Soviet power plus the electrification of the whole country! And I'm saying Communism is the electrification plus cornification of the whole country, from Pamyr to Taymyr. From Tadzikistan to the Arctic ocean! In Iowa, I saw corn grow three meters tall. What a joke! Six metres will be our goal. Full steam forward, Russia! We'll catch up with and outrun America! For over-fulfillers, I hereby introduce the order Hero of Sweetcorn Production!"

Although the order was introduced, sweetcorn disobeyed and flatly refused to grow on the shores of the Kara sea. Soviet citizens, especially women, were already used to spending most of their waking hours queueing for bread, but after sweetcorn replaced much of rye and wheat in the fields, the queues in the cities took such anaconda-like proportions that one foreign correspondent thought the country was stocking up on provisions before a nuclear attack.

When the floodplain meadows, which had provided excellent hay, were plowed for corn, cattle began to die.

And this is where Spiridon Pushistikov arrived to his glory.

Chapter 26: Taking Over America

SPIRIDON'S FRIEND, the one-armed war veteran Sergey Yershov, returned home from the war to become the head of the kolkhoz Lenin's Larks. He was always complaining to Spiridon that the damned sweetcorn didn't let him fulfill the state plan for meat delivery. To prove this, Sergey took Spiridon to a stable and pointed his finger at a cow. The animal was too weak to stand, supported by belts stuck under the belly and tied to a hook in the ceiling. The starving cow was mooing hopelessly and loudly, stretching her skinny neck.

The two friends sat down on a log. Each rolled himself a smoke and starting drinking, occasionally spitting into the rotten hay under their feet. Spiridon had brought some moonshine and two glasses; Yershov spread out a newspaper, put five gherkins on it, and took a bite from one. The cow was mooing just as loudly as before. "Oh stop that roar already! I wish you were fucking dead!" And he threw half a gherkin at the cow. The hungry beast caught the missile and greedily swallowed it. For a joke, Yershov threw another gherkin toward her.

"See, the starving beast will even eat pickles!" The head of Lenin's Larks grinned bitterly. "This year, we had so many cucumbers, I don't know what to do with them. My old lady's got whole barrels pickled. Anyway, let's have a drink."

And they drank again. And then again. And again.

"Listen!" Spiridon exclaimed. "You say you have no cattle feed. Well, what's wrong with gherkins? The salt will make them thirsty; full of water, they'll be heavier—and you'll fulfill the weight norm! Just order every woman in your kolkhoz to make ten barrels, and there you have the production all set up!"

Sergey gave his friend a stunned drowsy look.

"You serious?"

"Cross my heart," Spiridon said calmly.

The rumour about the new way of fattening cattle rushed from one kolkhoz to the next like fire. A month later, twenty collective farms were feeding gherkins to cows, pigs, horses, sheep, and even chickens. The land was blossoming! And then, on the crest of this unprecedented success, Spiridon had yet another original idea.

Mankind has long learned to transfer one kind of energy to another, Spiridon mused, fishing in Yershov's pond. Couldn't the thirst caused by the uncontrolled eating of pickles be transformed into a reproductive urge? "And this urge"—Spiridon gestured with excitement, almost letting his fishing rod drop into the water— "this urge ... Well now, the greed of Western capitalists has reached such a point that they don't shy away from the artificial insemination of cattle. Can't we do that as well?"

Soon, Spiridon was giving a speech from the stage at the House of Culture and Recreation of his kolkhoz. He was severe about the inhumane methods of capitalist farmers. "A soulless approach to animals is alien to the principles of communist morality. But as Comrade Lenin said, we cannot expect mercy from nature! We must take it from her! I propose to raise the morale of our cattle by introducing humane Soviet principles of fertilization. If you agree, please raise your hands!"

The vote was unanimous.

"But what exactly is it that you propose?" some daredevil asked.

It turned out that Pushistikov was proposing that every kolkhoz would welcome a cultural education team of four: a dancer, an accordionist, a general entertainer, and an inseminator. The entertainer would hand out a glass of vodka to every male farmer and a birch branch to every female one; the latter are to whirl in roundelays, the branches in their hands symbolizing fertility. The dancer will join them, and the accordionist will support the event with a thematically appropriate song, such as: "I enjoy a husband's duty, for my wife is such a beauty!"

Then, to the sounds of general joy, the inseminator would approach his bovine patient in a friendly manner, stroke her side and insert—at this point Pushistikov showed the audience his tool of production—this!

"What is the difference between a cow and a human?" he asked. "Well now, we can smile, and a cow can't! A man, damn it, he can laugh, can express gratitude in words! And what can a cow say? Nothing but moo. But, citizens, does this mean that the dumb creature does not appreciate the humanity of our approach? No, comrades, it doesn't!"

Soon Pushistikov proved his point. The success of the new method was total! At the exhibition of Achievements of the National Economy in

Moscow, cows were running out of their stalls at the first sounds of the accordion, licking the artistic team with their rough tongues in gratitude.

As it happened, at this very time the party ordered a leap in animal husbandry: the number of cattle was to be increased fifteen-fold. The concept of humane insemination (as Pushistikov called it in his report) was given a green light. As always, there were some fault finders. Out of pure envy, they objected to the use of artist teams in animal husbandry. However, economists won the dispute: this way, the problematic and difficult task of employing intelligentsia anywhere in the national economy would finally find its use for the collective farms—they could become the dancers, accordionists, and entertainers.

But while the new advanced methods were welcomed in the central kolkhozes, further in the countryside, the sluggishness and prejudices were still in the way. In some villages, Spiridon even made a personal appearance, nailing posters to the fences. "Fight sexual voluntarism in the breeding of cattle!" But neither village farmers nor kolkhoz cattle responded to the call. Illiterate bulls did not even attempt to fight their own sexual voluntarism. Obeying the whims of their stubborn nature, they kept on flirting with the opposite sex in the most direct fashion. Pushistikov was determined to put an end to this by keeping the bulls away from the cows and using them only to supply the sperm for insemination.

Over time, Pushistikov ceased to travel the kolkhozes in person, replaced by countless well-trained inseminators. Nevertheless, the syringe, which he now rarely used, remained dear to him as the symbol of his stratospheric social lift.

And even now, at Lyalya's party, spearing a pickled mushroom onto his fork, he quietly used his other hand to check if the syringe was still in his pocket.

Chapter 27: Robespierre's Snuffbox

THE HOUSEWARMING PARTY was in full swing when the mayor of Zaporizhzhia, Patermufti Obkomchik, appeared at the door with his wife, Januaria. Patermufti was balancing a large cardboard box tied with a white ribbon on his stomach, holding it tightly with both hands.

"A little present from us, dearest Larissa, a chandelier! Let there be light in your house, let darkness be banished!" The mayor puckered his lips for a kiss, but quickly pulled back after a glance at his wife. While Timmy was helping Januaria get her walrus body out of her fur coat, Obkomchik stood up on his toes (Lyalya was a head taller than him) and, reaching for Lyalya's ear, whispered quickly: "So sorry! That thing's out of plastic—for now. I'll replace it with real crystal later! Has shiny pendants, though, just as it should."

From a cabinet by the window, crystal glasses, vases, and swan-shaped candy bowls were firing their sparkling arrows into the mayor's eyes, clearly showing that Patermufti's former mistress disliked fakes. However, had the mayor presented Lyalya with such an expensive gift as a real crystal chandelier in front of his wife, his chances of surviving the day would have been catastrophically reduced. The diminutive mayor was no match to his armoire-thick wife. The cannonballs of her breasts were threatening to rip apart the crisp sparkling fabric. Her hips were those of a Stone Age Venus. Tim looked at her powerful shoulders in horrified awe. "She'll get stuck in the door!" he thought.

The table, set for many guests, was creaking under the weight of the delicacies. There were marinated pumpkins and pickled cucumbers, bean pâté and cabbage pie, herring and schnitzel, meat jelly and Russian salad, and, of course, Lyalya's signature dish, the Georgian *Badrijani*—eggplant pancakes filled with walnuts. Passionate about cooking, Aunt would begin to take care of the ingredients almost a year before the party, when the idea of a new apartment was but a bird trembling fearfully in the bush. Januaria was staring at the food, deciding at which flank to start the attack. She treated every dish like a personal enemy: the cabbage pies, the ragout, the cheesecake with sour cream—all these were to be annihilated.

Soon enough, the fatal mismatch between the heart's desire and the limited resources of the flesh became apparent. Januaria's ample stomach was groaning—she could take no more. This is when her trusty handbag came in handy. As greedy as its mistress, it began swallowing bagels, cakes, peppers stuffed with mushrooms, and, finally, two chicken drumsticks.

"Well now, that was nice!" Januaria said, licking her thick lips, leaning back into her chair and squinting menacingly at the hostess. Then she turned her mighty torso to her husband: "Come here, baby! We need to talk." Her thick, ring-covered fingers bore their nails into his ear. "Oh," he groaned, "my ear. What … oy … what have I done?"

"That, you know better! You've been playing pranks, kiddo! If you love to go down hill on a sleigh, you should love to haul it up the hill too!" All the while, she kept pulling at his ear clockwise, then counter-clockwise, until finally, trying to wriggle free, the mayor fell face down on the floor. There was some awkward laughter, immediately stopped by Lyalya.

"Cut it out! This is not some communal kitchen! Wash your dirty linen at home, if you please. Take the chandelier away, Januaria! Come on, come on, out of here!"

Lyalya helped the defeated man get up from the floor. Patermufti was standing there, rubbing his nose, bruised from the fall. The guests, frozen in various poses, watched—until the electrician Vardan knocked his knife handle against his glass. When all heads turned to him, he said: "Comrades, attention! I propose a toast! How hard is it for one woman to turn another woman's party into a wake? Not hard at all! Do we need even more tragedy in our long-suffering homeland? We need it like a horse needs ballet slippers! Like a dead man needs a bicycle! Like a Turkish sultan needs an empty harem! Like I need last year's snow! And like I need—whoops!—the Soviet power! So let's drink, comrades, to the peaceful coexistence of women with their rivals and their husbands!" The guests rose to their feet, and just as they were preparing to empty their glasses, there was a sudden ring at the door.

Another guest had arrived—the world-famous tenor Eduard Portugalsky.

***

Eddie Portugalsky had just returned from a triumphant trip across France, where he'd been singing Civil War songs at the Grand Opera accompanied by the Tula Ballroom Orchestra Guns and Cakes to celebrate the centenary of the Paris Commune. Entering Lyalya's hallway, he tossed his Tyrolean feathered hat onto the rack like a frisbee, hung up his new tricolor scarf, gave himself a wink in the mirror, adjusted the part in his jet-black hair, and stepped to the table at the very moment when the guests were raising their glasses to the peaceful coexistence of female rivals.

The glasses froze in the air, and a slight groan of amazement broke from the half-open lips, not yet whetted with sparkling wine. A foreign suit the colour of crème brûlée, a boutonniere, and a yellow-dotted bowtie—to those assembled, it was as if Champs-Élysées had moved into Lyalya's apartment. Eddie was holding a little package wrapped in shiny paper tied with a satin blue ribbon. Carefully, as if it was a living bird. "A present for you, lovely Larissa!" he announced in his clear tenor. Then he pulled out the yellow rose from his buttonhole, circled it in the air, and presented it to the mistress of the house, playfully tracing it across her cheek. Having emptied their glasses, the guests left the table and surrounded the famous singer. The wrapping paper was glittering enticingly. The guests stretched out their necks to get a better look.

"Back off, you all!" With his bottom, the singer pushed away the bodies that were breathing hotly onto his neck and gently liberated the gift from the wrapping. It was a luxurious snuffbox. On the lid, there was a picture of a nobleman in a powdered wig, with a black and white lacy jabot ruffled under the thick chin. "The snuffbox is handmade, enamel painting, nothing to sniff at!" Portugalsky said, aware of his pun.

The guests stared, shook their heads, and stepped back in puzzlement.

The practical use of the vacuum cleaner gifted by Seraphima and Spiridon was obvious. The radio from Vardan, the electrician, caused everyone's envy. The aquarium shaped like a whale presented by the construction trust girls was such a perfect present for Tim that his eyes got wet. No one doubted the usefulness of fashionable women's shoes, called manna porridge for their white porous soles, and even the octopus-like chandelier would have done temporarily, despite being plastic.

But what was the point of the snuffbox, this fragment of a long-gone bourgeois life? Eduard sensed the mood of the masses.

"That bijou had belonged to Maximilian Robespierre himself. You've heard of the guy, right? A personal present from the mayor of Paris!" he remarked carelessly.

"Really?!" The guests pulled back.

"Here, read for yourself: '*Li-ber-té, e-ga-lité*,' and so on …" Portugalsky poked at the Cyrillic inscription surrounding the wigged head of the nobleman.

"What's that supposed to mean?" Januaria squinted, chewing a bun.

"Liberty, equality, fraternity," Vanessa responded. She had been quiet so far. "But why in Russian letters?"

For a moment, Eduard was lost for words. "That idiot! To paint lilies on a revolutionary snuffbox and then to write in Cyrillic! Well, never mind." Playing with a key chain depicting the Notre-Dame chimeras, he shouted at the crowd, "You're asking why? Did you never learn history? Who's Robespierre? The leader of the French Revolution! And who's Radishchev? A forerunner of our Soviet revolution! So their Robespierre gives our Radishchev a snuffbox and has the inscription done in Russian letters, for clarity's sake. What's not to understand?"

"Didn't Radishchev speak French?" Vanessa inquired, implying that in the eighteenth century, anybody worth their salt in Russia spoke French and not Russian.

"When in Rome, do as the Romans do!" Portugalsky said curtly, feeling an irritation with this bluestocking, this marinated herring, as he had mentally dubbed the grey-haired skinny Vanessa. "Was Robespierre a total egoist, or what? He cared for us Russians, didn't he? He had us, like, on his list, revolution-wise."

"Must have been a great guy, that Robespierre of yours!" a mechanic exclaimed.

"I personally don't care that much for the inscription, but the little stones are pretty," Seraphima said.

"The little stones!? These are gems! This one is a real diamond, and this is a ruby!" Portugalsky carefully opened the snuffbox.

"Oh, the inside of the lid, just look at that!" Seraphima said. "What cute flowers!"

"Eh, the ignoramus. These are heraldic lilies, the royal emblem!"

"So that Robby Pierre guy was a king or what?" the electrician Vardan asked.

"A king?! No, Robespierre fought for the rights of workers and peasants! He came from the third estate, a peasant himself."

"A peasant with a diamond-studded snuffbox?" Vardan said. "Come on, how stupid do you think we are, Eddie?"

"Will you stop spinning those yarns of yours?!" Irena Bukhto exclaimed. Eduard had been her lover recently enough for her to be touchy.

"Whether Robespierre plowed or sowed is none of our goddamned business!" the singer said. "The thing is that ... it's that Robespierre got the snuffbox from King Louis—I forget the number—anyway, it was the royal snuffbox, and Louis had hoped to buy his freedom with it, so Robespierre wouldn't take his head off his shoulders. That's why he had a portrait of Robespierre engraved on the lid. You get it now, you bumpkins?"

The guests were mumbling, and not in an impressed way, but then Eduard made a cutting movement with his hand next to Vardan's neck.

Everyone was quiet at once.

"So what?" the plumber Gosha said, turning out to be a great erudite. "Did that bribe help him? The hell it did! He was quite a stinger, your Louis! Had he given away Tuileries Palace, maybe that would have clinched the deal. But to try and buy his life with such crap! And that Robespierre, why did he even take it? I mean, either you start a revolution, or you fuck around with snuffboxes!"

"Those French revolutionaries, they weren't joking! Hereabouts, things are not so bad. They'll put you in jail all right, but chopping off your head with a guillotine, just like that—not so much."

"They wouldn't know how to operate it, this thing, that's why!" one of the guests exclaimed.

The rest looked at him in shock. Somebody slipped into the hallway, reached for the coat hanger.

"Lisa, stay a bit longer, will you?" Lyalya said.

Meanwhile, Portugalsky went to the table. Somewhat squeamishly, he looked at the remains of the meal without touching anything. The tenor was suddenly saddened.

Saddened and disappointed, this is what he was. Disappointed by the ignorance of the mob on whom he depended for the success of his scheme. A man of a complicated biography, the famous singer was harvesting his daily bread and caviar from two departments at once: the Ministry of Culture and the Ministry of Love, as people used to call the KGB at that time.

Chapter 28: Che Guevara's Chessboard

Collecting his applause on the Parisian stage, Eddie did not for a moment forget his mission from the Ministry of Love: to study the stinking emigrant Parisian swamp, to find out who secretly shed nostalgic tears for the native birches hoping to see their golden leaves shiver back in Russia, their cruel stepmother, as they called it. Like any Soviet institution, the Ministry of Love was subject to a five-year plan. It required the ministry officials to catch a certain number of spies a year, to uncover so and so many anti-Soviet conspiracies, and to identify a quota of untrustworthy citizens. The salaries, bonuses and promotions of the huge staff depended on the fulfillment of the plan. The previous year, Eddie had been unlucky; he didn't manage to catch a single spy or discover even the tiniest conspiracy. And though he zealously fished in the emigrant cloaca, sniffing out this and that, even visiting the Russian-Orthodox Alexander Nevsky Cathedral in Paris, he found nothing but small fry.

Jasmilain-Letitia, with whom he occasionally spent a night, wasn't meant for his fishing net. It was her brother Apollo Razumovsky from London who interested Eddie. Apollo considered himself an illegitimate descendant of the Russian Prince Razumovsky. A forger famed in London criminal circles, he knew no equal. He could create a copy of a Breguet watch as easily as one of Mary Antoinette's gold pendants or a painting by Rubens. British newspapers kept announcing the discoveries of rare artworks and artifacts. For instance, in the Cathedral of Durham, in the tomb of Venerable Bede, Apollo found the very square and compasses that were used to kill the first freemason, Adoniram, the chief builder of the Temple of Solomon. And one rainy autumn day, in Paris, in the attic of 5 Rue Tardieu, near the crypt of Saint-Denis, where the first Jesuit, Ignatius Loyola, had given a vow of eternal poverty, he discovered under old newspapers … nothing other than the Holy Grail!

European museums and prestigious auction houses, saturated with Apollo Razumovsky's stunning finds, had already exposed many as fakes and were looking for the culprit. Apollo vanished from London and surfaced in Paris, where his sister lived.

Urgently needing to develop new markets, he decided to work in the East and in Latin America. He took up business with his usual energy. The first profitable deal was the sale of a chessboard to Fidel Castro himself: the very board on which ten-year-old Che Guevara had played against Casablanca, a Cuban, and almost won—which later helped Dr. Che Guevara become passionately attached to the Island of Liberty. The success with the chessboard inspired Arthur to new achievements. The chessboard sold to Fidel Castro still bore the traces of young Che's moist, trembling fingers. But what Apollo went on to sell to the Sandinista Ortego in Nicaragua was only touched by his own hands. Fifteen more boards with Che's forged signature sold like hotcakes across the Latin American continent. Dictators there were fond of playing chess as a relief from the burden of their duties. Inspired by the success in Latin America, Razumovsky turned his eyes to his ancestors' homeland, Russia.

To begin with, he decided to sell to the Soviet government a collection of insignia belonging to the imperial family (two real ones, the rest fake). However, the enterprise worried him. Wouldn't the Kremlin perceive his endeavours as ideological sabotage? Russian prison was not a holiday destination he had in mind. But Eddie, whom he met via his sister, assured him that the Kremlin, far from jailing him, would pick him up at the airport with bouquets of red carnations, provide him with a personal workshop in central Moscow, make him a member of the Union of Artists, and, with luck, make him a Hero of the Soviet Union. "Don't you fret!" Portugalsky assured the artist. "After all, we have the boots of Peter the Great exhibited in a Kremlin museum! Who can say they are real or not? And all kinds of crowns too! So why don't you try it?"

Portugalsky was lying shamelessly. Imperial regalia would only conquer Russian hearts later, with the collapse of Soviet power and the ascension of Eddie's former KGB colleague to the throne. While trying to net Apollo, Eddie could not know that, after a quarter of a century, the double-headed eagle would peck the sickle and hammer from the Russian coat of arms. No, that was deliberate provocation. Portugalsky suggested: "Let's sell a revolutionary snuffbox to a few museums! Say, one into which the great French revolutionary Robespierre literally stuck his nose. I've got connections in all big Soviet cities, and each has a museum of Revolution! Why don't you start with a dozen copies?"

Apollo was delighted with this plan. He had long wanted to con the curators of the Moscow Museum of Revolution, which had usurped a luxurious mansion in the city centre. This mansion had once belonged to his great-grandfather, Prince Lev Kirillovich Razumovsky, and later, it had housed the famous English club. Razumovsky's descendant did not object to the English club—after all, Count Leo Tolstoy himself had been a member—but housing a museum of revolution in his great-grandfather's mansion ... well, there are limits to everything.

Strolling along the Paris boulevards, an elegant cane in his hand, Apollo did not cease to feel an intimate connection with the soul of Lev Kirillovich Razumovsky. His ancestor's mind led the movements of his skilful fingers when he magically transformed junk into works of art that fooled the most experienced curators and connoisseurs. The master forger was a romantic; money wasn't everything he cared about. Apollo secretly envied his glorious ancestor. The name of Prince Razumovsky hardly ever left the gossip columns of St. Petersburg magazines thanks to a piquant scandal that brought him more fame than his title and wealth ever could. In his sunset years, the prince fell in love with the pretty princess Maria Golitsina. She happened to be married to someone else. So Lev Kirillovich invited her husband to play cards; Maria was the stake. The Prince won and married his trophy. How he had wrestled the required permission from the consistory remains a mystery.

Apollo Razumovsky saw himself as small fry compared to his ancestor, in whose soul cheating and honour interflowed so harmoniously. He was hungry for greatness. Portugalsky immediately paid him an advance from the Ministry of Love's subversion money. Having yet another drink with Apollo, Eddie was looking forward to the moment when he'd file a case against him as a ringleader of foreign intelligence who had infiltrated the USSR in order to overthrow the system.

Our tenor, as had been said, was a multitasker. While his job abroad involved uncovering conspiracies, back in the USSR, he had to identify the unreliable. Getting them arrested was easy enough. All you needed was to plant some illegal literature in their homes and accuse them of anti-Soviet propaganda, or else plant some antiques and accuse them of speculation.

Portugalsky was not particularly disappointed that the snuffbox didn't please the guests. He had far-reaching plans, and it was for their sake that he had appeared at the housewarming party. The case of Larissa Samsonova had long demanded active intervention; in fact, she had to be neutralized.

Eddie believed that the chance had finally presented itself.

It so happened that Portugalsky's wife Rita had been friends with Larissa, and Portugalsky long suspected that she had blabbed about his double life. The cold, even squeamish look that Larissa gave his gift reinforced the tenor's suspicions.

What could make tiny Rita, a woman with the head of the Greek goddess and the body of a twelve-year-old girl, blurt out the secret? And not just to anyone but to Lyalya, who, as Portugalsky had every reason to fear, might well share the news with his closest friends—that is, with half of Zaporizhzhia! The answer was simple: revenge. Rita had been told that her husband was renting a modest apartment in St. Germain for his mistress Jasmilain-Letitia, a dancer at the café Lapin Agile, which, translated from the poetic French tó a more prosaic language, means "The Quick Hare." Now his wife was trying to blackmail Portugalsky by threatening him with a divorce. (According to an unwritten but well-known law, employees of the Ministry of Love were to be married; if they failed to return from abroad, their wives would become hostages.)

The prospect of never seeing Leticia's lovely legs fly about at the Hare again filled the singer's heart with anger. And this, the tenor did not like a bit.

Fate is fickle: the tenor could forever lose the trust of the Ministry of Love—and then farewell to the eavesdropping, the surveillance, the denunciations and provocations, all this salt and pepper of life, without which he would be bored to tears. And most importantly, farewell to his second salary, the special distribution centres, the free vacation homes and the chance of receiving an apartment in a Stalin-empire-style high-rise, complete with servants. But even if divorce was an empty threat, Lisa's babbling was extremely unpleasant. If people find out for which department the tenor serves, they will get dis-acquainted and cross the street at the sight of him.

Once, Eduard Portugalsky had a dream. He saw himself wandering an endless road flanked with flat cardboard models of friends and acquaintances. And as soon as he neared one, it immediately fell face down, like a toy duck at a shooting gallery. The famous singer did not want to become an outcast. He loved the merry tinsel of celebrations, the ringing of glasses and speeches in his honour; he loved the chirping of female fans, the accidental touch of pretty diamond-studded fingers.

He could calm his wife by treats or threats. But Larissa Samsonova was another matter. It was not easy to intimidate the shrewd. He needed to deal with her the way he had with many unwanted people in his life. Robespierre's snuffbox would serve as a smuggled foreign good, which meant a good long time in prison. That's what Eduard had in mind while he was watching the guests leave.

***

The tenor had such a delicate constitution that he could never forgive even the slightest insult, and Larissa Samsonova had offended him three times. A year before, she failed to invite him to her birthday party, which was noisily celebrated by all of Zaporizhzhia. (This alone could serve as proof that she'd sniffed something out about him.) The second insult was pretty direct. She'd called him an asshole and a bastard. Not in his presence, but people were kind enough to immediately report the transgression to him. The third insult was the worst. The tenor considered it his duty to accost every woman he encountered between fifteen and seventy. Larissa didn't reciprocate in the least, which only whetted his appetite. With her, there was no point in beating around the bush: "Shall I compare you to a summer's dew, or we can do without?"

"Sod off," came her response. "I'd sooner sleep with a tarantula!"

Eddy laughed. Comparing him with a hairy spider! Not bad at all! In her eyes, he was dangerous! That stroked his ego. Women love danger; they love bad guys. Besides, it often takes more than one attempt with women. With this one, it might even take three. And he was ready. Except that there was no more time: the tenor was going on tour in Italy.

From Rome, he sent a reconciliation card with a fountain depicting Neptune strangling an octopus while surrounded by nereids, but Lyalya didn't pay much attention to the symbolism. She slipped the card into a phone book and forgot all about it.

Portugalsky, however, did not forget. She rejected him again. Twice now. In his mind, a plan gradually matured. He'd make Samsonova a mediator for the sale of Apollo's snuffboxes. Promise her a forty percent commission. And most importantly promise her Moscow which she wouldn't be able to resist: a luxury hotel, coupons to the best restaurants and the rest. Does she need a car? Fine, a car with a driver will be delivered to her hotel every morning.

In a feuilleton printed later about the discovery of a spy gang, Larissa Samsonova would be named the ringleader.

While Eddie was considering all this, the housewarming party had lost its lustre. Lyalya took off her high heels, put on slippers and an apron, and started collecting the dirty dishes. Eddie's wife went to the kitchen with Timmy to feed the goldfish. Eddie reached out, picked up the last sprat swimming lonely in oil.

"Look, Larissa, dear, I need a cozy little chat with you, just the two of us. The housewarming party was great. I wonder why people weren't impressed by Robespierre's snuffbox, though."

Lyalya shrugged in silence.

"Anyway, I think it's really cute," Portugalsky said. "Now listen, I've got an idea that concerns you." The tenor smiled, his face close to Lyalya's, and started whispering.

She shrunk back. "Yeah, it's a great idea, but keep me out of it, please. I need to fulfill the plan at work, can't spare the time."

"Oh, the plan ... You're not an opera diva, are you? A shock worker's plan!"

"Whatever ... but I'm not interested." Lyalya shouted for Tim to help her with the dishes.

Portugalsky's Adam's apple was bobbing.

"You'll be kicking yourself later! Attila forgives once. Attila forgives twice. Attila doesn't forgive the third time."

Lyalya sniggered. But the way he looked at her gave the creeps.

Chapter 29: Foreigners with Tiger Tales

HAVING RECEIVED FROM the state a one-room apartment in the heart of the city, an apartment with a parquet floor and a warm WC, one should be happy, right? And one would be if it weren't for the West Wind.

"How do you mean?" I asked my aunt as she was changing water in a vase with bougainvillea.

"You don't know anything about the West Wind? You want another story? I'll have to start at the beginning, then. This is how it goes. In the twenties, Stalin's secretary laid out the map of the USSR in front of his boss's feet. Stalin poked his boot into the left bank of the Dnieper. His architects—mind you, I wasn't there—measured out his shoe and ordered to have the greatest power plant in the world built in the area his shoe had covered. You remember the dam? Colossal. They flooded hundreds of villages around and during the war when Stalin ordered it to be blasted; thousands of locals perished. But in the twenties, they were building it with fanfare. They flooded its famous rapids where Zaporozskay Sech was. Thousands of tons flowing down fifty metres of concrete. That's when it all started in Zaporozje. Hurray to the blast furnaces!"

Fed by the electric power of the great river, a herd of factories and plants went to pasture in Zaporozje.

A menacing landscape of twenty of them sprang up in the heart of the city. The hellish flame was burning day and night, fatty clouds of smoke blackening the air. The Soviet leader apparently believed the proletariat should not be spoiled by the luxury of a tram: people had to walk to their jobs at the blast furnaces. Therefore, the living quarters were as close to the factory as they could get, in a new "barrack-type settlement No. 6."

In vain did sunflower heads turn left and right; there was no sun in the sky. Right at dawn, the city sank into a stinking brown-yellow haze. Unbidden tears ran down the cheeks of people in the street. Thanks to the poisonous fumes, a hard-boiled criminal could well be mistaken for the repenting Raskolnikov wiping a guilty tear from his unshaven cheek.

If a West Wind chanced to blow through the barrack settlement No. 6, loudspeakers would tune in a march popular since the 1930s."The smoke of furnaces, the breath of Soviet Russia!"

Those living on the very outskirts of the city were luckiest. They got their gas masks first. These were handed out from a warehouse with decommissioned military equipment. In the morning, there was always a fight. The old man in charge would only hand out masks to pretty young girls. "Where will the bea-u-u-uuty go if our cutest girls get poisoned?" he asked, raising his hands to the sky. Soon, a gas mask became a prestigious wedding gift: carefully wrapped, it was considered almost as good as the furniture set Helga, for which lucky newlyweds would often start saving in the hope of finally getting it at their silver wedding.

If it wasn't for one accident, who knows how long people would have survived the chemical attack of the blast furnaces and endure the West Wind?

Here is what happened. On Sunday, the sleepy residents of the barrack-type settlement No. 6, coughing spasmodically, stuck their heads out the windows, and saw that the streets were closed.

Equestrian police—a rarity in the city—were proudly prancing around the barrack, hoofs clicking on the cobblestone pavement, fencing off a line of people walking on the tram tracks. Even with poor visibility (the inky stinky West Wind was playing up this morning), these people could easily be identified as, to say the least, unusual. First, none were wearing black suits or ties. Instead, they were dressed in an entirely scandalous way: sports jackets, beige raincoats, white trousers, skinny jeans, long, brightly striped scarves and—in the icy November wind!— bare headed. Second, and even more strikingly, they had cameras hanging around their necks. Clearly foreigners, then; possibly hippies. The locals who dared open their windows to the wind could hear them talk their gibberish; foreigners gazed around, laughed, and gesticulated freely.

It wasn't just their cameras and jeans that caused the envy of the settlement. No, it was their gait! Not that the foreigners were limping, or dancing, or walking in some deliberately offensive fashion. No, they were simply walking. Not marching, but occasionally getting out of line. Turning their heads, nodding at the curious crowd in a friendly way. They were walking like … free people. That's what it was. Unworried. Unafraid. Which was insulting! Gawkers later claimed that some of the foreigners had tiger tails or donkey ears. But this seems improbable. Soviet border guards could let in donkeys in the guise of humans, but the tigers?

According to the plan, the group headed by the Secretary of the American Communist Party, the corpulent Mr. Buck, would first visit the Steely Fist steelworks and then the Hammer and Sickle plant. A few hundred metres before reaching the Fist, the delegation was met by a man wearing a fur hat and a thick woollen coat. Having politely run a step ahead and made a little bow, he turned to Mr. Buck and asked in his best English: "You like?"

"Oh yeah, it's great here!" Mr. Buck said, looking at Eduard Portugalsky with childish joy.

"Veit til you see!" Eduard said, running around Mr. Buck excitedly. "I sink is best vot you now see!"

"For sure, for sure!" Mr. Buck said, smiling.

And then there was a misunderstanding.

In front of the factory gate, the foreigners saw an electric concrete mixer. It was stuck. A worker, whose name was Stepan, was kicking it and commenting on its mother's alleged sexual relations with various people, animals, and appliances. In response to his rudeness, the mixer was rumbling and coughing, but the drum with concrete still refused to spin.

Stepan spat, picked up a stick, and began mixing concrete in the drum by hand (or rather, by stick). The American communists grabbed their cameras. This was something Eduard Portugalsky could not let happen. "No photo, plis, plis!" he said.

"We were allowed to take cameras, though?"

"Cameras, yes, but click, no!" Portugalsky said.

There was some confusion. Two policemen got off their steeds and approached the worker. "Hey, prole, what you doing here? There's a foreign delegation, don't you see? Piss off, will you!"

"Guys, the thing is, if the concrete hardens, they'll have my balls!" Stepan said, still stirring the cement with a stick.

"Why don't you stir it with your finger, dumbo? Get out of here!"

And Stepan submitted. He let go of the stick, grabbed the handles of the cart bearing the mixer, and wheeled it away.

The whole incident delayed the delegation for only five minutes, but these turned out fatal. Having spent three hundred seconds in the fumes of the five-year plan, Mr. Buck lost consciousness and crashed into the dust of the pavement. His comrades did his best to help: one took the striped scarf off his neck, another unbuttoned his leather jacket, the third began to press into his chest. But all was in vain. At the gates of the Steely Fist, Buck's communist heart stopped.

It's not fair to blame the poisonous West Wind of Zaporizhzhia, the Kremlin would later rule. Obese Mr. Buck had been suffering from a heart condition before. Be that as it may, he was now spread on the ground as if in flight, arms outstretched, eyes wide open and gazing into the smoky eternity of the Soviet paradise.

One can imagine the horror of the local authorities who had to inform Moscow about the tragedy, and down the chain, the grief of American communists, the grief of Buck's mistress and the displeasure of his wife. Perhaps unexpectedly, the simple workers of the Steely Fist, too, were crying real tears over the unseen Mr. Buck.

Lyalya personally knew Zina, a factory cleaner, who'd gotten no chance to show off the new overalls issued for the foreigners' visit. The welder Anatoly—who'd worked for Lyalya in the past—had to return the safety goggles he had received for this one day. The corpse of the unlucky communist was covered with ice and loaded onto a plane headed for New York. A separate plane was hired for the wreaths from fifteen Soviet republics that hurried to express their mournful solidarity with the Communist Party of America.

After this, the sensation might well have bubbled into oblivion without affecting the gloomy local lives. But no, the first secretary of the regional committee was given quite a dressing down and told to combat environmental pollution in case other foreigners with weak hearts ventured into Zaporizhzhia. And the administration began to act. It declared the stinking West Wind a war and implemented three separate countermeasures. First, every house of the settlement was adorned with a poster proclaiming "no smoke without a fire, but smoke without a smell!" Second, they attached a windmill to each blast furnace chimney. And third, they gave orders to fire cannons at the smoke, which, according to the authorities, significantly increased the effect of the other two measures.

"They did really well, our blockheads!" my aunt said laughing.

As a result of these coordinated efforts, the West Wind seemed to lose some of its umph, and the brown haze appeared somewhat more transparent. Still, despite the city's draconian measures, the number of deaths from respiratory diseases did not decrease. After some head scratching, the authorities concluded that there were only two options: they had to either ignore the Kremlin command or close all the factories. But stopping the production in Zaporizhzhia meant that Uncle Sam would win. Without this steel, the Soviets would never catch up with America, much less overtake it. Stopping production was a one-way ticket to a Gulag, and the same applied to disobeying the Kremlin order to fight pollution. Even if, by some strange fit of luck, the city authorities managed to keep their heads on their shoulders, their backsides would certainly leave the comfy chairs accompanied by better food, foreign trips, and free sanatoriums.

So after even more head scratching, the administration produced a brilliant plan known as "have your cake and eat it too." It was decided to set up a yoga camp on the island of Khortytsia, where, instead of breathing in fifteen times per minute, the locals were taught to only breathe in once. The trips to the camp were "voluntarily compulsory."

The most diligent, who reached the rate of one breath per minute, were awarded a medal and a gas mask. "That's where I first learned yoga!" Lyalya said winking at me.

Chapter 30: Do Not Write Letters to Brezhnev

On one such West Wind Monday, when it seemed to the weak of heart that it was easier to leave this world than take another breath, Timmy returned home from work. Lyalya heard him cough long before the key turned in the door.

"I … read this." Continuing to cough, he shoved a folded sheet of paper into Lyalya's hand. His own was trembling.

"You need a hanky? Here." She carelessly handed him one and started reading. In a second, her face froze. It was a summons to the local KGB headquarters.

"That's—no," she whispered, her lips white. "Why? How did it …? What did you do?!"

"I … I didn't do anything," Timmy said. "Nothing at all. Actually, it's not even addressed to me."

"But there is your name here!"

"My last name, yes. Have a look at the first name."

Lyalya didn't say a word while serving dinner. Timmy was also silent. Only when dinner was over did Lyalya quietly say, "It must be that KGB pig Portugalsky."

But she was mistaken. Surprisingly, Eddy had nothing to do with it.

The reason for the summons was Vasily, Tim's younger brother, who lived 5,000 kilometres away from Zaporizhzhia, in the village of Canareikino near the Altai Mountains. Vasily was a nice guy, and, like many nice guys, he had little luck in life.

When he visited his Zaporizhzhia relatives, which happened rarely enough, Vasily loved to tell a joke, with whose protagonist he strongly identified.

"There was once a poor man," he'd say, "and his rich relatives wanted to help him. But the poor man was proud and wouldn't take any money from them. So the relatives came up with a trick. They decided to leave a purse full of money on the bridge. The beggar walked along that bridge to the city every day to ask for alms."

At this point, Vasily would sniff with compassion for the poor man, pull out a bottle of vodka from a pocket of his greasy shirt, open it, and bring it into an upright bottom-up position over his mouth. A long gurgle followed, and then Vasily continued. "So the next day the relatives ask, 'Did you see anything interesting on the bridge today?' And he goes, 'What's there to look at? I'm so sick of that stupid bridge I always walk there with my eyes shut!'"

"That's me all right, huh?" Vasily guffawed, flattered to recognize himself in folklore. He really was an epic loser. The house that he spent ten years building burned down the day after he had hammered in the last nail. His bride cheated on him with his best friend a week before the wedding. If someone happened to hire him, he'd be fired within a month at the latest.

But once—only once!—Dame Fortune took pity on Vasily and presented him with a lottery ticket winning a thousand rubles.

It was an evening in the fall. The rain was pouring. Vasily was drunk and dying for a smoke. He sat down on a log, water running off him, and began to look for cigarette butts. Instead, he discovered a soaked piece of paper. He found some tobacco crumbs in his pocket and rolled them into it, but it wouldn't burn. Vasily turned it this way and that. On one side, there was the letter y, all that remained of the word "lottery"; on the other, a series of numbers. Just in case, Vasily stuck the piece of paper into his pocket and went home to sleep.

In the morning, sad and sober, he looked out of the window. Yesterday's icy rain had changed to a blizzard. Vasily remembered the piece of paper and got it out of his pocket. "You never know!" he thought, put on his threadbare *ushanka* hat and, staggering with yesterday's drink, stepped into the blizzard. He had missed the TV show proclaiming the winning numbers, but if his ticket had won, they'd know at the bank.

And it had! The young woman at the counter checked the number against her data: it was a thousand-ruble win. She gave the ticket and Vasily a closer look. "The ticket is defective, comrade! The edge is burned. The thing might well be forged. Now get out of here, or I'll call the police!"

And at this point, something broke in Vasily—something that, so far, had been holding together his life, such as it was, on a couple of rusty nails. No, Vasily did not hang himself. But having returned to his hole, he pulled a sheet of paper from the wall calendar, sucked thoughtfully on a pencil, and wrote,

"My life is bad, but Brezhnev's getting fat. I've got nothing to eat, but Brezhnev doesn't give a shit."

Then he put the poem into an envelope, addressed it quite simply "to Brezhnev" and threw it, unstamped, into the letterbox, having first scrubbed off ice and snow from its narrow slit.

Soon, the postwoman Glafira got out the letter and thoughtfully held it in her fingerless gloves. When she saw the word "Brezhnev," she blew on the letter as if the envelope could burn her hands in the frost. Then she looked around. Except for two or three sparrows, there was not a single soul to see. The snowdrifts were sparkling like giant breasts covered in glitter. The wires above her head were howling in the wind.

Glafira stamped about to warm her feet, mumbled a sad and quiet "fucking fuck," and started walking through the snow to the only stone building in the city: the local KGB branch. Having slipped the envelope into the slot of the tightly closed oak door adorned by bronze lion heads, the postwoman swiftly crossed herself and faded into the snowdrifts.

It must be mentioned at this point that Vasily had often asked Tim for help, and the soft-hearted older brother regularly sent him ten or twenty rubles in secret from Lyalya. Thanks to this, the KGB graphologists knew Vasily's handwriting as well as his usual addressee. The blasphemous calendar sheet came in an envelope with no return address, but the secret service specialists assumed the culprit would be easy enough to identify. All they needed to do was to summon Timofey Doroshenko for questioning.

Chapter 31: The Mayor's Advice

LYALYA KNEW WELL ENOUGH how easy it was to travel from Ukraine to Siberia free of charge on a one-way ticket. And Lyalya had no intention of returning to Siberia.

"So I had to go and see Obkomchik, of course," she now said, neatly folding the clothes I'd carelessly left on a chair.

In the oak-lined reception hall, Lyalya was met by a young secretary and a cat who began to rub against her leg. Without looking at the former, she picked up the latter and marched into the mayor's office. She started the conversation from afar, apologizing for the embarrassment at the housewarming party.

"Never mind, Laryssa, dear," Patermufti said. "We're two old sharks, you and me. Januaria got a chance to blow off some steam, and that's that. You'll get a crystal chandelier as promised."

"Forget the chandelier, Patermufti. I have bigger fish to fry."

As Lyalya's story progressed, the mayor's face was stiffening. His right shoulder began crawling up to his ear, as if to protect his head. The other shoulder followed. Having crawled into himself like a turtle, Patermufti jolted, called his secretary, and sent her home. Then he closed the door, rubbed his nose, and gave Lyalya a close look. "Anyway, how's the new apartment? Is the wallpaper holding on?"

"For now."

"Well, that's some good news … Yeah … So what do we do now? A bit much this time, huh?" Obkomchik came closer, his clever little eyes peering at her from amid the fat of his face. "They're idiots to take this seriously, of course. But that brother-in-law you got, he's quite something! You need him like last year's snow, frankly."

"Thanks for telling me. Any suggestions?"

"He looks just like a walrus without a moustache," thought Lyalya squinting at Patermufti.

"Look, now that the shit hit the fan, I'm to help, right? But I can't! You see, I can't! Not in my power. If they want that man of yours in jail along with his brother and with you, which seems rather probable, nobody will ask for my opinion!" And Patermufti gave the table a weak blow of his rather unimpressive fist.

Hearing "that man of yours," Lyalya dropped the cat onto the floor, and headed for the door.

"Oh hell, wait, wait," the mayor said. "No need to show character; I know you've got one. Well, if they summon you, deny everything. You're not in the know."

"Why? I can do better than that. I'd say I raped a kangaroo in a zoo."

It's hard to say what disturbed the mayor more: Lyalya's words or her malevolent laughter.

"What? Calm down, Larissa. We'll … we'll …"

"I'm perfectly calm. When they offer me a choice from a selection of crimes, I'll say I savagely raped a kangaroo in 1905. You don't read novels, do you? That's Aleshkovsky."

"Who smuggled this illegal filth to you? Must be Portugalsky? So, now, calm down. Let me think. Here's what you do … I've only got this one piece of advice: get out of here! Scram! Skedaddle! Or it's all out with you." He kicked away the meowing cat.

"Where do you want us to run to? Are you advising us to turn into LDTs?"

"What's that supposed to mean?"

"Long-distance tramps."

"Oh, stop with your sharp tongue already! It's not a time for jokes. You have to"—Obkomchik shook his head trying to control his shoulder that was trying to slap him on his right ear. "Let's meet again, brainstorm, think of something. Now I have to go home. Januaria will be cross, you know."

In a couple of days, Obkomchik called Lyalya. "Good news! You and Timofey are going to Crystal Goose."

"What? Is that even a real place?"

"Yep. Crystal Goose. You like crystal, don't you? The city is full of it. Or has been, at least. Was the capital of the Russian crystal production before the revolution."

"And now? What are we going to fucking do there now?"

"Well, you'll find out about now. You raised production in Siberia, didn't you? So now that's your new task. To raise crystal production to the pre-revolutionary level. They don't need it to be any higher yet."

Chapter 32: Timmy's Dreams

Timmy firmly believed that one day the USSR would collapse along with the idea of communism, five-year plans, socialist competitions between each other and against capitalist American sharks, half-day political information rallies, Red Square military parades, volunteer-compulsory shock work, and protests for peace in the Sahara desert. Then Timmy would become a free man. And having become a free man, he would see the world: London, Paris, Naples, all of it! Timmy knew the toponymy of Europe from maps as thoroughly as a passionate lover knows every curve of his beloved.

Timmy's premonitions did not deceive him. The USSR did indeed break apart and sink into oblivion; millions of its former hostages got to see the world. The only thing he had failed to predict was that he would not be among these millions—he would not live to see it all happen. But, as the poet said, hope nourishes young souls. Though Tim was not so young anymore and wrote no poems, he hoped for the future. His greatest treasures were the maps, an expression of his unquenchable thirst for travel. Having no corner of his own in the apartment, Timmy hung them all over the small bathroom. By the way, he was not alone in this. He was dreaming along with the whole country.

If we could go back to the 1970s and look into the tiny kitchens of the intelligentsia, we'd see precisely the same maps as Timmy's. There were some loftier dreamers, too, mental travellers of the entire universe: instead of geographical maps, they hung maps of the starry sky. And while their skinny offspring hurriedly absorbed noodles and herring, the walls of their kitchens and their tiny toilets were shimmering with constellations, spinning galaxies, and silently exploding supernovas.

But let us return to that modest apartment on Lenin Avenue in the glorious city of Zaporizhzhia.

Lyalya knew that Timmy went to the restroom not to satisfy the needs for which such a place was usually reserved. His needs were of a metaphysical order: conspiratorially flushing at unequal intervals, Timmy was sneaking around Europe.

Here he was in Paris. Early morning, a drizzle, the grey Notre Dame looming over his head. To the right, along the embankment, the book market trays were wrapped in cellophane on the occasion of the rain. Under the purple umbrella, young lovers were admiring the brown waters of the Seine. Another couple, much older, was running in the rain, a man and a woman holding hands and laughing.

A turn left, then right, and there came the famous café Les Deux Magots (or Gog and Magog, as Timmy joked to himself). He didn't go there for dinner—even in his fantasies, he didn't have the money. All he wanted was to talk to shadows. For example, to good old bearded Hem. Timmy was well read, which gave him, a quiet and insecure man, undeniable advantage over the uncultured, especially when he was sitting on the toilet and at the same time secretly strolling around Europe. Sometimes, he got on a train and rushed to the Côte d'Azur, to the city of his dreams—Nice.

Ah, Nice! Timmy knew precisely what to do with this legendary city, how to make the best use of the air, the sun, and even the mistral. Most importantly, he knew how talk to the shadows of the past about the meaning of the present. Who was that tall gentleman in a hat, a cane in his hands, walking along the Promenade des Anglais? Mon Dieu, was it Chekhov himself? Timmy adjusted his steps to the great writer's leisurely walk and found himself in a cafe opposite him. They got acquainted, shook hands, and Tim invited Chekhov to a cup of coffee. (For himself, he only ordered a glass of water.) Conquering his embarrassment, Timmy said: "Anton Pavlovich, how nice it is to sit here, enjoying the splendid view! Tell me, do you know what the name of Nice was in ancient times?"

"Alas, I don't," Chekhov said modestly, cleaning his pince-nez.

"It so happens that I have thoroughly studied this question," Timmy said, blushing with pleasure. "It turns out that ancient Greeks founded Nice and named it Νίκαια in honour of the winged goddess of victory Nike. See, there is Antibes in the distance, in Greek—Antipolis, which means 'the city opposite.' The Greeks had little imagination, really. But you, Anton Pavlovich, how would you rename Antibes?"

Chekhov's pince-nez sparkled ironically.

Timmy nervously pressed his old briefcase to his heart. "I'm sorry if I said something wrong … To be honest, I'm just so excited to meet you!" And he glanced down, sniffing. "You know, they're sending me to Crystal Goose, into the burdocks—as the Russian phrase goes, right into cockroach darkness!"

"Crystal Goose?" Chekhov asked. "Is this really a town? Never heard of it. And who, I'm sorry, is sending you there?"

"Well, my wife and her friend, she has that powerful friend, you see. I have no idea about Goose myself. But if you want, as soon as I arrive, I'll plunge into the archives and tell you all about it."

"That would be just wonderful," Chekhov said, and dissolved in the air.

"Timmy, you coming out there sometime soon?" Lyalya's voice, coming from the kitchen. "I've heard you flush four times! Get out already!"

Timmy pulled the chain again just in case, and, when the roar of the waterfall turned into a subtle murmur, opened the door.

"Get your suitcases from the top shelf!" his wife shouted. "We need to start packing!"

Chapter 33: Marriage Marathon

"Now this is when I had to make some tough decisions," Lyalya said, looking out from the Bogdanovich balcony at the sunset-lit mountains. "Whom to take along to that Goose town and whom to leave behind. My mother was quite fit and didn't want to go anywhere. Nikita was finishing school in Zaporizhzhia. And Lyuba was thirteen. The most difficult age. I couldn't leave her with her grandmother. Besides, she didn't want to stay behind without us, especially without Tim. He was teaching her cartography, watching the fish in the aquarium with her. Best friends, you know.

"So she'd come along. Fine. But what to do with the apartment? Officially, it belonged to Timmy. I wasn't registered in it. Well, suppose we left, and Nikita stayed behind. What if the police came: 'Show us your documents! What are your rights to that apartment?' None."

It took Aunt only one night to concoct a plan. It was a sleepless night all right, but by morning, all the details of the operation were in place. She managed to scramble together a hundred and fifty rubles—a month's salary—and went to a police station that was dealing with passports and registration issues.

"A bribe?" I asked. "How on Earth do you even do it?"

"It depends on the situation, and the rank." Aunt winked, happy to share her know-how. "If it's a secretary, you say, 'You love chocolate? Of course you do, my dear! Me too! I was going to get us both some, but I just didn't know which kind you prefer. Why don't you get your favourite kind yourself?' And then you slip some money into her hand."

"Did people ever refuse?"

"Refuse a bribe?" Lyalya chuckled. "Well, sometimes. Out of fear. But rarely. The thing is, you have to make it comfortable for them; they should feel safe with you. You know they've taken the bait when they avoid looking into your eyes and pretend to be suddenly busy, urgently writing something or making a phone call. Okay, once I screwed up. This woman at the police office, with whom I had asked to register Nikita in the apartment. With her, it went all wrong. Imagine, she takes the money but then turns all purple, gets up from the table, comes up close to me, and lowers her voice to a whisper. 'Put yourself for a moment into my shoes, comrade Samsonova. You're telling me Nikita is your son, that's fine, it's documented and can be proven in court. But who are you to Timofey Doroshenko? Nobody, as far as I'm concerned. You cohabit with him. Being a mistress doesn't give you any legal rights.'"

"You weren't married to him back then?"

"No, I wasn't. He was kind of reluctant. His cuckold's horns hadn't healed yet, I guess. And to be honest, I wasn't dying to marry him either. It wasn't as if he delivered me a starry sky every night, right? But when I heard this stupid girl speak like that. Me, a *mistress*? *Cohabiting*? Shameful words! After everything I'd done for him? So I came home dark as a thunderstorm and told Timmy, 'Either we get married tomorrow, or it's the last time you see me!' He didn't dare to say a word. So off I dashed to the registration office before it closed for the weekend.

"Once there, I took a good look around. And damn it, not a soul I knew, neither the chief administrator nor even a clerk! Now, how could I get married the next day!? But I'm not one for giving up, am I? So I sidled up to the first clerk I saw and told her that I *must*, absolutely *must*, get married tomorrow. The woman opened her eyes at me as if it were her first day on planet Earth and went, 'Excuse me! We are closing down for the weekend. Please come on Wednesday, that's the earliest that can be arranged.' And me: 'Wednesday? What do you mean, Wednesday? My bridegroom has cancer—his life is hanging by a thread.' I wonder now: Why did I make up such a stupid fib? Maybe it somehow affected Tim? Maybe that's why he died early?"

Lyalya shook her head sadly. "I shouldn't have said that. But we had to clear out of Zaporizja, right? And I was not going to leave my apartment to the state, was I? So I had to have a stamp, and to have a stamp I had to marry Tim Doroshenko, see? Who else would get things done the right way, solidly, so that they wouldn't be undone by a nose click? Anyhow, that woman wasn't a spring chicken. She must have seen terminally ill people getting married for legal purposes or because some women prefer to be called a widow rather than a spinster.

Nevertheless, she clearly took pity on me. 'Let's see,' she said. 'Maybe I can switch people around. Let's try for Tuesday, the earliest. Though I doubt it will work out.'

"At that moment, I slip an envelope into her hands. Two hundred rubles, a hefty sum in those days. She quickly shut it into her desk drawer and buried her head in her schedule. And what a chance. 'How lucky!' she exclaimed. 'I found a free spot for you. On Tuesday!'

"I clasped my hands together. 'Dear such and such'—whatever her name was, I don't remember now—'On Tuesday, I have more work than there are stars in the sky! That's when I make a schedule for sixteen hundred construction workers for a year ahead. They all depend on me!'

"She stared at me, forgetting to close her mouth. 'Well, then, I don't know where else I can put you. Monday is the first day after the weekend, and we're booked solid.'

"'I'm not talking Monday,' I said. 'He's having chemo on Monday. Tomorrow is the only day.'

"'Well,' she said, 'as far as I can see, tomorrow is Saturday. We're closed over the weekend, as you know.'

"So I made a face as if I'd just swallowed a frog. 'I'm very happy for you!' I said. 'So lucky that you have two days off every week! You know, I only had one day off all my life, and sometimes none …' And I looked not at her but at the desk drawer, thinking, 'You've swallowed the hook, and now you want to jump off?'

"So she started ringing her hands. 'Oh, you're putting me in such position, I'm quite at a loss. The week isn't made of rubber, you know, you can't stretch it.'

"'Oh yes, you can!' I said. 'I have to do it at work from dawn till dusk, and, unlike you, I don't get any extra money for overtime.'

"Then I shut up, and right in time—cause she was clearly about to start hating me—I slipped in another envelope. So she finally sighed and said, 'How about Sunday? I'll open the office just for you.'

"'Oh,' I said, 'the thing is Sunday is the official Construction Workers Mushroom Hunting Day. Half a city goes to the woods under my leadership. They'll be sure to pick some toadstools without me! And besides, that's my future husband's last wish in life, to go mushroom picking. We can't deprive him of his last wish, can we?' And the woman, now totally crushed, in a whisper: 'What do you want from me?' And I: 'Me? Do I ever want anything from anybody, in my whole doleful life of misery? It's people who always want something from me. Simple: you've got to marry us tomorrow!'

"And the woman finally surrendered. 'You know what? I've seen enough in life, but I never saw a bride who has no time to get married!'

"I can only recall running to three hospitals that night to get Tim a wheelchair. I told him to put on some pyjamas and get in, wrapped his legs in a cotton blanket. 'You better not ask me any questions, just close your eyes and make a sick face,' I said. 'And be glad you don't need to buy a wedding suit!'

"That's how I got two stamps in my passport, one confirming my marriage and the other registering Nikita, my son, in Tim's apartment. As my husband's stepson, he now had the legal right to it.

"So we shut down one life to open a new one." Aunt sighed, pressing the cigarette butt into the ashtray.

PART III

Chapter 34: Life in Crystal Goose

As a Muscovite, I could never fully appreciate why the Russian capital seemed so attractive to so many people. Thousands were trying to get to Moscow by hook or by crook. But the way to the dream was blocked by the stony breast of power; you were only allowed to live in the heart of Soviet Russia if you had a Moscow residence permit. The megapolis could not feed itself: dozens of villages, hamlets, and towns supplied Muscovites with provisions, condemning their own residents to near starvation. The people who created all the food on Moscow's tables had to fight hard to get at least something back from the capital. And they did. Villages sent messengers, "the sack people," who, after a long railway journey, would storm Moscow's half-empty stores. Seeing the villagers with their bags and sacks, the Muscovites would squeamishly move to the other side of the street. The non-locals spent the nights at railway stations (if they were lucky enough not to get shooed off by the police). In the mornings, they besieged the shops and spent countless hours in the queues, with slavish obedience, waiting for sausages, sugar, buckwheat, flour, salt, pasta, and sunflower oil to be later distributed among the village relatives and neighbours. The Muscovites rushing to the shops after work complained that the counters had been emptied by the unwashed smelly hillbillies.

Why was Aunt so drawn to Moscow? Did the food shops do it, or the pretty teeth of the Kremlin, or perhaps the conservatory and the theatres? Yes, it was all of this, separately and together. "A stroll through Moscow, and suddenly you feel like a human being!" She must have secretly envied us, her Moscow relatives. The idea that Crystal Goose was only two hundred kilometres away from Moscow was a great consolation for her.

Lyalya, Tim, and the teenage Lyuba arrived in Crystal Goose in mid-winter. The city seemed deserted. The empty streets were dark, the streetlamps missing their glass fronts. Behind snowdrifts the height of a tall man, houses with plywood-shuttered windows were shyly peeking out.

On the outskirts of the town, a flock of hungry mongrels started following the newcomers. Lyalya threw them a half-eaten sandwich; they fought over it and fell behind.

When the barking finally subsided, they were stunned by the silence, interrupted only by the dry squeak of snow under their feet. From time to time, they slowed down to take a breath. From the unfathomable blackness above, the stars were looking at them, brighter than ever. Like furry rubber balls suspended from a thread, they pulsed, seemingly moving closer and back again. The icy air burned in their lungs.

At the porch of a wooden blockhouse, the newcomers came across something solid. Timmy shoved the snow apart with his foot, and stumbled on a half-naked female corpse. Lyalya gave out a cry. She knocked on the dark windows, running through the streets in the snow. No one opened.

The fronts of the streets looked irregular, with stubby one- or two-storey houses stepping out of line and alternating with abandoned shacks, half-buried in snow. Some of the red-bricked buildings with hipped roofs, solid and with a hint of a brickwork decoration on a façade, seemed to have belonged to a pre-Soviet era and, though neglected, still stood their ground. It was in one of those houses that Lyalya and Tim were assigned a small one bedroom flat number three. Tim struggled with a rusty lock that finally succumbed to his efforts and let them in. Lyalya touched an unresponsive switch in the vestibule.

"The wiring needs to be fixed, possibly replaced," she said indifferently. After stumbling on a dead woman in the street, the disrepair—familiar and to be expected—failed to stir any emotions. She rummaged in her bag for the candles they prudently brought from Ukraine.

"We still have a couple of hours of light," Tim said. "Let's see what else we've got here."

There wasn't much in the kitchen. The absence of a stove or a fridge or countertops was, however, compensated with by a tap that ran cold water. Half the living room was taken up by a Dutch stove with shepherdesses playing flutes on white-blue tiles.

"Bloody cold here," Lyalya said, rubbing her frozen fingers. "I wonder where our neighbours are getting their firewood from."

Three days later, Lyalya went to inspect the glass factory, walking there over an ice-covered river. Half-destroyed brick buildings with black pipes stared at her as she hiked along the shore, past a few fir trees and birches. From the fog, a crumbling church arose like a ghost. She came closer. White-stone trim, twisted columns, and patterned window cases hinted at better days. Lyalya looked up: instead of a cross, a silver goose was sitting on the dome.

"A goose, imagine!" Aunt said, pressing her hands to her head. "Well, I think either I'm mad, or the whole city is! So I say to Timmy, 'Well, look where we ended up thanks to your genius brother! The city is like after the bombing, and now, a goose on top of the church! How does your toponomy explain the goose?' And Timmy says, 'Toponymy has nothing to do with it. Though it wouldn't hurt to go through the archives. Tomorrow, I'll check things out. Living in a city and having no clue about its history? That's moral decay.'"

Listening to my aunt, I couldn't help but laugh. "Moral decay" was lifted right from the Soviet propaganda playbooks; it was newspeak jargon of the seventies. It referred to the woeful condition the collective West was rotting in. Like the last stage of a corpse decomposition. I shook my head and asked, "Is that what he said?"

"That's exactly what he said. And I go, 'You better lift your eyes to the ceiling!' And he goes, 'What's so special about it?' 'I can count the stars of the Milky Way through the holes in it! That's your moral decay! Are you going to fix the ceiling, or are you going to rub the seat of your pants in some dusty archive?'"

As it turned out, the first place they put us in wasn't fixable. We then moved into a house allocated by the city council. Ancient masonry with stone carvings, patterned platbands, all kinds of architectural bells and whistles … Initially, we thought it was an improvement. The factory owner had built some fancy houses for his workers, but that was back in the eighteenth century! And since then, as we soon discovered, nobody thought to fix them. Wind was howling through the rooms like in a desert. The doors were squeaking so bad they seemed about to snap off their hinges! Timmy could be so good with his hands when he wanted to, but he had other priorities! Instead, he up and went to Vladimir, the nearest big city, to dig in the archives."

Chapter 35: First Letter to Chekhov

TIMMY LOVED TRAINS. After all, one can dream much better when listening to the rolling wheels and gazing out of the window than when sitting on a toilet at home. On his way from Vladimir back to Crystal Goose, Timmy began his first letter to Chekhov.

Dear Anton Pavlovich,

I would like to inform you that the first thing I did upon arriving at my new place of residence was hurry to the archives, as I promised. Crystal Goose! An intriguing name indeed.

Let me be honest: the information preserved in the archives is so overgrown with myths that separating the grains of truth from the spit of fiction takes stamina. After reviewing countless documents, I had to conclude that they most clearly mirror the Soviet period. A good thing you didn't live to see it. I'd rather tell you about the olden days!

In the ancient chronicles, the first mention of the tribe that settled on the bank of the Gus River dates back to the twelfth century. They lived among the dense forests and professed pagan Christianity. "What is the strange combination?" I hear you ask. I'm afraid I won't be able to explain the subtleties of their faith, but it seems they believed that Christ would save them—and depicted him as a bear, a wolf or a fox.

The chronicle mentions two free thinkers who denied the Bear-Wolf-Fox Christianity. Not surprisingly, these nihilists were expelled from the congregation and driven away into the impenetrable thicket of the forest. There, they built a hut and lived as hermits, eating nothing but roots, mushrooms, and berries. You won't be surprised, dear Anton Pavlovich, that, like all good hermits, they were tormented by temptations day and night. But they resisted and never lost hope of seeing the true God face to face.

But God would not show up. Instead, He chose to test them and sent a variety of trials. The worst thing—the fire—came in the tenth year of their hermitage. The fiery hell burned down their miserable shack. But a huge pine tree collapsed nearby, and its roots turned up a whole slice of land. The hermits hid in this funnel and watched as fire tornadoes jumped from tree to tree, falling century-old giants with a terrible noise.

When the flame finally subsided, the hermits came out of their hiding place. Light-headed from hunger, thirst, and the fumes, they looked around. The whole world around them burned, nothing but soot, and the black leaves were moving uncannily under their feet from the heat, as if they still had life in them.

Oh, oh, I think I should be getting out now … Sorry, Anton Pavlovich, I almost missed my station!

Chapter 36: Second Letter to Chekhov

Dear Anton Pavlovich!

Sorry for the long silence. In my absence, my wife managed to close up the roof, install new doors, and put glass into the window frames. Now, while she and her daughter are tiling the bathroom, I decided to take a minute to talk to you. For this purpose, I excused myself into the garden under the guise of weeding carrots.

Now, where were we? I remember we left our miserable hermits sitting on the stump, waiting to die. And just as they were getting ready to part from this world, a goose, untouched by soot and white as an angel, dashed into the smouldering coals a few feet away from the stump, honking in agony before being roasted. "God has finally appeared!" cried out the monks. "He descended onto the scorched earth to save our lives! Manifested as a goose!"

Struck by this revelation, they partook of their new God's roasted flesh and were saved.

The desire to share their new faith with the villagers was burning stronger in them now than the forest fire had burned. Having finally left the woods, they preached the new faith to whoever would listen. Christ didn't resemble a wolf at all, they said. He wore the flesh of a goose and had sacrificed himself for humanity.

But villagers were no fools: they roasted the new prophets alive and threw pieces to the dogs. Which, naturally, caused panic among the martyrs' followers. To avoid prosecution, the followers of Goose God pretended to be mute, emitting nothing but strange hisses and honks. These noises were in fact Honkanook, a secret language they had invented to communicate with each other.

The survivors proclaimed that eating geese in the memory of their God was a sacred duty of each believer and that each Honkanookie—as they called themselves—should pray in Honkanook to the image of a goose painted on a tree or cut out of bark.

When, five centuries later, the rich merchant Chmokov came to the river Gus, there were hardly any traces left of the Honkanookies or their bizarre cult. Except for two: the Gus inhabitants had a striking predilection for goose meat and a custom of wearing a goose feather behind the left ear. As nobody in the settlement showed any signs of literacy, these were clearly no quills …

Goodbye, dear Anton Pavlovich! The hammers went silent. Lyalya and Lyuba must be done with their carpentry and will be coming for me now!

Chapter 37: Third Letter to Chekhov

Dear Anton Pavlovich!

I promised to describe to you the history of Gus-Khrustalny or Crystal Goose, but only reached the wild, primitive times so far. You will forgive me. Every day, my chores grip me in their claws. Now, to move from poetry to prose: My wife and I are having a hard time feeding ourselves. Thank God, she has a green thumb: potatoes, beets, carrots, cabbage—everything grows in her garden. She dug up the ground herself too. Only in the end, for appearance's sake, I took up a shovel as well. What can I say about our second winter? It was no better than the first one. Blizzards, snowdrifts … So much snow can fall overnight that the gate is snowed shut, and our house is buried. Then my wife takes a shovel and starts digging us up. It's like morning exercises for her, but in a couple of hours, she loses her patience "Where are you?" she shouts. "Counting the flies on the ceiling or what? Your figure badly needs some snow gymnastics!" Luckily, she usually only calls for me after most of the work is done. The truth is she really likes to shovel snow; good for her waistline, she says. She doesn't really want me there, but if I don't come, she won't talk to me for the rest of the day. Everyone has their flaws; why should she be an exception?

Last time she called, I had to interrupt my letter and go out into the cold. And what did I see? My wife had prepared a mountain of snowballs—and before I could even blink, she started pelting me! Like a little girl! All red in the face, her eyes aflame, her warm headscarf off, her curls scattered on the collar of her fur coat. Oh, how I admired her! A pity I'm not an artist. That's how I would've portrayed my Amazon wife, a snowball in her hand.

Though her photograph at home, on a cupboard, is also beautiful. Nothing special, it seems, and yet, she's utterly lovely. Or I imagine her at her desk. She always works hard, even brings work home on Sundays. Imagine her wearing a bathrobe on top of a nightgown, one slipper on, the other foot bare, doing math, driving a pencil over a big sheet of paper, or standing at the drawing board, working on a new project, or fixing an old one. I'm not young, but I love her like a teenager! Only I don't know how to express this love, or so she tells me.

This time, I go out into the yard, wrestle her into the snow, she gets up, we start throwing snowballs at each other, laughing. The neighbours look out of the windows: "What's the fuss? Ah, those two at play again! Well, good for them." And up go the shutters.

Once a week, Lyalya heats up the banya for me. We've got one, a real little Russian sauna hut. Anton Pavlovich, you know everything about the banya, don't you? Lyalya breaks some birch branches in the forest for the proper massage to improve the circulation, steams them well, pours some hot water over me from a vat. And gives me lashes. Sometimes it's hard to take, but I squeeze my teeth, not a moan, after all I'm a man, that's what my wife says. Besides, it's an ancient ritual. What can one do? Then I run onto the snow in the costume my mother had given me birth in, as the tradition demands. And then again, and again. Afterward, you walk on the clouds! As good as new!

Are you perhaps surprised, dear Anton Pavlovich, that I am writing about such trifles, throwing the garbage of life onto your artistic millstones? But I've heard writers can make use of all kinds of useless bits and pieces. Call it the notes of an ethnographer from Soviet life (that you had very good luck not to taste, God forbid!). You can turn these bits this way and that and find a diamond in a pile of dung, for all I know. And then it will look like we didn't live in vain … ah?

Did I tell you that we left Zaporizhzhia without telling anyone our address? The KGB is no one's sweetheart … What's this, you may ask? Some cagy thing? My dear Anton Pavlovich. I will leave you with your ignorance. So you can still sleep at night. Enough to say we knew nobody in town at the beginning. I, for my part, love silence and peace, but my wife can't live without people, and a bit of brouhaha, you see. Before I could blink, she managed to befriend half the town.

Anton Pavlovich, You've been to Europe, got even to Ceylon. What's it like? I've never been in the West, but I suspect life there must be better than here in every way! Yet, will you agree if I say that Russia, too, has some goodness about her? What exactly? Hmmm. We launched the first Sputnik with a little doggie Layka on board. She never came back. Science over animal rights, I'd say. Our cosmonaut, Gagarin, was the first man to orbit the earth. Returned in one piece, eternal glory to his courage! Mind you, he crashed to death several years later during a routine training flight. Some say he was drunk. I don't buy that! Though ... do our folks not drink? Of course they do! And how not to? You said, one should squeeze out of oneself the slave mentality drop by drop. Binge drinking is just the first step to that noble goal. I must say, vodka takes people's edges away, their harshness. That's when Russians show their true colours, and lots of superior qualities. Boundless hospitality for one. Take my wife, for example.

About once a month, she invites all our neighbours. At first, she and Lyuba stop by every house and knock on every door. For instance, they'd ask Zina Makhina, "Will you bring salted mushrooms?" And she'd answer, "Sure thing! Chanterelles, milky caps, honey fungus? I've got all kinds!" Then they go to Tanya Shverko, the wife of Peter the Glassblower: "Tanya, could you bring sauerkraut with cowberries?" "Of course!" "And you, Vera, will you manage a meat jelly?" "Yep!" This way, they agree on a dish at every house. As for Lyalya herself, she's great at pirozhki and dumplings. She'd make hundreds of them with the neighbours and put them out in the cold, on the windowsill. There'd be homemade cherry vodka too, and honey moonshine, everything local, nothing from the store. To be honest, I'd rather have some sausage and cheese, but where would I get such delicacies? That's a paradox for you: the shops are empty, but our table is groaning under the weight of the food.

And the neighbours don't just get together to eat and get drunk! No, they follow ancient customs. They dress for the feast. Women put handkerchiefs on their shoulders, red roses on a black background, mostly. They have also sewn and embroidered white shirts for us men. And when we finally sit down to the table, all dressed up like that, the toasts are raised: to the homeland, to world peace, to the freedom of fiery Angola, Mozambique, Ethiopia, Ivory Coast, and Nicaragua; against Israeli Zionists threatening the Communist Party of Greenland; against American nuclear ambitions in New Guinea and so on. Then, we start eating. Not until we sate ourselves to the gills would women begin their songs. Rather sad, most of them, about the harsh female fate, the broken hearts, the separations and departures.

After another drink or two, the women usually get tearful, and then somebody says, "Well, enough with the melancholy! Fleas and lice love a sad face! Come on, where's our accordionist?"

So Fedor, one of the neighbours, takes the accordion, and then the men start dancing. My younger brother, Nikolai, tap dances like anything. He visits us sometimes here, from Moscow. And our dear little Lyuba—well, she's just best of all! When she's in a roundelay, slowly turning in a circle. The beauty of it!

When guests leave, my wife snuggles up against me, my exhausted warrior woman. She's the one doing all the work, organizing everybody, you know. So I embrace my sleepy Lyalya, but there's still my brother Nikolai's bed to be made: he usually doesn't go back to Moscow same day. My wife always liked Nikolai; they joke around. She goes, "Next time, warn me in advance if you're bringing your wife or your mistress. I can't tell them apart, what with both being called Masha and looking like twins!"

But some time ago, a terrible thing happened. Nikolai was supposed to come from Moscow; it was getting dark, and still he wasn't there. We were getting worried, and right we were.

Finally, in the night, they arrive. My brother, whiter than a wall, won't say a word. So we ask his illegal Masha (his legal Masha being at home this time): "What happened?" And she says, "Nikolai ran someone over." "Is he dead?" She nods, silently. "An old man, drunk, really smashed, walking right into us. Nikolai didn't see him at full speed, in the dark." And my brother, he's still sitting there as if he himself was dead. So I tell my Lyalya, "You see the way Nikolai is? You have to run to the police and draw up a statement." I mean, who else but her?

Off she is to the police, then to the coroner. With a bribe, as usual: "Take care of this, please!" And he says, "You don't need to worry; the old man was very drunk indeed, and your relative is not to blame." But he takes the money anyway. By the time she's home, Nikolai and Masha have already left for Moscow. Did not say as much as goodbye. Lyalya couldn't sleep from that day. Could get no rest. Finally, in secret from me, she decided to meet the family of the victim. He had a son and a daughter, middle aged, both of them; the old drunk had been over seventy.

She told them that, though it wasn't my brother's fault, she still wanted to help the family. Here, she said, is some money, for the funeral, or whatever.

But this didn't turn out well at all. The son and daughter were offended. They could manage a funeral well enough without her, they said. "And don't you try to shut us up with a bribe; we will sue our father's murderer anyway!" Though this money wasn't meant as a bribe at all. The law is on my brother's side, we don't owe these people anything—my wife simply wanted to help them from the kindness of her soul. She has a soft heart, you know. She only seems harsh. A put on.

So by and by, they began to threaten her. They said Nikolai wouldn't get off scot-free, that if the court wouldn't do them justice, they'd avenge their father themselves, an eye for an eye, a tooth for a tooth. In short, this thing is not good. And my brother hasn't been coming to see us since. As if he had disappeared from the face of the Earth. I do not want to overload you, dear Anton Pavlovich, with all these mishaps that you may find totally useless for your writing.

But in case you decide to use any part of this sad story, please know that my brother is not to blame. The drunkard himself walked under his car's wheels.

Sincerely yours,

Timofey Doroshenko

Chapter 38: Fourth Letter to Chekhov

Dear Anton Pavlovich!

Sorry, I got carried away in my last letter—back to the history Crystal Goose now. All archival documents suggest that the real history of the town doesn't begin with the wild Honkanookies. It begins with the merchant Chmokov, who lived under Catherine the Great and founded the Goose glass manufactures. Among the documents I found, the most precious is his diary. What a flamboyant character he turned out to be! To wit: the son of a serf who bought his freedom and then got rich selling wood, Chmokov had inherited his father's business abilities but also "his mother's tender heart," as he puts it. He goes on to say, "Despite my respectable age, I fall in love as easily as a seventeen-year-old boy" (Provincial Archive Fund № 208).

The merchant dreams of entering the boudoir of the Empress herself—a daring desire, but not particularly original, judging by the number of young men who succeeded in fulfilling it. Chmokov, though, dreams of Catherine the Great not for the sake of a career or an aristocratic title. He writes that he had "fallen victim to the arrow of the prankster Amor" (Chmokov's Diary, p. 27).

But what were his chances of competing with Orlov or Potemkin? Zero! The enterprising merchant decides to impress the Empress with his literary genius instead. For a long while, Chmokov had been pouring his passion into heartfelt sonnets. But how could his poetry reach the royal eyes of his beloved?

The merchant contrives to make such a gift to the Empress as to outshine all other gifts in her collection, and smuggle a few lines of poetry into it. As it happens, at the same time he has to travel to Europe for business—to Venice, to be precise. There, Chmokov trades in oak and larch, used by the Venetians to fix the rotten piles "on which this mirage city was erected, and whose destruction would send it right to the bottom of the sea, much like Atlantis," he writes in his diary. Having made a good deal, he visits the Palazzo Ducale. The Hall of Jewelry takes his breath away. In a vitrine, on black velvet, he sees four goblets made of ruby-coloured crystal with gilded facets.

Catching the light with their mysterious depths, the goblets shimmer and sparkle in crimson and gold. "There it is, the miracle," mutters Chmokov, and his knees become weak. "I came here to sell some logs, I thought, but my true destiny was to behold eternal beauty, to find a gift worthy of my beloved."

"Cos'è quello? What is this?" Chmokov asks the treasurer in broken Italian.

"This is a gift from Pope Paul the Third to Silvia Ruffini," the Italian answered, smiling mysteriously but clearly proud of the Pope. "Four sons did she give him, and four times did he thank her with a precious goblet."

Chmokov's heart gave a jolt when he imagined his royal beloved bringing this precious glass to her lips, sipping some champagne—and then noticing the dedication engraved on the golden stem of the glass in an elegant curly script:

"A Pledge of Love and Bliss of Passion,
This Goblet Is a Poet's Due.
Oh Drink from It and Give the Nation
A Child That Looks Like Me and You!"

Blood rushed to the merchant's giddy head. Wasn't that too bold? But then again, nothing ventured, nothing gained.

The next day, feverish with dreaming, Chmokov adjusted his wig, fluffed up his jabot and demanded an audience with the treasurer. Usually good at bargaining, he was stunned that the stubborn old man plainly refused to sell the goblets.

Returning to his quarters in the evening, the irate Chmokov broke his favourite walking stick over the head of his serf and only then read a letter that his valet submitted to him on a silver tray. His beloved daughter Anastasia, a playful girl with a great singing voice, was getting married. Accepting a suitor without first asking her father's permission? He had to return to Russia right away! But how could he flee the battlefield! No, let them wait—he has to win the fight!

In the morning, wearing a new camisole with gold plumes, he tried his luck again at the Palazzo. To no avail! The treasurer remained deaf to all his propositions. Neither golden ducats nor the promise to send him fifty pretty and pliable Russian serf girls could convince the old man to part with the treasures entrusted to him.

With a bitter heart, the merchant left sublime Serenissima and returned to gloomy Russia. The familiar cheerless autumn landscape weighed heavily on his soul. The plains, the swamps, and the gullies bred his melancholy. Then he saw a river glitter in the distance.

"What's that?" Chmokov inquired moodily.

"A river," the cabman answered. "'Gus' or 'Goose' in vernacular, they call it."

"'Goose'!? They call a river 'Goose'? Now that's Russia for you!"

The merchant sighed and ordered the cabman to stop. While the horses were drinking from the river, he lay down on a meadow to rest. And, perhaps because he could smell his native land all around, his moping turned into full-fledged Russian ennui. "How could I miss the wedding of my beloved daughter in pursuit of a phantom!" Chmokov complains in his diary. "What do I care about those cursed goblets!" He even had a little cry, that's how upset he was. But by and by, the tart aroma of the spruces and the sweet smell of the grasses calmed him down. The merchant did not notice how he fell asleep.

And in his dream, he saw a swan. The royal bird walked about him, spreading her wings. Chmokov looked closely and saw that it was not a swan after all but a goose. On her head, a crystal crown was glimmering, shimmering with many-coloured facets. With a hollow human voice, the goose spoke to him: "Is our motherland lacking in mastery? Why are you, nincompoop, chasing after the papal goblets? Leave the moping behind and get down to business!"

"What kind of business?" asked the merchant in his dream.

"The crystal business!" the goose allegedly answered. "Russian glassblowers shall make a goblet just as good as those you admired in a foreign land."

"Start a new business? Hmm … But who would take care of my sawmills and factories?"

The wondrous bird gave no reply, and the vision disappeared.

Chmokov woke up, embarrassed and confused. He went to the river to wash his face and drive away the feverish dreams. As he was scooping up a handful of water, something fell out of his pocket and into the river. He leaned down and managed to catch the glittering thing before it drowned—it was a little crystal crown. The merchant gave out a cry and examined the crown that fell off the goose's head. Shaken to the depth of his soul by these mysterious events, the first thing the merchant did when he arrived home was order a public prayer to purify his soul. But the prayer service did not help: the goose order haunted his imagination, and he did not dare disobey her.

Chapter 39: The Goblet

Dear Anton Pavlovich!

I must inform you that, unfortunately, here Chmokov's diary abruptly comes to an end. Whether he was tired of writing or got busy establishing a crystal manufacturing in town, that I can't tell. However, I managed to piece together his story from different sources and especially the notes of his son-in-law, who unexpectedly turned out to be his right hand in his new enterprise.

A month or two after the mysterious encounter, Chmokov handed over his paper mills to his son and started building a glassblowing manufactory at the very place where the crowned goose had appeared to him. The location turned out suitable: the dense wood supplied fuel for the stoves; the river contained the white quartz sand needed to make glass.

Chmokov did not skimp on his money. He had solid houses built for his serfs, after the German fashion, and sent four men to study glassblowing in Venice and Bohemia.

And so it began. Coloured glass boxes with filigree ornaments, enamelled dishes, and intricate, gem-studded flower bouquets made from opal, milky white, and azure glass astonished the customers at Russian fairs. For his own amusement, Chmokov made funny mirrors. In a convex one, he saw himself as a short man with tiny arms; in a concave one, he seemed to be a giant. He even managed to create mirrors in which his whole figure disappeared while his room was clearly seen: the furniture, the oven with Danish tiles, and, on the wall, a portrait of Catherine the Great with a blue ribbon over her shoulder, a copy of the painting by Rokotov.

In less than a year, the glory of Chmokov's manufactory reached the capital. He was showered with orders for mirrors and carriage glass from the Moscow nobility. The royal courts of Europe, too, heard about him and were ready to pay handsomely for crystal chandeliers and vases with double-headed eagles. But so far the masters had no success with Chmokov's greatest dream, ruby-coloured crystal goblets. Still, the merchant did not give up. He himself made sketches of goblets and spent whole days in the workshops, watching gold being poured into the glass mass and crystal being cut with a diamond. And finally, it happened! Shortly before Easter 1792, Master Shustrov presented the merchant with a goblet that was a precise copy of the papal one.

That day, Chmokov did not go home to sleep. The ruby miracle was like a living being to him. In semi-darkness, by candlelight, Chmokov watched the mysterious shimmer of purple rays, drove his moistened finger over the thin rim, extracting gentle moaning from the glass. The sound was so sweet that he began crying—crying as hard as he had only done the day his wife died, just before Christmas. Then he wrapped his goblet in a rag and carried it home.

Meanwhile, a rumour spread that Catherine herself intended to see the famous manufactory. For this purpose, she would stop in Goose on the way from St. Petersburg to Moscow. Chmokov rubbed his hands. Finally, the capricious Dame Fortune was giving him a chance.

While considering how precisely to present the Empress with the goblet, he developed yet another fantasy. A goblet was not enough for Catherine. No, he would create the eighth World Wonder in Goose for her royal delight!

Day and night, the serf masters worked erecting a marvellous crystal palace. Crystal dishes on crystal tables were glittering in all the colours of the rainbow, porcelain maidens in gilded and enamelled dresses were gently touching crystal harp strings. In the alcove, by a crystal cradle, a nurse in a Russian folk dress was giving a crystal baby her crystal breast. In the evening, when the sun left the sky in its fiery chariot, candles lit up, and the fingers of a porcelain maestro touched the keys of a harpsichord made from ruby crystal, wondrous sounds enveloped the palace. In the night, the glassblowers covered the palace with a dome woven from star-studded brocade.

All kinds of rumours surround our Goose. They say that no less than Pushkin visited the town and saw the remains of the unprecedented palace. They even say that the crystal cradle he noticed inside the crystal palace gave the great poet an idea of the fairy tale about a beautiful princess sleeping in a crystal coffin. Why should the great Russian genius visit Goose in the first place? Oh, dear Anton Pavlovich! You can't imagine what kind of gossip and tall tales made their way to respectable archives! For example, the archives recorded evidence of some policeman who personally saw Pushkin grabbing a goose in the street, plucking a feather from it and going on to write Eugene Onegin with it. But I have digressed.

What about Chmokov, you may ask?

The news that the Empress herself intended to examine the famous glass manufactory had the deepest effect on the merchant. The night before her arrival, he went to the crystal palace and walked around it, adjusting the starry brocade like a mother tucking in her sleeping babe. Then he laid out a camp bed by the palace and waited for the morning, never closing his eyes.

Oh, insidious fate! Oh, royal will, more changeable than weather! Instead of coming herself, the Empress sent to Goose the twenty-two-year-old Prince Zubov, her newest favourite, the newly baked owner of fifty thousand serfs and a co-ruler of the empire in all but name.

The numerous retinue of the prince included two trained monkeys in gilded uniforms, with little rapiers on their sides and aiguillettes over their shoulders. The fun-loving young prankster never parted with the monkeys, whom he had taught to steal wigs from noble heads and spit at the revealed baldness.

Now, imagine Zubov with his retinue, including the monkeys, approaching the crystal palace. He opened the doors, unleashing utter chaos! In the blink of an eye, the monkeys were breaking and destroying everything around them. Under the blows of their rapiers, clavichords were moaning and harps were crying. Precious vases were exploding into glass fireworks. Chandeliers were flying to the floor, showering beheaded porcelain maidens with splinters. By a miracle, the cradle was the only thing to survive. It continued to swing in the corner with a quiet moan.

That evening, Chmokov's body has finally given up. Chmokov has suffered a stroke. Did he immediately pass to his eternal rest, or did he suffer for years, trying to complain to the world with a disobedient tongue? No one can say. All we know is this: when Catherine the Great sent the first guild merchant Illarion Chmokov her gloves, a sign of special royal favour, along with the highest command to rename Goose into Crystal Goose, he couldn't respond to the royal mercy. His dead eyes were contemplating the better world, and his soul praising with the Almighty.

The question now is whether the famous glassware business stop its existence with the death of its founder. Luckily, Chmokov's descendants were an enterprising bunch, not prone to chasing phantoms. His great-grandson Gregory was especially crafty. He is said to have come up with the idea of Goose tourism, an idea far ahead of its time. From all over the world, gapers and gawkers came to admire the wonders of nature: a Chinese goose with a triple growth on its beak; a beautiful Toulouse bird with a goiter the size of a purse. The bloody fights of battle geese from Tula gathered such crowds that five inns, complete with stables, were built to accommodate them. A construction boom began in the city, and white-stone mansions with openwork masonry were growing like mushrooms. The famous artist Vasnetsov arrived from Moscow to paint three new churches. Was it perhaps then that a silver goose appeared on a dome to attract tourists?

Crystal palaces and ruby goblets, sweet dreams and the glorious past … Oh, dear Anton Pavlovich! I should not be telling you what happened to the town later! Your premature death has spared you the burning shame for your homeland. And who is to blame? The people. No beast is as cruel as the human being. Gosh, I think I've missed my station! Off, I have to be off! Let us say goodbye, then. Let us turn off the lights and lower the curtain.

Chapter 40: Commander-in-Chief Takes Charge of Production

LUCKILY, CHMOKOV'S DESCENDANTS didn't live to see year 1917. The year of revolution. They never saw the leather-jacketed commissars storming the glass manufactory just like Zubov's monkeys had stormed the Crystal Palace. Nor did they see the commissars hanging three glass blowers to bring home a message to the rest: rather than indulging in useless luxury, the new *Homo sovieticus* was supposed to tilt Mother Earth and forge steel for the glory of the state.

But those who came after the commissars soon realized that building the first dictatorship of the proletariat was a costly affair. The much-needed foreign currency didn't grow on Russian birches. Nor could executions generate dough. But what Russia still had were the precious art collections in its museums, its silver-cased icons, the golden goblets shimmering in the semi-darkness of the few churches that had miraculously survived. Needless to say, the glassware from Crystal Goose couldn't compete with Scythian gold from the Hermitage in terms of sales to the West, but it was worth peddling to the rapacious capitalists anyway.

And so it came to be that the new Soviet power ordered the glass production in Goose to be revived, and the machinery to be restored.

The order of the Party is not to be trifled with! Soon enough, crystal ashtrays with Russian fairy-tale motifs and porcelain dishes with hammer and sickle started flowing westward, and foreign currency began travelling in the other direction—into the pockets of Party bosses. But why did the production of crystalware stumble again in the seventies? The first five-year plan was fulfilled in seven years, the next one in ten ...

The party bosses blamed three things for their lack of profit: the outdated machinery, the constant drunkenness of the glassblowers, and the intrigues of foreign spies. While the KGB set about to fight the third problem, Lyalya was sent to Crystal Goose to deal with the first two.

There, I thought, what a mighty life force, what a grip, what abilities this woman has! Ready to do anything, never one for giving up. If she'd only been born in another country, under different circumstances, what success she'd have achieved, how much money she'd have made! Instead, she ended up in need and in Siberia.

"But tell me, how did you manage things in Goose?" I asked after our third day in Kotor. "Did you get used to it?"

"Well, you get used to anything. And you can find good people anywhere. One thing bothered me though: the boozing in Goose was rather too much, not only among the men but even among women. And children, too."

"It's amazing the KGB left you alone."

Lyalya was silent for a minute. "I'm immensely grateful to Patermufti, really. He saved Tim's life, nothing less."

"Yes, but how you were supposed to increase production in that Booze Goose town all on your own!"

Aunt shook her head. "When we arrived, there was not a soul on the streets, half of the houses were nailed shut. In one window—it was Lyuba who noticed it—instead of glass, there was an udder!"

"What do you mean, an udder?"

"I mean precisely that, a cow's udder! I guess it was meant to keep the cold out in winter. The whole town had only two shops, both empty as the desert. I went to inspect the factory: total desolation. All equipment broken. Darkness. One man was sitting by a dilapidated melting furnace, drinking from a bottle, all swollen with booze. Still, he wasn't quite beyond talking.

"'Where are the workers?' I asked. 'Where are the famous master glass blowers?'

"'Off to the woods.'

"'What?'

"'Don't what me! Off, like I say. They live in the woods, that's that, hand to mouth. I guess the wood spirits feed them.'

"'The wood spirits?'

"'Yep! That's our tradition, see. If things get nasty, we're off to the woods.'

"'And the city authorities, the police, what are they doing about it?'

"'City authorities, my ass!

"'So why are *you* still here?'

"'Me, I'm guarding the furnace.'

"'What for? It's broken, isn't?'

"'It's good enough for Vargun to use.'

"'Who?'

"'Vargun. A devil, kinda. Every night, he tries to start a fire in the furnace, to burn down the whole town. It's a punishment for our sins. And I'm not letting him. I say, if we people have sinned, it's not our fault. It's our damned bosses.'

"Was he only drunk, or mad for real, this man? Hard to tell. His jacket was full of holes, as was his boot—he was wearing only one, must have lost the other one somewhere. His shaggy beard was reaching almost to his waist.

"'Well,' I say, 'that's a fine kettle of fish you have here! Look, old man, I came here to increase production. I need all the working hands I can get. Can you convince the people to come back? They'll get a good buck too!'

"At this, he laughed so hard that the bottle fell out of his hands. It rolled toward me. I got it and gave it to him.

"'See,' says I, 'your Vargun seems to like you: the vodka's still inside.'

"'Sure he likes me! Sometimes we have a little drink together, you know.' The man winked at me and continued. 'You're a pretty wench. Pity something's wrong with your head. Convince the people to come back! Are we really supposed to believe you'll reopen the factory? It has been shut for five years!'

"'And now it will open again. I'm not one to break my word.'

"'Look here. If you have that kind of power, you're a boss. And we don't trust bosses! They keep screwing us. It's all pie in the sky, their promises. You know what the commissars did to us? They hung us from lanterns! They said, our work was all crystal bling-bling for the rich. The motherland needs steel, they said, not your bourgeois shit.'

"'That was a long time ago.'

"'Yeah, well. The people have memory.'

"'After the war, the factory was restored, right?'

"'Sure it was, cause they needed foreign money, the bosses. Everything went to the West, and the workers got a big fat nothing! Arise ye workers from your slumbers, sure … Do you know who you're talking to? Stepan Butuzkin, that's who! Stepan Butuzkin, he's nobody's fool. Stepan Butuzkin is a master glassblower, that's right. Made a human-sized firebird once! After his own sketches. And what did he get for his trouble from the Soviets? Another big fat nothing! A letter of commendation for his hard work! What good is a letter of commendation? They can wipe their asses with it!'

"'I will pay all workers honestly, Stepan. Let's restore production, let's fix life in this town. Come on, master glassblower, we'll drink to our meeting!'

"So there I am, coaxing him, and all the while thinking to myself, 'Why am I casting pearls before this half-mad drunk?' Then again, you have to start somewhere, grasp a string to unravel the whole. So by and by, I learned from Stepan what had happened in Goose."

Chapter 41: Glassblowers

LYALYA BROUGHT STEPAN a new pair of boots and a cotton-padded jacket, along with a heater, a spirit burner, some canned food, tea, and gherkins against hangover. And smokes, of course. Puffing on her cigarettes, Stepan told her the whole story.

About ten years before, party bosses from Moscow started coming to Goose for hunting. There was plenty of game in the dense woods back then: partridges, foxes, hares, deer, even wild boars. So the bosses came, demanded a feast, a well-heated sauna. Spent a week guzzling vodka and cognac. Once they sobered up, they'd always turn up at the factory and start looting, carrying off the best dinner services to their women back in Moscow. Then it got even worse. Celebrating weddings in Goose became a thing. Marrying off their sons, daughters, friends. And, according to good Russian custom, throwing goblets on the floor after every drink. Quite a few times, they dragged the whole tablecloth from the set table just for fun. Coloured glass, crystal—bang! bang!—all in pieces! Meanwhile, the factory has to report to the state, to fulfill the five-year plan or say goodbye to the wages. But what could they say? These were party bosses from Moscow, top brass! So people were paying for the losses out of their own pockets.

Once, during a wedding—it was autumn, it got darker early—the groom's drunken friends ran out into the street like a pack of hounds and started shooting at lanterns. Once all the lanterns were in pieces, more fun was needed. A live shooting gallery, that was their plan: they grabbed a passerby, tied him to a pole, put a brick on top of his head—and took aim! This time they missed and ran on, firing at the windows from about three metres, and all the while, there were people inside. In one house, a woman with two small children was killed. Now that was enough. The people rose up against the bandits, caught them and tied up. Two were strangled to death, and the bodies thrown into the river, hidden under the ice. The frosts were fierce that year, the river was frozen in late October.

The next day, a commission from Moscow came to look for the guilty parties. But the Goose people kept mum. And maybe the whole thing would've been hushed up, but one of the dead had a distant relative who was a really big cheese. So the bosses began trumping up a case, and then the whole town of Goose just off and fled into the woods. Like they did in the past, centuries ago.

When Lyalya told me this story, while I was lying on a sofa, and she was fussing in the kitchen over 'nectar', that is our dinner, I could only shake my head: "So it was hopeless, wasn't it?"

"Not quite. Maybe that Vargun devil helped me!" Aunt laughed. "To begin with, I persuaded Stepan to come with me to the woods, to show me the fugitives' camp."

"They could've murdered you."

"Oh no! I have my technique. You have to look them straight in the eye, never avert your gaze first. Besides, I was bringing them a nice present: five crates of vodka on a sleigh. Promised that everyone would get a quarter litre after work if they restarted production. They told me, 'We're not leaving the woods.' 'Fine,' I say. 'Stay here. I myself will come here every day, take you to work, and bring you back to your camp in the evening. I don't even want to know what kind of thing you have going on with Moscow, that's not my business.'

"They frown at me, fidgeting. There's no trust in their eyes. What if it's a trap? So I try to calm them down. 'If they start digging, I'll close your case,' I say. 'The prosecutor is my chum.' A fib, of course! But I had to persuade them somehow! Still they had doubts. 'No real glassblowers among us anymore, all dead,' they go. But here, Stepan interrupted them: 'Come on, guys, that's not true, is it? There's Yakov, and here's Petr—did you think I wouldn't recognize you? Come on, maybe we'll have luck this time! Look what a fine wench they sent us!'

"So he convinced these two to come back to the factory.

"And so we started—Stepan, Yakov, and Petr, my first team. Gradually, others joined them. A month later, I had fifteen people working for me. The only trouble was that many were heavy drinkers. You know what a really bad hangover is like? The headache, the nausea. How can you work at the furnace like that? We'd have accidents all over the place. So I thought, 'Okay, let's go for the lesser evil.' Right in the morning, before work, I loaned the guys a ruble each from my own pocket for a quick drink. Go get some vodka from Zina at the shop, and then back to the factory, that was my rule. I had an agreement with Zina that she'd sell half-litre bottles to my workers an hour before the shop opened, at 8 a.m. And I must say, my men never cheated me. As soon as they got their salary, they always returned my rubles."

"And that Zina, she came to work an hour earlier every day especially for you?"

"Sure she did. We were friends, after all! I was helping her as much as I could too. When her house collapsed, I sent some workers her way for free repairs. She was a single mother; her husband had left her. The middle son was on his way to becoming a criminal, and I straightened him out, made him an apprentice with the glassblower masters. My Lyuba helped, too. When Zina was at work, she babysat the youngest child, gave him lunch, helped him do his homework."

"And Timofey, did he find a job too?"

"At first, I didn't even let him try. The KGB was after him, remember? Stay at home, I said, and be as quiet as a mouse. So he was our housekeeper for a while. He spent a lot of time with Lyuba too. Back in Zaporizhzhia, Lyuba used to save money and skip school lunches so that she could give her stepfather another goldfish for his birthday. All these fish survived and moved to Goose with us. They were named after small rivers: there was a Zusha, a Zizdra, a Tsna. Timofey would teach Lyuba: 'See, Tsna is swimming close to the surface, gulping air. Means she isn't getting enough oxygen. Let's check the temperature. If the water is too warm, it has less oxygen.' They were just one heart and one soul, the two."

"But wait, if you were the only one working, where did you get the money to live, and to buy whole crates of vodka besides?"

"If you can't ride two horses at once, you shouldn't be in the circus! I didn't need much for myself, Lyuba and Tim, anyway. The real issue was where to get funds for the workers. I went to Vladimir, to Moscow, never let the ministries alone. 'Do you want the glassblowers to work again, so that we can show the bloody capitalists what we're made of? Well then!' I had the school refurbished, a new hospital built, even a concert hall opened. Goose became quite a fancy town, let me tell you!"

Chapter 42: Lyuba

I HARDLY KNEW MY cousin Lyuba; we had always lived far apart. What kind of person was she?

"Until she turned about fifteen," Aunt told me as we were watching the sunset from the balcony, "my daughter was my best friend and helper. All those twists and turns started later. She had never been at a loss for words, but in her late teens, she grew a tongue sharp enough to cut a piece of wood. Oh well, time flies like an arrow, fruit flies like a banana! Before I could blink an eye, Lyuba was finishing school and considering higher education. Stubborn as anything, she was. She'd go to medical school, and that's that! But first, there was no medical institute anywhere near Goose, and second, everyone knows that you don't get to study medicine without the right connections. So I tell her, 'Nothing going, sorry. Let's set the bar lower. I'll get a place for you at the Goose construction college, easy!'

"'Didn't you hear?' that daughter of mine says. 'I want to go to medical school, not a construction college!'

"'If wishes were horses!' I answer. 'I wanted to design beautiful buildings and not to stand around in dirt among drunk workers on construction sites. I'm an architect, and I work as a foreman.'

"'So what?' she goes. 'If your life has been ruined, let's go ruin mine? Besides, my passport doesn't call me Jewish, so I'll have an easier time than you!'

"The way she talked to her mother! Reproaching me with my profession! I won't be ashamed to die, I told her, I'll be leaving a few things behind when I go: houses, schools, hospitals. Besides, this work of mine had been feeding Lyuba her whole life! Yeah, so I was rather angry at this kitten showing her mother the claws! But I also thought to myself that I couldn't really argue with her. If a crackpot idea hit her head, that was that. So, for tactical reasons, I took a step back.

"'Okay,' says I, 'if you want to go and study in Zaporizhzhia, why not? Your grandmother is alone there. You can help her.'

"By the way, when I explained to my mother why we were leaving

Zaporizhzhia, or rather, why we were fleeing, she didn't say a word against it. 'Do as you please, don't worry about me. If they knock on the door, I'll pretend I don't understand.' But of course, I was worried to leave her alone. Nikita was away, and they could easily take Timmy's apartment. So if Lyuba wanted to return to Zaporizhzhia to study, maybe it wasn't such a bad idea. But there, I had quite a rude awakening coming. She wasn't going to Zaporizhzhia, she said, but to Kiev.

"Kiev of all places! Why? To get as far away from me as possible? I ask her, and there, the shit hits the fan. All her old grudges come out. It turns out that she always hated Goose: no movies, no discos, no friends, all the people she liked left back in Zaporizhzhia. Well, what should I have said? That Goose had probably saved her beloved stepfather from prison or worse?"

And then, without a break, Aunt proceeded. "Tell me, how many languages does an elephant speak?"

"W … what? What elephant?"

"Any elephant. African, Asian, take your pick! Well, I'll tell you. A trained elephant understands commands in four languages. And my daughter, she couldn't find a single shared language with her mother! The kind of grudges she had, I couldn't believe my ears! I'd been treating her like Cinderella, she says. Me! She had only one pair of tights, she says, mended all over! What do tights have to do with anything? Sure, we weren't exactly rich in Goose, especially at first: I was the only breadwinner, and I had to spend quite a chunk of the money on vodka for the workers. But gradually life got better, right? Then that darling daughter of mine says, 'You've been sending me, a thirteen-year-old girl, to bring money to your drunkards at the factory before dawn, in the blizzard and the cold!' That I'd deprive the child of sleep before school? Never! Well, maybe a couple of times. Was it such a tragedy to help her mother a bit? Long story short, off she went to Kiev. And then you know what happened? Remember when you came to see us? To say goodbye?"

Chapter 43: Farewell

In the last summer before leaving Russia for good, I went to Ukraine to say goodbye to my family. Back then, going to the West was tantamount to leaving for the other world. There was no hope of ever seeing my relatives and friends again. I was especially eager to say goodbye to Grandma Adelle, of all relatives my favourite.

The summer in Zaporizhzhia was as hot as usual. I remember my grandmother rushing to make me some quince jam (to provide a jar—at least one—for my trip "to the other world"). Just as back in my childhood, she was wiping off large drops of sweat from her forehead with a corner of her apron. Bees were flying in through the open balcony door, attracted by the tart smell of quince, and grandmother was spooning their curly bodies from the bubbling surface of the golden brew.

Lyalya, too, was there. I remember how she weighed sugar for jam on what she called her "duck scales." She filled sugar into a pillowcase, put it on the one aluminum plate, and assembled a whole family of weights on the other, one by one, from small to large, adding one, removing another, until opposing flat duck bills finally stood level.

As usual, Aunt was complaining about her husband, and grandma was sighing quietly, stirring the jam in a large aluminum pot. She laid the straining spoon onto a saucer, by then covered in scarlet sugary patterns, and moved away from the stove.

"How many times did I tell him, 'If you can't finish a job, don't start!" Lyalya grumbled. "He keeps trying all kinds of things and then stopping halfway through."

As always when Grandma Adelle faced what she saw as unfairness, she bit her lips, and her cheeks reddened: "Lyalya dear, don't forget he raised your children! Look how he cares about Lyuba! Who's without flaws? Have patience."

"Mom, you've told me this a few times too many. The children have grown up, and now all that remains is him and me—and utter boredom!"

At this moment, her husband entered the room.

Timofey and I hadn't seen each other for many years. He smiled awkwardly at me, lifting his eyes and immediately lowering them, as if sensing he'd just been the subject of gossip.

Lyuba followed him in. I was amazed at her pallor, her exhausted face, and an expression of indifference so strange in such a young girl. She had blue shadows under her eyes, and her hair, which I remembered wavy and golden, was hanging down her sunken cheeks in dirty wisps.

I knew that Lyuba had tried to enrol at the medical school in Kiev twice, both times unsuccessfully. Then she returned to her grandmother in Zaporizhzhia, and, as far as I could puzzle together, made her money with some medical massages …

And then "things went sour."

The rumour whirled through every town and city where her numerous relatives lived: Lyuba was pregnant, and nobody knew by whom. That is, Lyuba probably did, but she flatly refused to reveal it to her family.

She had been avoiding a confrontation with her mother for a long time, and it so happened that the talk finally took place during my farewell visit.

Timmy was sent to the grocer, and Lyuba wanted to join him, but Lyalya blocked her way.

"Sit down. We need to talk." She looked at her daughter brusquely and lit a cigarette.

I remember grandmother asked her to go out on the balcony: smoke was bad for Lyuba, after all.

Lyalya quickly put out her cigarette.

"Well, tell me about your plans for the future," she said to her daughter. "We're all here to listen. Even your cousin, see, came all the way from Moscow."

"Bullshit! She came to say goodbye to grandma," Lyuba said.

"How far along is it? Two months?" Lyalya said in an indifferent voice.

"Ten weeks."

Lyalya drummed the table.

"Not much time left, but it's still doable. You won't feel any pain, I promise. The head of the department is a friend of mine, she'll arrange anaesthesia. I'll call her right away."

"Thanks, but no thanks. I'll deal with it myself."

"What do you mean, you'll deal with it? In what sense?" Lyalya said very quietly and squinted at her daughter.

"In the literal sense."

Grandma and me were the only ones preventing a caravan loaded with rocks from falling into the abyss. One careless word—and it would all be over.

Grandma hastened to intervene. "Lyalya, calm down! Maybe Lyuba is right. Somehow things will work out. We'll help. Have some peaches, here!" And she reached for the cupboard.

"Work out? So tell me, how does she"—Lyalya was now speaking about her daughter as if she weren't there—"how does she picture the future? Who's she counting on? Timofey and me? That we'd raise her child?"

"The hell I need you!" Lyuba said with a snort. "I'll bring up my child myself! Stop fucking with me, will you?"

Lyuba took a peach, plunged her teeth into the juicy pulp, and methodically finished off the fruit. After sucking the last bits of pulp from the stone, she threw it, aiming at the garbage can, but missing. Grandma bent down to pick it up.

"The cheek she has!" Lyalya was shouting now. "Mom, leave it alone. Let her pick up that damned stone! Every beast is clever enough to give birth, as Chatsky said. Sure, why work or study if you can have a child at eighteen?"

"Nineteen. And stop with your stupid quotes already!"

"You're a bit young to be teaching me!"

"Lyalya, calm down!" Adelle stepped in for her granddaughter. "Don't you know how eager Lyuba is too study and work? She just had no luck. It isn't easy to get into medical school; they take one out of thirty there."

"Didn't I warn her? But why would she listen to her mother! So they failed you at the exam, and now you have to get pregnant by hell knows who?"

It was at this point that the caravan rattled into the abyss.

Pushing away an empty plate, Lyuba screamed, "And you ... Did you have to get pregnant by hell knows who?"

"What?"

"Don't what me! Did you have to get pregnant by that alcoholic Samsonov?"

"He's your father!"

"Well thank you very much indeed! Should I be grateful for his holy sperm or what?"

Grandmother covered her face with her hands, but in a moment she caught herself, got out three glasses, and started pouring us strawberry drinks, urging Lyalya and Lyuba to stop: "Such talk. Look, it's not some kind of a disaster, not a war! I still have strength. I'll help! We'll bring up the child together somehow."

"Sorry that I'm leaving," I said, "or I'd help too."

"You'd what?" Lyuba said, laughing in my face. "I didn't hear you!"

"Don't listen to her," Lyalya said and reached for her drink. "She's just a brat!" She took a sip. "You want to ruin your youth? Go ahead! It's your life, after all."

But it wasn't like Lyuba to leave the last word to her mother. "You pharisees! Who helped you get into architecture? If it wasn't for my grandfather, a war veteran, the hell they'd let you study! But for your daughter, you wouldn't bend a finger. You knew they wouldn't take me at the medical school if I don't know anybody there—and all of a sudden you're all honesty and principles!"

"Oh, the jam's burning!" grandmother exclaimed and hurried to the stove.

Lyalya took a wooden spoon from her hands. "Where's the second pot?"

She deftly poured the bubbling sticky golden mass into another pot, and Grandma Adelle kept reproaching herself for almost spoiling the jam, for causing the trouble.

Chapter 44: Grandma Adelle

I've met my lucky share of kind, generous, and sympathetic people, but never anyone who could compare with Adelle, Larissa's mother and my grandma, in selflessness and tireless sacrifice.

The lives of the saints have long ceased to be popular reading matter, and their strange world (in which few of us believe) has nothing to do with our concerns today. But if I were asked what kind of people the saints were, I'd say they must have been like Adelle. This quiet, small, seemingly unremarkable woman, who'd worked as a draughtswoman in a factory all her life, was neither particularly educated nor a brilliant conversationalist. She loved to read but rarely allowed herself the luxury, considering housework and helping her loved ones her primary duties.

Was she intelligent in a conventional sense? I couldn't tell. What she certainly had was wisdom and encompassing tolerance for the follies of us, her human fellows. I never heard her criticize anybody, though deep in her heart, she understood things without words and could tell a fool, a braggart, a cad, with half a glance. I think she pitied people and forgave their follies. Loved, pitied, and forgave. The energy of her love was so powerful that, in her presence, everyone, including me, couldn't but believe themselves truly special. Back then, I thought I was her favourite grandchild; now I believe that Adelle was giving her generous warmth and abiding love to everyone she encountered in life.

We lived in different cities, then in different countries. My grandmother's letters flew to me over all borders and continents with their questions about my health and well-being, with wishes of everlasting joy and happiness. She died at ninety-eight, in her sleep, as the righteous should die. The last letter—written by someone with a clear mind, every comma in place—was sent off a week before she died.

Now, Aunt was all that remained from my past life. For some reason, it was hard to start talking to her about Adelle, much as I wanted to. Once again, she and I were descending the hill following the strawberry trace to Kotor, along the beach. At the entrance to the city, two chestnut trees, which I hadn't noticed before, had finally lit their bloomy candles in honour of spring.

"Imagine," I said, embarrassed to look at Lyalya. "I'm still missing grandma."

She slowed down, and I saw her face twitch. "Mom's gone. Just gone! It's been a long while, but I can't get used to it. I had her headstone improved lately, the inscription refreshed, and there I was, sitting on the grave and bawling. I mean, what a life she had! Three revolutions, civil war, dispossession, terror, then war again. She had been wounded, did you know? Her parents, sisters, uncles were executed. Shot dead in the pit. Constant hunger, never enough to eat, not during the wars, nor after. And not a word of complaint. Spartan endurance."

"Yes, she was extraordinary in every sense. I'm trying to grasp her essence, to put it into words and can't. Can you?"

"What for? I simply loved her."

"I don't know … but somehow I feel that if we remembered her every detail, her movements, her words, we'd preserve her somehow … for eternity, or something. Nonsense, of course."

Lyalya looked at me with bewilderment: "Are you suggesting that you believe in some sort of afterlife?"

"I don't know, really. I wonder, did grandma believe?"

"She never talked about it. But she always fasted on Judgment Day, remembering her murdered parents. Never told us to fast though. And if she ever prayed, she prayed quietly."

"Didn't you have a feeling that she was praying for the absolution of her sins? I mean, she'd been dropping bombs on Germany, probably killing people."

"What are you saying! War is war. We weren't the first to attack! Anyway, Mom didn't talk about her feelings. She was secretive this way. How she burned in the plane, how she survived the wound—not a peep. I know all this only from my father. And if somebody asked, she'd only smile and spread her arms, like nothing special, things happen."

"Wait, and what about you? When she was flying that plane, you were a little girl, weren't you?"

"My grandma took us in. I was three, my sister twelve. Mom didn't have to go to the front, since her children were young, and father was against it too, but she insisted. She knew she'd be useful. She'd been in an aviation club—they were a big thing in the twenties—so she knew how to fly, and how to parachute."

"You know, what's most astonishing in the hindsight is that I never heard her say a bad word about anybody. For her, everyone was good. She felt compassion for everyone."

"Good, I don't know. Mother could take a measure of a person pretty quick. It's just that she was even better at forgiving. She forgave our Ukrainian neighbours, who betrayed her parents to the Germans. She forgave Ruth too. More than that, all her life, she took care of Ruth and her daughter."

For a while, we walked on in silence, each with her own thoughts. Then Lyalya said, "No, your grandma wasn't some kind of angel. She was something else. Iron will. If she decided something, quietly, with herself, that's how it was going to be. Not always easy. Say, she'd make some borscht and wouldn't eat a single spoon herself so that the family got more. And try persuading her to have a morsel of some food she considered special—a piece of cheese, say! Half her life, she was forced to starve, and then she … it became a habit of sorts, as if she forgot how to eat. By the way, grandmother literally saved Lyuba in that story with Irakli. Without her, I don't know what would have happened."

Chapter 45: Lyuba's Baby

THE DAYS ARE LONG in May. The sun had sunk behind the mountains, but there was still light. It was as if someone had thrown a net with a thousand orange fish scales over the sky. It gradually dimmed, sliding sideways and throwing shivering pink highlights onto the water. In the air, there was that peace that precedes the twilight, as if the day, before vanishing forever, was hesitating to give way to the night. Unwilling to return to the Bogdanovich boarding house yet, I persuaded Lyalya to have dinner at a restaurant.

The waiter laid out the menu before us. Lyalya, as usual, did not look at it, and while I was choosing for her and for myself, she hurried to splash out what, apparently, had been nagging at her heart.

"You think Lyuba believed me?" she asked.

"Believed you what?"

"That thing with the medical school."

"Oh, that … Shall we order some oysters?"

"It's up to you, my girl. I don't really care. By the way, I told her I didn't have any connection in medicine, no way to help her get a foot in. I only started building hospitals later. Actually, I'm not even sure I could've arranged the anaesthesia for her abortion. I told her I could, but that was just so she wouldn't worry. You remember what kind of anaesthesia we had back then? And who ever got one? Only the party bosses' wives."

"Yes, that always astonished me," I answered and went on to taste the wine. "The state had money for missiles, but not for anaesthesia for women."

"Oh, they would've found the money all right if they wanted to. No, it was punishing women for having sex!"

I had a sip of Etna Bianco. "A little tart, but I like it. Have a taste!"

"I actually prefer red."

"Why didn't you just say so? I can reorder. Though white goes better with oysters."

"Oysters? Don't they have any proper food?"

"You've never tried them? You can order whatever you want. Octopus salad, minestrone; a stew maybe? Anyway, I'm still curious about Lyuba. The father, I suppose, he never materialized and she had an abortion?"

Lyalya froze, glass of wine in her hand. "Don't you know? Lyuba gave birth to a boy, but he died."

It was the first time I heard this, and I was lost for words.

"How long did he live?" I finally asked.

"Five days."

"And what did he die of?"

"We'll never know. I've tried hard to get at the truth but didn't. He wasn't born prematurely, the weight was good, the skin looked healthy. You know they wouldn't leave the newborn with you back then, only bring it over for breastfeeding? Well, for three days, they did, and on the fourth day, they didn't. Too weak to suck at the breast, they said. On the fifth day, they said he was dead. How did he die? Why?! There was an infection in that clinic. There were several deaths, but the truth was concealed so as not to spoil the statistics. They wrote 'birth defect.' What kind of birth defect? You know, like during the siege of Leningrad, people starved to death by the thousands, but you couldn't write that on a death certificate. We can't have starvation when we're building communism, never mind the siege! Same here. An infection in a Soviet hospital? Never! Yesterday, a healthy baby, and today—here's the body to bury. Well, there I said no! Let my nineteen-year-old girl have a child's grave in her life? Nothing going! 'You killed the child, so you bury him!' I told them. Lyuba got mad at me about this at first, but then, many years later, she said, 'Mom, you were right back then. Who'd be taking care of the grave when I'm in Germany?'

"But she grieved for a long time about this baby. It was only when she had two daughters in Germany that it got better. And you know how strange life can be: the baby's death reconnected us. We became as close as we had been in her childhood. Lyuba even said she was sorry about our fights, said she knew I had wanted the best for her. And I said, 'Lyuba dear, water under the bridge.' Since then, she always asked me for advice. When she fell in love with her Irakli too. Mommy, what would you do in my place?'"

As we finished dinner, I felt that I hardly knew my cousin, and later, when we were returning along the dark embankment to Bogdanovich, I asked Lyalya what happened to Lyuba after the death of her baby.

"Well, Lyuba tried the medical school exams again and failed for the third time. Then, Perestroika started. For the first time, the borders opened, and people ran like rats from a sinking ship. Lyuba decided to leave too. She said, 'I want to be a doctor, and here, they won't let me.' You know, if she has an idea in her head, she'll hold on like a bulldog.

"I was in Crystal Goose with Timmy back then, and she was in Zaporizhzhia. She was supposed to be taking care of Grandma Adelle, who wasn't well, but after the baby's death Lyuba changed. Spent days and days shut in her room, lying on the couch, watching the ceiling."

"Somehow I can't imagine that. She's more like you, I thought."

"She'd never talked to us about the father of the child. There was some drama there, some betrayal, I'm sure. But she buried it deep inside her. Whole days, weeks, she was doing nothing. That death got her down something terrible. Besides, Lyuba always needed a clear plan in life, and there was none. I didn't know how things were back then, Mom didn't tell me. She didn't want me to worry. But I think that's when my daughter decided to leave the country."

I rushed to offer a positive explanation. "Maybe Lyuba was subconsciously saving her strength for emigration, preparing for a decisive leap?"

Lyalya paused. I could feel her perplexed look in the dark. A woman of action, she did not believe in underground rumbles, in deep hidden emotional work.

"If you have such grand plans, you shouldn't be lying around, you should be doing stuff! Learning the language at least. Am I right, or am I right?"

"I understand that kind of passivity," I said. "Have you never had a feeling, a sixth sense of the future, which you can't put in words? And look what Lyuba went on to achieve: quickly mastered the language abroad, got an education, became a doctor."

"And she didn't stop there, either," Lyalya said. "She continued studying. She decided to become a neurosurgeon, and she became one. Not to mention that she had children, raised two girls in Germany. Yes, my daughter is quite the iron lady. Nothing can drag her down. Well, except for the baby's death and the whole Irakli thing."

Chapter 46: Lyuba's Love

On our fifth day, as we often did in the evenings, we settled down on the balcony. A bird squawked in alarm and fell silent. In the darkness, I could only see the contours of Lyalya's face by the burning light of the cigarette moving from her lips to the ashtray and back. Neither of us felt like talking for a while, but Lyalya was the first to break the silence.

"To think of it," she said, "we're so similar, my daughter and I. Maybe that's why we fought so much. Like me, she had only one true love in her life, that Irakli. Before, I didn't think she was capable of love at all. Though her name means 'love,' I often thought she had an ice cube for a heart, like the Snow Queen. But with Irakli, Lyuba lost her mind."

"Irakli," I said. "I've heard the name from your sister. Was he from Ukraine?"

"No, he was from Moscow, but he sometimes came to Ukraine for work, and this is how they met. One day, they visited us in Goose. So handsome he was! The height, the build! Eyes like the king of Babylon! Curled eyelashes, raven-black hair, a waist like a girl's. He'd look dashing on horseback. Half-Ossetian, you could see that. And Lyuba—you remember your cousin—a miniature, blue-eyed blond. They looked good together in their difference. She adored him, hung on his every word. You wouldn't recognize her! I managed to get hold of some tangerines for their visit, and when they sat down to dinner, she peeled one and fed him, slice by slice, never taking one herself. And that's my daughter! Imagine!"

"He came to Ukraine for work, you said? Who was he?"

"A nuclear physicist."

"Oh yes, everyone fell in love with physicists in the sixties! But by the eighties, they fell out of fashion again, didn't they?"

"Well, not for Lyuba. She was in awe of Irakli. And he really was a gifted guy, that has to be said. A physicist, and a lyricist, as they used to say. He wrote poems, and he painted. In Moscow, he took her to avant-garde exhibitions in private apartments. They had the strangest things there, like black paint smeared on cardboard, a crushed tin hanging over it, and dried banana skins glued all around. The whole artwork was called Dying Civilization Swinging Over the Abyss. For Lyuba, all that was new. She had never met anyone like this before.

"So all that would've been just dandy, only her Irakli had two major flaws. One was irreparable, and the other—well, it depends. The irreparable flaw was that he was fourteen years older. As for 'it depends,' he was married. And if that wasn't enough, he'd decided to emigrate to America with his wife and daughter."

Chapter 47: Give Me Another Globe

AUNT GREW SILENT, tilted her head, and looked at me significantly, checking if I was aware of the traps insidious fate had set in the path of her daughter's life. I shook my head suggesting that yes, fate was insidious indeed.

"You tell me," she said "Who's setting people up with all this crap! I guess the devil is sitting cross-legged on a cloud, waving his foot and playing tricks on us. So well, Irakli had applied for a permit to emigrate a year before he met Lyuba. And you know, once you apply, you can't work, you become a pariah, basically, until you get your permit—which might be never. He left his institute so as not to taint his friends. Became a refusenik."

"A nuclear physicist, was he? At famous Kurchatov Institute? But what hope did he have they'd let him go abroad after working at such a place?"

"Precisely. Do you see what I'm getting at now?"

What Aunt was usually getting at was the same thing: money to survive. No, she wasn't greedy; on the contrary, she was ready to "give her last shirt away," as she said, but life had taught her to always be cautious. People who tried to leave the country under Soviet rule became outcasts, and in the long waiting period (for some, it lasted for years and ended in rejection), it was impossible to earn money or to be part of society in any way. Doomed to poverty, refuseniks had to take money from friends—those, that is, who had the courage not to turn away from them.

Her daughter, attaching herself to a man who had voluntarily chosen such a path? Lyalya was vehemently opposed to that, of course. It seemed to me, however, that there was something she liked about Irakli.

"I must give him credit," Lyalya said. "He did not sit idly by. He moonlighted as a cartoonist; not under his own name, of course. And he went on to publish articles in physics, also under fake names."

I'd heard many stories of emigration with all its torments, but even against this background, Irakli's was unusual. As the euphemism went, he had an "interesting biography." Or rather, an interesting family history. It concerned his maternal grandfather, an Ossetian, in whose honour Irakli was named.

When the Treaty of Brest-Litovsk gave part of Georgia to Turkey, his grandfather managed to escape to America—thus avoiding the fate of his brothers, whom the Turks forced into Islam. In America, he got married and joined the Communist Party. And in 1937, he went to Russia with his two children to personally participate in building the most just society on Earth.

The American wife did not share her husband's enthusiasm and stayed home.

"Nineteen thirty-seven!" Lyalya exclaimed, lighting another cigarette. "Couldn't have picked a better time! Who said 'I left Russia, not the USSR? I can't go back, those capital letters won't move apart to let me in?' Or something of that sort ... That's right, Tsvetaeva. See, you haven't forgotten Russian literature yet!"

Aunt slammed a mosquito on her naked arm.

"What are all these damned beasts doing here on the Adriatic Sea? In May, at that! Well, anyway, the wife refused to go, but the husband still went. And what he saw ... Well, it was just like in that joke, you know? A foreigner drives to the USSR in his car—and soon enough, the car falls into a huge hole in the middle of the road. So the foreigner's outraged, of course. 'How come you didn't place a fence around it, or at least a red warning flag or something?' And the Soviets say, 'Didn't you see the huge red flag when you crossed our border?'"

Aunt chuckled.

"Same thing with Grandfather Irakli. He wanted to watch his former countryman, Comrade Stalin, build communism all over a sixth of Earth's land. Serves you right, if you're so clever! But leave two poor kids at home. Well, he didn't." Lyalya knocked on her right temple, and then she asked suddenly, "By the way, how many books do you think Lenin wrote, speak not of the Devil?"

"Dunno. Lots. About fifty volumes, I guess."

"And what about Stalin?"

"No idea. Why?"

"Stalin didn't write a line himself! Not a line! It's proven now. He had no use for ink. He wrote in blood. So he sent Grandpa Irakli straight to the Gulag. Will you stop with the cookies already? You get fat at your age, you won't get thin again! That was the third one, enough."

She pushed away the plate with cookies that she herself had brought to the balcony along with her tea and strawberries.

"Explain this to me," she said excitedly. "Why did everybody believe the propaganda? I mean fine, Grandpa Irakli was almost illiterate, a cobbler or something—but Romain Rolland, Feuchtwanger, all those famous writers, how could they believe Stalin's tales when the show trials and news of executions were out there in the open?"

"I used to think about it a lot. But I still don't have an answer."

"Were they just idiots pretending to be smart?"

"Idealists is more like it," I said reaching for another cookie while Lyalya looked away. "Idealists need to believe in something. To have faith. Life in the West has its pitfalls: inequality, injustice, crime. Is this the best humanity can do? They don't accept that."

But Lyalya wasn't convinced: "But even so! Didn't they see our poverty, our humiliation, our total lack of rights? Didn't they see how much better things were in the West?"

"They were shown exactly what they wanted to believe in: Potemkin villages. Things didn't look bad at all at first sight, not like in Africa. The trams running, the people wearing shoes, no beggars on the street like in big Western cities."

"Sure! Because for begging you to go to prison, or to an island—you know cripples were sent to that island after the war?"

"I do, but all those Feuchtwangers couldn't have known that."

"Didn't they have heads on their shoulders? No, they didn't *want* to know! As you said, they saw what they *wanted* to see!"

"Maybe … But slavery is often invisible. There were no plantations in the USSR, and the real life of collective farmers was not shown to Westerners. I'll tell you about one incident I had. My customer, who really loved my work, a French-Canadian woman, an interior designer, was once throwing a big cocktail party. She invited me over. After perestroika, Russia was in fashion, and the editor of a leading Canadian newspaper—a sleek man with a well-groomed beard, a glass of wine in his hand—had me cornered, and I just couldn't get rid of him. He said that, though the Soviet Union had collapsed, the advantages of the Soviet system were undeniable: free education, medicine; the state offered free daycare so women could work. And you know what they were like, Soviet daycares? When I was still in Russia, I heard enough stories from my friends. 'Okay,' I said, 'would you drop your one-year-old off at a nursery with one grown-up taking care of forty babies and toddlers on a meagre salary? A woman who opens the windows on purpose when it's minus twenty degrees so that the next day, half the children get ill and she can somehow cope with the rest? Would you?' So he mumbled that his wife doesn't work. 'Well, you see, Soviet women are legally required to work. They don't have a choice. By the way, when was the last time you were in Russia?' 'Never,' he said. That didn't surprise me. Why would he go there? Such people are never convinced by facts. They have their system of beliefs. You can't argue with that."

"Yeah, faith was exactly what got Grandpa Irakli in trouble. It killed his son. See, the war started, the father was in prison, and the son was drafted, despite his American citizenship. He died in the first few days. Alice, the daughter, remained an orphan in a foreign country, eighteen years old, with hardly any Russian. She was renamed Alyona. Later, she worked in radio, broadcasting Soviet propaganda to the West. She married a Russian and gave birth to a boy whom she named after her father, Irakli. So Irakli was half American."

"Didn't his mother Alice/Alyona try to go back to America?"

"Many times, but she wasn't even allowed to visit. In the late 1980s, Irakli—the younger, I mean—decided to leave, all the while wondering which would be the stronger force in the decision: his work at a secret institute or the fact that his mother was American. All this Lyuba described to me in detail, and I thought, my poor girl, what are you getting into? All this dangerous, alien stuff!"

"So Irakli's mother was never allowed to go back home to the US?"

"Yes, she was, during Perestroika, as a very old woman. But she'd spent her whole adult life in Russia. She still spoke English, of course, but she had no idea how American life worked. Felt really lost there."

"If she was released, his chances of leaving wouldn't be so bad. Family reunion and all that."

"Well, yes. Only this is when he met Lyuba. He met her, and, like Hemingway said, the ground floated away under their feet. Or maybe it swam away, or jumped away, or something. Anyway, he was an honest man, told her everything, about being married and emigration and all, and Lyuba felt quite lost. Imagine her crying on her grandmother's shoulder. 'I can't live without him! What should I do?' Adelle advised her not to give up hope, but also to hold on to the idea of building her own life too, getting an education in Germany, like she wanted. You see, my mother, unlike many people of her generation, was broadminded, didn't consider emigration a betrayal of her homeland. She also believed it unlikely that Irakli would dare break up the family, and that it was for the best. To be the culprit of divorce—she didn't want her granddaughter to carry such burden. But Lyuba took her grandmother's advice her own way. She cried and cried, and then took the bull by the horns. Made Irakli decide: either he gets a divorce, marries her, and they go to America together, or she applies for a permit to go to Germany.

"Like in that joke, you know," Lyalya said laughing, anticipating the pleasure of telling yet another one. I heard a few from her every day. "So a Jewish guy, say, Moishe, is finally released from the Soviet Union, gets into the airport with his belongings, rubs his forehead. 'Phew! Finally, I got out!' And the airport clerk asks, 'Your destination? Israel?' Says Moishe, 'What are you, crazy? They have wars there, Arabs! I'm saving my son from Afghanistan, and you want to send him to another war?!'

"So the clerk suggests the States. 'Oh no,' he says. 'High unemployment, race conflicts … Though Hollywood is as Jewish as Jewish can be—but who needs me in Hollywood, right? No, not the States.' 'Okay,' says the clerk, 'maybe Australia, then?' 'Walking on my head? It hasn't come to that yet!' So the airport clerk loses her patience. 'I'll bring you a globe, and you point where you want to go.' Poor Moishe takes the globe, turns it this way and that, sighs, and finally asks, 'Do you happen to have another one, by any chance?'

"Same with Irakli. How do you make such a choice? With his wife, he probably could go to America; if he divorced and reapplied with Lyuba, the whole process would begin again, total uncertainty. But love! Besides, he's in Moscow, and Lyuba in Zaporizhzhia. Suppose he gets a divorce and stays in Russia. Then what would Lyuba do? Move to

Moscow instead of Germany? Plus, he cares for his wife and daughter! Would they go to the States without him, perhaps never see him again? And how could they possibly cope there? And so Irakli turned silent. Stopped answering Lyuba's letters, poste restante, and she didn't dare call him at home. All this exhausted her so badly that she sought a bit of solace with a boyfriend on the side. She didn't really care for him—that was just despair. But while Lyuba didn't take Oleg seriously, Oleg was ready to go to the end of the world for her. Kept asking her to marry him and move to Germany together. What to do?

"How many sleepless nights the three of us had spent talking, Mom, Lyuba and I, turning things this way and that, discussing, like the two of us now. And one morning, I say to her, 'I know how hard it is for you, daughter, I know! I've been in your shoes, but my dear girl, sometimes you have to choose between love and your future. Besides, feelings are unreliable. Today, the earth burns under your feet, or floats, or jumps, and tomorrow, love's gone, and you are at a broken trough. Imagine, you break up with Oleg, stay in Russia for Irakli, and he up and goes to America after all? You stay behind with no profession, no nothing. You need a profession for independence!' And grandma, she said you couldn't have everything. You always have to sacrifice something. If Lyuba didn't love that guy Oleg, as she said, wasn't it better to tell him?"

Chapter 48: Knot Severed

"Lyuba's rationality won in the end," Aunt said. "'Mom, you're right,' she said, 'Irakli's building his life, and mine got stuck. I'll go to Germany with Oleg. We'll have children, a family of our own.'

"She was in no hurry to announce her decision to Irakli though, waiting for a chance to talk face to face. For two months, they didn't see each other. Turns out that during that time, Irakli had received the permission to leave for America. As usual, he was given the barest minimum of time to pack. And Lyuba, she had no idea.

"There she sits, in Zaporizhzhia, waiting to hear from Irakli. Nada! So off she goes to Moscow of her own accord. Calls him from a friend's phone, says, 'Here I am.' Irakli comes to the apartment. Lyuba's friend had left her the key, as usual. You know, Lyuba told me later, 'Mom, he knocks on the door, and it cut through my heart. Right away, I know something is wrong. This was not the way he used to knock. I rush to open. He is standing at the door, silent, his face a closed book. No embrace, won't even look me in the eye.'

"They went in, closed the door, and Lyuba told him that it was over. That she had another man in her life, that he loved her, and wanted to come to Germany with her. That she had decided to marry him. Irakli gives her a strange look and goes to the window without dropping a word. Lyuba waits. He keeps quiet. She gets angry—imagine her getting angry at her idol! She shouts at him to say something. And he goes, 'What's there to say if you—you've made up your mind, haven't you?' 'Sure.' 'Well, you're probably doing the right thing.'

"For Lyuba, that was a big blow to her ego. She didn't expect him to let her go so easily. I'm sure she hoped he would talk her out of it. 'Is that all our love is worth to you? Do you even realize I'm doing this for you? To clear the way?' she asks. And he goes, 'Well, I'm not stopping you. You're young. I'm old. You need to live.' With 'old' meaning just under forty. Lyuba then told him frankly, 'They are letting people emigrate now. I know you'll leave sooner or later, and what about me?'

"Then Irakli finally spilled the beans: why he had not written, why he had avoided seeing her. It turns out that three days before the permission to leave for the US was granted, his wife had stumbled upon Lyuba's love letters. Irakli didn't try to make excuses, and his wife flatly refused to go to America with him. Why would she build a new life in a foreign country with a man who'd betrayed her? She decided to go without him, to bring her daughter to the West. They both wanted their child to grow up in America and get an education there. The only reason they refrained from divorce was that they'd need to reapply for emigration, always a risk.

"Lyuba listened to all this, plopped down onto the floor, pressed her head into the sofa, and bawled away. She was ready to swallow her words. 'I'll stay with you, just say you want it!' But what he said was not what Lyuba wanted to hear. He said he was a finished man and couldn't accept such a sacrifice from her."

Aunt sighed.

"Well, what was Lyuba supposed to do? She returned to Zaporizhzhia, asked Irakli for time to think. He kept away from her, didn't want to influence her decision. Lyuba pondered and pondered and then married Oleg. The rest you know: she went to Germany, had her daughter Anya. You'd think she'd forget all about her beau. It was a whole new life, after all. But no! She called him from Germany, said she couldn't live without him, said she'd be sneaking off to Moscow to see him."

"Well, well, well!"

"Well, well, what?!"

"It's a long way. Ukraine was closer. When she was still in Ukraine, I mean. And what did her poor husband think of all that?"

"Stop with the sarcasm! You've never been in her shoes. My daughter had been mean to me, and I can't forgive her—but I still feel sorry for her. I still love her. You didn't get married, you never wanted kids. For you, the main thing is work. You said so yourself, but for her …"

That's how fate decreed it, but I didn't remember ever saying that. She was cruel, my Aunt. "Me not getting married doesn't mean I don't understand how people fall in love," I said.

"Sorry, my little one! I didn't mean … it's just that you're dealing with those quilts of yours. The little circles and squares, the bunnies in the grass, the kitties on the porch, what a clean pretty life! Perhaps you don't need anything else. But love—it's when the ground burns under your feet!"

Aunt found my profession weird and didn't conceal it. I regret I once went into details with her about selling vintage Amish and Mennonite quilts, which my art gallery specialized in. That they were in great demand in the States and Asia seemed crazy to her. Aunt couldn't understand why people were willing to pay a hundred thousand dollars for an old blanket (the older, the better) when any Ukrainian babushka could sew a few old shreds together just as well for a single dollar.

I felt sorry for Lyuba. I hadn't known anything about this drama before and suddenly saw it in a new light. "And Irakli's wife and daughter, did they ultimately go to the US?"

"Sure. Who would miss that chance?"

"How did they fare in America? Did she manage to find a job?"

"No idea. Probably ended up washing dishes. She's an art historian by profession. That's no good. Irakli was their only hope."

"So did Lyuba start visiting Irakli in Moscow?"

"She didn't get to. He killed himself. It wasn't until a year later that Lyuba found out."

PART IV

Chapter 49: Orphans

I'd be leaving for Canada in two days and was secretly glad to finally get back to my life, but Lyalya was obviously sorry that there was so little time left, that we had to part soon. She fussed, wanting to do something for me, and kept fishing in her suitcase, trying to present me with cardigans, kerchiefs, and other things without which she believed my life would take a totally miserable trajectory. She even started asking me about quilts, to humour me a bit before our departure. She was astonished that I led seminars on quilt history and organized international exhibitions. "Quilts are still being made," I said. "There's a new fashion for natural dyes. Master quilt makers make dyes from bark and roots, grow marigolds, black walnuts."

Aunt couldn't resist. "There's no end to human stupidity! Have they gone mad or what?"

I rushed to switch from marigolds to her favourite theme: how she heroically changed the face of Crystal Goose.

I opened the window. The sweet air of the Adriatic, that blue print of happiness, caressed my face with its gentle fingers. Below us, pale-pink, yellow, and white houses were stepping down to the sea, sun upon them. The soft breeze carried to me the dry whisper of palm trees and the voices of people walking along the promenade. They were tall and well built, these Montenegrins, people of the Black Mountains, with dark hair and dark eyes, their strong features hinting at Turkish rather than Slavic origins, at ancient forces that violently collided and mixed both together. But in the sound of their language, I could discern the Serbian backbone, easily recognizable to a Russian ear.

I was reluctant to leave this small country, even though we only had a glimpse of it, "pushing blood to our hearts" on short promenades along the sea.

The Crystal Goose seemed to be a phantom, a fruit of somebody's ailing imagination. Except that it was my Aunt's reality for so many years that it welled up in her and looked for a release in endless mournful tales.

Aunt took a deep breath, as if someone had pumped the oxygen out of the room and was now letting it back in. There were still so many stories to tell before parting.

"Well, what can I tell you? Sure, life gradually got better. The town grew, became more modern, a bit less criminal. There were fewer violent murders. Before, whole families had fought against each other, whole neighbourhoods.

"When I was offered to become the head of the construction trust, I said no at first. The regulations, the estimations, the responsibility! Imagine: hospitals, schools, kindergartens, a nursing home—whatever gets built rests on my shoulders. Do I need all that? But you know, you just put one foot in front of the other, as they say, and walk right into the abyss. I took the job. Of course, I often got objects with defects—a leak here, some crumbling plaster there. The local administration was always in a hurry to put all facilities into service. 'Come on, come on, quick!' And never enough material. And then they tell me, 'Your next project is the construction of an orphanage.' And I say, 'I won't let you push orphans around! This time, everything needs to be first class. I'll check every brick myself! By smell and taste, if need be!' So I got together the best construction crew, the best building materials, everything. It was ready in time, and my trust took over. When the orphanage opened, I told the director, 'If you need anything, don't try the ministry, just come to me!'"

"I remember reading somewhere that Soviet orphanages spent something entirely ridiculous on children's food," I said. "Let me see if I can convert the number in my head … Under a dollar a month! About as much as a bullet costs."

"Well, certainly not at my orphanage. I wouldn't have had that! For my orphans, I got the best plumbing, new furniture—everything for free. And when I came over to have a look, I'd always march right into the kitchen and stick a spoon into the pot. To see if the stuff was edible. They feared me a bit, I guess, and they respected me. They didn't feed kids rubbish, didn't steal food from them. When I visited, I always brought candy and toys; all the children used to follow me around. The littlest ones would ask, 'Are you my Mommy? Will you take me home?' And their housemother would say, 'Your mother's on a work trip. She'll come back and take you home.' They used to say that to the little ones. The older kids didn't ask anymore. They knew no one would ever come for them. It was like this in Soviet times. There was no fashion yet for selling children to foreigners, like now."

"Selling? You mean that people from the West are allowed to adopt Russian kids?"

"To adopt! You know how it works? The foreigners pay out, and all the money goes right into the director's pockets! The orphanage gets zilch."

"But these children get a life abroad, in a proper family!"

"Well, let's hope so! Anything was better than Soviet orphanages. So I came to visit once again, brought candy and gifts, as usual. And one little kid especially just seemed glued to me. I told him, 'You've got your portion. Go now, sweetheart, let the others have a chance.' He stays silent. Just keeps standing there, looking at me with these big black eyes, eyelashes curled like a girl's. Keeps standing and staring. When the other kids spread away, he throws himself at me, presses his head into my skirt, as if there were only him and me in the world.

"Children in orphanages always lag behind in their development. He was three and looked about two, a big head on a thin neck, and so scrawny, skin and bones … He smelled of loneliness, and sorrow; you know the smell of sorrow? Kids in orphanages have that smell … Like other orphanage kids, he was a blade of grass grown in a cellar—pale, weak, tiny. They rarely run about, these children, rarely smile. But this one did. He was beaming at me. Shily, slyly, but radiantly. Why? What did he have to smile about? Something inside him, it seemed. He had blue rings under his eyes, and his olive skin was greyish from malnutrition. He was a mulatto, the colour of milky coffee."

"How did a mixed-race child turn up in Goose?" I asked, surprised.

"Wait, I'll tell you. His name was Daniel. Danechka, I called him. He takes me by the hand, presses his cheek into my palm, and just won't let go. What am I to do? I tell him again, 'Go play, sweetheart. I need to talk to the director.' He got it, stayed behind the door when we went into her office. But I heard him cry outside. So I asked the director, 'What's wrong with him?' And she said, 'He's just weird, spaced out. Too sensitive, I guess, or maybe it's because he's black.'"

"That's how she put it, 'because he's black?'"

"Sure! Apart from this boy, the people in Goose had only ever seen dark skin in pictures."

***

Elena had been eighteen when she gave birth to a son by a Congolese, a student of the Patrice Lumumba University, created in the USSR specifically for African students. In those years, the Soviet Union did all in its power to promote communist ideology in post-colonial Africa. The free tuition of African students was part of the plan. The Congolese said back home he was a prince; his father had five thousand buffaloes and seven thousand goats. The average African student was rich in the eyes of Muscovites and had privileges that they did not: money, access to special stores, and freedom of movement. A few dollars, a pretty dress, even a bottle of shampoo helped win a girl's heart. Daniel's mother soon became the prince's concubine and maid.

After graduating, he went back to the Congo, to his flocks and wives, leaving Elena eight months pregnant. Her parents threatened to kick her out if she didn't send "the darky" to an orphanage. Eventually, she gave in. Why in Crystal Goose? She thought the housemothers would be kinder away from Moscow.

"And so," Lyalya said, "there I am, stroking his springy curls, and he says, 'Are you my Mommy?' and just won't let go. He couldn't remember his mother. He wasn't yet two when she gave him away … But he won't let go, won't 'run off to play,' as he was told. He's reaching out to me, asking 'uppy,' poking his face into me like a kitten, holding on with arms and legs, a wave of that terrible orphanage smell hitting my nose. His curls smelled worse of all. It was the smell that decided it. I thought I'd take him home, give him a good bath, and return him the next day. Honestly, there was no other thought.

"So how did you end up keeping him?"

"His eyes. If you had seen his eyes, you wouldn't have asked."

Chapter 50: Daniel

No one in the family could understand Lyalya's motif. Neither her children nor her husband endorsed it. Perhaps Lyalya was affected by the tragic fate of her first husband, Samsonov, who'd grown up in an orphanage. Perhaps conversations with Seraphima, who'd been abandoned by the inseminator, contributed their share; disillusioned with men, the beautiful Seraphima found her happiness by adopting a little girl.

One way or another, Lyalya's life was turned upside down. This strange, dark-skinned child became the focus of all her desires and thoughts. The relationship with her husband suffered greatly at first. Tim had helped her raise two children. Bringing up yet another one, and a stranger at that, was not part of his plans. He tried to talk her out of it: the only dark-skinned child in Goose will be teased, even mobbed.

Lyalya concluded fiercely: "'Don't worry. My child will have none of that,' I said. 'Anyone who picks on him will be mincemeat!'"

***

Daniel stayed. Lyalya did for him what no one else would be allowed to do. She spent half the day in kindergarten with him until he was old enough for school. In first grade, she sat with him in class, at the same desk, keeping at his side even during breaks. He was shy, and other children wouldn't play with him at first, but they didn't dare bully him. No one wanted to cross the "boss lady." However, Lyalya didn't stay a boss for long. She switched to working as a regular engineer, part time, to dedicate herself to the child.

Soon, she discovered Daniel's unusual musical abilities. Nobody in her own family, except Uncle Haimele, had ever been musical.

"When we went for a walk," Lyalya told me, "he'd always pick up a stick or an iron rod and try out all kinds of sounds—swoosh it along the bars of an iron grate, knock it on a tree, drum on a stone. He listened to the world around him, teasing out its sounds, repeating them. And how he sang! Songs of his own, non-stop, melodiously, like a thrush.

"We used to go to the river—very early, at sunrise. There were always birds in the reeds, teals, yellow buntings. Daniel would sit on a stump, very quiet and just wait. I'd say, 'Keep your back straight, Danechka, you'll grow a hump!' He'd whistle, copy bird's voices. Then we'd go to the forest, listen for thrushes in the pines. Can you imagine me just sitting and listening to birds? Danechka taught me this."

When Lyalya started saving money for a piano and a music teacher, Tim grumbled only for appearance's sake. By that time, he, too, had become attached to the child.

By the age of eight, Daniel was a competent pianist. He began composing music before he learned how to write it down. Lyalya had no doubts about his future. She needed to move to Moscow so that he'd go to the music academy there.

"Truth be told, my own children never made me as happy as Danechka," she said. "He had this—how shall I say—natural compassion for things in the world. His sensitivity was often his enemy. He'd be concerned for the cat next door that keeps meowing the whole day. Is it perhaps lonely? And what happens to spiders over winter? If they die, who would move into their mazing house, their web? It's so rare for the child to pay any attention to nature; they are still part of nature themselves. But Danya was different. We had a wood stove, and he'd bring wood from the shed, help me light the fire. When I put plates into the drying rack, he'd stand beside me and do the same. Other kids want to run around and play, but he … he was always either at the piano or at my side. And caught my mood instantly. As soon as I thought of something sad, he'd quietly take my hand and stroke my palm with a finger. That was our secret sign. It meant, 'Don't be sad, Mummy, I'm here with you!'

"We've only ever had one spat, and it was all my fault!" Lyalya continued after a long pause. "I should never have lied to him! But you see, I didn't want to upset him."

Her face sagged. She looked bleached, faded. Her eyes were staring ahead blindly.

"I remember it was a warm spring day. Danechka and I were going to a pet shop. Tim had promised him a pigeon for his birthday; he'd long wanted one. We agreed it would live in a neighbour's dovecot. His son was a friend of Daniel's. They'd feed and fly pigeons together. So there we were, looking at the birds. So many breeds! Your ordinary blue rock pigeons, white frillbacks with black stripes, brown rollers—they turn somersaults in flight—and lots more. There was one breed so white it hurt your eyes, without a single speckle, like a picture of the holy ghost. A 'dove,' you have to say; 'pigeon' sounds too dirty for it. Lifts off without a run-up, like a helicopter. That's the one Danechka liked. He wanted it perfectly white. Without a speck.

"And suddenly on the way back from the shop, he asks me, 'Mom, when I grow up, will my skin be white like yours and Daddy's?'"

"Where'd he get that from?" I asked, surprised.

"Well, he saw he was different. He seemed like an anomaly to himself. I didn't understand how serious he was. I just grinned. 'Sure it will!' But he took my words literally."

Lyalya shook her head sadly.

"Half a year passed or so. He was happy with his music and his pigeons. And I forgot all about it. Then I see, he's got abrasions above his elbow. 'What's that, Danny?' He stays silent at first. Then he admits he'd been trying to scrape off the brown colour of his skin with a pumice stone. Trying to help along what he expected to happen anytime, 'as you promised, Mom.' 'Promised what?' 'That when I grow up, I'll be like you.' I had to explain to him what was what. That turned out to be a tragedy for him. 'Why did you cheat, Mother?' After this, he didn't come close for three days, only talked when it was absolutely necessary. Stopped believing me, you see."

Lyalya covered her face with her hands.

"If I'd told him the truth then, maybe things would've turned out differently. Maybe all that happened wouldn't have happened?"

"I don't see the connection."

Lyalya made a convulsive sobbing sound. I pretended I hadn't noticed. She pulled herself together quickly.

"He caught me lying, don't you see? I had been everything to him, a fortress—and suddenly, there was a hole in the wall. When you lose faith, you're open to all troubles, prey to misfortune …"

***

Trouble first appeared in the form of Elena, Daniel's mother, who came to Crystal Goose to pick up her son from the orphanage.

"What should I do?" the director asked. "I have Daniel's biological mother sitting here. I won't tell her your name or address, of course."

"What?" Aunt said quietly, her breast heaving. "I'll be right there."

In the director's office, a portrait of Brezhnev was scrunching his immense brows at a young woman with a flat, blank face. She was wearing a home-knitted cardigan and a long, dark skirt. A light kerchief was covering her hair. Perched on the edge of a chair, she was afraid to face the director across her massive table and looked sideways.

"Why do you suddenly want the child?" the director demanded to know.

The woman didn't raise her head. Her fingers were crumpling a dirty handkerchief.

"It's been eight years," Lyalya said, disguising her inner turmoil with external severity. "Daniel has now a home. Loving home. Loving parents. You want to take all this away from him?"

Elena threw a nervous glance at the women on whom her fate depended. She spoke hesitantly, with frequent pauses, as if she didn't have the strength to reach the end of a sentence. What she said was this: she'd recently "found God." In this, she had followed the example of a friend who went to a convent after two failed marriages. Orthodox churches and monasteries were springing up like mushrooms after the rain on the shaky soil of perestroika.

In the morning, before work, Elena prayed. After work, she washed the church floors, changed candles, cleaned the silver. Her confessor, Father Nicodemus, said he wouldn't absolve her of her sins until she repented. And the repentance was to take back Daniel.

"God is merciful," Nicodemus had said, "but He will not forgive a mother who breaks the laws of God. You have behaved like a cuckoo in the woods. Worse. A cuckoo is an ignorant beast, but you're a human being created in God's image. The only way out for you is to take the child back and do penance."

When Lyalya heard that, her fear was replaced by anger. New converts would never find favour with her. "She abandoned Danechka, and now she wants to wash herself clean! No chance!"

"What's your job?" the director asked, giving Elena an icy glance. "Where do you live?"

It turned out that Elena was working as a cleaner at a railway depot near Moscow and living in a dorm.

"How are you going to raise a child under these conditions?" the director demanded.

"Father Nicodemus promised to help," Elena whispered. Her hands were clenching the handkerchief so hard that the joints of her fingers turned white.

It turned out that Father Nicodemus had a friend who was Father Superior at the Pechora Monastery. He had promised to take the boy in.

"So that's the plan!" the director exclaimed. "The child is to be torn away from his adopted parents to rot in a monastery!"

At this, Elena slipped from the chair and begin crawling toward Lyalya on her knees. "You're kind, you're good!" she said. "Give me my son back, I beseech you in the name of God!"

"Stop that nonsense!" the director shouted. "Get up right now! You gave the child away of your own accord, didn't you? Enough with the comedy!"

"Help me, for Christ's sake! I'll pray for you all my life. Give me my son. Save me!" Elena kept repeating this as if in a trance. Her handkerchief fell from her head, revealing mousy hair. She kissed the hem of Lyalya's skirt.

"What's wrong with you?" Lyalya said, pressing her back into the chair. "What do you mean, 'save you'? No one's threatening you."

"I'll burn in hell for my sins if I don't get him back! Have mercy, I pray!"

"Oh, there it is! You see how these damned clerics fool the people!" The director heaved herself from the table and loomed over Helen. "Okay, enough! Get a grip. Come back tomorrow, and we'll settle this."

"So you—you'll give me my son back?"

"I told you to come back tomorrow!" the director shouted, losing her patience. She smoothed out the skirt that had gotten stuck between her thick nylon-clad thighs.

"God give you health! God give you eternal life!" Elena was babbling, making signs of the cross and backing out of the room.

When the door finally closed behind her, the director took a few mighty steps toward the cabinet and pulled out a bottle of Armenian cognac.

"Crazies are an occupational hazard with us, aren't they? That's what I call unsafe working conditions, and we don't even get hardship money! Come on, let's have a drink." She put two crystal glasses on the table and emptied hers in one gulp. "Aah, that was nice. But really, that things have come to that. People want to go to heaven at the expense of their children. I won't let her get anywhere near Daniel tomorrow! If she tries anything, I'll call the police right away."

Lyalya felt that something had sunk into her, her fear and disdain replaced by something equally unpleasant: a mixture of disgust and pity.

"You haven't registered the adoption, have you?" The director wiped her mouth with the back of her hand, leaving a bloody lipstick mark.

"No," Lyalya breathed out.

When Lyalya had decided that Daniel would live with her, she considered official adoption, of course. But she didn't want to complicate her relationship with Tim, who had initially resisted the idea. Besides, adoption required a formal waiver from the parents. She put it off until "better times."

"N … now, that's not good, is it?" the director said. "Now we're sure as hell getting no waiver from this fool. We could file for forfeiture of parental rights, I guess. We'd need to claim she's a drunk or a prostitute, though. Or we could just scare her off. So you aren't drinking with me? Shall I clean away the cognac?"

***

Lyalya didn't go home right away. She wandered the streets for a long time until she found herself in the factory district. The day was overcast, the river gleaming dully. Unsightly vegetable gardens stretched along behind their rickety fences, interspersed with square buildings of dirty red and black bricks. Suddenly she was terribly tired. She entered a courtyard and found a bench. Its back sported an inscription done with a penknife: "Petr fucked Masha rite hear!" Cigarette butts were lying under her feet. A light wind swept up and carried off some newspaper scraps. A few metres away, a group of men was playing dominoes. One, in a dirty sleeveless sailor shirt, finished his beer and threw the bottle into a scrawny bush under the fence. Lyalya heard glass break. Another man went to the barn to pee.

"And at this moment," Lyalya told me, "I was gripped by such sadness, such disgust at life! What for? Everything, what for? Here I am, trying, running my head against the brick wall, building houses and hospitals for them. And all around me—the Middle Ages, obscenity, rudeness, dirt. Nothing changes. So now a woman wants to take Danechka away from me. How can that be? Why? Believe it or not, for the first time in my life, I felt sorry for myself. I know it does no good. But I just couldn't stop pitying myself, and this made me feel even worse. And strangely enough, I started feeling sorry for Elena too. After all, I'm a mother myself! I understand! She was the one who gave birth to Danechka, my little sweetheart. She gave birth to him, yet had no chance to see how he grew. No chance to see how good he was, how gifted, just how wonderful, on the brink of youth. His voice would soon start breaking. I mean, what did this poor Elena ever see in life? Nothing but humiliation! To start believing in hell, with flames and frying pans and all that—this is some last degree of despair, let me tell you."

"Someone had broken her will …"

"Just imagine the horror she has—not of life, not even of dying, but of what comes after! At least we don't have that worry. We've always had enough of a hell on earth. So how could I give her the last blow? Did I have the right to do that? There I am, sitting on a bench among the drunkards, trying to figure out how to tread a fine line, to be fair to her, to Danechka, and, well, to myself too."

Lyalya felt silent for a few moments. Then, she said, "First I thought, let her come to school, look at Daniel from afar at recess. But then … then I came to my senses. Too much of a risk. Who knows what she'd do? Maybe she'd try to steal him? What to do? Whom to ask for advice.

"In the end, I went home, still no decision made. Daniel immediately felt I wasn't quite myself. He watched me closely but was too delicate to ask. I distracted him, asked him to play something of his own. He was very much into composing at that time, Bach-like sonatas. I bought him records, and he listened and composed. I looked at him, and my soul melted. My boy, my sunshine! I'm not giving you away.

"I set the table. We had dinner. There was a thunderstorm that night. You know, I'm not afraid of anything—apart from thunderstorms, weirdly enough. Some kind of animal horror. We went to bed, I dove under the blanket, clung to Timmy, embraced him. He wasn't getting much affection from me in those years. And there I was, thinking, 'God, we're not old yet! We're fifty. Life isn't over. At least my man is with me; he's not perfect, but who is?' I smelled him, I felt how close we were, caressed his chest, twisted a hair on it, he laughed … He was a ticklish one. This was my man. The only one I had and the only one who … well, cared about me. Yes, he loved me, maybe not the way I needed, but the only way he could, the only way he knew how. And I was no birthday cake either, but he somehow put up with me. I snuggled up to him and then spilled the beans, told him everything about Elena, and my fears. And suddenly, he pulled away and sat down in bed. 'I don't understand,' he said. 'How can we keep someone else's child when his own mother shows up?'

"'What … what are you saying? If you love Danechka, you can't …'

"'Of course I love him. But we have no right to keep him. We have to give him up.'

"It was … like a bucket of cold water was poured over me. 'What do you mean, give him up? Our Danechka? Don't you understand what would happen to him?'

"'What's so bad about it? He'd sing. In the monasteries, the choirs are quite professional.'

"I was stunned. How could Tim say that? How could he think that? 'You always wanted to get rid of Daniel,' I said, 'and now you're happy to get a chance.' The reproach was unfair, and I knew that. Tim had long grown to love the boy. But everything inside me was boiling, I couldn't help it. In short, we had a big fight."

"In Canada, foster parents usually keep in touch with biological ones," I said. "They even allow them to visit their child."

"Really? Now, how would that work? What I would say to Danechka, huh? 'I'm nobody to you now; here she is, your real Mommy!' Wouldn't that mean I'd been lying to him all those years? Lying again? I'd never told him he was adopted, and he soon forgot his early childhood."

"How did you manage to keep it a secret? No neighbours ever told him he wasn't yours?"

Aunt covered her eyes with her hands and shook her head. "Yes, that's the thing. That's the thing! He was five or six when he came running from the yard sobbing, 'You're not my real Mommy! Vera just told me!' And me—you should have seen his face, I just couldn't!—so I said, 'Sweetheart, don't you listen to such nonsense!' After that, how could I back out? So anyway, he didn't know. I couldn't have him meet his mother. And so I decided: if Elena wants to see her son, let her come to his concert. He was giving a solo performance at the house of culture. Chopin, Rachmaninoff. Let her rejoice at her son's success. But you can't trust these religious fanatics, so I was taking a risk. I put forward the condition. 'You can watch him, but from afar and under my eyes.'"

"You're quite the Solomon!" I said. "Remember, when two women were contesting the right to a child, and Solomon said, 'Let them tear the baby in two and each take half?' And the real mother said, 'Better give the child to the other one.'"

"What does that have to do with anything? It's not like I challenged her motherhood! Anybody else would have told her to eff off! Me, I allowed her to come and see him."

But Elena didn't show up for the concert, and no one saw her in town again.

Chapter 51: Misfortune

In all the years I knew my aunt, the Daniel chapter of her life was never discussed. There were some rumours in the family that Lyalya had adopted a child, but nobody knew exactly why. It was a very rare and unusual thing to do in the Soviet times, but then Lyalya was an eccentric.

Daniel was twelve when he disappeared from home. Lyalya's life was crushed.

The police combed the whole town and the surrounding forest—to no avail. There were some suspects, relatives of the drunkard Tim's brother Nikolai had run over years before. But it turned out they had moved to Rostov a year before the incident.

Then Lyalya thought of Elena. She sent some men she trusted to the suburb of Moscow where Elena lived. The biological mother was found in a mental hospital. She kept raving about the flames of hell, spoke in tongues and hid from the visitors under her bed.

Crystal Goose was a high-criminality town. People were killed for a glass of vodka, for an old fur coat. Many crimes remained unsolved. But everyone in town knew Daniel—and loved him. After the initial rejection of the dark-skinned boy, his warmth and his talent had won over the hard-nosed inhabitants of Crystal Goose.

What could have happened? There wasn't a trace, not the slightest clue to the mystery. In the very first days of search, Lyalya's hair had grown grey.

She thought he was dead when she got the call. "Your nigger," said the voice on the phone, "has five days to live. You hand over ten grand, you'll get him back. If you don't, we'll bury him alive in the woods. Five days, remember. You call the police, he's dead."

Lyalya and Timofey had nothing close to such a sum. All day, they walked around the house dazed, as if walking through deep waters at the bottom of the sea.

The next day, Lyalya opened the door early in the morning and saw a letter without an envelope on the doorstep. She recognized Daniel's handwriting right away. He was begging his parents to save him.

Three months before, Lyalya had bought a car. She could sell it for about four thousand rubles. The TV was relatively new and could bring in another five hundred. She had three hundred on her savings account. Lyuba promised to send as much as she could spare, but she was a student and had a child, so she was living hand to mouth too. Also, the transfer would take time. There were still five thousand missing.

Lyalya started knocking on doors, asking for a loan. She was well loved, her story was horrifying, and people gave what they could. But most of them could hardly make ends meet.

Neither Lyalya nor Tim slept at night. When the kidnappers called again, Tim picked up the phone. Stuttering and struggling to find the words, he began to explain how they were collecting the money. He asked for a reduction and for two more days to sell the car. The man on the phone answered with a dirty curse and hung up.

"Do you believe in miracles?" Aunt suddenly asked me.

"I don't know. Why?"

"Well, I didn't until I got a call from—you'll never guess—Victor."

"Who was that?"

"Remember, the Admiral? That's what you and I called him when we were kids. Chocolate ice lollies, remember?"

"I didn't know you had stayed in touch."

"We hadn't, at first. Victor was living in Zaporizhzhia, working on veterans' affairs. He was still friends with my father back then. As for me—you know my life had taken a different turn. Siberia, Samsonov, my children, my work … But at some point, I met Victor in Zaporizhzhia, by chance. Daddy had died by then, and I came to the cemetery on his anniversary, as usual. There, I saw Victor—he, too, had come to pay respect to his best friend. Slim he was, just as before, but all grey. We sat down on a bench at the grave, remembering my father. I got some water for the young birch I had planted at the head of the grave, cleaned up the flower bed. Victor was watching me in silence all the while. Then he said, 'Lyalya dear, sit down for a minute.' And he looked me in the eyes, like in the old days.

"I heard him say 'Lyalya dear,' and my heart thumped. He put his hand on mine. We sat there silently for a while. Then he asked for permission to call me sometimes, to meet the children—he had never seen them, after all. I said yes, of course. Tim was not in the picture yet, or not that much, let's say. And Victor started calling me, and sometimes he came to visit. He made friends with Nikita, got him interested in the sea. It's because of Victor that my son is an electrical engineer with the navy. Well, not anymore. But still, Nikita had spent almost ten years at the job, made good money. And when we moved to Crystal Goose, Victor even came to visit us there a couple of times. He gave me good advice. When I started the glass factory, I felt like I was going to sink —but he gave me faith. And you know what? I've had my share of admirers in life, and Timmy had never been jealous before. I thought he wasn't the sort to even notice. But Victor did make him jealous. Nothing was said, but Victor felt it and stopped coming. Stopped calling too. It was a pity, but, well, Life goes on. And all of a sudden, on one of these terrible days, there's a call. I can't pick up, I'm too afraid. Tim goes to the phone—and hears Victor's voice. He hands me the receiver, and … You know, I'd been trying to keep it together. But when I heard his voice, tears just started spouting, rivers of them. And through the tears, I somehow managed to tell him what had happened. And Victor said, 'I have an urgent matter to attend to in Crystal Goose anyway. I'll come tomorrow.' That was so transparent I could almost laugh. An urgent matter? In our poky hole? But that call calmed me down a little bit. I fell asleep for the first night that week. The next day, Victor came and handed Tim the missing five thousand."

Lyalya fell silent, took a breath.

"Victor stayed at our place for two days. He took upon himself negotiations with these monsters. He and Tim met with them, gave them the ransom, and took Daniel home. It was in the woods; I didn't go in. I was waiting a hundred metres away, by the car, half dead with tension. And then I saw Victor and Tim coming out of the forest, holding Daniel under the arms, almost carrying him. He was dragging his feet strangely. When he approached me, he didn't say anything. He just looked at me and looked away again. Now, that was scary. I picked him up like a baby, carried him to the car. He didn't resist; his body was kind of sluggish. At home, I was afraid to ask him anything. I thought, 'Let him come to; give him time. He'll speak when he gets better.' But he didn't get better, and he didn't speak. Most of the time, he was half asleep, but sometimes, I couldn't tell ... he was not responsive. I put on records with his favourite pieces of music. No reaction. His eyes especially frightened me; before there was so much life and excitement in them. Now he never looked at me or Tim. Just stared at one spot, above the horizon, somewhere far away. What did he see? What did he think? Once I lay down with him, I stroked his cheeks, his arms, no reaction. What have they done with him? What?"

My aunt was sobbing. What I puzzled together from what I had heard between the sobs was this:

Daniel suddenly developed a fever that nothing could put down. He was hospitalized, but that didn't help. Lyalya was at his side all the time, sleeping in the hospital. She wanted to talk to the boy, even to ask his forgiveness for having failed to protect him, but was waiting till he got better. He never did. Daniel lost consciousness, and a week later, the candle was extinguished for good. The doctors couldn't determine the cause of death. There were signs of beatings on the child's body, but they were not lethal. The medical staff concluded that the death was the result of a nervous shock.

Chapter 52: Life Without

After Daniel's death, the lives of his foster parents were never the same. They began avoiding each other, grew silent, and ate at different times so as not sit at the same table.

"I never told anybody much about that time," Lyalya said. "You're the first."

And I thought this was probably the main reason why she'd so badly wanted to meet—to tell me about Daniel, to tell me how she managed to survive.

"After his death, I felt nauseous all the time. Whatever I tried to eat was poison. Fresh air burned my lungs. Bright things hurt my eyes. Everything made me sick, you know? Crystal Goose isn't a beautiful town, but there are wonderful places even there: the forest, the river, the ponds with the lilies and reeds. I tried to go for walks. I thought it would ease the pain. But Danechka had loved nature, and so it hurt me to look at a sunny meadow. I'd go back home, and the first thing I'd see would be the neighbours' dovecot. Daniel again. This fluffy white thing hurling itself into the pure azure, higher and higher until it turned into a dot. Just imagine, in such a tiny body, at such a height, a heart was beating. And Danechka's wasn't. I looked closer, wanted to see which one was Daniel's pigeon. This one, fluttering about? That one, turning a somersault? Anyway, it didn't know that his master is no longer in the world. Or maybe the dove is Daniel's soul? Watching me, watching this sinful land. At that moment, I—well, I still didn't believe in God, but I felt with all my soul that there must be another life. That it wouldn't end with this."

Lyalya gestured dismissively at the universe.

"And immediately I felt better. For a while, that was my shred of hope. Then it left me. Again, there was nothing but a scorched plain. I came home, I saw his piano in the corner, and I felt a red-hot rod ramming my chest. Thank God we sold the piano later. Pain, but also guilt. I know now how my mother felt all those years for failing to save her parents. Where did my guilt start? The day I said he'd turn white like us when he grows up? Or when I didn't give him to Elena? And here's a strange thing: I kept hating myself for that, but when Tim once said, 'If you had given Daniel to his mother, he'd still be alive,' I was ready to strangle him.

"Not like him at all, to speak like that. Not like him before Daniel's death, that is. From the day he died, we quarrelled non-stop, for no reason. Never before had Timid Timmy raised his voice against me. Now, everything I said annoyed him. And he had developed a disgusting habit: if something fell to the floor, he wouldn't pick it up. He'd just kick it away. I wanted to run, run far away, to never see Tim or that apartment or the town where my child had been tortured. Not to see anything!

"And then Lyuba invited me to Germany. She wrote tearful letters, begged me to come and help. She was studying medicine, had two little girls. She needed help. Who is there to help but your own mother, especially when you're in a strange land? I came twice. I was well received then."

Lyalya took a breath and stopped.

"Let's sit for a while," she said, sinking onto one of the benches spaced equally along the quay. It clearly wasn't so much the walking as the memories that had taken away her strength.

"Did Tim go to Germany with you on one of these visits?" I asked.

"No time. He had to finish that chicken coop of his."

"He bred chickens?" I asked.

"Nah, that's what I called his little hut. See, we had a vegetable garden two kilometres away from home. I grew my own fruits and veggies, barely ever bought any. Every day, I schlepped myself to the garden, worked there, walked home in the dark—we had sold the car, remember? So Tim decided to build a hut near the garden. 'It'll be easier for you,' he said, 'you can live there in summer. Fresh air and all that. We can rent out one room of ours for that time to help with the debts.' And I think, 'Come on, be real with me! When were you ever interested in money?' I could see right through him: all he wanted was a bolthole, somewhere to be alone.

"Timmy, of course, would never admit it to me. And I didn't mind the idea, really. But I asked him this: 'Where will you get the building materials and the labour? Are you counting on me, as always? I'm out of options.' After adopting Danechka, I had switched to working as a regular engineer, I told you, right?

"But he said, 'I'll build it myself, with my own hands.'

"'Yeah, right,' I think. 'The hell you will! You're a dreamer, not a doer. A rooster will lay an egg sooner than you'll lay a foundation!' Besides, it really wasn't easy. A simple nail you couldn't get in the store. You hire workers. They arrive drunk or not at all. But I didn't try to talk him out of it. He has a bug up his ass—fine. Probably helps him think less of Danechka.

"So he'd be off to his shack every day after work. That's about three kilometres from the city. He'd come home later and later. Got a sheepdog guarding his 'palace.' I brought him food twice a day on weekend, as if I didn't have enough on my hands.

"One night, thieves climbed into that hut, shot the dog, and cleaned it out. The radio, tools, even the old shoes were taken. Thank God, Timmy was sleeping at home then. After this, he bought two more dogs and started spending the nights in his little witch hut. 'Nothing to be done!' he said. 'The place must be guarded.'"

***

Aunt and I bought our usual load of strawberries in Kotor. Then, from sheer boredom, we watched the crowd leave the womb of yet another cruise ship.

"Do you believe that people can change? Say, under special circumstances?" Lyalya suddenly asked, chewing on a strawberry.

"I don't, really. Superficially, sure, but not essentially, I think. Why?"

"So a person is the same from the cradle to the grave? How do people adapt if they don't change? All I do is adapt."

"People adjust, of course," I said. "But that's just temporary mimicry."

"No, it isn't. You, for instance, have changed."

"Yeah? I think I'm still the same."

"Nope. You were talkative. Now, you're so closemouthed, I have no idea what you're thinking."

"I'm just watching the steamer. Not really thinking much of anything right now."

"That's fine, but I'm telling you when I came back from Germany for the second time, my husband was unrecognizable. Kept running around me like a puppy, trying to please me. 'It turns out I can't live without you,' he said. Rather touching, really. Like a second honeymoon. Only we never had a first."

Chapter 53: Letter from Canada

THE FARTHER FROM KOTOR, the fewer tourists we met. The bay gradually took on softer features, the mountains gently sloping to the water. The endless expense of the sea can be frightening and hostile, but the curving contours of a bay suit the eye, feel peaceful. The warm air was caressing us, chasing away sad thoughts.

Lyalya felt it too, and the tone of her voice softened. "I remember it was May, as it is now. The nightingales were already singing their clicking song, and bird cherry flowers were smelling like ... do you still remember that smell? Bitter and yet sweet. In a hollow near the witch hut, a stream ran, with cherry thickets along the banks. Tim and I were sitting on the unfinished veranda. There was no porch yet. Half the floorboards were missing. Inside, the workers were hammering away. Us, we put out a folding table and had a picnic. I had brought a bottle of schnapps from Germany. And some other things for Tim—shoes, clothes, old German maps; that was his special treat. I was telling him how Lyuba and her kids were doing. He wanted to know all about Lyuba, as always. They weren't rich and worked hard, but things were well enough, I said. Lyuba and her husband had even taken me to Paris for three days. Timmy's eyes caught fire at that. He'd been dreaming of Paris for a long time. So I'm painting him a picture, but all the while, I'm afraid to say the main thing: that Lyuba had asked me to move in with them. First I thought she was joking, but no. 'Things will be no good in Ukraine, you'll see. There'll be a war. Move to Germany, Mom, before it's too late.' Right she was, too. A war really started. Look at all this fight in Donbas. Already thirteen thousand dead, and there is no end in sight.

"You know how after perestroika, Germany opened the borders to Soviet Jews? Especially to those whose relatives had been victims of the Nazis. So Lyuba tells me, 'Mom, we have the documents on the deaths of our relatives. I'll have them translated, I'll hire a lawyer, I'll find the money. Come. I miss you terribly, and so do the girls.' To tell you the truth, that put me in a bind. I was happy she needed me, missed me, of course. Yet to visit was one thing, but to move permanently? To leave behind my recently widowed son who had lung cancer? How could I? I argued that I was too old to learn the language. Lyuba said I didn't need to. That she'd interpret for me, and that I could talk to all the Russians. There are Russian newspapers, a Russian choir. She said I'd have fun singing in the choir, imagine!

"A choir was just what I needed, right? And Timmy, he'd suddenly start singing too? I knew he wouldn't move. He wouldn't leave his pet project, his hut he'd never finish building anyways. Besides, what would he do in Germany? But Lyuba's offer stayed on my mind. On my way back, on the plane, I thought, 'Why shouldn't I leave even if Tim doesn't? Why not do as I want?' Of course, starting all over again at my age is scary. But after Danechka's death, the whole town made me vomit. I'll never know who stole my dear boy and killed him, but someone in town did! How could I live with these people after that? After I had restarted glass production, after I had given them a way to make some money again, after I had a whole block of new apartments built—this was what they did to me?

"Well, so Tim and I were sitting at this half-finished veranda and we were having a wonderful time. Nightingales were singing their tiny heads off, a lovely evening indeed! Tim hugged me and said: 'I love you, Lyalya! Do you know that?' 'I do.' 'Well, let's drink to the success of all our hopeless enterprises!' And he glanced sideways and gave me a little sad smirk. And I felt sorry for him, because he knew. He didn't talk much, but he understood what was on my mind. We drank some more. Maybe the booze had loosened my tongue, or maybe I got sentimental with the nightingales and all, but I told him everything. I said, 'See, Lyuba has invited me—I mean *us*—to move to Germany. They are there alone, they need help.' Timmy gave a low whistle, as he used to do when he was confused. The fork with a bit of herring didn't reach his mouth. The colour drained from his face, and he quietly asked, 'You want to go to Germany for good? Did I get that right?' I half nodded, half shook my head. 'Well, go ahead, if you need to. Why not?'

"'And what about you?'

"'What about me? You seemed to mean you want to go alone.'

"'Well, I didn't say that.'

"And he goes, 'Let's not play charades. I know you want to go solo.'

"Well, that was too much for me. I backtracked, said I didn't really mean it, it's just talk. And to change the subject, I told him some stuff that Lyuba had read to me from German newspapers. It was an article about war criminals, how Germans hunt them around the world. 'Well done,' I said. 'They take responsibility for their past! Old age is no excuse for war criminals.' Tim's face suddenly went white. I go, 'What's the matter? You're drinking too much!' And he: 'Age is no excuse, you say?' Oh, yeah, they'd just put a ninety-year-old on trial.

"He suddenly had a coughing fit. I hit him on the back, he pressed his hand to his chest. 'What's wrong with you?' I asked. He said his heart was not feeling right. He had probably drank too much. And when he felt better again, he began talking—at length, as he rarely did, this time about his father.

Chapter 54: Tim's Father

Tim was a rather recent acquisition to our family, and the family lore had few entries detailing his pedigree. I myself had met Tim only a couple of times in my life and was eager to find out more about him now. It was getting late. A sudden wind rippled the waters in the bay, and a single cloud drifted across the sky, which was darkening before our eyes, transforming from ultramarine to pale blue.

"If I felt pity for orphaned Samsonov," my aunt said once we returned to our abode. "what did I have to feel for Tim, once I found out his whole story, which he, by the way, kept mum about for many years? Just come to think of it! No matter whom you take, of the war generation, if their parents have somehow survived Stalin's executions, and children survived four years of war grinding machine, and then avoided Gulag, these children would be mentally if not physically damaged. Men especially. Though women fared no better. It was up to them to raise their children, single-handedly. The whole generation of boys grew without fathers. As somebody quipped, the only man present in those households was a portrait of Stalin on the wall. Tim's case was hardly different. His parents separated shortly before the war; his mother was left alone with three sons. Irritable and bitter, which I understand. Her sudden outbursts frightened the hell out of them, that's what Tim told me, this part anyway. And when, once in a while, she began to cry and hug them, clutching them to her breast convulsively, that made them feel even more lost and confused. The father, on the other hand, was adored by his children. He was Tim's hero. He visited every Sunday, brought delicious gifts, never raised his voice. Tim remembered one detail in particular, how he loved to climb into his lap, gently taking off his glasses. They were always a bit crooked, Tim said, as his Dad's left ear was underdeveloped from birth, and looked like a little pink worm. His light eyelashes blinked helplessly, his soft Ukrainian face seemed defenceless and childish. Tim's father was Ukrainian, his mother, Russian, you see.

"His dad taught geography and German in high school. I think this passion for maps, Tim got it from his father. When his father visited his children, he'd empty his briefcase onto the table—paper, pens, gouache, erasers—and start drawing. Castles with embrasures, moats, draw bridges grew under his quick pencil. Crusaders beat back every attack, hot resin flowed onto enemy heads from the toothed walls. You know those things that boys love. Father got some ancient maps from somewhere, with no America yet, before Magellan, before Amerigo Vespucci, exciting, right? 'Can you draw the contours of Australia from memory? And how about India?' That's how his father taught Tim world geography. And Tim carried it on later with our Danechka. I can just see little Danny sticking out the tip of his tongue with eagerness, drawing the continents with coloured pencils. Sorry, I got off track … We were talking about Tim, right? Anyhow, his two older brothers usually would run off to play in the yard, and Tim, I can imagine how thrilled he was to have his father to himself, along with the continents—the known ones and those to be discovered together."

"Looks like Tim's father was a nice man," I said.

"Nice man? Well, I never met him of course, but in those pre-war years, he was a patriot, or a Ukrainian nationalist, depending on your take. There are lots of those in Ukraine now. Nothing wrong with loving your own land, don't get me wrong, but look, half of the population speaks Russian as their mother tongue. Yet, it's a forbidden language."

"Doesn't surprise me. A natural reaction to Putin's meddling with Ukraine. Biting off Crimea."

"This is now. But back then, Ukraine was part of the Soviet Union, and nationalism was forbidden by the Soviets. It was actually dangerous to express such views. So, for example, Tim's father would teach little Timmy Ukrainian history, not the Russian or Soviet History. 'Here's a Cossack with a musket. Here's the seal of Bogdan Khmelnitsky. Here's the trident of St. Vladimir. And here is the coat of arms of Hetman Doroshenko himself, our ancestor. Kyiv is the mother of Russian cities. Back before no one had heard of Moscow, Kiev was already a great city, the most beautiful place'—all of that in Ukrainian to boot. Once his mother entered the room, he would switch over to Russian: 'Remember, son, Ukraine will be free! The day will come, she will breathe in the air of liberty.'

"Tim's mother would explode. I told you she was Russian, not Ukrainian.

"'What rubbish are you putting into the kid's head?' Mother scowled.

"Tim wanted to visit Daddy at his place sometime, he told me, and he didn't understand why that never happened. Once, he overheard his dad tell his mother, 'You should wash the floor sometimes, Valya. Children can't live in such dirt!'

"At this, she screamed: 'Oh, now you've got a complaint too! Get out! Don't you dare set foot here again!'

"Tim especially remembered one bright evening of the last spring before the war. Father had put his sons to bed, but for some reason he did not leave the flat. The children's room was a corner behind a room screen. It had lilies on it that looked like skulls. Timmy had long poked a hole in the fabric. Now, he looked through this hole and saw his father and mother sitting opposite each other at the bare table with long, strange faces covered with lacy, flickering shadows from a kerosene lamp.

"His father spoke quietly: 'Give me the kids, Valya. It will make things easier for you. Timmy at least. Olesya is ready to take them in. Please consider it.'

"Tim heard his mother start whispering in response, but soon enough, she began screaming: 'Let your bitch touch my kids? That's not gonna happen! Can you be honest for once in your life? You don't care about me or my kids! You destroyed everything … You took away my life! Now you want to take my boys too? To have a nice life with that bitch of yours at my expense! Get out! Get out of here!'

"Timmy didn't know what female dogs had to do with his father, and he dived under the blanket to block out the screaming. But he heard that his father had singled him out among his brothers, which meant he loved him best, and wanted to live with him. And he yearned for his father and hated his mother for not letting him go, for saying so many bad things to his hero.

"Mother began crying, and Timmy felt sorry for her too. Now he wasn't sure whom he pitied more. His father was strong, he always brought food, somewhere in his other home he must have had lots of food. And they usually didn't have any food, and mother counted every crumb and boys fought because they were hungry. Tim wanted to come into the room and make things better for both of them, somehow, but fear had chained him to his cot. Under his blanket, he tried not to move, not to breathe.

"He also remembered a time very long ago, before Daddy had left them. When everything was good and he played with the neighbour's puppy. He also remembered how his parents let him crawl into their bed on Sundays. He was the youngest, after all. Once, Daddy pretended that his mother was a car. He pressed her nipple and said, 'Beep, beep, let's go!' She giggled. 'Not in front of the child!' But Dad wouldn't let go, and they both laughed.

"Then Father left them. At the beginning, Mother cried all the time. But then, the war came. And Mother stopped crying.

"Dad was not drafted because of his bad eyesight, but he stopped showing up at home.

"The cannonades, the explosions made Dnipropetrovsk shudder for weeks and weeks. Then it all stopped. Germans had taken the city. The strange silence scared the inhabitants no less than the sounds of war. The city seemed extinct. The few people who dared go out into the street did so at a run. Behind closed shutters lurked a quivering life.

"Then, columns of German motorcycles and trucks rushed along the pavements. Something new was beginning. Something, the meaning of which little Tim could not understand. He only learned it much later.

"The Germans were throwing leaflets. The word 'Jews' came up in every one of them. Tim remembered this one: 'Stalin is a Jew, death to Stalin!'

"Jews were fined thirty million rubles for 'robbing the Ukrainian people.' The blacksmith Haikel-Khaim Tsymburg was burned alive in the synagogue for helping the Red Army.

"The census of the Jewish population was carried out quickly and efficiently, with the help of Ukrainians and Russians. Local policemen helped SS soldiers break doors. They burst into apartments, smashed everything, grabbed the silverware and jewels, beat up the people. Women and children screamed, men covered their heads with their hands, some prayed. There was no ghetto in Dnipropetrovsk. There was no need: the fifteen thousand Jews of the city were killed quickly. Shot, most of them. The shootings took place in shallow ravines. Then, a little earth was thrown over the corpses, and trees were planted. If there was no ravine at hand, the doomed would dig their own graves. Sometimes, pits were covered with planks. People were made to stand on the planks, then shot right into the pit. Children weren't worth the bullets. They had their heads smashed with rocks or were thrown to a ditch alive.

"Five hundred kilometres away from Dnipropetrovsk, in a forest near the city of Orel, in the same autumn, the Soviet military was also engaged in transplanting trees. Thin birches with cigarette-paper thin bark, aspens with fluttering leaves, rustling maples—all were lying prepared, roots up.

"Under the rapid onslaught of the German army, the Soviet units were retreating. On their way, they shot thousands of compatriots: victims of the Stalinist terror who were serving their sentences. The head of the NKVD, which was renamed 'KGB' in the fifties, regularly sent people to the burial places to check if everything was in order, if the dug up and newly planted trees were standing correctly. The checkers pretended to be hunting for mushrooms.

"But Timmy's family was spared the searches and the shootings. It was as if someone had covered them with an invisibility protective cloak.

"And then things changed for the better. Mother let Father visit the family again. He only came in the evenings though, in the dark. But he would bring food: a loaf of bread, some tinned meat. And Mother never shouted anymore. She stood there, her eyes down, and silently accepted the gifts. Father wore a uniform with a white bandage on his sleeve. Through the thick glasses, kids could see the puffy bags under his inflamed red eyes. Now Father never sat down to draw together with the boys. He left quickly, tousling his boys' hair on the way. Once he opened his backpack, and out crawled a shivering grey kitten. 'That's the Weinsteins' cat,' he said and gently scratched the kitten behind the ears. 'Nice eh? You'll take good care of him, eh?'

"Shivering with fear, the kitten left a stinking yellow puddle in the corner. This, it also did on all the following days, until Mother took it outside and left it in a funnel from a bombed house.

"That was the father's last visit. Timmy would never see him again. He kept waiting though, waiting with dismal persistence. He kept waiting even after his mother told him that father had been shot as a collaborator. Timmy didn't know what a collaborator was, but a neighbouring boy helped him figure it out. He did so by screaming 'fascist bastard' while kicking him in the groin. Timmy was weak and did not resist, but he believed neither the boy nor his mother. He was not a fascist bastard, and father couldn't have been shot as a traitor. No, he certainly died the death of the brave, on the battlefield, single-handedly fighting a tank or something like that. The way heroes die.

"When the city was liberated from the Germans, a new misfortune came. Mother was arrested as the wife of a collaborationist, though father had left the family before the war.

"The three sons were taken in by relatives in different cities.

"Mother only returned from the camp after Stalin's death. Once of imposing stature, she now weighed no more than forty kilograms. Her fits of quick temper, that Tim had found so scary as a child, were now replaced by a total lack of emotions. How did she survive in the camp, twelve years away from her sons? She didn't say. Indeed, she could hardly speak at all. Something was wrong with her throat. The doctors could not determine what it was. This mysterious disease justified her dumbness, protecting her from talking about the past. But she didn't really lose her voice. She simply didn't find it necessary to talk any more, it seemed. Yet when Mother thought she was alone, she whispered something to herself all the time. Tim overheard her once, and it seemed like a sign of madness.

"The family's old house had miraculously survived, but now it was home to another family. So Tim took his mother to live with him in Donbas, where he had managed to get a job as an equipment adjuster. The son of a traitor, he was lucky to have work of any kind. 'Tick-tock, tick-tock,' went the cuckoo clock. The mother sat at the window, immobile. She refused to go outside. To entertain her, Tim once put on a record of pre-war songs. Mother stood up, and suddenly finding her voice, began singing—then she grabbed the record, dropped it on the floor, and began to stomp it. 'Don't you dare! Don't you ever dare again!' And she sank down onto her chair in exhaustion again. What had happened in that hell from which she had returned, the hell that was now inside her? How did it relate to music? Tim never found out.

"Two years after her release, Mother died.

"Timmy's childish belief in his father's heroism slowly eroded; it had to die, and it did, covering his fond memories of his father with the ash of shame. Tim could not stop loving his father. But he couldn't understand how his father became a traitor either.

"Painstakingly, Tim taught himself to accept the lot that fate had thrown at him in her ruthless indifference. And in the end, he found a way. He tried not to think about his father anymore, to erase him from memory. By betraying the motherland, Father had betrayed them all: his brothers, his mother, his childhood, his present, his future. Wasn't his death a form of redemption before them all?

"And so the time came when the son inwardly agreed with his father's death as just retribution."

Chapter 55: Vlasov's Army

Official Soviet historiography hardly ever mentioned Vlasov's army (also known as The Russian Liberation Army), which fought against its own people on Hitler's side. The famous general of the Soviet Army, the division commander Andrei Vlasov, switched sides and managed to unite under his command an army of many thousands, including former Soviet colonels, generals, and professors of the General Staff Academy. Together, they fought against their own compatriots.

Even before their official unification into an army, police units of collaborators in the occupied territories of the USSR, consisting of Ukrainians, Lithuanians, and Estonians, fought against the guerrilla movement. They interrogated, tortured, made lists of Jews to be murdered, and participated in executions.

There is no doubt that they aroused the hatred and spite of the people who laid down forty million lives to liberate their country and Europe.

Solzhenitsyn, the commander of a sound-ranging battery in the Red Army, was one of the first to write about the Vlasov phenomenon in *The Gulag Archipelago*. But before the collapse of the USSR, his books were inaccessible to the general Soviet reader. Owning one meant a sentence in a labour camp.

What made Vlasov and his army fight against their own people? The twentieth-century Russian history does not spare us excruciating questions.

Like General Vlasov himself, many of his soldiers had been peasants. Before the war, they had witnessed the purposeful extermination of their compatriots by Stalin: the forced collectivization and the artificial famine had cost millions of lives. In Ukraine, women with starving children staggered to the roadway, only to meet death from commissars' bullets. Mad from hunger, mothers ate their own children. There was no one to bury the blackened corpses.

Vlasov and his officers considered themselves the liberators of the Russian people. They stated this at the trial, when, after the end of the war, the Soviet units managed to catch the general and bring him to Moscow. The interrogation lasted without interruption for ten days and nights. But even after this period of torture, Vlasov still declared, "I'm not a traitor, and I'll never say otherwise. I hate Stalin. I consider him a tyrant and will say so at court. Our torment is not in vain. Time will come when the people will remember us kindly." After this, the authorities didn't dare hold a public tribunal. Vlasov and five other generals of the Russian Liberation Army were hanged.

Stalin demanded that his Western allies produce the other Vlasovians, and the allies, unwilling to antagonize Stalin, satisfied his demand. Only the tiny kingdom of Lichtenstein refused to obey.

Over ten thousand collaborators were shot without trial. According to eyewitnesses, truck engines were used to muffle the sound of the shootings.

The collaborators could not forgive the Soviet power the enslavement and murder of the Russian people. The Russian people, in their turn, could not forgive the collaborators for cooperating with the enemy—an enemy who considered Russians a lower race, who enslaved, tortured, and exterminated them.

Collaboration was one of the taboo topics during the Soviet times. The murder of six million Jews in death camps, was another. The word "Holocaust" did not exist in Russian until the 1990s—that is, until the collapse of the Soviet Union. Three post-war generations grew up knowing nothing about the gas chambers. Even those who survived the war kept mum. And yet it was impossible to fully conceal a genocide of such a magnitude. Thus, as it often happened, the Soviet propaganda resorted to half-truths.

While it was acknowledged that fascists kept prisoners of war, communists, and gypsies in concentration camps, there was no mention of Jews. The killing of one hundred thousand Jews near Kiev in Babi Yar was silenced. Singling out one nation—and Jews were considered a nation, as the passports said—from the happy Soviet family was considered a relic of bourgeois chauvinism. The Germans exterminated not Jews but "Soviet civilians" in the occupied territories, the official version went. This was partly true: women, children, old people, scientists, engineers, artisans, doctors, bakers, mechanics, blacksmiths, librarians, teachers, musicians, journalists—all of them were indeed civilians, defenceless against a bullet. But civilians who did not happen to be Jewish were usually left alone unless they were suspected of helping guerrillas or hiding ammunition. Jews were killed not because they were civilians but because they were Jews.

Too indecent to be used in the press, the word "*jevrej*"—"Jew"—was never neutral, like "Russian," "Georgian," or "Kazakh." A dirty word, it was unpronounceable in polite society. During the short-lived thaw of the sixties, a documentary novella about one of the few successful uprisings in a Nazi death camp Sobibor slipped through a somewhat relaxed censorship into print. In spite of the fact that two hundred and fifty thousand people killed in Sobibor were Jews, the word "Jew" never appeared in the novella. Nor was it mentioned in connection with the organizer of the uprising, the Soviet officer Alexander Pechersky, who was transferred to Sobibor from a war prisoners' camp when it turned out that he was Jewish.

Vasily Grossman, a great Russian twentieth century writer, was the first to enter Sobibor and Treblinka with the Soviet troops as a war correspondent. Testimonies of the survivors and his personal observations were included in *The Black Book* compiled by him and another famous writer, Ehrenburg. By 1948, the manuscript was assembled and prepared—but by Stalin's order, the book was never printed. Members of the Jewish anti-fascist committee that assembled *The Black Book* were executed. Grossman survived, but his own book that documented the fascist and Soviet camps was seized by the KGB, as later was his masterpiece *Life and Fate* compared in its scope and significance to Tolstoy's *War and Peace*. Unable to get back the only existing copy of his life's work, Grossman soon died.

Chapter 56: Natasha

THE YEAR WHEN HIS first marriage broke up, Tim was haunted by nightmares.

Loneliness weighed like a boulder on his chest. Life seemed precarious, as if he was walking on a wire, balancing with a shaky bar, with the abyss yawning to the left and right; that's how it felt to him.

Once he dreamt of the foldout couch that had served as a marital bed to Natasha and him. In his dream, Natasha was asleep on the left. Next to her, in Timothy's place, there was the muscular back of his friend Aleksey. Tim knew it was him, though he couldn't see his face.

Aleksey had lived with them for a whole year back then. For reasons of money and bureaucracy, he had no place to stay, and Timofey himself had offered him the chance to move in. He could use the tiny room—a closet, really—where nine-year-old daughter Vera had slept before. Aleksey offered to pay rent, but Tim refused.

Now, all of them had dinner together. Aleksey brought sprats, sausage, sometimes a piece of ham. Timofey was a shy melancholic, and Aleksey a witty bon vivant. Instead of the usual everyday drabness, there was now a spirit of reckless fun in their kitchen gatherings. Natasha became noticeably happier, and Tim was grateful to his friend for it. The spouses' life now centred around Aleksey, it seemed.

But time went by, and Natasha began to complain: Vera was getting older; how long was the girl supposed to sleep behind a screen in the dining room? Tim tried to hint at the situation to his friend, looking away and stuttering slightly. But Aleksey ignored all hints, and Tim did not have the courage to say straight away that it was time to move out. And so the three of them, plus a child, spent almost a year together, mostly in merriment. And throughout this year, unwittingly, Tim was sharing his wife with his friend.

An additional blow came later. When all this came to light and Tim left his home, neither his wife nor his daughter seemed to regret it. Never mind Natasha, but Vera didn't want to see him either.

"How could that be?" Tim asked himself, rubbing his temples and whistling in bewilderment.

He was attached to his daughter, and of the thousands of injustices of life, this one seemed to him the cruellest. Perhaps his wife had concealed the true reason of the separation from their daughter? Unwilling to disgrace her mother, Tim did not tell Vera the truth either. The child must be offended that he suddenly left, thought Tim. He hoped he'd find a way to talk to her honestly when she grew up, to tell her everything as it was. This thought comforted him a bit, but not for long. Somehow, it all fell apart through no fault of his own. But he still felt guilty. His heart seemed to know that nothing would change even if his daughter believed him.

Injustice was like a cast, only soft in the first moments, then stony hard forever.

Chapter 57: Encounter with Clavdia

Timofey's deceased mother increasingly frequented his thoughts now. He saw a strange symmetry in their lots. Both of them had been betrayed. Just like him, she walked on a wire, balancing with a pole. She had lost her balance in the end, had fallen into the abyss. He saw all the cruelty, all the injustice of her life. Still, he had never felt any special warmth for her, unlike for his father, who had deserted them so early, whom he tried not to love and could not help loving. A feeling of guilt, ubiquitous and incessant, oppressed him.

After Natasha's betrayal, he felt a dismal emptiness. Everything got mixed up so hopelessly: love mixed with hate, trust with suspicion. It was like walking through a scorched desert: a mental thirst tormented him.

For a long time now, he wanted to go to the city of his childhood. To find people who knew his father. Perhaps those who'd witnessed his death were alive? It wouldn't be the first time he'd tried to get information about his father. He'd searched through archives, sent inquiries, but to no avail.

In the early 1970s, a year after his divorce, Timofey went to Dnipropetrovsk in order to meet Olesya Smeluk, a woman his father had left them for before the war.

She must've been very old by the time Tim went to see her, that Smeluk. He couldn't blame her for the past. He simply wanted to meet her, to be in touch with somebody who'd known intimately his father, and perhaps was the last to see him.

Timofey approached a solid wooden fence, kicked up a deflated rubber ball from between the burdocks. Surely, she'd been aware of taking a father from his little children back then. But had she cared? They weren't hers, after all. Father was to blame too, wasn't he? All water under the bridge now. The main thing was to find out how he perished, thought Timofey, as he went ahead, passing ancient merchants' homes, which miraculously remained there since the last century, with their porticos, columns, plaster coming off to leave lichen-like patches behind. If Father had not left Mother (a tough person of principle), who knows, perhaps she wouldn't have allowed him to embark on the path that ended in his death.

More old merchants' houses, and finally Timofey reached a park that appeared familiar to him. There'd been a lookout tower somewhere there formerly, but someone had evidently demolished it. The tram tracks were gone too. He found himself on a broad asphalt-paved street with nondescript prefabs.

"Olesya Smeluk?" a girl in the inquiry office asked. "Such a person isn't registered with us. We have a Clavdia Smeluk though. A relative, maybe?"

He went to find the given address, passing a park with a cast-iron Pushkin's bust. Sparrows were taking a dust bath by the granite base. Along the boulevard, Stalin's empire-style buildings had risen—grey monoliths built by prisoners of war. He turned into an alley, away from them, and in ten minutes he found himself back in his childhood. A speckled hen with three chickens was pattering on the cobble pavement; sunflowers were resting their frizzy golden heads on lopsided wattled fences, and behind them, in lilac bushes, he could discern old huts with carved frames that had miraculously survived the war.

It was one of these old wooden two-storey houses that Clavdia Smeluk dwelled in. Timofey ascended the squeaky steps to the second floor. The number of buttons over the entrance door covered with artificial leather suggested that more than one family inhabited the communal apartment. He rang four times, waiting after each ring. At last, a tall old woman, her face like parchment, opened the door. Her sharp wrinkles astonished him. Deep grooves seemed to be cut across her forehead and along her cheeks with an axe.

"Hello. I'm looking for Olesya Smeluk; here, I was given your address. Are you a relative of hers?"

"And who are you?"

"You see … Olesya was, so to speak … well … the common-law wife of my father."

The old woman took Timofey in with an inquisitive and gloomy eye. Unable to stand her hostile glare, he hurriedly averted his eyes.

"What's the name of your father?"

"Doroshenko. Kasyan Doroshenko."

The old woman gave him a stern look-over with her pale, frosty eye, then beckoned Timofey to follow her into a dark hallway. The door of a room alongside the hallway opened, releasing a man in an unbuttoned police uniform jacket.

"I see, you're having young visitors!" the policeman said, impudently examining Timofey. "An old crone! Feeling like fresh meat?"

Clavdia proceeded along the hallway without replying. Timofey followed her sideways, trying to move clear of the beggarly communal property: basins and troughs hanging from nails, a child's tricycle. Smell of human congestion, borsch, rancid sunflower oil, household soap, pungent medicines.

A child was crying behind the wall.

Timofey recalled how he had let a stray cat smell his mother's vial with valerian as a boy, and how the unfortunate animal arched its back and scratched the floor, howling.

Finally, the old woman ushered Timofey into her room and tightly closed the door.

"So you're saying Kasyan is your father?" she asked, fixing her expressionless eyes on him again.

The contrast between the musty darkness of the hallway and the rural coziness of the old woman's clean little room amazed him. The room was somehow very Russian fairy-tale like. You'd expect a ruddy girl here, with a waist-long flaxen braid, touching balalaika string perhaps—not this old hag of waxen face. "She must come from the countryside," thought Timofey.

The only window faced the backyard and was curtained with lace. The table was covered with a white lacy tablecloth; a heap of big and tiny pillows was towering under an equally lacy cover on the bed with a nickel-plated back. In the corner, a gold-mounted icon hung between two towels with red roosters cross-stitched upon them.

"What's your name?" asked the old woman without bidding him sit down.

"Timofey. I wonder if Olesya knows anything about my father, his death?"

"You're too late, Timofey. Olesya had been dead for, let me see, almost thirty years."

Timofey briskly glanced at the old woman, her tightly shut lips, her dark low forehead. He could see nothing in this closed, masculine face.

"I'm sorry," he said. "I didn't know."

"How could you? And why should you be sorry? The son doesn't answer for his father."

"I didn't mean that … I … So you knew my father?"

"Sure I did. I was like a mother for Olesya. I was the older sister, we lived together. I told her back before the war: 'Don't get involved with a married man! This will never lead to any good.' She didn't listen! He ruined her. Yes, he did."

And the old woman turned and quickly crossed herself before the icon.

He felt awkward.

"Well, excuse me for bothering you. I thought, maybe …" He crumpled his cap, ready to get up and leave, examining the room for the last time. "It's nice here. Cozy. Do you live alone?"

"Who should I live with? My first husband is dead, and so's the second."

"If you ever need something repaired or any help," Timofey said, trying to expiate his intrusion, "please don't hesitate. It's right up my alley. A broken TV or something,"

Clavdia scowled at her visitor. "I don't have no TV. A sewing machine though."

"Let me see it."

"You'll really get it working?"

"I'll give it a try."

The old woman became animated. "Well now, sit down, don't you stand there, give your feet a rest. I have an old, pre-war Singer. Worked fine. And now it's dead, kaput. Won't pull the thread. I can't go without it. You see, I do some work at home, get things done while the neighbours are gone."

Clavdia approached the dresser by the window and revealed her old Singer from under lacy covers.

"A policeman moved in this year! There's no peace with him around. Keeps trying to sniff out something. It's worst when he gets drunk. 'What, private enterprise under my very nose? I'll lock you up, you'll see!' So fine, put me in jail! Will that help the state? Ah, whatever." Clavdia waved her hand. "I guess he's all bark and no bite!"

Timofey turned the machine upside down, inspected the spool, checked the shuttle, tightened some screws. "Some lubrication wouldn't hurt. Have you got any oil?"

"None at all."

"I can bring some tomorrow. Give me some rag. I'll check it."

He lifted the foot, and the machine started to make stitches on the rag smoothly and gently. "Here you are."

"You really are a jack-of-all-trades! I don't know how to thank you, Timofey. Some tea, maybe? With currant jam?"

While she poured tea, Timofey noticed that her dark, bony, veiny hands were shaking.

"Do you perhaps have a photo of your sister?" Timofey asked, sipping. "They say she was a beauty." He'd actually heard no such thing, but he wanted to please the woman somehow.

"A photo? There, in the trunk under the bed. Only my back won't bend. Come, help me!"

Timofey pulled a trunk with an iron lid from under the bed, extracted two old albums, and watched his hostess arrange them on the table. The photos were inserted into oblique slits cut into the thick pages.

"Well now, how old is she here? About seventeen, probably." Clavdia brought the open album close to her eyes. "That's her, my sister, Olesya.

Even the faded black-and-white photo couldn't steal away the radiance from the girl's delicate, almost childish oval face that was looking at Timofey with such inviting innocence.

Studying her face, Timofey understood why his father had left them.

School photos, white turndown collars around thin necks. Three friends, their arms around each other's shoulders, with the smiling Olesya in the middle. Here she was in a boat, with oars in her hands, a garland of wild flowers on her head, squinting at patches of sunlight on the water. Its glimmer was still discernible on the time-faded photo. Here, too, she was all openness, purity, light. At whom was she smiling? Whomever it was, the one who was taking the picture must have smiled back.

In each photo, Olesya was different, but one thing was the same: that glow in her eyes, and that openness, that tenderness, that sweetness.

"Do you have a photo of my father too?" Timofey finally asked.

For some reason, Clavdia threw a nervous glance at the door. Then she silently took a package wrapped with old newspapers and tied with a coarse string from under the albums. While she busied herself with the string, Timofey couldn't help but stare at her quivering hands.

And then Timofey saw his father. His bulging near-sighted eyes looked at him evenly, seriously. There was Olesya sitting in a chair, him standing over her, his hands on her shoulders, wearing an embroidered Ukrainian shirt. A bright, carefree Olesya in a light, sleeveless dress ... and this much older, thick-set, short-sighted man with round glasses on his meaty face. His father.

The other photo showed a group of German soldiers and officers against the background of what appeared to be a high palisade, or a shed. They seemed to be on vacation. All of them were looking into the lens, the hands behind the backs, self-satisfied smiles on every face. It took Timofey some time to recognize his father in a chubby man on the fringe of the group; his military uniform and a white band on his arm changed his appearance. But it was him all right. The thick glasses over his bulging eyes were unmistakable. His father was the only one who looked away rather than into the lens. But he, too, was smiling. Diagonally to him, in the first row to the left, there stood two blond women who appeared local, Russian. Both of them were wearing jackets over their flowery dresses. In the younger one, he recognized Olesya. The other, older one, in strap sandals, had some reckless cynicism around her lips. She clearly knew her worth. It was impossible to connect that image with a stony face of an old woman sitting across him. But somehow, the shape of the face and the brow told him he was looking at a much younger version of Clavdia.

"Well, don't you recognize me?"

Timofey moved his glance from the photo to the old woman.

"Sure I do!" he said, lying. "Yes, this must be my father, this is Oselya and this ... this is you."

As Clavdia gathered the photos scattered in a semicircle, one escaped to the floor. The old woman wanted to pick it up, but Timofey was quicker. "Let me help!" And he bent over the small faded square.

The soldiers on it were armed with assault rifles, their faces could not be seen, only backs and profiles. The present captured by the picture seemed insignificant compared to the past left behind the frame and evidenced by a ditch gaping a few metres from the group with something frightening, bulging in a formless heap, inside.

A black forest stood behind the ditch.

Again, Timofey recognized his father in one of the soldiers—by a slight stoop, a characteristic inclination of his head. And like in a group photo with soldiers during the break, the father was looking away, aslant from that common dead in which he appeared to have just participated and which mainly interested the photographer.

What was he doing there? What was he doing a minute before someone took the picture? Half an hour before that? An hour? Executioners at rest, the group photo near the shed with the sisters. Was that before or after? Are these soldiers the same? How does Clavdia dare keep it? Today, in Soviet Russia? Timofey turned the photo over. It did not have any dates on its back.

"How did this turn up here?" Clavdia said as if she saw the photograph for the first time.

"This forest, where was it?" Timofey asked, feeling his voice would not obey him.

"This isn't a forest. It's the Botanical Garden. There was a gully before it. The Krasnopovstancheskaya gully behind the Transport Institute."

"So she knew, she knew all about it," thought Timofey with trepidation. He pointed at the figure on the right, standing apart from the others. "Is this my father?"

"I don't see well, and I can't tell."

"What kind of work did my father do? Do you know?"

There came a long silence. "Your father worked as an interpreter for the Germans." She fell silent again, for a moment. "Well, you couldn't say no to the Germans. One had to do all kinds of work."

"Whom were they shooting here? Communists? Captives? Jews?"

"Sure, a lot of kikes." Clavdia turned the photo this way and that. "Why are you asking?"

"I used to live in Dnipropetrovsk before the war. I remember places. And I don't recognize this place."

"They gathered them in the Karl Marx Square and chased them to the botanical garden from there." Clavdia sighed, poured some tea into her saucer and began blowing at it. "Drink your tea before it gets cold," she said. "Anyway, Jews had had all the power in the city before the war! Bled us dry, the kikes. In villages, it was even worse! They didn't pity our children; why should we have pitied them? Who had forced people into kolkhozes before the war? Kikes, that's who. And who starved us? Kikes again. A commissar came to our village on a requisition trip. Mothers grovelled at his feet, begging him to leave some grain to children so that they wouldn't starve to death. Fat chance! Kikes ruined Russia, yes they did!"

Clavdia sipped her tea off the saucer, the way peasants do.

Timofey lowed his eyes avoiding looking at her.

"Whatever blame the government put on him," she said, "your father was a good man. My sister loved him. There's war around, hardships, but those two were like two doves. Maybe he wasn't the best-looking man in the world, a bit on a chubby side, but he took care of us; wouldn't let us starve. Her and me, we shared the same room. When Kasyan moved in, I had to sleep in the kitchen. But with him, we were never hungry. Olesya was three months' pregnant. If it wasn't for the war, you'd have a brother or a sister. Only your mother wouldn't give him a divorce."

Clavdia fanned off a fly sitting on the sugar bowl, finished her tea, and gathered the photographs. While she was tying a string around them, Tim furtively put one photo into his pocket. Then helped her to push the trunk under the bed.

The next day, keeping his promise, he brought an oil can to Clavdia to lubricate her Singer. He also mended a shelf over the washbowl, and repaired the old samovar.

But again, he found out nothing about his father's death.

***

In 1943, not long before liberation of Dnipropetrovsk, the SS-Standartenführer Klueger, the chief of Kasyan Doroshenko, took to visiting the Smeluk sisters.

"He cut a fine figure, this Klueger," Clavdia said. "A tall, well-built man, his hair parted razor sharp, his nails polished, wafting of cologne. A pity he was a German. He tried to visit when your father was not around. Brought wine, chocolate, even coffee. Olesya was the one to serve at the table. That's what Klueger wanted. Ordered her to do her hair, dress up, not to run about in an apron in his presence. As Olesya put the samovar on the table, he'd screw up his eyes at her. Then he'd settle in the armchair, his legs stretched out under the table in the boots, puff at his pipe, and stare at her. During dinner, he'd only address Olesya, even joked with her. If Kasyan happened to be around, he interpreted. Once, he kissed her hand, I remember. She blushed but didn't withdraw it. And Kasyan just kept smiling. What could he do? You don't argue with your boss.

"So Klueger began to come about twice a week, in the evening, after his work, whatever that work was. As things were getting bad for the Germans at the front, Klueger changed. He was now often irritated and brusque. He didn't joke anymore and drank a lot. If Kasyan and I happened to be home, he'd bark: '*Gehen! Hinaus gehen!*' That is, 'Desert the room! Don't come back for at least an hour!' Kasyan hesitated first, but Klueger only looked at him, and that was enough. And so it went. When Klueger came, Kasyan and me went off. I'd go to a friend, and Kasyan, I don't know—perhaps he waited it out at your place. Visiting his kids.

"This continued for several weeks, until the Red Army retook the city. One night, there was heavy bombing, the ground shook under the feet. I didn't go to my friend that time but lingered in the vicinity waiting for Klueger to get away. But where to hide under bombing? I rushed home ahead of time. And what do I see? Klueger in his underpants and Olesya half-naked, crying, and him slapping her face, screaming '*Russische Schweine!*' See, what happened, she had wanted to put an end to all this for a long time, but was afraid of Klueger. And Kasyan … she didn't want anything to happen to her man. As I said, Kasyan kept pretending he knew nothing. In the meantime, our army was getting closer. If they found out about her, sure deal, they'd execute her. What was my poor girl to do? I kept telling her, 'Tell your German you are pregnant. Maybe he'll leave you alone.' So finally she did.

"Did my father know?" Tim asked.

"About what?"

"Her pregnancy."

"That, I can't tell. Long time ago, that was. But for Klueger it meant we, Russians, had duped him, stained the honour of a German officer. He just flew off the handle and beat her up pretty bad that time. She lost the baby the next day."

"What happened with them, then, my father and Olesya?"

"Kasyan? I told you already. I don't know what happened to him. When Dnipropetrovsk was taken, the Red Army executed everybody who helped the Germans. If the Russians were short of bullets, they hung them on trees. But I didn't see your father among the hanged. We never saw him again."

"And your sister?"

"Well, she was sick after that miscarriage and all. Then ... then she persuaded the Russian command to take her in as a nurse in a field hospital. She had had some training before. And then I didn't hear from her. Not a word. Only when the war was over, we got a note: DIED A BRAVE DEATH DEFENDING HER MOTHERLAND."

Clavdia got on her feet, walked around to the corner where the icon of a saint was hanging, and whispered a prayer, crossing herself and bowing.

Chapter 58: Kasyan's Childhood

PYRAMIDAL POPLARS WERE FLASHING by in the train window, interspersed by white huts. Rich, Ukrainian soil; generous, the Ukrainian sun. Luxurious, the apple, cherry, peach orchards. The train ran on and on, rapping out its usual Morse code :"Who's-he-what's-he-who's-he-what's-he …"

It began drizzling.

Timofey watched oblique drops plant themselves on the glass, and the accursed questions kept tormenting him. Who was his father? A near-sighted crank? An affectionate daddy? A spineless amoeba? A passionate teacher of German and geography? A heartless sadist? A killer shooting the innocent and bringing death to Timofey's mother and, inadvertently, the bright beauty Olesya, who would not have gone alone to the front to be killed if he hadn't first betrayed her, then abandoned her, one way or another? That photo, hidden between the pages of Shevchenko's *Kobzar*, a book of poetry taken on the journey for courage and communication with the father's spirit.

"Girls came together
To wipe away tears;
Comrades came together
To dig deep pits."

He remembered his childhood well enough, the intuitive sense of the people he could trust, the ones who truly loved him. More than intuition, it was instinct. His father had loved his three boys, loved them tenderly, in a manner Mother didn't or couldn't. He took care of them, didn't let them starve … Had the war made him into what he became? Had he been forced? On that terrible photo, he doesn't look at the ditch. He is looking away.

And he, Timofey, what would he have done in his father's place? If you have three children … and a gun aimed at your back? But then the doubt gripped him again: What if he did that of his own free will?

Rat-tat-tat, went the wheels. And Timofey recalled a fairy tale his father had once told him. A *bogatyr*—a Russian hero—named Sviatogor travels the world. His steed is as high as a mountain, his helmet touches the sky, pine forests can hardly reach his ankles. And Sviatogor encounters a wanderer, homely in his appearance. "What do you have in your sack?" asks Sviatogor, happy to meet another human during his lone wanderings through forests and mountains. "Lift my sack and you will know," answers the wanderer. The *bogatyr* dismounts, gets hold of the sack—and cannot lift it. "How can that be?" he wonders. "I can root out a three-hundred-year-old oak with one hand, and yet can't lift your sack! What did you put in it?" "The weight of the Earth, its soil, is in the sack. This is why you can't lift it," says the wanderer and goes his way.

This weight, this love for one's home soil, for Ukraine, had always permeated the Doroshenkos. Their family had been peasants from time immemorial in the village of Zhmerino. There, they were born and died. Kasyan Doroshenko, Timofey's father, had nine brothers and sisters, and all of them worked the soil with the parents. The soil bore well and did not let them perish during the revolution and the civil war.

***

Out of the ten children, only his father overcame this weight, this pull of the soil. When he was thirteen, he left for the city. He pulled himself up by the hair, learned German, became a teacher, a respected person.

Kasyan didn't leave his home of his own will though. Near the Doroshenkos' farmstead, the old widow Glafira lived at the edge of the village. Her two sons and her husband were killed in the civil war, fighting for Budyonny. Glafira was short and thin; but her legs were swollen elephant-like. She moved with difficulty. Though Glafira was the mother and widow of war heroes, she wasn't well liked in her village. Maybe it was because she was offish, aloof. She did not sing songs with others and, most importantly, never asked anyone for anything. "Since she never asks for help, she must be an arrogant bitch," the village women thought. But the Doroshenkos, her neighbours, helped

Glafira without her asking. When Kasyan's mother saw the old woman, carrying water from the well and hardly moving her stubby legs, she ordered her children to run and take her yoke from her. The older Doroshenko—Kasyan's father and Timofey's grandfather—mended the widow's roof, and Kasyan himself chopped wood for Glafira since he was tiny. He liked this work, the more so as Glafira never let him go home without a piece of lard or a newly baked loaf.

Once Glafira fell badly ill. The twelve-year-old Kasyan suggested he'd earth up her potatoes, chop wood—in a word, help her manage the household. Glafira had no money, so she paid him with a duck. Unfortunately, on his way he met the village elder Petro Tsybuy. "Where did you get this from?" he said, laughing and nodding at the desperately quacking duck that thrust its red bill out of the sack. "From Glafira," answered Kasyan.

"If she's so kind, maybe she wants to give me a piglet?" Tsybuy smiled good naturedly and went on his way.

But this innocent interlude had grave consequences. Tsybuy later accused Glafira of using hired labour—and thus being a capitalist exploiter.

After Glafira's arrest and banishment to Siberia, Kasyan's father said to him, "You better run, boy, they might come for you next. Go to the city. There, you'll be like a needle in a haystack."

Out of the entire big family, only Kasyan, future Timofey's father, survived. Did he realize then that he had killed Glafira by babbling about her duck? She was his first, though unintentional, victim …

Kasyan's father, brothers, and sisters were *dekulakized* and banished to Solovki.

Dekulakized! What a word, thought Timofey, looking at the fields and coppices flying by in the window. You could say, then, that to *dekulakize* means to compel a person to unclench a fist. Literally, *kulak* means fist. But was there anything much in that fist? In Soviet speak, *kulaks* were the evil capitalists. The *dekulakization* entailed arrests, deportations, and executions of millions. After the revolution, the once robust Doroshenko household disintegrated into nothing. One barren cow, an old horse, two piglets, and half a dozen hens were all that was left to a family of eleven. When the rooster died, there was no money for a new one; they'd borrow one from the neighbours. They had nothing to feed the livestock; the old mare became so emaciated it couldn't pull the plow. Kasyan's father and his sons loosened the soil by hand, with nothing but spades. But that was just the beginning.

The kolkhoz also demanded the piglets, the horse, the hens, all the tools: the plow, the pitchforks, the scythes, the horse collars. The state wouldn't let the Doroshenkos have a single potato, a single ear of corn. When they refused to give up what was most vital—the cow, without which the children could not survive the famine—they were called kulaks, the category of successful farmers to be exterminated.

Kolkhozes were formed by force. The work there was slavery. Instead of money, kolkhozes paid by ticking up workdays in a notebook. The ticks meant remuneration in kind, if there was any. Most often, one got a bit of grain; if there was no grain, one got nothing. Failure to fulfill the norm entailed punishment: fewer workdays were ticked. The peasants under attack preferred to burn their households, to kill their livestock rather than hand it over to the state.

When peasant revolts broke out throughout Ukraine, they were suppressed with executions and deportations. But why did Stalin endeavour to purposefully destroy his own people? This was the question that Timofey could not answer.

Many tried to escape, but there was no escape. It was prohibited to move from place to place. Before the late 1960s, peasants were not allowed to have a passport. Without a passport, you were a non-person. Just like in the times of serfdom. Timofey, who had studied the archives, understood this well. Serfs had had their allotted land, at least. Kolkhozes took this away from peasants too. In case of diseases or famine, landowners who owned serfs had been obliged to take care of peasants, to feed the families. The Soviets not only provided no food—more than that, they made Ukraine starve, killing thirty million. Ukraine was not the only region subjected to planned starvation, though probably the largest.

Lenin and Stalin had made no secret of assigning primary importance to the proletariat, and above all, factory workers. Stalin wanted to turn a backward agrarian country into an industrial colossus to be respected and feared by the world—overnight, with a wave of the iron sceptre.

He was giving the finger to that fallen, corrupt, criminal world of capitalism. And he desperately needed to prove that communism beat capitalism in every respect: in the height of corn, the production of steel and iron, human longevity, and the everlasting enthusiasm and hysterical joy of his people. To keep the cities under control, he needed to feed the proletariat. But who would feed the city if not the village? Taking away goods earned by hard labour from individual farmers is not easy. The mass confiscation was easier to organize through kolkhozes.

This is what Timofey was musing about on the train. But now he couldn't catch the main point: Why did Stalin want an industry created at the expense of millions of lives? Five-year plans, socialist emulations, the fictitious overfulfilling of five-year-plans, the punishments for under-fulfilling, jail time for a single ear of crop stolen by a starving child, shooting from age of twelve. Why all that complicated engineering built on blood?

Gradually, Timofey accepted the conclusion he had tried to refuse. Violence, destruction, and public executions accompanied by glorification were to attain a single purpose: absolute power over lives and deaths of millions.

This terrible truth was hidden from the eyes of most of his contemporaries. 'They were simply duped,' thought Timofey. 'We were all duped!' The impenetrable layers of propaganda, slogans proclaiming a bright future of the new Soviet man, served the only purpose of satiating an insatiable craving for power. This trip to Dnepropetrovsk presented the truth with such merciless clarity that Timofey couldn't deny it any more.

The train stopped at a substation, and the trees stopped with it. It ceased raining, the sky cleared, and Timofey saw a pale pink foam appearing here and there in the window: apple trees were standing in full bloom in the slanting sunrays.

But where does that craving for power come from? How is it born? Timofey tried to think his thought to the end while examining women selling things on the platform. They were hung with strings of dried mushrooms like necklaces. Each had heaps of pickles laid out on a newspaper. Where does the craving come from? Where? Well, where do these blossoming apple trees, these faraway clouds come from? As long as there is that, there will be this. This is the law of nature, thought Timofey. And this tangle cannot be unravelled, the truth cannot be reached. The answer seemed silly, worthless to him, but he had no other.

When, in 1933, commissars came for Timofey's grandfather, he did not resist, did not set his house on fire. They took him, his wife, and all their children from their home. Their neighbours raided the house, took everything.

The family was sent to the Solovetsky Islands. Nobody returned.

Fields, coppices, white houses running in the window again, the train now doing a new tap dance: "What-for-what-for?"

To get rid of the bitter tune, Timofey began thinking of Natasha.

He wanted to talk to her out of habit, tell her about his journey. But then he remembered that there was nobody to talk to, that he was alone in the world. Why? This question had no answer either.

Chapter 59: Timofey's Two Marriages

WHEN TIMOFEY TRIED TO THINK back to his life with Natasha, his friend Aleksey invariably appeared before his eyes, as if Natasha and he had not existed before Aleksey moved in. He recalled the most important things poorly, but trivial, irrelevant stuff lived in him and hurt him. For no reason at all, he, for instance, remembered that Natasha used two towels at once to dry herself after a shower and threw them into the laundry bin. Did towels really become dirty from a single contact with a freshly washed body? But it was impossible to persuade her to change her ways. Or that ridiculous army of bottles and vials on the shelves. She could not part with them even when they became empty. Or the concert programs, some useless tickets, even the bus tickets, she used to impale on a long needle attached to a round wooden stand. She was never able to throw away anything, cluttering a tiny apartment they shared. It used to annoy him then, so why now—when that life was broken and no more—why did he recall it with such nostalgia?

Sometimes he tried to persuade himself that his wife could not love that traitor Aleksey as much as she had once loved him, Timofey. After all, she had asked for help. ("Our apartment is too small. Tell him to go!") If only he'd listened. But he had ignored her, had failed to understand the hidden meaning of her words.

Timofey was most amazed by the fact that he still worried about Natasha, though he hadn't forgiven her. She was delicate, vulnerable, like a little girl in her appearance and habits. Often feeling weak and unwell. Sure, she played it up too. But with time, it became hard to discern what was real, what was not, and now he thought that perhaps she was really suffering, but he had ignored her. The moment that thought pricked his heart, he would mentally slap his hand: a cheat, a woman without any moral scruples, that's what she was.

In their relationship, he was good at everything, and Natasha was good at nothing. Timofey cooked, shopped for food, and, of course, repaired and mended everything in their household. He got accustomed to that and got irritated only rarely. He fulfilled not only the needs but also the whims of his wife—happily, most of the time. Now that she'd left him, left for his friend (these thoughts were never apart from each other), there was nobody left and nothing to live for.

He was told that Aleksey ended up marrying Natasha. This both calmed him (she was too helpless to be on her own in this world) and became a source of another, stronger pain. Whether Aleksey prohibited his stepdaughter from visiting her father or whether this was Natasha's idea (so as to let the girl get used to her "new Dad"), the result was he never got to see his daughter anymore. Once, he tried to pick her up after school, and she stuck her tongue out at him and ran away saying that he was not her Daddy anymore. The pain of this new betrayal was concentrated in two syllables: "Daddy." It was not him but his rival whom his daughter called this now. Timofey could not grasp how a ten-year-old could have bought that.

***

Some two years after the divorce, Timofey met Larissa. This woman was quite the opposite of Natasha. The enormous vital force emanating from her knocked Timofey off his feet. It carried his melancholic, slow, doubtful soul upward. Having submitted to Larissa's irrepressible energy, voluntarily given up the reins of power, he at first relaxed and rested. Many things were new to him. He was amazed and somehow touched by how easily Lyalya handled pliers, a hammer, an electric drill.

If he asked her how she felt, whether anything hurt, she only raised her eyebrows with a puzzled look and shrugged her shoulders.

He made their storage room into a small workshop, installed electricity. Larissa came in every now and then, watched him make, mend, repair something, her arms folded over her chest. She did not hesitate to give advice. Often, she took something out of his hands. "Look, this way's better." Timofey nodded, smiled feebly. Soon, the fun went out of working in his workshop. For a while, he could not decide what to do while Lyalya cooked, and he was told to keep away from the kitchen. Then he took a liking to playing patience with his new mother-in-law. At this, he again saw Larissa's raised eyebrows. When he busied himself with maps and books on topography, he also feared her sarcasm.

When did he begin feeling like a burden to her? The changes in family life accumulated unnoticeably, like water wearing away lime. "What a loser you are! You can't stand up for yourself!?" Lyalya flung at Timofey when once again he had been passed over for promotion. He disliked conflicts and avoided them at all costs—but the more he submitted to his wife's will, the less, it seemed, did she respect him.

Both in appearance and character, little Lyuba resembled her mother. But she was a funny, amusing child. And he did love her, with the love he couldn't reach his own daughter with. When Lyuba left for Germany, another void crept into his heart. There was Daniel, and his daughter and now step-daughter. He pushed those thoughts away, thinking of some exciting discovery he made in a local archive. It turned out that some German was sent to Russia from Berlin by the famous Tsinnendorf no less, to start a Masonic Lodge in Crystal Goose.

Chapter 60: Second Letter from Canada

The letter that Timofey showed his wife that lovely May evening on the porch of his unfinished little hut had spent almost a year in a drawer. Back when Timofey had received it, Daniel had disappeared, and nothing else mattered. Then, it took some time for Timofey to understand who the letter came from. The envelope and the stamps were foreign; the return address was in Canada. Timofey knew where Saskatoon was, but only theoretically—he had neither relatives nor acquaintances in Canada. The photo inserted between the sheets of strange thin paper told him nothing. A thin, bald old man. A melancholically drooping mouth, a gloomy glance from behind his glasses. "Who is this creep?" Timofey thought. "Looks like some Soviet bureaucrat. In Canada?" The letter was written in Russian. Timofey scanned the uneven lines, the handwriting was difficult to read.

"Hello, dear son.

I hope very much this letter finally will reach you and you'll respond. I have repeatedly written to your brothers Vasily and Nikolay, but I didn't receive any answer. Maybe the address is wrong? If you receive this letter, please tell your brothers, help me to contact my sons. I hope you are all alive and ... "

Timofey gulped, listening to his uneasy heartbeats. Then looked at the photo more carefully. The round, good-natured face of his father held in his memory was nothing alike that thin and gloomy old man. But then—there it was, that worm-like deformed left ear, the one that made the glasses wonky on the father's face! Could it really be him?

So he'd survived, escaped reprisal, taken refuge in Canada? Out of habit, Timofey went to the bathroom to read the rest of the letter.

His father wrote that he had been living in Canada for about forty years, that he'd been a schoolteacher and kept a farm, but was retired now. There was a large Ukrainian community in Saskatoon, he said. He'd married a Canadian of Ukrainian descent. He added he was not in good health; in fact, he was very ill, and he invited Timofey to come and see him, meet his wife, his daughter, Angelina—Timofey's thirty-year-old sister. The travel costs would be on him. Timofey thrust the letter far into the drawer and pretended to forget it, focusing all his energy on searching for his stepson. But he could neither forget nor devise how he should answer.

Three weeks later, Danny was slowly slipping away, staring at the wall, reacting to nothing. It was at this time of hope and despair that Timofey decided to write an answer. Trying to describe his life briefly, to tell what he knew about his brothers, he tore up two drafts. All that remained were two sentences: "Dad, do you recognize yourself in this photo? The soldier looking away, the first on the right—is this you?" As soon as Timofey put the copy of the photo into an envelope and dropped the letter into a mailbox, he repented. Surely, his father would not respond to this challenge! Now he had deprived himself of the last chance to learn the truth.

When the second letter from his father arrived two months later, Timofey opened the elongated blue envelope with a strange mixture of eagerness and caution.

His father wrote that Timofey had deeply hurt him with his suspicions. Yes, he had worked as an interpreter for the Germans. He had worked, he wrote, so that Timofey, his mother, and brothers would not starve during the war. He did not have any idea of what that photo was. It goes without saying that he had not taken part in any shootings, though he had heard of German punitive operations.

He wrote that there had been a clandestine patriotic organization in Dnipropetrovsk. It had struggled for the separation of Ukraine from the USSR. Being a Ukrainian patriot, he had secretly supported that organization before the war; communists led by Jews had fought against it. The Germans had justly punished these communist Jews, he said. But the figures were exaggerated, and the photo sent by Timofey was surely a fake. Then his father expressed hope that his son would not yield to Zionist propaganda spread by the perestroika. Global Zionism had invented the so-called Holocaust, he wrote, in order to collect money for the Israeli army. For this purpose, Jews had added three zeros to the six thousand killed to obtain their six million victims.

He proceeded with new family details: both his wife and his daughter were nurses. His wife Sylvia had retired long ago, and his daughter Angelina was taking care of him. He had bad kidneys, was on dialysis. Nobody knew how long he would live. He repeated his invitation for his son to come earlier rather than later. Volunteered to pay all the expenses. In a postscript, he asked if Timofey's mother was alive and, if she was, asked to give her his regards.

He did not mention Olesya.

***

Lyalya ran through the first letter from Canada, studied the stamp closely. "So you received this a year ago, didn't you? Why didn't you say anything?"

"You know what went on at that time ..."

Lyalya darkened, reminded of Daniel's death. Instinctively, she reached out for a cigarette.

Timofey took the pack from her.

"You get through twenty a day. Don't smoke so much!"

Lyalya obeyed silently. "You are a lucky one, aren't you! Yesterday a pauper, today a king! Your father turns out to be alive, and there's a sister thrown into the bargain! So you should go to Canada rather than to Germany, especially, if he is willing to pay all the expenses." She was secretly rejoicing that the question of her moving to Germany alone had been relegated to the background for a while.

"So why so gloomy?" she said. "When it comes to deciding or organizing, it hits you like a ton of bricks. Poor thing, he's invited to Canada!"

"Can you hold your tongue just once? Can you keep out of it?" Timofey flared up, angrily pushing away a plate with unfinished food.

"What ... How do you mean it?"

"Literally! Don't decide for me! Don't judge what you don't know!"

"Okay, sure," she said, taken aback by the resolve she'd never seen in her husband before. "No need to raise your voice."

It was dark by now. Nightly freshness was wafting from the garden. Lyalya stood up and was about to leave without glancing at the dirty dishes on the table.

Timofey straightened up in his chair. "Look, I'm sorry. I talked rashly. Stay a little longer, okay? You aren't in a hurry, are you?"

He had never told his wife about his visit to Dnipropetrovsk. He had not considered it necessary to let her into a dubious family story: his meeting Clavdia, stealing the photo—all that was before the "Larissa era." His father had perished in the war like millions of others: this was his version of the past for his wife. Having concealed the truth, Timofey felt embarrassed for years, like an accomplice in a crime. And now, he didn't want to be left alone in this unfinished hut, with the night approaching. He needed to coax his wife back somehow, to retain her if only for a while. More than anything, he now wanted to take her into his confidence, to be reassured by her in his doubts. He told her about his visit to Clavdia, then showed her his father's second letter.

Lyalya put down Tim's laundry, which she was preparing to take back home for washing, and she looked at her husband, lost.

"Maybe it really isn't him in the photo?"

"No, it's him all right."

Timofey nodded.

"I don't know what to answer him. What would you do?"

"It's really up to you. You said you wanted me to keep out."

Timofey looked into his wife's eyes anxiously, askance. "I know it's up to me. But … would you cut him off completely? Or would you rather …?"

"I repeat: I wouldn't give any advice in this business." Lyalya began to pull on her cloak, preparing to depart. She picked up a bundle of laundry and two empty bags in which she had brought food.

"Wait a bit, Lyalya, where are you hurrying? Can't you for once … Let's talk a bit."

Lyalya put the bags and laundry on a bench. "What's there to say? If you really want to know my opinion, here goes: you should inform Germany that a war criminal was found in Canada."

Timofey looked at his wife fearfully. "But he's over eighty … and he's ill."

Lyalya shrugged. "As I said, it's up to you to decide."

"Yes, I know. But if it was your father, would you?"

Lyalya stood the bags on the floor and squinted at him. "My father liberated a women's concentration camp! And my grandfather crawled on his knees in front of your father, quite possibly, who was translating while they whipped the old man before shooting him. And you want my advice? What you do is up to your conscience. Don't involve me in it. Okay?"

Chapter 61: Burning the Bridges

A WEEK AFTER THAT CONVERSATION, Lyalya went to Zaporizhzhia to return the money she owed to Victor. Instead of five thousand, she had only two. She hoped to return the rest gradually.

Nothing had changed in the colonel's flat since those distant years when Lyalya came here in secret from her parents: the same narrow cot, a chair by a desk with tidy heaps of files, bookstands along the walls. In a glazed cabinet, there were the same ancient knickknacks: army field glasses, a brass sextant, a miniature copy of the first English steam locomotive. The desk sported a group military photograph: the young Victor with his comrades-in-arms, Lyalya's father to the right of him. Separately, in the corner of the desk, there was a picture in a wooden frame showing Lyalya as she had been forty years ago.

While Victor arranged some simple food on the coffee table, Lyalya extracted the money from her bra in the bathroom. She put the heap of crumpled bills onto the table.

Victor looked at them askance and shook his head.

"Darling, don't even think of it. I won't take it, and that's that."

Lyalya hesitated. She knew it was no use to try to persuade Victor.

They said nothing for a while.

"Are you going to stay for long?"

"A few days. I came to see my son."

"I talked to Nikita recently. The latest X-ray is good."

"All the same, I worry about him."

"Everything will be fine," Victor said. "You'll see. Four years elapsed, a long time. He's cured now. Are you going to stay overnight with him?" He gazed at Lyalya with that special, intent look that had attracted and slightly frightened her as a girl.

She nodded.

"Okay. I hope he won't make you sleep in the kitchen!"

"He'll find a bed for me somehow."

"If you wish, you can stay with me. My homemaker went to see her relatives in the countryside for three days. Her room is vacant. Why aren't you eating?" Victor put some fresh cucumber and a few pieces of cervelat sausage onto her plate. "What has upset you? I told you: it's okay with Nikita's lungs."

Lyalya said nothing.

"I know what a hard time you're having, darling ..." He did not spell it out. He knew she'd understand. "I'm going to say something very banal, and I know it is, but trust me: time's the best healer. Let it do its job. But you have to help yourself."

"How?"

"Stop blaming yourself."

"I don't ... I try not to."

"I'm not saying it because it won't help, and won't bring him back. That you know. I'm saying it because you're unfair to yourself. And you shouldn't be. You've done more than anybody could for Daniel." Victor put his hand on her shoulder. "Shall I turn on some music? Something old, to raise morale? Georg Ots, maybe?"

"Who?"

"Well, my dear, you became quite uncivilized in your backwoods!"

"Yes, I've drifted away from everything somehow."

"How don't you remember Ots? The Sevastopol waltz? 'Chestnut trees are in bloom again/And I'm waiting for you again,' he quietly hummed in his soft baritone, which had always made Lyalya's heart palpitate.

"This ... Yes, I remember. But I'd rather listen to something else."

Victor turned on his gramophone, put on a record.

Ots tantalizingly intoned, "I can clear all obstacles without shyness/ I'll contend with any adversity/Just mark on the globe/The place where I can soon meet you."

"What's the big deal?" Lyalya thought, trying to protect herself from the past. "The lyrics are rather stupid, actually." But the sillier these words seemed, the more did they touch her heart. Suddenly, she felt sorry for herself, her youth, her waning strength, her thrashed hopes. She held back her tears. This was not the right time to let go. There never was the right time.

***

Victor had stolen her away from her school prom. They were running along the waterfront, him in his uniform, her in her low-cut ball gown. A fresh breeze blew from the sea, but she did not feel it, so enchanting everything seemed to her. This handsome colonel with his chivalrous manners, his prematurely grey hair, his smile, his voice, his words, the way he threw his tunic over her shoulders, and how a medal slightly scratched her naked shoulder. She loved everything about him. She remembered the masculine smell of that tunic, its unexpected heaviness on her naked shoulders, its warmth. Big raindrops fell onto sand, and a heavy shower began. They ran to the nearest coffee shop on the pier, the first coffee shop in her life. The silk of her wet skirt clung to her hips, and she noticed his glance, noticed how eagerly he looked at her body, and she blushed, pretending not to notice.

On a small stage, there were four musicians with saxophones, and in the middle, a tall, broad-shouldered man in a white tunic intoned in a mellow baritone:

"Bright is my way across the mountains,
I'll ascend on wings into the blue,
And to everything I'll do from now on,
I'll give a bright name of you."

This was Ots. Couples stood up from their tables, began dancing. Victor and Lyalya approached the orchestra, and it seemed to her that everybody was looking only at them—a stately military man with decorations and a thin girl, almost a child, he embraced.

***

The record stopped. Victor bent down to Lyalya, took her face in his hands, and quietly kissed her lips. She tried to free herself, but he lifted her from the chair, and they stood silently, embracing each other. She had no strength to pretend anymore. Pressed against his chest, she couldn't hold back her tears.

"Why?" he whispered, his lips brushing her forehead, her cheeks and lips and hair. "Don't cry, my darling. Everything's all right now, isn't it?"

"What's all right?"

"You do know that I have never loved anybody but you. I tried, and I couldn't."

"But why then, why did you … give me up?" she whispered faintly without moving her face away from his lips. "Why? I didn't care if we couldn't have children together. All I wanted was you! You obeyed my father like a boy! God! All my life is broken because of that, do you know? All my life." She sobbed uncontrollably.

"Calm down, my darling … calm down." He pressed her face to his chest. "You know the truth. It wasn't because of your father! You were twenty. How could you have married an invalid? You had your whole life in front of you. And now you have your wonderful children, you have your husband."

"Don't! Don't say this!"

Victor released her from his arms. Lyalya stood unsteadily, then came to the table, took a powder box from her bag, powdered her nose, wiped her tears with a handkerchief.

"Lyuba invited me to Germany," she remarked in a far-away, cold voice. "To come and stay."

Victor glanced at her sharply. His cheek was twitching. She'd never noticed such a thing on him before.

"Will you go?" he asked. "And what about Timofey?"

"Why shouldn't I go? What keeps me here? You don't need me, and Timofey will be okay. Since Danny died, we are strangers to each other. Besides, it turns out his father had been with the Gestapo. Timofey had been concealing this from me throughout our life."

"Gestapo? Are you sure? How did you learn that? I thought his father had died long ago!"

"Nope! He had escaped to Canada, imagine, and had been flourishing there all those years. I told Timofey he had to inform the authorities, let Germany deal with that. But he has his head in the sand, a veritable ostrich. I can't stomach being with the man!"

And she told Victor all about the letters received by Timofey.

Victor remained silent.

"Just imagine!" Lyalya was becoming increasingly agitated. "He can't make the decision by himself and asks me for advice if he should forgive his father!"

"And?"

"Thank God, I'm not in his shoes and will never be. But how can one forgive that? Would you forgive?"

"I don't know … I've been invited to Germany, you know, and I wouldn't go. I have nothing against Germans per se, but I can't. I lost everything in that damned war. I had lost my health, I had lost you, my love, my happiness! And I'm not one to forgive people like your father-in-law!"

Lyalya jumped up, clung to his chest again, pleadingly looked into his eyes. "Victor, love! Do give it a chance, for the last time! Not all is lost as yet, a piece of life is still ahead. Nobody can tell us how to live! My father is dead, my children are grown up. Just say the word, one word, and I'll give up everything! I'll follow you like a dog. I'll crawl on my knees after you! Don't reject me! Don't give me up again! Just look at me! Nothing has changed since then, only we have turned grey. But what do we care! Nothing matters anymore … just you and me, happy, finally, at the end of our lives, my only one!" And she began to cover his hands with quick kisses.

Victor gently withdrew his hands from her and pulled her close. "What about Germany? What about Lyuba?"

"Lyuba will do without me fine. I don't need Germany! If you … even if we have only a year left together, I'd …"

"Calm down, my darling. There is also Tim."

"I told you already! His happiness is in the damned hut that he'll never complete."

Victor stepped aside, and said, without looking at Lyalya, "I can't do that, Lyalya. You understand, I can't."

"But why? Now that we're our own masters, who would judge us?"

"Of what use am I to you? I'm seventy-five. I'll go soon. You'll desert your husband. What will happen to you then?"

"Victor, love! I only want to live a little bit in the end, I never did … to have a gulp of happiness, and then I don't care about what happens! I was never happy without you, not with anyone, don't you know? I lived like a robot: do this, do that, work, work, work, raise children. But there was not a single day when I didn't think of you! In the taiga, in the snow, in the construction mud, you were always my only light.

I knew that there was you, and I could live and breathe. And now you abandon me again?"

"I'm an old man. I have no right, my darling. I may get sick. I don't want that for you, understand? The past cannot be changed. You can't step into the same river twice."

"Is this your last word?"

"Yes, it is."

Two months later, Lyalya left for Germany. Timofey knew she would never come back. But he was wrong. Fate dealt Lyalya a totally different set of cards: unable to understand what had happened and at the apogee of despair, three weeks after her arrival, Lyalya returned to Ukraine.

***

More than ten years elapsed. All this time, Lyuba kept calling her mother, sending packages, inviting her again and again. But Lyalya flatly refused to go to Germany even for a visit. When I attempted to find out what had happened during her stay years ago, she invariably answered, "Ask your cousin. They didn't explain anything to me." Her bitter words suggested the fatal certainty that all was over.

"Come on," I said, still hoping to play the role of reconciliator. "With your memory, I'm sure you remember! Maybe you said something wrong?"

"I really don't know." Aunt sighed and shook her head. "I came, rolled up my sleeves, and got to work at once, as always. I washed, cleaned the house, cooked, took the girls to the school. Everything was okay in the beginning, and then, after a while, they began excluding me from meals. I was served separately, or rather, my daughter dropped a plate onto the table silently and disappeared so quickly I couldn't even ask what the matter was. I try to start a conversation; she just wriggles away. Obviously, she waited for me to guess that it was time for me to bug off. Well, I guessed, all right. I began to pack my trunk, deliberately, so she would see, in the evening. I was hoping she might try to dissuade me or at least ask why. Not a sound. And still I hoped. Perhaps she'd say something at parting? All she said was, 'Oleg will take you to the airport.' She had her residency. She said, 'I have to receive patients,' or something."

"And then what?"

"Nothing. I said goodbye to the girls and left."

"You know, a medical residency really cannot be cancelled on a short notice."

"Sure! And one's mother can be cancelled, right?! My whole life can be cancelled! After that, I all but killed myself. I had burned all bridges behind me at home. Did she think about that? And now she calls, pretends that nothing had happened!" Aunt lifted her eyes, squeezed tight with pain. "Who kept asking me to come to Germany? Lyuba. Whose plan was it? I keep all her letters from Germany as proof. She didn't spare the money for a lawyer either. She had copies of documents translated, about thirty relatives of ours that were shot. She said, 'I'll get it done, you'll see.' And she did—the Germans found confirming materials in their archives. Everything was right: the place, the dates. They are a well-ordered people, you know. Each execution was registered. Finally, I received a permit to live in Germany. And all for what?"

"Perhaps she decided that you wouldn't adapt to Germany, that you'd feel more comfortable at home?"

"Did she ask me where I felt more comfortable? Why should she decide for me?"

"How did Timofey let you go?"

"I told you. I invited him to join me, but he wouldn't go."

And so my aunt returned.

When she appeared with her two trunks at the threshold of the house in Crystal Goose, Timofey was, as my aunt put it, "befuddled, totally."

At night, Lyalya was awakened by her husband's muffled sobs. She would never have imagined that the quiet, phlegmatic Timmy was able to cry into his pillow like that. It was the first time she saw it. From surprise and from the shock of what had happened in Germany, she too burst into tears. This very night, the spouses reconciled passionately. Timofey asked his wife to forgive him, blamed himself for the whole mess. Lyalya repented, said it was her fault, that she had a bad, commanding temper, that Timmy was an angel, kindness itself, that nobody else could live with her. It was like sudden awakening, you see! "What fools we've been! Why quarrel? When so little is left?"

"You know how children hook their little fingers together after a quarrel and say, 'Make friends, make friends. Never, never break friends. If you do, you'll catch the flu. And that will be the end of you.' Just like that, we made friends with our little fingers under the quilt that night. We agreed to live the rest of our lives in peace and quiet. We were going to celebrate this by going to the Black Sea."

In the morning, Timofey went to the vegetable garden to dig out some potatoes for lunch. In an hour, Lyalya found him dead. He had died from cardiac rupture.

Chapter 62: The Parting

OUR LAST DAY in Montenegro came. Early in the morning, we went to the airport. Bidding farewell, Aunt tearfully thanked me for our journey, which she called the greatest gift in her life. Now and then, she gripped the trunks, hectically checked and rechecked the tickets and passports. Something awkward, unsaid could be felt in her gestures. Finally, she lifted her moist, farewell eyes at me and told her worry with an ingratiating half-smile. Could I solicit the Canadian government to issue her a visa? She wanted to see all her relatives before she died. I hesitated at first, but promised to try it by writing to my representative in Parliament.

Lyalya brightened up. "You do that, my girl! Tell them about my life, the Siberian construction work, about Norilsk and Crystal Goose. Tell them what we had to endure! Don't I have a right to see my relatives one last time after such a life?"

"That's not the issue. You need to prove that you don't intend to stay. The last time, they didn't let you in because they feared you wanted to immigrate."

"Do they think that everyone dreams of immigrating to their stupid country?!" Aunt exclaimed. "Here, I have my son with cancer! The graves of my father, my mother, my husband! We don't desert the graves of kin."

I smiled. "Well, graves are a weak argument for the immigration service."

I boarded my plane with a heavy heart. Both of us secretly knew we were parting forever.

On my way to Canada, I had to change planes twice. In Belgrade, three huge Serbians with shepherd dogs approached the gate. The policemen questioned the inspectors for a long time, and the flight was delayed for almost an hour. I feared I'd miss my connection in Munich to my flight to Montreal. And my fears came true. Gasping and panting, I ran up to my terminal just at the moment when the boarding for the Montreal-bound plane ended. The Customer Service people sympathized with me, smiled, provided me with a water bottle, a toothbrush, a comb, vouchers for two meals, and a taxi to the airport hotel. My baggage remained in the airport until the next day's flight.

The lack of baggage was balanced out by unexpected excess in time. I left the airport hotel and entered a cozy, toy-like world of paved streets, one-storey houses with tiled roofs, many-coloured shutters, lawn gnomes, and, of course, geraniums in their flower boxes on every windowsill. In the middle of the street, there proudly loomed a pole with brightly painted bird houses fixed at different levels. At the end of the pole, animals reminiscent of the Town Musicians of Bremen sat atop each other—a wooden rooster, a dog, a cat, and a donkey. I turned into an alley leading to a Catholic church. A field and a small grove behind the churchyard—all of it was so unlike the environs of North American airports with the mechanized pragmatism of their enormous highways and parking lots; their lifeless glitter of steel and glass.

I returned to the hotel, into my room, empty except for a narrow bed, a single chair, and a small table. There was nothing to do, and on the spur of the moment, I decided to find Lyuba. I remembered that she had moved to Munich with her family a few years ago. A search on Internet finally gave me the name of a doctor: Luba's name—Dr. Samsonov—stood out among the German names.

My cousin promised to visit me at my hotel in two hours. She didn't invite me to her home.

We hadn't met for a quarter of a century. I didn't recognize my cousin in that lean, classy, close-cropped woman. Her hair was styled into spikes like platinum needles. She was wearing a black leather skirt and a leather jacket crisscrossed by iron zippers. I noticed her black knee-length jackboots, and her bag hanging down on a golden chain. Lyuba took off the tinted glasses, which covered her entire face, and looked at me with her coldly glittering eyes surrounded by crows' feet. It was Samsonov's gaze. There was something stern, inflexible in the expression of her thin, tightly compressed lips, her pointed chin, high cheekbones. We compared our memories of each other with reality. Each of us apparently thought the time had changed the other beyond recognition. Lyuba sat down on the only chair in the room. I perched on the edge of the bed.

"I'm glad you could come. You see, I got stuck here by accident. They delayed my flight in Belgrade and I ... I mean, I wouldn't have intruded if ..."

"Yes, right, a blessing in disguise," she interrupted. Her movements were brusque, birdlike, and she chattered nineteen to the dozen. "I've got half an hour. Awfully busy these days, but as you see, I managed to come. After all, we are cousins, aren't we?" She looked at her watch. "Well, tell me about your holiday with Mom, and, you know, how do you do. Wait! I'll show you the kids first ... You only saw Anya when she was little, right?"

She began to fish in her handbag. Took out a pad, a pen, a powder box, some spray.

"What's that?"

"Pepper spray. I don't leave the house without it. Since Merkel let in two million Muslims, the streets have become dangerous."

Finally, she got out her iPhone and began to quickly tap on the screen with her forefinger. "That's not it, no, not this one. Here she is, my Anya! Quite adult already. She's moved in with her boyfriend. He's German. Born in Germany, I mean. They're renting an apartment. The boys and girls don't marry nowadays. Here is her Andreas. And this is my junior, Rita. Looks like Oleg, doesn't she?"

"Beautiful girls," I said.

"Yes, can't complain. So how do you do in Canada?"

"I can't complain either."

We remained awkwardly silent for a while.

"How is Oleg feeling after the surgery?" I finally asked. "Your mom told me."

"He's okay. I keep him in line, of course—exercises, walking, they are a must. A special diet, too."

"You must get tired sometimes. How do you manage everything: the household, your work?

"Who doesn't get tired?" she said defiantly.

I felt I could not give the conversation a neutral course, however hard I tried. She pulled her black creased jackboots down to her ankles.

"How did you find Mom?"

I became alert. Lyalya told me that Lyuba was jealous. She, not me, should have taken Lyalya to a resort.

"I think she enjoyed the visit. Only her knees and back were aching a lot of the time, I noticed, though she wouldn't talk about it."

"What does she want, a painless life at the age of eighty? No chance! I keep telling her: swimming like you is madness! I mean, whole kilometres, in cold water, in winter?! A no-brainer, right? But she won't listen to me! I'm a physician, but I'm not an authority to her."

"You see ... She doesn't want to yield to old age. She makes every effort to resist. And she never complains."

"That's not what I call it," Lyuba said. "I call it denial. She probably brought all her swimming medals along to show you, didn't she?"

"What's wrong with that?" I asked timidly.

"Nothing. You say she didn't complain to you, but every time I call her, she tells me about a pain here and a pain there. Fine, her back aches, sure. Whose doesn't? She doesn't know what suffering is. I have to deal with patients who really have it bad!"

Though I had difficulty to imagine Lyalya complaining, I said, "Sometimes, one needs to get things off one's chest. To unburden oneself. You're a doctor, maybe that's why."

"Exactly! One must do something, not just quetch! I say, 'Mom, take an antiarthritic medication.' She says, 'No, I'd rather do without it.' 'How do you mean that?' 'I don't trust the medicine here. They mix God knows what into this stuff.' 'Okay, let me send you some medicine from Germany.' 'No, never mind. I'll manage without.' Well, a no is a no. If she wants to be, I don't know, some heroic tortured partisan, let her!"

"I'd offer you some tea," I said, at a loss to reply, "but I have nothing here."

"Did they give you anything to eat at least?"

"Yes, they did. At the airport, I was given meal vouchers."

"Excellent," Lyuba said, having glanced at her watch again. "As a matter of fact, I should go. Come visit sometime! We'll talk properly."

"I guess we won't meet that soon. Can I ask you something, just one question?"

"Well, sure. Go ahead!"

"What happened back then, when your mother came to Germany? Ten years ago?"

"You should've asked her. You had a lot of time to talk, no?"

"She said she didn't know what happened."

"She knows perfectly well. But she always has to put on an act."

"She's your mother though."

"She's a drama queen. She gets bored. And me, I have no time for dramas. I have to work."

"Still, what happened? Did she order you around? Did she meddle too much?"

"Well, one can hardly order me around. She tried though. A tigress doesn't change her stripes."

We remained silent again for a while.

"Look," Lyuba said finally, "she shouldn't have deserted Timofey. She abandoned him. She decided she could get away with it."

"Wait, wait. Aren't you meddling in her life now?"

"Her life? Who brought up her children for her? Who was there for Nikita and for me? Tim, that's who! He was like a father to me, and she threw him away like an old glove. That won't do."

"But …"

"There are things you don't know. Okay, here goes. While she stayed with us, I called Timofey. He told me he had 'a little trouble with his heart.' And when he says 'a little trouble,' it means things are really bad. I know him, his tact. He had heart problems and heart pain before, but he never complained, never even wanted to talk about it. This time he asked me what medicine he should take. I told him to see the doctor right away. I worried, of course. I wanted to tell Mother, but he made me promise that I wouldn't spoil her holiday. Her life in Germany he called a holiday. I promised, and kept my word. But the one thing I know: a person should not be left alone in such a condition. So I made her go. I had no alternative."

"Lyalya told me she had all but killed herself."

"Well, she likes to exaggerate."

"Don't you believe that this affected her terribly? It still pains her!"

"Of course it does! Still, for her it's just drama, and my dear stepfather? Where is he now? Dropped dead on her arrival."

"But it's not her fault if he had heart problems!"

"Yes it is! Heart problems are curable if not neglected. Look what I do for Oleg! Heart attacks are caused by stress, both negative and positive. After Mother left, Timofey kept it together somehow—and then she returned all of a sudden, and his heart simply gave up. I'm sorry for both, I really am! His death was a crushing blow to me, and I pity her too. But I'm not to blame! You see, I wanted to spare her. That's why I didn't tell her the whole story all these years. She's had enough things in her life. I think she must have caught on by now though. Okay, I should go. By the way, you didn't tell me anything about yourself. How are your quilts selling? Do you remember the one with lotuses and dragonflies you gave us for our wedding? We still have it!"

Lyuba quickly pulled her boots up her calves, crackled with the many zippers of her jacket, and disappeared from my life. I undressed and got into the unfamiliar cold bed.

I had to get up early the next morning to catch my plane back home.

****

Three years after my aunt and I met in Montenegro, Putin launched a full-scale invasion of Ukraine. My aunt's city is located twenty-five kilometres from the front line and close to the largest nuclear plant in Europe. The Russians took it over in the first days of war, and the explosions at the plant put the world on edge. The first thing Lyalya did when she heard the news was take a shower and wash her hair. Then she sat alone at her kitchen table, head in her hands, hair still dripping. She later told me she thought, "Why did I bother? So they won't need to wash my body after my death? But who will be left here, and what difference would it make anyway?"

When, in the first weeks of war, I volunteered on the Polish-Ukrainian border helping hundreds of refugees to reach the countries of the European Union, my aunt was not among them. She refused to leave her cancer-recovered son behind. And in any case, with the train lines and bus routes constantly shelled, it was no longer possible for her to make it alone all the way from Zaporizhzhia to the safety of Poland and then Canada. So we talked on the phone, when we could, and I, for one, imagined we were sitting on the balcony in Montenegro, watching the sun sink behind the mountains and pour scarlet over the bay.

Acknowledgements

My thanks go to Michael Mirolla of Guernica Editions, who, for more than ten years, continues to give book form to my flights of fancy.

I'm especially grateful to my excellent editor Paul Carlucci for his sharp and benevolent eye. Working with him was a real pleasure and an inspiration that every writer needs on their long and often lonely journey.

I'm always grateful to Wlodzimierz Milewski, who manages to summarize, in one brilliant cover image, what takes me three hundred pages to describe.

About the Author

Marina Sonkina is the author of several collections of short stories, children's books, and works of non-fiction, including *Rupture; Ukrainian Portraits: Diaries from the Border; Tractorina's Travels; Runic Alphabet; Stalin's Baby Tooth; Expulsion and Other Stories;* and *Lucia's Eyes and Other Stories.* She was born in Moscow (USSR) and now lives in Vancouver (Canada).

Printed by Imprimerie Gauvin
Gatineau, Québec